Icearaus Flight

Icearaus Flight

Published by Leaky Pen Publishing

Printed in the U.S.A

Cover art by Melkor3D/Shutterstock
Bible quote: New International Version, Biblica, 2011. Biblegateway.com
Drop cap font designed by: Dieter Steffmann
Map images: Joe McDermott, Star Raven, Lileya
Edited by: William Lovan

Second printing July 2018

ISBN-13: 978-1-7321186-0-7
ISBN-13: 978-1-7321186-1-4 (e book)
ISBN-10: 1-7321186-0-4

Library of Congress Control Number: 2018903104

Visit our website at JRHarris.net
Leakypenpublishing@gmail.com
www.Facebook.com/JRHarris

Acknowledgments

This book is dedicated to my wife, who always offered words of encouragement even in the darkest of times, and to my beta readers; R. Harris, B. Lovan, G. Hamm, T. Koch and P. Harwood. Your critiquing and suggestions were invaluable.

Quotes

"I enjoyed reading book one, *Icearaus Flight*.
Thought it was well written, and enjoyed the adventure that was brought forth through each chapter and look forward to the sequel, *Birth Right.*"

-B. Lovan

"The prologue gets you right from the start and the story leads you through a very interesting world full of creatures and characters that will capture you imagination. A story based on good and evil, and a sacrifice of one to safe many."

-T. Koch

"An absolutely beautifully described world which drags you in kicking and screaming, then leaves you thirsting for more as the last page ends."

-G. Hamm

"J.R. Harris has taken a classic fantasy theme and sent it on a long needed detour through his twisted imagination. He provides enough vision to create a unique world while engaging the imagination of the reader, yet never allows the story to become mired in excessive detail. A brilliant first effort from a soon to be well known author."

-R. Harris

Icearaus Flight

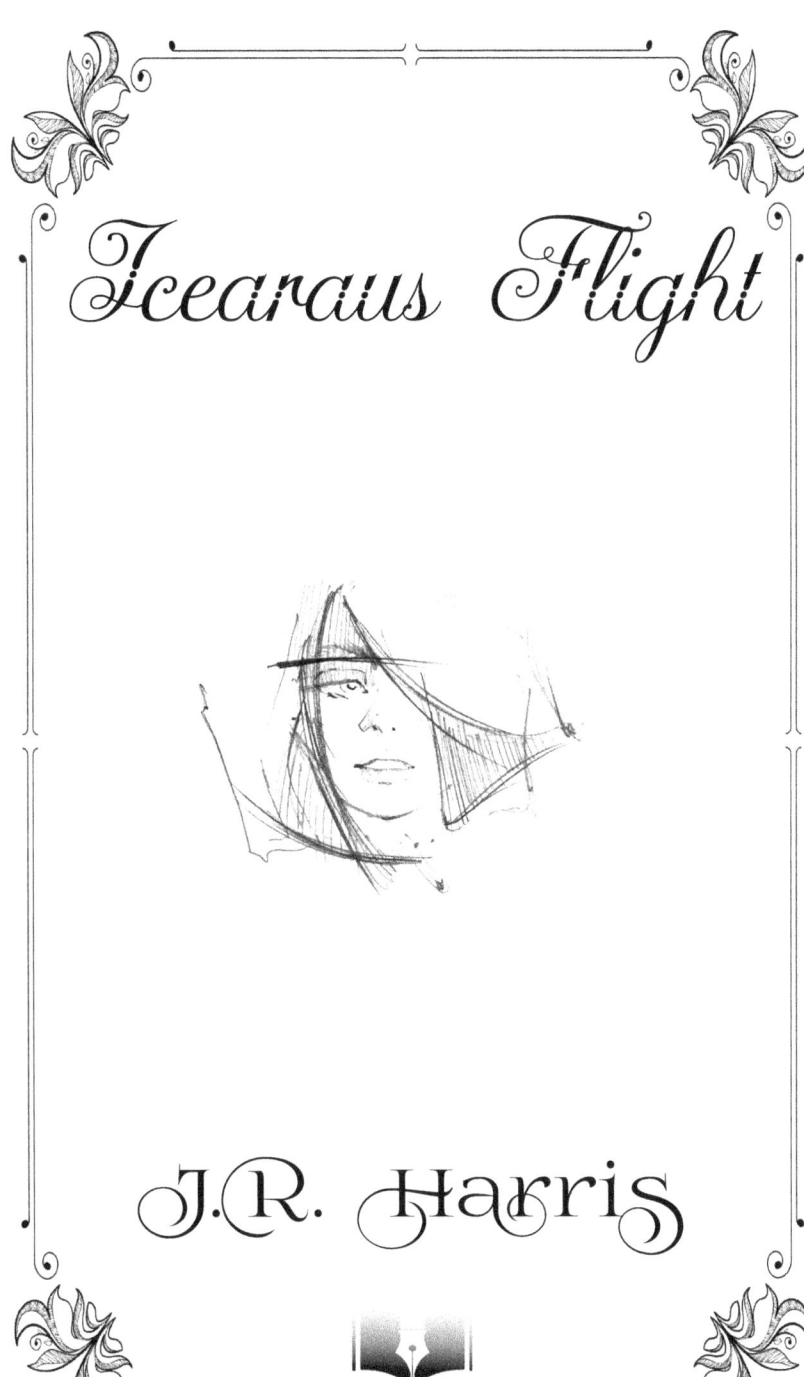

J.R. Harris

Leaky Pen Publishing

The saddest kind of sad is
When your tears cant even
Drop and you feel nothing.
It's like the world has just
Ended, you don't cry, you don't
Hear, you don't see.
You just stay there,
And for a second the heart dies.

~Anonymous

Icearaus Flight Maps

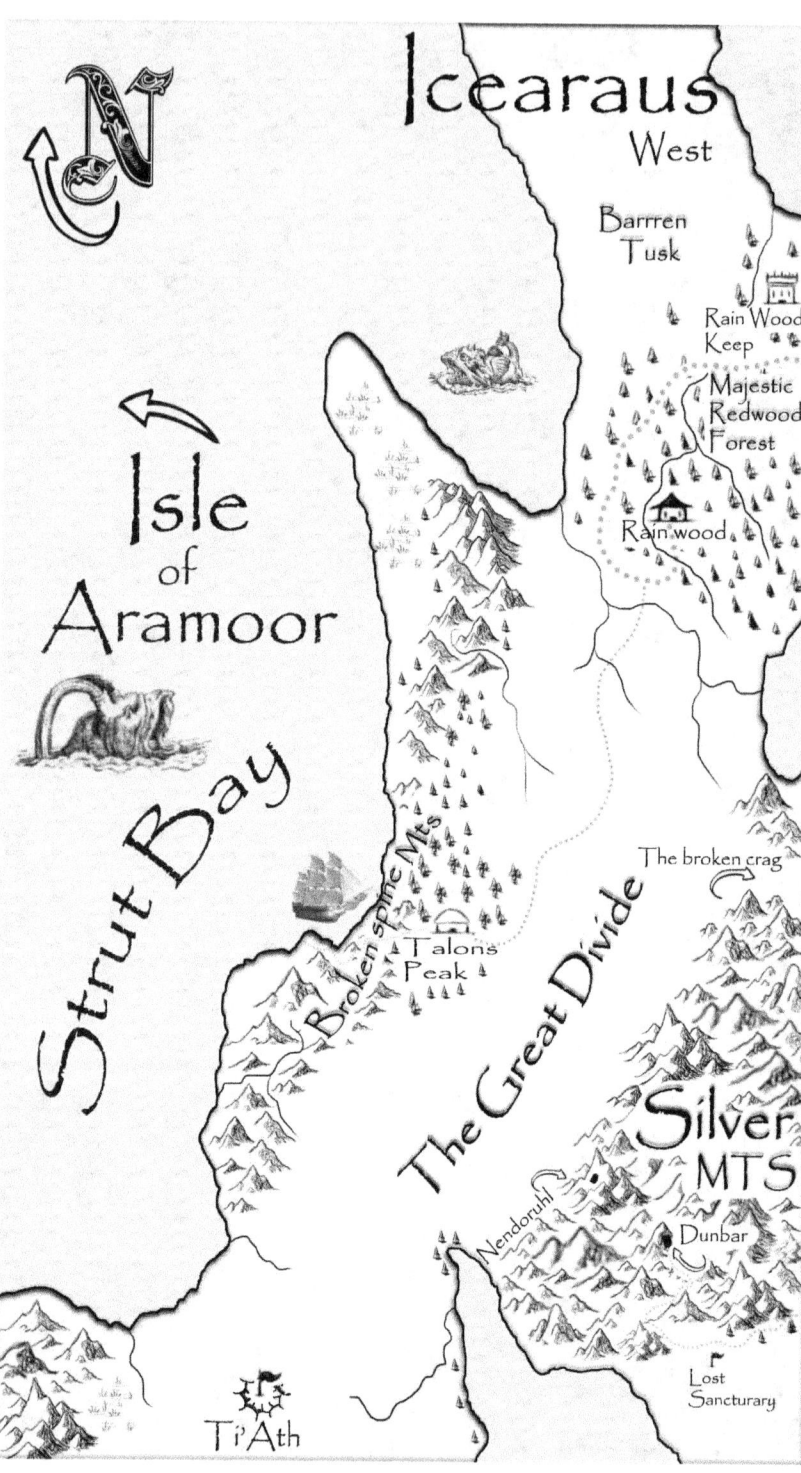

Isle of Aramoor

1/4 Mile

Portal
Calvery Mnt

Kings
Watch

destiny Ln.

Prologue

Twenty five years ago…

emetrius felt the wicked presence of a tormented soul enter the room.

"Did she suffer?" The voice dripped with a sick, sadistic pleasure. Demetrius never looked towards the sound. Instead, he kept his eyes fixated on the smooth mahogany table, or more precisely what lay on it. Besides, he didn't need to look, only one man produced such drivel.

"Enough," Demetrius responded, a hint of disgust in his voice.

"Good… good," the voice cackled. "We must not, and shall not allow the filth of this world go to their grave unpunished for their sins."

"Well tell me this, what exactly was this woman's sin?" Demetrius asked the man who materialized from the darkness.

"What were her sins?" Karayan raised one eyebrow. "Have you learned nothing through-out the years I have used your services?" He pulled back his darkened cowl and shook his long black mane revealing a pale white face. Prominent jaw, chin, and cheekbones appeared rigid in the dim candlelight and two piercing blue eyes held a catastrophic promise. "Her sin is that she's a bearer, a carrier of disease. Impregnated by a creature of the underworld she only has one purpose, to carry the fetus until birth so the demon child can spread pain, disease, and suffering… even death if enough time is given."

"So why must she suffer? Why not simply kill her?"

"Must we continue with the lesson?" Karayan snarled. "Every time you see a good man become sick, you have these to thank." He pointed at the dead body still tied to the chair. "Every time a child is stillborn, it's because of them," he continued.

"So she must suffer for her crimes against society. To feel some of the pain she caused?" Demetrius asked.

"Exactly, and I take the fetus back to the palace for destruction." Karayan approached the corpse. "What a waste," he said, and then poked at the corpse with the blunt end of his gnarly staff. "She was a beautiful girl."

Small pointed ears poked through bloodstained silver hair as the head sagged.

"An elf?"

Demetrius nodded, but his eyes remained focused at the pair of eyes on the table.

"Very unusual," Karayan said.

"Yes... yes, it is."

"I can't recall an elf ever being chosen."

"Nor can I," Demetrius agreed.

"The underworld grows desperate," he chuckled.

Turning her head in multiple positions with his staff he examined the wounds. "Another job accomplished with surgical precision, a skill few have mastered and even less perfected,"

Between them, a painful silence formed.

"Enough with the idle talk," he focused his attention back on Demetrius. "You know why I'm here, do you have what I desire?"

"In the basket, under the table," Demetrius motioned with a small dagger.

Karayan pulled back the bloody towel and examined the contents. "Its heart still beats, still fresh," he whispered. A broken smile came to his face. Satisfied, Karayan placed the towel back and tucked it neatly around the edges careful not to touch the creature inside.

"Are you okay, you seem distant?" Karayan asked. He fondled the baskets handle.

"They say the eyes are the doorway to the soul," Demetrius's voice was cold, the words calculated. "Do you believe even in death, the soul can look back through those very eyes, back into the soul of those who killed them?"

Karayan laughed. "No. When the physical form dies, so does the soul."

"Then why do we close their eyes before we bury the dead?"

Karayan laughed, "I don't." He snatched the basket and made for the door.

"Leaving so soon?" Demetrius asked. A streak of silver flashed across his eyes as he moved past the candle. "Are you forgetting something?"

"Oh yes... yes. In all my excitement I seem to have overlooked your umm, shall we say reward? Yes, a reward for a job well done." Karayan retrieved a large leather coin purse from his pocket. "I believe you will find this more than enough," and tossed Demetrius the bag. "Now, if you don't mind."

Demetrius snatched the bag and watched Karayan vanish into the night, the secret door remained open. A tug on the thick purple string allowed the contents to spill out on the table where he spread them with his dagger. Quickly he counted them and then recounted them. "You bastard!" He slammed a fist against the table. He was five gold short of the agreed fifty.

Demetrius slid the coins into the bag then picked up the eyes and gently placed them in as well. It was still dark outside and a thick cloud layer had every star veiled. From the east, a cool breeze carried the promise of a warm day but the air still had a chilling bite.

Demetrius ran. He didn't know where he was running to or what he was running from, he just ran. The sun broke the rim of the land painting everything it touched in blue and pink fragments that reflected off the dew covered grass. Shaking off the cold he ripped open the purse, reached in and pulled out the eyes. Even though life left them hours ago, their color still shined as bright as the hour he plucked them. They moved as he moved, as he gazed in, they gazed back.

"*I know what you did,*" something whispered.

Demetrius searched for the voice.

Something came over him, a feeling of despair, or malice. Whatever it was draped a blanket of shame over him and both eyes watered. In his mind, the words came clear as crystal, *murderer... killer...*

Shaking his head he tried to make it stop.

Murderer... killer... The voice attacked him.

He couldn't comprehend what happened. Killing came natural, even at a young age. Ever since he was a child, he followed the leadership of Lord Rayne, Master of the Brotherhood. He spent decades training and continued to train long after others retired. His muscles were perfectly toned and his agility superb. Eventually, he climbed to second in command and only one remained better at killing, and even he grew concerned.

Throughout his life he had killed hundreds, dispose of an ex, collect payment for a debt in blood, or make a witness disappear. To him it was business, and business meant money.

The elf girl was different though, the moment she died something happened. Something from her, some sliver of magic entered him. Demetrius looked into the eyes, even now they sparkled with life. He hated himself for taking them but it was too late now, the body would have long since been removed. He tried to throw them but an unseen force kept his fingers closed. Unable to discard the eyes he wrapped them in the cloth and returned them to the bag.

Rested, he continued east until the road forked. South led home to the Lost Sanctuary, except he had no intentions of going there. Minx, a secluded village on the banks of Nye Lake known for the riff-raff who didn't fit anywhere else seemed more like, a fitting home.

Murderer... killer... The words hounded him.

As the sun rose so did the temperature and by noon large beads of sweat dripped from his brow and his black tunic clung to his back. A shady spot just off the beaten path offered the perfect spot to rest.

Murderer... killer... The words rattled in his mind.

Leaned back against a stump he let his mind drift. He re-lived every word Karayan spoke, and none of it made sense anymore. Above him, the limbs of the trees formed a living latticework.

Murderer... killer... The words came, only broken by the sound of a hurried hoof: A horseman approached from the east. Demetrius had few enemies and of those none would have considered challenging him.

The highly polished armor reflected the sunlight like a mirror and the vibrant purple plume that fluttered in the breeze told him this man was a member of the Royal Guards, Karayans personal protectors, the best of the elite. "Quite far from the palace?" Demetrius asked as he stepped out onto the road.

The horse reared kicking with his legs and screamed a loud neighing sound. Launched free, the rider landed flat on his back snapping the plume which fell forward covering the horse masters face.

On his feet, in a flash, his hand went straight for his sword. "My location is none of your concern, peasant." His eyes rolled like marbles following the plume. "And look what you caused," he screamed, plucking the broke plume from his helmet. "Now remove yourself from the road and retrieve my horse, before I lay you open."

"Peasant… Karayan would be highly upset if he knew you called me that."

The guard's eyes squinted. "First, you startle my horse and make me take a tumble, and now you disgrace the Kings name?" The metallic hiss of his sword echoed through the forest as it came free of its sheath. "You'll taste my blade you insolent slug."

"Put that away before you hurt yourself," Demetrius chuckled, trying to keep a stern face. "I have no desire to fight you."

"As I see it, you don't have a choice," then swung the blade in a memorized routine and approached aggressively. "I'll give you one last chance since I'm feeling generous. Retrieve my horse then kneel and pay your respects," he snarled.

"I'll never kneel to that swine."

"What did you just—"

"You heard me. I won't bow to that pig, or anyone else."

"Blasphemy," the guard screamed. "And the penalty is death." Without warning, he lunged with his sword aimed directly at the heart of his foe.

He was quick but Demetrius proved faster and both daggers leaped to his hands and parried the strike.

"You got some skill," the guard snarled bearing his teeth at the botched attempt. His knuckles popped, and the color drained as he gripped the sword. Thrusting once more the clash of steel broke an eerie silence as Demetrius deflected the attack.

Their eyes met and time froze. Demetrius's lips curled at the end.

The guard tried to focus on Demetrius but was mesmerized by the lightning quick movements.

Demetrius darted in slicing the meaty part of the throat just under the helmet. As quick as they appeared, the daggers vanished.

Grasping at the wound blood squirted through his fingers while blood-red tears leaked through the eye holes. Staggering, he fell at the assassin's feet... dead.

For most it would have been a hard choice, but not Demetrius. A plan quickly developed and sweat dripped from his body as he pealed the corpse from the metal can then re-dressed him in his own clothing.

For once in his life, he felt clean and looked rather handsome. If he was to do this, he had to do it right and give up his most valuable possession. Hesitantly, he unclasped his belt and fastened it on his dummy. There was one more detail not to be overlooked.

The long sword was clumsy but effective and with one swing the head rolled away As if he was a ghost he looked upon himself. He had finally met a better foe.

Demetrius mounted the horse then looked into the bag and saw the eyes. Somehow in the fight, they had come unraveled, and they looked back through the opening at him.

Murderer... killer...

Weeks later...

"They got him," Arlin said, his voice lacked emotion.

"Got who?" Lord Rayne asked. Leaned back in the chair his feet propped up on the ornate oak desk.

"Demetrius, he was found a fortnight ago... beheaded. I ordered his body taken to East Haven for burial."

"Impossible," Lord Rayne hissed. "Who's responsible for this?"

"No one knows. Rumor is he was killed in his sleep and discarded like trash along the eastbound road."

"Foul work is at play," Lord Rayne screamed. "And you're positive?"

"Without question. I saw the body myself."

"Begone from me," he screamed then leaped to his feet and pounded a fist against the desk.

Chapter 1

The tips of her fingers went numb hours ago, and the dried blood painted her jagged nails a crimson pink. The ground was cold, hard, and the search for food was tedious, but tonight's catch was rather nice. Three brownish worms, two gray pill bugs, and one large ripe slimy slug covered in yellow spots. *"Ahhh,"* she let out a long-winded moan and rocked back on her heels ignoring the grumbling in her stomach. "Well, it's more than last night."

Placing each morsel on the windowsill she looked at the woman staring back at her in the dirty, rain-streaked window pane. "What have I become?" she whispered to the reflection. Patiently, she waited, tapping her fingers on the rusty metal bars that had not always been there. At first, her eyes were drawn to them. They mocked her, kept her from the outside world—*it's for the greater good*—she could still hear her father's deep throaty voice say—*someday you will understand*—he would remind her. Over time she had grown used to them. No longer did she see them, she saw through them.

Just outside the window lightning flashed and thunder crashed leaving wicked shadows dancing along the buildings. Angry, thick, rain clouds arrived earlier punishing Lynn Brook with a rare summer storm, the like of which none had ever witnessed. Wagon wheel ruts became rivers and mud to quicksand.

Normally the streets would be crowded. "Don't run too far ahead," a woman would yell at her children as they played. The squeal of an axle as an undersized mule pulled an overloaded cart. And every hour the pounding of leather on dirt echoed as the Royal Guards marched past making their rounds. They were beautiful. Polished armor fastened tightly with blood red straps and their purple plumes dancing in the breeze, a smile crept across her face. There was always eleven, five to either side and one in the center barking orders. She would sing along with their cadence until they were gone from sight.

With the onset of this storm, she had not seen the patrol in hours. Averie scratched her cheek, it must be bad because the guards never missed their rounds.

Years ago Lynn Brook would have been considered a quaint quiet town. People came and left as they pleased, a simple life for simple people. All that changed when King Karayan moved from the Rain Wood Forest to Lynn Brook. Enormous walls were constructed and topped with sharp metal spikes impregnated with steel barbs to keep anybody from climbing in, or out. Barracks were built to house his Royal Guards, services had to be increased, and the population exploded. A town roster was created. One large portico was built to regulate the flow of wagons and carts, while a smaller man door was used for foot travelers. Those coming or going had to check in with the roster guard. Both gates were closed at sunset and would not be opened until morning. Overnight, the quaint town of Lynn Brook became a thriving metropolis, complete with all the usual riff-raff that follows.

Pulling back knotted clumps of thick dirt-encrusted hair, Averie look around her room. The stark nakedness of it all was depressing. At one time large colorful pictures lined every wall and the finest furniture filled the room. Oil lamps offered a warm yellow glow, and the floor was made of wood and held the softest rugs. Since her infliction, all that remained now was one three-legged stool and a small pail that leaked.

Outside the window another bolt of white-hot electricity ripped through the sky momentarily lighting her personal prison cell. It was kept dark for a reason. Given the opportunity, people would peer inside to get a view of the creature that lurked within. The thunder that followed shook the very core of the house and dust fell from the ceiling like rain.

A wiggle on the windowsill caught her attention as a worm tried to escape. She was that proverbial worm, trapped, waiting for death. Just like the worm, she was no longer in control. Every decision was now made for her by the keeper, her father.

With one gulp two of the worms were devoured. The third however would not go without a fight. She watched it wiggle and squirm in a desperate struggle to survive. She held the worm up and observed it more closely, who am I to take the life of something that fights so hard. "Be free," she whispered and tossed the worm into the darkness. The pill bugs went down smoothly but the slug retaliated. It left a trail of sticky slime all the way down her throat she could taste long after it was gone.

The shriek of a rusty hinge caused a shiver to race up her spine and she trembled, wondering what her punishment today would be. The silhouette of a monster filled the doorway. In three long strides, he covered the distance and grabbed her by the neck with large, hairy, sausage-like fingers then pressed her face against the windowsill. The wood tore into her face and she expected at any moment to hear the sound of bones snapping and feel its bite. The floor spun and large black spots invaded her vision.

Startled back to consciousness, she felt her face slide along the wall as large splinters drove through her cheek then buried into her tongue. She could feel the warm blood stain her chin and both eyes watered.

Satisfied, he jerked her to within inches of him, "you wish to know what you've become?" His voice was ragged and hateful.

Discarded like a used rag she landed hard on the flat of her back emitting a loud thump. A cloud of dust rose causing her to choke. Her chest burned as she gasped, fighting for air that so easily evaded her. Water streaked from the corners of her eyes leaving trails of glistening wetness down her dirt-stained cheeks. From where she lay she could see the door remained open. The possibility of escape was slim, but she had to try. Get up, she commanded herself, kicking and flailing every limb.

The sudden outburst startled her attacker for a moment then a broken smile etched across his face. He followed her gaze towards the door. "Thinking of escape?" His laugh was coarse.

The way he gracefully darted across the room and took to flight left Averie astounded. For such a large man he moved with the swiftness of a cat and landed with one large thick knee to her left side. The sounds of ribs cracking echoed off the walls as if they were in a deep, hollow cave.

Blood-curdling screams shattered the silence.

Her mind swooned and head wobbled as if attached by a spring as he punched her face. She had lost count after the first but many followed. It should have hurt, but she had lost feeling and shut down. Like a doll, she hung in his grasp. Slamming his other knee onto her chest he moved in close as if to kiss her.

She gagged as his breath filled her nostrils.

"I'll tell you what you are," he snarled. Small pieces of food fell from his maw sticking to the bruised leather-like skin. "You're a diseased filthy creature that's unworthy of life. You steal air from those who deserve it. You're a disgrace."

Averie glanced away. His breath was bad enough but the food that fell into her mouth made her nauseous. Doing so, she noticed another man now stood in the doorway. Smaller than her attacker but larger than a woman, she guessed it was her brother but dizziness filled her head and he faded.

"Just kill her now," he said. "Save us the trouble of watching her," his voice dripped with a sickening pleasure.

She recognized the voice. It was not her brother or anybody else she would have expected. Instead, it was Ilteris, her suitor. He swore an oath to be at her side in good times and bad times, in sickness and in health if she would be his wife. Now was her time of need and he abandoned her, thrown her away like garbage. Her mind drifted to a place where she still found comfort. Maybe I am garbage, but I am still a person. She realized though, with him working for the keeper any hope of being rescued diminished. She would be left to fend for herself, whatever that was worth.

"I can't," he responded, "King Karayan wants her alive." Drawing back he slapped her, "Don't look at him, don't ever look at him again." The impact turned her head. "Your vision might infect him as well."

His fingers grasped onto her hair like a rope and lifted her head, "you've disgraced the family." He slapped her, "and brought shame upon our name. People look at me and whisper hateful things. Friends no longer visit, they avoid me and it's entirely your fault." He smacked her with the back of his hand. "Ten more days, you hear me?" He hawked a large slimy glob of spit onto her forehead and watched it run down the side of her face. "Ten days," he snarled, and then slapped her again.

She made no effort to move until the door closed. Fighting back the pain she needed to get up, laying there was not an option. Finding the courage she climbed to her feet. The pain forced vomit to fly from her mouth and a stream of water ran from her eyes. Stumbling like a newborn fawn she used the wall for support. The loud click of the lock confirmed he was gone leaving her to ponder what he just said—*ten days*. Quiet as possible she moved to the corner, the farthest she could get from the door, and the farthest she could get from him.

Chapter 2

Pegan Rhoe sat on a fallen dogwood log on the west side of the narrow ravine that didn't exist. It was only accessible by a narrow crack in the side of a jagged wall near the very peaks of the Ash Mountains. He learned about it by accident nearly forty years ago when he was a young man still in training. The charred parchment clung to life at the edge of a hearth. Intrigued by the name, Dragon Downs, he set out to discover its location but the details were vague.

Having spent years searching and on the verge of failure he came upon a trail he had never noticed. The trail led him through terrain that ripped and tore at his clothes and left long, nasty red scratches on any exposed skin. At the end, it led to a crack just wide enough for a man to slide through. The farther he went, the tighter it got, and he had all but given up when the crack opened wide into a saucer-shaped valley. As far as he could see dense vegetation covered everything except the middle where a ravine was visible. "Dragon Downs," he whispered.

This had to be the place and thoughts of riches beyond belief filled his mind. In his research, he discovered that a great battle took place here and a golden dragon was slain, leaving behind a horde of treasure. Having spent the next few years searching no treasure was located, or proof a dragon was even slain and eventually he wrote it off as folly. Decades passed, and the thought faded from memory. That is until he came home to a rolled up parchment attached to his door.

He chose a spot far enough off the trail to have plenty of time to see who came. This particular spot was perfect, not only did he have a clear view of the ravine, it also kept him completely concealed. To either side was a thicket overshadowed by jagged rocky walls that reached the clouds while a narrow trail snuck through its center. Lightning in the distance and slow rolling thunder told him tonight was going to be wet. Pulling his cloak tight he tried to find comfort from the nasty breeze that infiltrated every seam.

His mind drifted as he wondered who might have scribed the note. It must be someone old, much older as the name had long since been erased from existence.

The time came to a standstill. Nothing moved except the black clouds that blotted the sky and darkened the night. The breeze whipped the thicket creating eerie shadows that brought the dull gray stone to life.

An uneasy calm filled the ravine when the lonely clop of a single horse caught Pegan's ear. The rider, whoever he was made no intentions of concealing his arrival. From his perch Pegan watched as the rider drifted into view, fading in and out of a fog that seemed to creep just inches behind him.

"Impossible," he whispered, there was no way to get a horse in here. This must be some kind of evil magic at work. Still, his curiosity got the better of him and he waited.

Completely draped in a pure white robe the cowl was pulled low and he seemed to sway with the horse as if permanently attached. As he neared Pegan could see that upon the robe there were threads of gold that danced upon the surface in some magical mesmerizing pattern. Weaving in and out of each other the thread moved in a mystical dance then merged to become one. Only then did it explode into an array of different patterns that lined every edge.

Pegan watched as the rider brought the black steed to a halt and dismounted. Long strands of silver hair spilled midway down his back when he pulled back the hood. Dense wrinkles on his stark white forehead revealed the man was old, impossibly old yet he moved with a purpose. Leading the horse by the reins the rider vanished into the thicket of pickle berry bushes and cattails.

Something was strange about him, something not natural. A figment of imagination sprung to life by an alcoholic stupor. So real, so vivid you could touch it but yet gone the moment you reached for it. Pegan was not sure to chase it or run. The fog which followed the rider filled up the chasm and engulfed the area. Swirling in the breeze it surrounded him, covering his face like a cool wet towel, and terror entered his heart.

Unfolding the parchment he examined the seal one last time, searching for some clue of who its author might be. Drawing no clues he held it up to the moonlight and read it one last time.

> *PEGAN RHOE...*
>
> *Your presence has been requested. Meet me at Gilford Gorge, heart of Dragon Downs at midnight on the first Full moon after receiving this parchment. The time has Come to forget the past and create the future, Be alone, Be prepared.*

Pegan drew in a deep breath and read the note one more time, the simplicity was astonishing. Folding the parchment he placed it back into his pocket and debated his options. He could simply forget the whole thing and leave. After all, whatever this man wanted he had no obligation to help. Besides, there was a good chance this would only lead to trouble, something he didn't need or want.

Curiosity got the better of him though and he slipped from his perch. Sneaking through the fog he made a calculated move which should have placed him directly behind the stranger. He wanted to make sure he held an advantage if things turned bad. Nearing the location where he expected to find the stranger he crept low and slowed his pace to a crawl.

"Join me," the stranger said, his voice was pleasantly warm.

With the element of surprise gone, Pegan jerked out the small knife he carried.

"You won't need that," the stranger said, "at least not yet." His back was still towards him

Pegan scanned the ravine, how did he know? He must not be alone. Someone else must be watching from afar. It was at this moment he realized this was all a trap, it was all planned out, and he walked right into it. What a fool I've been. Now it was too late and the chance of escape had passed. Gripping the knife he would not go without a fight. Thoughts raced through his mind and sweat rolled down his brow. Contemplating his next move he crept backwards then turned to flee but his legs froze. He felt as if he had died and rigor mortis was upon him, yet he was very much alive. "What kind of trickery is this?" he screamed. The knife fell from his grasp. Trapped in some immobilizing spell or paralyzing poison he never felt the sting of a dart. Unable to move he was left for this man to do with as he chose.

He could sense the man. Felt the stranger's hot breath upon his neck as he circled. Eventually, they stood face to face and their eyes met. They struck Pegan as something from a dream. A piercing deep blue which penetrated both skin and bone, peering deep into the soul of the one they gazed upon. Pegan felt naked, ashamed.

He recovered the knife and slid it back into the sheath. "I believe this belongs to you," he said. "I am Elwrick, spiritual guide, and friend, keeper of the book of portals, and you must be Pegan Rhoe?"

Pegan never answered, instead he chose to study the man, searching for a weakness.

"I come in peace and with counsel," Elwrick said.

Pegan felt life reenter his body instantly after Elwrick snapped his fingers.

"Come, we have much to discuss."

Hesitantly, he followed Elwrick to a fire which burned with a chromatic colored flame but kept a slight distance between them.

"Sit," Elwrick motioned.

Unsure why, Pegan did as instructed. A painful silence fell between them.

"Why am I here?" Pegan finally asked.

"You are here because this is where you need to be," Elwrick answered.

This was no ordinary man and the more he listened the more he became intrigued. There was something in his voice, something that reminded him of a past long forgotten. Maybe something in a dream, that was it, this must be a dream.

"And also…" Elwrick paused for a moment to gather his thoughts. "You are here because I have need of your services."

"What can I offer you?" Pegan said. Both eyebrows shot skyward. "I'm a simple farmer pulled from my bed in the middle of the night."

Lightning flashed off into the distance and thunder rolled through the ravine rattling any stone not firmly fixed. The first drops of rain hissed as they hit the flames. "And on the worst night possible, I might add."

"A simple farmer who knows of this place, I think not," Elwrick chuckled.

"How did you get that horse in here?"

"Never mind that," Elwrick said, his words became serious. "Pegan, a new bearer has been located."

"Bearer…" Pegan hesitated, the words rolled off his tongue.

"You know of which I speak."

"Is that not the King's problem?"

"What King?" Elwrick's face scrunched up in confusion.

"King Karayan, the ruler of Icearaus." Pegan looked startled.

"Oh, him," Elwrick sneered. "He's no King, he's a steward."

"Steward." Pegan's mouth opened wide as if making an O sound.

"You have no idea how the world functions," Elwrick said. "A veil has been woven over your eyes for decades while the true nature of the bearer has been forgotten. That is why I am here, to reveal to you the truth, to remove the blindfold."

Pegan placed his hands towards the fire.

"A bearer is not destined to remain within our world. She is impregnated by the Creator who then takes her child to another world to be born. It is there they grow and learn. When the time is correct, they return to share their knowledge with us. It has to do with improving our world, that's all. They are not diseased, in fact, only the purest are chosen. You see all these stars," Elwrick said pointing up to a few places in the sky where the darkened clouds had yet to cover. "People come and go, passing what they've learned from world to world. She is a gift from the Creator. This world's though has been forgotten, as we no longer have anything to offer. We have been left behind."

"You really expect me to believe this. Don't drag me into your dark sick fantasies." Pegan's face flushed red. "Everybody knows bearers are diseased creatures that need to be eradicated from this world lest they infect the population as a whole."

"I am sorry you believe this."

Pegan shook his head, "Fine, the bearer is not a diseased creature but a woman pure of heart. You still haven't said why I'm here."

"Because you're going to save her."

Pegan leaped to his feet, "what did you just say?"

"She needs to be saved," Elwrick answered.

"Well if you're so concerned, why don't you save the wretched thing?"

"I would love to but I reside in a distant realm and thus bound by different laws. I begged the Creator to let me aid but unfortunately, I must remain an observer. It is only now after many decades I have been given permission to intervene, but only with counsel and direction. I have been given authority to find who I believe has the ability to end this tyrant's rule, and move the world in a positive direction."

"And you found me."

"Yes."

"And what if I say no?"

"I can't force you," Elwrick said. "But you are the only chance this world has to keep from being forsaken." His eyes narrowed as his vision fixed onto something Pegan could not see.

"Forsaken?"

"Yes, the Creator is on the verge of total destruction of our world. We are the only world where the people have failed. Chaos runs wild." Elwrick looked towards the sky.

"I beg to differ," Pegan said. "The people have not failed."

"No," Elwrick said. "Look around, what do you see? Very few remain who are not bound by some dark corrupt desire."

Pegan shot him a wicked glance. What he said was true.

"Even now, having been told the truth you still refuse to help. I can see it in your eyes. I know you have questions but are frightened of the answers. Terrified it will alter your whole reality of the world you live in."

"You're wrong," Pegan answered.

"Then hear what I have to say."

Pegan nodded for him to continue.

"All other worlds treat their bearers as royalty as this one once did as well. But something went wrong and I don't know what or when. For some unknown reason, Karayan has convinced the populace that bearers are diseased and has them killed but not before the child is cut from the womb and given to him as you are well aware of." Elwrick wiped the water from his face and rung it from his long beard.

Pegan rose and walked a few feet away shaking his head. *Why did I answer that stupid note? What have I got myself into?* Facing Elwrick once more he asked, "why me?"

"Why you?" Elwrick gasped. "Because there is something special about you, something that tells me you will succeed where all others will fail."

Pegan shook his head, "this is not my calling. People die every day, this has nothing to do with me, I'm sorry. I won't risk my neck to save someone I don't know."

"Nothing to do with you, this has everything to do with you, is the past so easily forgotten," Elwrick erupted like a volcano. "Or do you need some coin to remind you?"

Pegan let the words melt into him, and each one stung like the crack of a whip.

Elwrick knew Pegan was not convinced but balanced on the edge of a knife. Wrapping Pegan in an arm he pulled him tight, "It's time, time to forget the past and forge a new future, time to end this reign of terror, time to become who you were meant to be." Elwrick clenched a fist in excitement.

The last words hurt as his past came rushing back, this man was right, he had no choice but to right his wrongs. "What must I do?"

"Travel to Lynn Brook, kill the keeper and rescue a beautiful young woman named Averie. She needs to be taken to the Isle of Aramoor where the portal can be opened. It is there I will join you."

"Averie," Pegan whispered, *such a beautiful name*, he thought.

"Yes, it is," Elwrick answered as if he read Pegans mind.

"We have one problem though," Pegan groaned. "Lynn Brook is not just a town, It's a fortified city, guards everywhere, no way in or out without being noticed. Even if I do make it inside how do I find her? There must be a thousand houses there. It would take me a year of searching to locate her. Surely you cannot expect me to do that? I need more, tell me her location."

"I cannot tell you, I must show you," Elwrick said. "Sorry I must do this and he rose."

"Do what?" Pegan tried to retreat but Elwrick was upon him, grabbing his wrist with deadly force. Pegan screamed. His head swooned and every muscle in his body twitched and jerked. Electricity drove through him, his shirt smelled of heat and sweat oozed from every pore. He no longer felt the rain on his face or the beating of his heart. Fading, he felt the last breath of air escape his dying lungs.

A blurred house came into focus. It was small but well-kept with a manicured front yard lined with bushes and shrubs each sprouting flowers of different colors. Between the shrubs, a cobblestone walkway led to the front door. In the blink of an eye, he stood at the door. A wooden plaque carved with numbers read *one... one... four...* hung from a thick rope.

As that image faded another formed. First, a child appeared, young, energetic, full of life running through the house, playing and laughing, and then the image changed to that of an older woman. Beaten down and starved Pegan was not sure if it was the same girl or not. He reached out to the woman, but she was gone.

"What kind of trickery is this?" Pegan screamed from his knees.

"Pegan," Elwrick said, his voice changed drastically. It had gone from a warm pleasant reassuring tone to one of foreboding.

He tried to listen but the pounding in his ears blocked the sounds.

"What you just saw is taking place as we speak. That woman you saw is the bearer. I do not know when, but she will be exterminated. She will be tortured, have her stomach ripped open, and the fetus destroyed. When all that's complete she will be thrown onto the street like garbage to be eaten by stray dogs and other carrion. You know I speak the truth."

"You still have not told me her location, only a vision, a vision I cannot interpret."

"Think," Elwrick said. "I have shown you all you need to know."

"How am I to do this, I have no true weapons?" Pegan asked.

"This is indeed a troubling situation," Elwrick responded, "and one I did not foresee." He ran his fingers through his gray beard. "Dire situations call for extreme actions," he finally spoke. "Take this," Elwrick said as he unclasped a dark brown leather sheath from his belt and handed it to Pegan.

"I won't take your weapon," Pegan said, he put his hands up and backed away.

"Take it," Elwrick demanded. His voice struck like lightning.

As if under the control of a superior being he reached out and snatched the item. It felt good in his hand, light, yet strong and sturdy. Without sound and effort, the blade slid from the sheath. The handle was silver, bellied for an improved grip and wrapped in fine black suede. The double-edged blade was made from a strange bluish tinted metal and was perfectly symmetrical. A thin groove lined the center of the blade creating a spine that provided both strength and a place for blood to exit. The Quillion was adorned with jewels that sparkled and each end formed into the shape of a three-clawed talon grasping a translucent orb. The first orb was clear and contained a swirling blue smoke while the other was a solid red and emitted a faint pulsating hue.

"This is a fine dagger," Pegan said, "but, I cannot accept it." He slid it back into the sheath and handed it back.

Elwrick turned away, "the dagger's name is Fel-Strike, Keeper of Light, crafted in a long forgotten era by the Silver Mountain Dwarves. Given as a…" Elwrick choked on the words "a keepsake for my family who perished while defending Nendorühl from the demons at the end of the Great War. Today, I pass it on to you for helping rid the world of Karayan. There is magic in that dagger, but how it will affect you I don't know. For it senses its owner and conforms to their needs. Keep it, use it, until we meet again my friend," Elwrick said as he left, leading the horse by the reins.

"And what if I fail, what if this dagger falls into the hands of the enemy?"

"Have faith in yourself," Elwrick spoke with a calm voice, "I've already placed mine in you."

He watched Elwrick mount the steed and trot away taking the fog with him then pondered what he saw, relived every detail in the vision. "The answer is in the vision," he whispered.

Pulling out the dagger he felt strange. No longer did he feel weak, His vision cleared. Every fiber was immersed in energy that pulled at him, tugging at his very soul like a snake coiling around its prey. Revitalized, he faded into the night heading east, towards Lynn Brook.

Chapter 3

The storm seemed unnatural, violent. It lashed out at anything and anyone. Pegan pressed onward directly into the heart of the storm. His heavy black cloak offered little protection from the pounding rain and howling wind. The trail he followed became mud and threatened to suck the boots off his feet with each step. Hours passed before the familiar cobblestone road between Fairdenn and Lynn Brook found his feet. It was a welcome sight, from here his destination was only hours away.

Pegan stomped the mud from his boots and set off on a slow trot. Normally, it would have been packed by travelers heading in both directions but not now, the storm had everything stalled.

In the distance, the looming walls of Lynn Brook grew from the mist. The pointed spikes that topped the walls jabbed into the blackened clouds. His eyes followed the road to a large portico which was currently closed. The obsidian black bars spotted with rust glistened in the dim light provided by a single lantern. To the left was a large wooden man-door bound in steel.

Pegan pounded on the door.

"Who's there?" The raspy voice came through a slot in the door. "And what do you want?"

"I seek refuge," Pegan said, "from this blasted storm."

A bolt of lightning sizzled across the sky lighting everything for a brief second, a thundering boom followed.

"Go away," the voice yelled back through the opening. "The town's closed for the night."

Pegan pounded again on the door, this time harder, and longer.

"I said go away," the voice snapped. "I won't tell you again."

"Where am I to go?" Pegan pleaded. "I have no supplies, nor shelter. Do you wish me to die out here?"

Pegan stepped back as the door swung inward. "Well, get in here," the guard snarled. Using his hand to block the rain he studied the stranger as he entered. "Guess I did my good deed for the day."

"State your name?" A second guard groaned from the shack. In his hand, he held a large book opened to a blank page.

"Blair," Pegan lied. He learned years ago to keep his identity secret.

"Blair what?" The guard asked, spitting on the ground. "Why do I always get the stupid ones?"

"You just seem to get lucky that way," the drenched guard laughed.

"Oh, sorry," Pegan said. "Blair Sherwood... from Fairdenn." Pegan watched the guard log his name into the book.

"State your business?"

"I come to visit my sister," Pegan grumbled, wiping water off his face. "I should have moved faster but this blasted storm overtook me." Pegan pointed to the blackened clouds. The rain fell sideways and more lightning lit the sky off in the distance, thunder followed. Pegan waited till the guard finished writing, and closed the book. "Is there an inn near where I can find refuge?"

"Down there," the drenched guard pointed. "Second left, can't miss it."

"Wait," the guard yelled from the shack. "You said you were coming to see your sister?"

Pegan was caught in a lie, something he had not anticipated. He would simply kill them if needed but the bodies would pose a serious problem. Once discovered questions would be asked, and alarms sounded. No, he needed to get in and get out without drawing suspicion or raising questions. He thought quickly before the guard got too suspicious. "Like this?" Pegan pointed to his muddy boots and drenched cloak. "I don't think she would appreciate me stomping around her home in this condition. I'll get a room and wash then visit her first thing in the morning. The storm should have broken by then."

Squinting his eyes suspiciously, the guard eventually nodded his approval. "The Smoking Pig is the place you want." Then sent him away with a wave of the hand.

"Thank you," Pegan said. Behind him he heard the guard grumble about having to polish his armor tomorrow, and how he should make him do it as punishment.

Pegan followed the direction until he arrived at a hand-carved wooden sign spinning like a top from a single piece of twine. The other had snapped and lashed out like a whip at all who passed. Gripping the sign he cut it free and observed the image. A fat pig with smoke simmering off its back. *This must be the place*, he thought, then dropped the sign.

Pegan entered and shut the wind and rain out. The tavern was dark but his eyes adjusted quickly and he took a long look. One wide center aisle led to a bar against the far wall while long tables lined either side. To the right, a narrow staircase led to a small balcony that overlooked the main floor. Leaning on the balcony a single man studied the crowd.

Men of every shape and size filled every chair and scantily dressed women roamed the aisles carrying trays overloaded with drinks and food. Along the walls, men stood in small groups and spoke in hushed voices. Lanterns suspended by thick chains provided the only light while chocking pipe-weed lingered on the stagnant air. The whole tavern reeked of stale ale and broken dreams.

People scampered out of his way as he approached the bar. Conversations died to a whisper, and every eye followed his path. A single seat remained open at the bar which he filled. Behind him, the conversations started again as people spoke of the stranger who entered. Patrons were unaccustomed to having strangers intrude upon their domain, especially rovers.

At the far end, the bartender was filling the mug of another and appeared quite intoxicated. He was shorter than most, maybe five foot if he stood on a box, balding, and thick around the belly. Wide suspenders snaked over a filthy gray shirt and held up a pair of filthy brown trousers.

Working his way down the bar filling glasses as he went he eventually arrived at the new face. "Howdy stranger," he said reaching out to shake hands. "Never seen you around these parts before. Must be one of those rovers from the South?"

Pegan knew instantly he referred to the multiple settlements that formed at the giant fissure south of the Ash Mountains. Rapists, thieves, murderers, and any other criminals that were banished from society called it home. Actually, Karayan had no problem with the criminals, only those who got caught.

"If you say so…" Pegan answered.

"Well then," he said. "I'm Jake Cadweld, owner, operator… and you are?" His voice slurred.

Pegan gagged as the thick smell of whiskey crossed his nose. "Blair," Pegan said, taking the hand in a firm grip. "Blair Sherwood."

"Got caught out in the storm, did ya?"

"I did," Pegan said as he looked around the room. "Place always this crowded?"

"Not normally," he answered after he took a swig from a dark colored bottle. "Usually dead about this time but the storm pushed everybody in."

Pegan studied the patrons, "I'm here to meet an old friend but I don't see him."

"Perhaps this freak storm has kept him home." He took another swig.

"Perhaps," Pegan agreed.

"I got a plan, why not stay here for the night? I got one room available if you can afford it."

"I would much rather stay in the company of friends," Pegan said. "But thanks for the offer."

"Well if your looking for company, I got you covered," he chuckled. A quick whistle brought two girls over from across the room wearing clothes that left little to the imagination. "That's all I got left for the night, but since it's late, I'll offer you a good discount."

Pegan studied the pair. He could see it in their eyes they were not there willingly. "Sorry ladies, I'm not looking for that kind of company," Pegan said, then handed each a gold coin. "Now use this money to find a more reputable job," he scolded them.

Cadweld's eyes widened as he saw the coins flicker in the light. "Perhaps I can help you find your friend. You know where he lives."

Pagans plan worked perfectly. He understood a few coins could make someone talk even if they didn't want. He also knew they would stay quiet because it effectively made them an accomplice. On a sheet of parchment, Pegan scribbled *one… one… four* then slid it across the table. "Any idea where this place is?"

Cadweld's face went pasty and his palms dripped with sweat. "There are many places with that number, it's a big town, I'm going to need more if you want my help." He wiped the sweat from his brow.

Pegan described the place from the vision.

"Can't say I recognize it, perhaps a little jingle might refresh my memory. Seeing as you're so concerned with the welfare of my, shall we say, workers," he chuckled low under his breath. Then took another gulp.

Pegan slid three gold coins across the table.

Cadweld motioned for more.

Pegan slid two more.

Cadweld knew better than to push his luck, "follow me," he whispered, then led him to the back of a small storage room and secured the door. "You must be here to see the creature?" Cadweld said excitedly.

"Creature?" Pegan raised a brow. "I am here to see an old friend I have not seen in years. He lives at *one… one… four*. I can remember the place, but not its location."

"Well," he said. "I do believe I can help," taking another swig he offered Pegan the bottle.

"No thank you," Pegan pushed it away. "Never touch the stuff."

"Each their own just leaves more for me," he said.

"So where is it?" Pegan asked bluntly.

Cadweld cocked his head slightly. He knew the story was a lie but didn't care. Five gold coins were more than he would make in ten years and more important, there was a good chance he had more, and he wanted it. On a parchment, he drew a map then explained the fastest route before handing it to him. "And remember." His face lost all expression, "make sure you take this turn," he said and pointed to a section on the map. "Otherwise, the guards will catch and question you."

Pegan waited till the door opened, "by the way," he tucked two more coins into the bartender's shirt pocket. "This conversation never took place, and you never saw me. I want it to be a surprise when I arrive."

"What conversation… and you are…" Cadweld said. A smirk stretched across his flabby cheeks.

With the map safely put away, Pegan vanished in the shadows.

Cadweld looked towards the balcony at the young man leaning over it and gave a quick nod.

That was the signal he waited for and raced out the door after him. Strangers were not welcome here, that is unless they had money.

Pegan knew he was duped when the directions led to a darkened, dead-end alley. He also knew he was not alone. Pegan stopped and listened to the footsteps approach and when the moment was right he sidestepped a blow from behind, ducked another from a large left hand then jumped back to get a better look at his assailant. He was a young man about his size, tanned skin, and black hair worn in a short, military style cut. Instantly, he remembered him as the one who stood on the balcony back at the inn, no doubt sent by Cadweld.

"Give me your money," the kid yelled, his voice was quite gravely and laced with a thug mentality.

"You want it, come and take it," Pegan growled back, baiting him with the brown leather coin purse.

The kid came in fast with a huge right hand that would have killed him had it landed.

Pegan dodged the haymaker then grabbed the arm as it flung past. Twisting it back he kicked the kid's legs out knocking him off balance. Tumbling backwards he landed on his back in a giant puddle. Pegan held fast to the arm and twisted it a bit more. The kid spat out a mouthful of water then screamed as if he was being tortured.

"Shut up," Pegan hissed, then kicked him in the mouth. He needed to be silenced before the whole town was alerted to his presence.

Gagging and choking, the kid coughed up teeth and blood.

"Quiet," Pegan whispered into the face of the frightened man. "Unless you feel like dying right here, right now in this mud hole."

The kid's eyes looked like saucers.

"You're will take me here?" Pegan shoved the parchment in the kid's face.

"I don't—"

Pegan punched the kid in the side of the head. A loud pop echoed down the vacant streets as the eardrum ruptured and the head wobble as if the neck was made of rubber. With both hands, he shook the kid by the collar till it ripped free. Angered, he reached down and slapped him two more times. "Tell me," Pegan yelled again drawing back for another punch but lowered his arm. He reached into his cloak and pulled out Fel Strike and showed it to the kid. "You'll take me there or I'll send you home in pieces, starting with your ears," Pegan snarled. He stepped on the muggers head and smashed it deep into the mud and pulled the ear away from the head and placed the blade against it to allow the victim to feel the cold steel.

Tears broke from his eyes as the stench of feces floated on the wind. His lower jaw trembling to the point his words were barely understandable. "I'll take you there, please don't kill me," he gurgled.

"If you run you'll experience more pain than you could ever imagine. You will beg me for death a thousand times but it won't find you." Pegan jerked the kid to his feet by an ear.

They walked for hours and Pegan began to think the kid was leading him astray. Looking for an opportunity to slip away and get help. "I should just kill you now and save the trouble," he smacked him in the back of the head.

"We're almost there," he sniveled.

A few blocks later they arrived at the house. "Can I go now?" The kid asked through broken teeth. "I did what you asked."

"Sure," Pegan said and hit him between the eyes. Pegan grinned as he watched the eyes roll back and the kid crumbled. "So you can go warn your friends, I think not," he said. Pegan tossed the body into a thick patch of bushes to hide the evidence.

Chapter 4

The house was exactly like the vision, every last detail was exact. Pegan glanced in each window as he scouted the house. Only one person was home besides Averie and he was a giant of a man. Seated at the table with his back to the wall he would be difficult to surprise. Not that he feared the man, he feared that the man would get to Averie first and kill her.

A break in the rain offered the prime opportunity as the keeper rose from his seat and left out the back door to the outhouse.

Now was his chance. He slipped inside and quickly extinguished each candle. The glowing embers in the fireplace cast eerie shadows providing the perfect environment, and he melded into the shadows behind the table and waited.

In the darkness, the clunk of a door shutting reached his ears. Moments later a silhouette formed and Pegan followed it with his eyes, watched it check the locks on Averies door. Watched it circle the table and sit no more than five feet in front of him.

"Damn weather, I can't bel—"

Pegan emerged from the shadows like an apparition and clasped his hand over the keeper's mouth. The blue hue of a dagger lit the kitchen.

The keeper struggled frantically kicking his legs and flailing his arms.

Pegan smiled at how easily the blade cut into the flesh. He held tight as the body convulsed, then slumped over lifeless. His lifeblood spilling away down the front of his shirt.

With the candles relumed he focused his attention on the door that kept her captive. Removing the big iron rod he tossed it aside then flipped the lock open. Painfully slow he cracked the door open only a few inches and peered inside. It was pitch black and the pungent smell of decayed flesh and old feces forced him to back away where he bent at the waist and vomited.

Pegan rubbed the water from his eyes and wiped the snot from his nose before going back to the door. Using the rod this time he pushed the door open all the way and waited. This delay had two purposes. One, he could see if anything darted from the room and two, it placed some distance between him and that fowl funk. He waited for the stink to lessen then used a candle to light the room as he peered in. To the left, Averie sat on a rickety three-legged stool which looked as if it would collapse at any moment just from its own weight. Pegan believed he had seen some of the foulest creatures that ever walked, or crawled Icearaus, but he was not quite ready for this.

Large clumps of matted hair spilled out over a half torn, flea riddled, and feces-stained robe that hung on a wire-thin frame. Upon her skin were wounds that had not yet healed and leaked yellow pus while large black and purple bruises dotted her face and arms. A few fingers had doubled in size, swollen from having their nails ripped off. She looked like something that died months prior and had yet to be placed in the ground.

Pegan's eyes went wide as she rose from the stool. She moved in an awkward twitchy fashion like a puppet and somebody else was jerking the strings.

Pegan waved for her to come, "I'm here to save you," he said softly.

Emitting a groan she backed away to the farthest corner of the room and raised her hands in a defensive posture.

How can this still be alive," Pegan thought, then his face flushed red and he clenched his fist draining the blood from his knuckles. Her condition drove a dagger straight through his heart and he hated himself at this very moment. Hated himself for all the things he had done in the past.

"Come." Pegan waved to her, "I mean you no harm."

Averie looked at him as if he had spoken a foreign language, head cocked sideways she leaned against the wall for support.

Pegan entered ignoring the overpowering stench. He tried to prevent the contents of his stomach from spewing forth but it was of no use and he vomited again.

His stomach churned again as he stretched out a hand, "I'm not here to hurt you," he reassured her.

Time stood still as she debated her options but then reached out and took his hand and with great care she was led from the room.

She walked slowly and leaned on him for support. Unsure of his intentions they could be no worse than the keepers. Entering the next room though she stopped. Both hands raised towards her head when she observed the keeper. It was only now she understood. The time had finally arrived, and she was only moments away from being delivered to the King. Days prior she decided to go with dignity and pride. She would not give him the pleasure of watching her cry.

Pegan noticed her discomfort, "he's dead," Pegan said. "He will never hurt you or anyone again."

She looked around him at the man in the chair. He slumped slightly to one side as if sleeping. His shirt was covered with blood and a puddle formed below the chair. He had told her no lie and she could see the wound, a large gash from one ear to the other almost decapitated the man.

"You can't go like that," Pegan said as he looked her over. Her deep blue eyes had sunk deep into the recesses of her skull almost turning them black. "Do you have any clothes?" he asked.

She shook her head.

"Well, we need to find you something." Pegan ransacked the house and found a thick robe, cloak, hat, gloves, and a pair of boots. "Put these on, we don't have much time."

As he waited for her to change the glint of metal from a candle caught his attention. A small dagger sat on the mantelpiece. With a hiss the blade slid free of the sheath The construction was exquisite and it felt good in his hand, well balanced, and extremely sharp.

Pegan laughed when he saw Averie, the clothes hung on her like a sheet, "It'll work for now."

Pegan cracked the door open and peeked out. He had to make sure the road was vacant or all this work would be for not. Satisfied, he took Averie by the hand and they vacated the home. As quick as possible they traveled down the darkened street to a back alley where the path turned south.

Averie knew these streets well, she could have been anywhere in the city in hours but time had caused those memories to fade. Faster and faster they traveled to the point she could not keep up and in a frantic scream of pain, everything came to a halt. Her chest heaved to the point of explosion and sweat dripped like candle wax. Her left side burned like fire as she gripped it then collapsed on a crate. Supporting her ribs she fought through staggered breaths. Instinctively, she lifted her robe and placed her bare hand against the large purplish black colored bruise.

Pegan took a few minutes to examine the wound, "they may be broken," Pegan said.

Fighting for air she didn't disagree.

"You can't keep walking like this, you need a mount," Pegan said as he lowered the robe.

She groaned as it made contact.

He came unprepared for this. They would have to wait for morning to buy a mount when he remembered a few roads back a mule slept in a small stable just off the road.

Backtracking they found the stable. No lights burned inside and all was quiet. Sneaking in he managed to put the reins on just as he heard someone yell for him to stop. Behind him, the owner held out a large pitchfork.

"Thief," the man yelled.

"I'm not stealing it," Pegan said.

"Sure looks that way to me," the owner replied. He was an older, fat-faced man with long shaggy white hair wearing nothing but pajamas.

"I'm buying it." Pegan pointed to the two gold coins on the railing. "My wife is sick and she can't walk."

His eyes shot to the coins, "double that and you got yourself a deal. Otherwise, I call the guards and you'll be hung before daylight."

"Two gold is more than enough; you can easily buy ten mules for that price."

"I'm done arguing, four is my price or I call the guards."

"Fine," Pegan said. He reached for his coin purse but pulled out his dagger instead.

The man screamed for help and raised the pitchfork but was too slow.

Pegan knocked the weapon aside and buried the blade to the hilt into the meaty neck. Simultaneously, he covered the man's mouth and lowered him to the ground.

Pegan knelt and waited to see if any heard the struggle but when no one came he recovered the gold and quickly buried the body in the hay.

The rain had yet to slacken and now a dense fog filled the streets like an apparition by the time Averie was ready to travel. Except for the clop of hoof on cobblestone, they traveled in silence. Street after street passed, and it seemed as if they were walking in circles when the familiar sight of the gate came into view.

Averie clasped tight to the mule as it lumbered side to side.

"Halt, who goes there?"

Pegan never saw the guard but heard his bellowing, gruff voice.

Averie whimpered from the voice. To be discovered now so close to freedom, she shivered at the punishment she would have to endure.

Pegan sensed her distress, "they won't harm you, I promise," he whispered. He slowed their pace in anticipation.

"Answer me," the guard hollered, followed by padded footsteps.

The hiss of swords leaving their scabbards warned Pegan of a potential fight. "I seek passage out of Lynn Brook," Pegan answered. "My sister is very ill and I am taking her to Fairdenn where her mother lives. She has arranged for a healer to provide care."

"Come closer, into the light," the voice cut through the obscuring fog. "Let me see your face."

Pegan's approach was slow and calculated. Two guards stood at the ready, light reflecting off their armor from the lanterns they carried in one hand while swords—shiny, sharp and ready for use—occupied the other.

Pegan sighed, they were the same two guards who offered him entrance. With the fog and lack of sleep, he hoped to go unrecognized. Regardless, he was inside now and had access to the gate. If they refused to let them leave, he would simply kill them. After all, what are two more bodies?

The problem though was the roving patrols. Eventually, the guards would be discovered, alarms sounded, the King notified, and searchers sent. What he needed was time, time to get far enough away from the city before her escape was discovered. And the only way to do that was for them to allow them to leave unchecked.

Holding the lantern high the guard first looking at Pegan, and then turned to the rider, "remove her hood." The guard pointed towards Averie with his sword.

"My sister is ill and the cold will only pain her more." Pegan refused to comply.

"Wait, don't I know you," the other guard said. "He's the man who came through earlier. Blair... Blair Sherwood if I remember correctly."

The other guard took a better look then agreed. "Nobody leaves till morning. Come back when it' light and the storms broke. Be gone from here." The guard waved his sword.

Hanging their lanterns they returned to the shack and closed the door. Through the window they watched him.

Patiently, Pegan waited.

"Be gone from here, I won't tell you again," the guard yelled through the open window.

"I won't stand here idle and watch her die due to your ignorance," Pegan answered the threat.

"I'll handle this," he said. His partner already sat against the far wall.

Thwack, the sound of the door slamming was muffled by the rain as the guard left his post, a look of disgust on his face. As he neared his blade slipped free of the scabbard.

Pegan's hand found his own weapon. "I'm not looking for trouble," Pegan said. He placed himself between the guard and Averie.

"If you're needing a healer, you must have some coins?" he whispered.

"Some," Pegan answered.

"Give me half," the guard stuck out his hand.

"I won't have enough for the healer?"

"That's not my concern... now is it," The guard snarled. His crooked teeth appeared yellow in the lantern light.

"Fine," Pegan agreed. He counted the coins and gave him half. "Now open the gate so we can leave."

The chain groaned as the porticoes rose. "And don't come back, ever, or it'll be off with your heads," he screamed as the pair vanished in the fog.

"Crazy fools," the guard said as his drenched supervisor returned to the shack.

"Sometimes you need to break the rules and let the crazies out," he said, his fingers fondling the gold.

Chapter 5

verie turned. Behind her, the town of Lynn Brook, her home of twenty-one years faded. The towering high walls with its razor-sharp spikes and the gatehouse with its ever-burning light would soon be nothing more than a memory. The beautiful palace to the north, time square with its enormous fountain… everything was gone, replaced by a swirling mist and heavy downpour.

The consistent rocking motion of the mule took its toll and her eyelids gradually closed. On more than one occasion, she jolted herself awake just in time to keep from falling. Before her, the stranger, her savior, led the mule by the reins, his motive unknown.

Pegan led the reluctant mule from the cobblestone road out into the plains. The clop of hoof on stone quieted to a squish as both guide and mount sunk into the soggy ground. Pegan stopped and studied the vast expansion looking for something, or someone. Hesitant, the mule grunted and tried to turn back but Pegan held fast to the reins.

The sudden change in direction hadn't gone unnoticed, and it crossed her mind to ask where he was leading her. She also understood the consequences of speaking without being spoken to and remained quiet.

Pegan exerted great care and led the mule around holes, boulders, stumps, and logs. With each step, he could hear a groan escape her lungs.

The temperature rose as the day passed. The sky cleared, and the fog dissipated. In the distance, the vague outline of large trees loomed. With the lumbering beast in tow, he found most paths unsuitable and backtracked several times until he found one which they could safely use. He knew before leaving Lynn Brook this forest oasis would be their first break. It was both secluded and secure.

To Averies surprise, the grove was quite elegant, complete with thick shade trees, lush green grasses, and a crystal clear pond ringed in cattails and snippet weed grasses. The glass-like surface glistened from what few rays snuck through the dense canopy of leaves and branches.

Carefully, he lifted his charge from the mount then created a small fire, large enough to cook on yet not so big as to draw attention from the heavy smoke.

Drawn like a moth to a flame she located a suitable spot and sat.

It seemed like an eternity as they each starred at the other. "I'm Pegan Rhoe," he said, "but call me Pegan."

She never spoke, instead, her vision refocused on the fire. The heat felt good against her ragged skin.

"It's okay," Pegan said. "I understand you've been through more than I could ever imagine. And I know trust is something that is earned." Pegan retrieved a large piece of salted pork and skewered it. From the corner of his eye, he watched her study the food. Drool glistened on her chin and she licked her lips. "When did you eat last?" he asked.

She didn't answer but instead turned away.

With the meat warmed he held it out for her to take, "here, eat."

She had seen this treatment before. Weeks earlier the keeper prepared food and offered it to her. As she reached for it he pulled it back, called her a thief, and then whipped her into unconsciousness. She had no desire to relive that moment.

"Here, you can have it." Pegan held it closer.

Averie forced her knees against her chest and both eyes remained focused on the fire. The urge was strong to take it, but her will was stronger.

"You look famished, you need to eat," Pegan said. He wouldn't force her to take it, but also knew the consequences of starvation. He cleaned a rock and placed the meat within her reach and walked a good distance back. "Now eat," Pegan said sharply. "You're nothing but skin and bones and the journey is long. It will do neither of us good if you die from starvation."

Seizing the opportunity she latched onto the stick and gnawed on the meat like a wild animal. Her jagged teeth tore away large chunks and she swallowed them whole. She could not remember the last time she had eaten anything besides, bugs, worms, spiders, slugs or anything else not quick enough to escape. Let alone it being cooked.

"Slow down," Pegan said, he sat beside her. "Eating like that will make you sick."

Ignoring his warning she tore the last bit of meat from the skewer, licked the grease from her fingers, and then slurped on the stick, nothing went to waste.

"When you're ready to talk, I'll be here," Pegan said, placing more meat near her. "But now I must tend to the mount before he roams."

The growling in her stomach ceased and her headache calmed. At one time she dreamed of fleeing, running away and hiding in a place she would never be found but not anymore. When he was near she felt an overwhelming sense of calmness, as if no harm would befall her. Lying by the fire she closed her eyes and faded off into a peaceful slumber. The nightmares that haunted her dreams nightly never came.

Pegan crept to the edge of the grove and looked out towards Lynn Brook. He wanted to make sure they had not been followed. As the last rays of light faded, the grove went dark. They should have left by now, been halfway to the Ash but she needed rest, sleep would do her good. Throughout the night Pegan kept the fire burning. Somewhere in the darkness, a coyote howled while a million crickets sang. Pegan let his vision drift towards the stars as he leaned back against a stump. The words Elwrick had told him echoed through his mind—*around each one of those stars are other worlds.* "Sleep well, my lady," he whispered.

It was well past noon when Averie woke. Beads of sweat ran down her face and a thick black cloak covered her body. The fire dwindled to gray coals mixed with glowing embers and stunk of charred wood. Pegan was nowhere to be seen. Fear struck her heart and she climbed to her feet in a rush, ignoring the pain from her ribs as she spun in a complete circle. The grove was empty except for the sleeping mule.

"He abandoned me," she said in a panicked voice, one trembling hand went to her lips.

The splash of water caught her attention as a naked man climbed from the pond. His wet raven black hair hung straight down at the sides highlighting his stern angular jaw, chin, and prominent cheekbones. His face told a story of years of training and his thin body rippled with muscles offered immediate proof to that claim. Deep emerald green eyes shadowed by thin, but visible black eyebrows told a story of seriousness, but yet also held a twinkle of compassion. Not one detail was overlooked as she watched him in the distance. From the way he laced his boots, to making sure each dagger hung just right, Averie could see he was a true perfectionist.

She knew he could tell she was watching him when his mouth transformed from one of seriousness to that of a crooked smirk. Not a smirk of intimidation but rather a look of embarrassment for being caught naked, vulnerable. He was a man women dreamed about and why he chose her, she couldn't understand.

"Where are we going?" She called out in a weak, labored voice.

"You're awake," he said, his lips broke into a grin, "and to answer your question, deep into the Ash, for now." Pegan pointed towards the large mountains to the west then watched as her eyes saw past him to the range.

"You told the guards we were going to Fairdenn, you lied," she said.

"My lady, I had no choice. Your disappearance will not go unnoticed forever. Once discovered, search parties will be dispatched. If a lie buys us more time to put distance between us and them, then I would say the dishonesty was well worth it," Pegan smiled.

"Do you think they will catch us?" she asked.

"Eventually," Pegan said. He could tell she didn't like his answer. "Karayan's reach is far and wide. Word will reach every town and village to be on the lookout and a large reward will be offered for your capture."

"You mean King Karayan?" She asked.

"No," his words turned a deadly seriousness, "he is no King," Pegan replied. "He's just a steward."

"So what then, we surrender?" she gasped. "You don't—"

"We fight, and we never stop fighting till we get to the Isle of

Aramoor," Pegan said as he used his foot to spread out the last few embers. "On another note, I still don't know your name?"

Averie was oblivious to what he had just said. One location jabbed into her like a sliver, "The Isle of Aramoor?" she asked.

"Where Elwrick will meet us," he said. "But right now we need to get as far away as possible. The trail I'm taking travels deep into the Ash Mountains."

"Have you traveled it?"

"Many times," he answered. "I still don't know your name?" It was a lie, but he needed her to say it. A simple confirmation he rescued the correct person.

She paused a bit, "Averie, my name is Averie," she said with a smile. It was a name that she had not spoken in a long… long… time.

"Well, Averie," Pegan took her hand and knelt. "I have taken an oath from Elwrick to see you safely to the isle. Upon my life or death, I will do what I must to guide you there."

This was the second time she heard that name, "whose Elwrick? And why didn't he come?"

Pegan thought a moment, "I'm not sure who he is. And he didn't come because I don't think he can. He's not from our world, but another. We spent hours talking about the old magic and the world. At first, I never believed him, he talked crazy. I hated him for telling me the things he did, but I realized there was truth in his words. That's why I offer you my life today, to see the wrongs of this world righted."

"I don't understand?"

"Neither do I," Pegan said. "No one does, but what I do know is the reason you were to be killed."

"Why?"

"Because of the child you carry," Pegan said.

"Child." Averie's nose wrinkled. "I'm a diseased filthy creature who needs to be destroyed before I corrupt civilization. That is why I must be destroyed."

"Listen to me," Pegan said. "You are not a filthy creature but a woman perfect in heart, spirit, and mind; this is why you have been chosen to carry the child, a gift from the Creator. The child will someday restore Icearaus to its former glory. I don't know when, or how, but it will."

"I have never been courted by a man, how can I be with child?" She rubbed the small bump on her belly. "It can't be… you lie. I am a filthy creature infected with a demon, or plague, or something."

"Filthy creature," Pegan repeated the words. "Don't you believe that for one moment, don't you dare," Pegan said. "You have been lain to, we all have. A web of lies has hindered our vision for decades but now the truth has been revealed. You must take my word. You are far from a filthy creature, only treated like one."

She smiled. Beyond the dirty lips and broken teeth, clumpy hair and recessed eyes, he could see that beauty remained.

Pegan drew a deep breath, "It's hard to ask, and if you can't answer I'll understand," he said. "When were you to be exterminated?"

Horrified by the question she winced, drawing large wrinkles across her forehead. "I don't know," she said. "Before you came, he said something about ten days."

Pegan counted the days since they left. "Excellent, if all goes well we'll travel a great distance before you're discovered missing."

Averie tried to stand but doubled over in pain. A small trickle of blood seeped from her mouth.

"Can I see the bruise again? In the light, I can better assess the damage."

She bit her tongue as the robe passed the massive blue, black and purple splotch that covered her entire left side. Pegan began his examination by poking here and there, each time she jerked as a finger made contact. "They're not broken," he said. "But I think a few are cracked."

"So what does that mean?" she asked.

"You need a healer," he said. "You won't make it to the isle in this condition. Lucky for us our path takes us right by one. Well, pay him a visit before we leave the ash."

"Can he be trusted?"

"I think so, he's an outcast like me," Pegan answered. "Do you wish to bathe before we leave?"

"I am not going in there."

"I won't look," Pegan said.

She thought for a long moment. "No thank you," she said again. "I can't…" A slight trust for men still lingered.

"Someday you will learn to trust me."

Averie smiled, she was sure eventually she would.

Back on her mount and the sun at their backs, Pegan led them out of the grove and towards the towering peaks of the Ash Mountains.

Garrien woke to the high-pitched squeal of a wagon as it passed. From where he lay branches created a finger thin latticework against the bluish backdrop making his head spin. His fingers dug into the soft ground and his head slumped back into the mud. "Make it stop" he begged, his vision faded to darkness and his eyes slammed shut.

Hours later Garrien woke not knowing where he was. What he did know though was the saliva that ran down his face was not his, but that of a large canine licking the sweat and blood from his face. The air was heavy, thick and his shirt clung to him like a second layer of skin.

"Get away from me," he grumbled through a slackened jaw. The dog snarled as it backed away, a white froth dripped from its lower lip. Not ready to give up just yet on dinner it stayed close.

With the aid of a few limbs, he pulled himself from the ground and stumbled out towards the road. People gasped and scattered out of his way. Women grabbed their children draping one hand over their eyes while grown men stepped back in disgust. "What are you all looking at," he screamed before running off down the street and disappeared into a darkened alley.

Shadows were long by the time Garrien made it home. Not wanting to show the shame he snuck through the back door and straight to his room.

The dim light from a single candle reflected off the gold coins stacked on the counter. Cadweld lifted them off the counter then let them fall, pleased with the clang each one made as it landed on the other. Using both hands, he straightened the stack till the alignment was perfect. Garrien should be back soon with the rest.

"Has he returned?" Sharmayne asked as she entered through the swinging door, her eyes drawn to the glint of gold.

"Not yet."

"What's taking him so long?" she asked, leaning on the bar she twirled her long red hair with one finger. "It's been over a day now."

"This ain't his first job," Cadweld snarled. "He knows not to come straight home when the job is done, less likely to be followed."

"And you sure nothing went—"

"Listen," Cadweld slammed his fist down spilling the stack. "You questioning my boy, saying he's not capable?"

"No," she said and backed away. His temper had grown out of control since their marriage, right along with his drinking, and more than once it turned physical. "Every other time he's always back by morning."

"Garrien's the best darn fighter this side of the Ash. Kicks hard as a mule and bites like a crocodile," he spat. The tip of his tongue hung from his mouth as he focused his attention on rebuilding his golden tower, "and besides, ain't no rich dignitary gonna beat him."

"That was no dignitary."

"Then rich vagrant. Whatever you call him. I bet he stole the money anyway."

"Why would a vagrant or a dignitary be interested in that creature?"

"Who knows," he said, sliding the coins into a brown leather purse. "Regardless whether he is a dignitary, vagrant, or criminal, he has money and I want the rest of it." A crooked smile found his face.

"I hope you're right," she said.

"Hope is for people who don't have capabilities," Cadweld said tossing the bag up into the air, he caught it with the other hand, "he'll return."

Chapter 6

Even though the kid was young and in shape, the trek across town left him winded. The pain in his side forced him to bend at the waist as he reached the palace. His long shaggy uncombed hair clung to his sweaty face and his dirty, undersized pants exposed socks of different colors. He stopped at the guards who waited by the stairs. Gasping in long drawn-out breaths, "I need to see the King."

"Go away… street urchin," the guard yelled, looking down at the disgraceful dirt ball. A hiss rung out as he slid the menacing looking curved sword from its sheath. "Before your filth permeates the palace."

He waited his entire life, all twelve years of it living on the streets but no more. Things were about to change and in his favor. An errand placed him directly in destiny's path and there was no way he would let this opportunity pass. After tonight, his family would be a respectable member of society. They would finally live where the houses shine and the streets where clean. A place he always dreamed of living and now he had the means to make it happen and refused to let this guard ruin it. "This is very important," he said.

"Well tell me and I will make sure King Karayan receives it," the guard said.

"And let you take all the credit and the reward. Not on my life," he argued.

"Fine then, be gone from my sight," the guard snarled.

"When it's discovered that the information I have about the escape —"

"When what's discovered? And what escaped?" The guard demanded.

Even at his young age he was extremely streetwise and knew the power of words. "Ah... maybe it's nuthin but then again, maybe not," he said and turned to leave.

"Let him pass," the other guard said. "I ain't risking my neck for that urchin. What if something did happen and he speaks the truth? Are you willing to take full responsibility for turning him away? Besides, the King's policy says he is to be informed of everything that goes on in this town."

"And if he's lying?" The guard slid his sword back into the sheath.

"Then he'll be made an example for all to see. And we come out clean as virgins."

"I guess you're right," he said. "Hold up," the guard yelled to the kid. "I've changed my mind, come tell the King and collect your reward."

A grin crossed his dirty face as he walked up the stairs towards two massive double doors.

"Wait here," The guard said and slipped inside, only to return moments later and resume his post.

Soon, a woman appeared and ushered him in.

The boy leaned back as the figure in black stood from the chair. He was the tallest man in the world.

"The guard tells me you got something very important to say, something that cannot wait?"

"It's true," he said. "I was hoping with this information my family would be moved off the streets and placed in a nice house in the good part of town."

"Is this a bribe?"

"No," the kid pleaded.

"Well then," Karayan said, "if I feel your information is important enough, I am sure new living arrangements can be made."

"Okay... okay. I was outside the creature's house when I saw two men approach. I hid in the bushes so I don't think they saw me. One I recognized as Garrien—"

"The man who lives in that nasty brothel?"

"Yeah, that one," he said. "Well, I never saw the other one before, big ugly guy all dressed in black with a cowl pulled low blocking his face. When they got to the house the guy in black hit Garrien hard with something shiny knocking him out cold as a fish then he tossed the body into the bushes."

Karayan's eyes opened wide. "Continue," he said eagerly.

"Well, this stranger waited outside for a long time then went around back. I couldn't see what happened next but as I was getting ready to leave something strange happened. The front door opened, and he stepped out and had another man with him, at least it looked like a man."

"Was it the diseased creature?" Karayan demanded.

"I don't know," he said, "but I got more. A bit later I saw the same two at Ray Keats place. Mr. Keats had a pitchfork out holding it towards him. The man did something and Mr. Keats went limp and dropped the pitchfork. A bit later they left and one was riding a mule."

Karayan moved at a blistering pace. The sound of material ripping echoed off the walls as the kid flew from his feet. The only reason he didn't sail away was Karayan snatched him by the neck with his other hand. His grip tightened like a vice as he shook him.

Unable to resist he flopped like a rag-doll. His shoes launched through the air as if hurled by a catapult.

"Answer me, boy." He pulled him in close and screamed in the kids face.

He tried to answer, but the grip was so tight breathing stopped.

At arm's length he held the child straight out and with his other hand he smacked him across the face. Blood sprayed from his nose painting the wall a grizzly red. With the return swing, the lower lip was all but ripped from the kids face.

"Was it the bearer?" Karayan screamed again.

Even if the kid had the answer it didn't matter, life had slipped away before the second smack.

Karayan gripped the kid by the crown of his skull and twisted the body until a grotesque pop echoed. Satisfied, he threw the boy into the corner. The squishy sound of the impact confirmed few bones remained intact.

"Guess I need to go check myself."

Less than an hour later they arrived at the keeper's house.

"There's no need to knock," Karayan said as he stepped past the Royal Guard, his head tilted to one side and his nostrils flared wide from a foul stench that leaked out from behind the door, "he's already dead, I can taste it in the air." The locked door offered little resistance as Karayan leaned against it and gave a shove. A snap could be heard as the door swung inwards littering the floor with shards of wood.

The air was alive with the tune of a million flies and the bloated body of the keeper was slumped to one side, as if possessed by a demonic entity it convulsed. Below it a pile of maggots squirmed, falling from the gut which burst open hours earlier. The stench of decay penetrated every pore as it raced by filling the vacuum created by the open doorway.

Oblivious to the flies, Karayan entered the keeper's tomb and walked right through the pile of the maggot on his way towards the other room. A quick glance told him what he already knew, "she's gone," he said.

"Impossible," the Royal Guard replied, "how did she… kill him?" He asked from the doorway.

"She didn't," he said. The slice was perfect and left the head dangling, attached only by a fragment of skin. It extended from ear to ear in an eerie mocking grin as if saying I won. "A razor-sharp instrument guided by a skilled hand created this wound. There are few trained…" Karayan walked out.

"Search the place and bring me anything of value," Karayan demanded. "Then burn it to the ground."

"My King, shall I inform the gravediggers they have a job to do?"

"No. I believe a cremation is in order," Karayan said as he made his way to the exit. "And I believe she is still in the city. Find her, or you'll take her place," he snarled.

Silence filled the tavern when six Royal Guards walked through the front door, five of them drawing their swords while the last unrolled a long parchment and read it. "It is by decree of King Karayan that Garrien Cadweld shall be taken into custody—"

"You can't barge into my establishment and haul off my son like a common criminal," Cadweld yelled. With his fist clenched he rounded the bar making his way towards the guard.

"He can, and we will," the guard said as he stepped between them.

"Out of my way," Cadweld yelled as he reached for the guard.

Screams filled the room as the guard buried his sword deep into Cadweld's chest. Unsure of what just happened Cadweld reached for the embedded object only to lose three fingers as the guard slid the blade free. A thin trail of blood leaked from each corner of his mouth as he tried to speak. Time halted as he stared straight into the guard's face. His face went pasty and his eyes locked in a glassy stare. In silence, he fell at the guard's feet.

"Tear this place apart till we find him," another guard screamed.

Patrons fled the tavern searching for safety along with his wife but she got snagged at the door and pulled back inside. She tried to fight but was no match for the guard who slapped her multiple times then placed his blade against her throat. A slight trickle of blood leaked down her bosom. "Where is he?" the man snarled, their faces mere inches apart. Her beauty brought on a rage of passion and he ran his tongue up the side of her face.

"He's not here," she cried. Her neck felt like it would snap at any moment the way her head was being twisted.

"You lie," he slapped her. His grip slackened just enough giving her the opportunity to break free and try to crawl away. Angered, he kicked her in the face. Throughout the bar, the sound of furniture being smashed could be heard. In one motion he dropped all his weight onto her back while jerking her head back by the hair. "Tell me where he is or I'll cut your throat?" he demanded.

"He's not home," she begged.

"Wrong answer," he said and was about to cut her throat when a guard yelled from the back, he's been found. "You got lucky," and shoved her face down on the floor.

A guard emerged leading the frightened man out at knifepoint.

"King Karayan wishes a word with you," the guard said. "But judging from how you look, I would say he's already paid you a visit. None the less, take him." Bound with thick, black chains that bit into his skin he was led from the tavern to a waiting cart.

The palace was to the north of town and built upon a large terrace that allowed King Karayan to overlook the town. To either side, large trees lined the roadway and only allowed brief glimpses of the grassy fields and the large stone decorative fountains beyond.

As the road reached the palace, it widened to twice its original size then stopped at a large stone encased pond. Overlooking the pond was a fountain shaped like a dragon perched upon a waterfall, from its snout came a cool mist while water rushed by its feet spilling over the edge into the waiting pond.

To either side of the fountain were large curved stairs constructed of black marble wound up to a large landing that ended at the base of the dragon. A pair of large mahogany wooden doors appeared to be the only entrance. Four guards stood at the bottom of the stairs while the landing had another pair of guards, one to either side of the door.

The palace was astonishing with its pointed roofs that reached high into the sky, magnificent yellow stone walls, decorative stained glass windows, and gorgeous landscaping.

Nearing the fountain the wagon was brought to a halt and his bindings removed. Escorted up the stairs a single female stood motionless waiting for his arrival. Even being this groggy her beauty was unmistakable. Dirty dishwater blond hair flowed clear to her rump in waves that curled at the ends. She bore the deepest hellfire red eyes Garrien had ever seen. From neck to toe she wore a fire ash gray silk colored robe and a simple twine rope belt that highlighted her perfectly shaped bosom. A silver dagger hung on her left hip.

"My name is Lilith," she said, "and you must be Garrien?"

"Yes, my lady—"

"We've been expecting you," her voice was like a dove singing. With a wave the door swung inward, and they entered. Behind them, it closed by itself.

The main hall of the palace was bright as many windows fitted with stained glass lined each wall. Light refracted by the color's filled the room in rays of reds, blues, and greens. In between each window hung a large tapestry depicting different battles long before his time. Pure white marble stone infused with silver veins covered the entire floor except for four large steps constructed of black onyx which led to a platform.

A single table made of mahogany sat in each corner surrounded by four chairs and a lone candle burned on each table. The centerpiece though was the throne on the platform. It was carved from one solid piece of granite with thin gold veins snaking their way around the surface. Huge diamonds lined each arm and giant red rubies formed the base. The silhouette of a man filled the seat.

"My King," Lilith said, bowing low on one knee. "Our guest has arrived."

Unsure of what to do, having never been among royalty Garrien just watched.

"Thank you, Lilith," Karayan said, rising from the chair.

Garrien's mouth dropped open as the figure rose. He was expecting a man all scared up from battle, missing a few fingers with a large sword swung over his back. Not the well-spoken, charismatic and devilishly handsome one who greeted them.

With his eyes fixed on Karayan, Garrien failed to notice Lilith take up a position behind him, resting one hand on the hilt of her dagger.

"It has reached my ear… that you aided a strange man?" Karayan said. A slight hint of hostility floated on the words. "I have it upon good faith you led this man straight to the house of the bearer?"

Small beads of sweat percolated on his forehead and ran down his face in glistening streaks. He tried to step back but a sharp object prevented his retreat. Lilith was there with her dagger.

"This is true," Garrien responded, his voice shaken. "But I did it against my will."

Karayan eyes narrowed. He hated to be addressed improperly, but decided to let it slide until the questioning had finished. "Then tell me this," he motioned with his hands, rolling them in a circular pattern. "When were you planning to inform me?"

"When I felt better, perhaps in a few days."

"A few days… Do you not realize the importance of this information? She's now escaped and her capture will be costly?" Karayan hissed. As he finished, he motioned for the guard in the corner to come. "Go to the gatehouse and bring me the roster for last week," he whispered.

"Yes my King," The guard bowed then left the room.

Karayans focus was back on Garrien, "if you are innocent, then tell me what happened?"

"I ran into him outside the tavern. A big bastard, the kind you only see in nightmares. He said he was looking for an address, *one… one… four…* to be exact and asked if I knew its location. I told him I didn't, and he called me a liar. No one calls me a liar, and we fought. I fought like hell and landed my fair share. He bested me and said he'd kill me if I didn't take him there. Next thing I know I woke up the next morning laying in the shrubs." Garrien's voice shook, his eyes focused on the ground.

"Hmmm," Karayan said. A good hour passed while he debated on the best course of action.

A sigh of relief escaped Garrien's lungs as the guard returned carrying a large stack of papers. "Here are the rosters, my King," the guard whispered, "but there's more."

Karayan motioned for him to continue.

"I paid a visit to The Smoking Pig as well and talked to his mother."

"And?"

Over the next few minutes, he explained everything in great detail what occurred.

"Thank you," Karayan said, dismissing the guard back to his post.

"Well… the part where I get confused is when you left the bar to rob him," Karayan said.

"That is a filthy lie, I never—"

Lilith slapped him in the back of the head with the pommel of her dagger dropping him to one knee. "Never address the King with that tone," she said. "In fact, you have disrespected him ever since you entered the palace."

"Do you think I would make up unwarranted accusations?"

"But I—"

"Silence," Karayan yelled. "I will get the truth out of you. Bring him here."

Garrien had no choice but to comply with the guards or have his arms broken.

Karayan met him half-way up the platform then landed a punch square to Garrien's face. The impact ripped him free of the guard's grasp and sent him reeling backward where he landed with a loud thud on his back. Blood ran from his nose and mouth painting the floor the color of a pink rose.

"Bring me a block of wood," Karayan hissed.

Forced on his back a guard stood on each arm while his feet were placed on the block leaving a large gap between his knee and the floor.

"Now… I'll only ask once," Karayan placed his large foot on the kneecap and applied pressure. "Who was he?"

"I don't know," Garrien cried out. His body convulsed and tears ran down his cheeks.

"Do you like pain?" Karayan asked. "I can make this last until you beg me for death but it will never find you. In fact, given the opportunity most my prisoners take their own lives. Unless you want this to continue I recommend you start talking?"

"I already told you all I know," Garrien begged through quivering lips.

"Hmmm," Karayan mumbled rubbing his chin. Then without hesitation, he jumped and landed with both feet on Garrien's knee. A sound followed like gravel breaking and the leg lay flat while his foot remained on the log.

The scream sounded almost demonic and vomit launched from Garrien's throat.

"Now let's try this again." Karayan knelt by the broken knee and lifted the foot while adding a slight twist for added pleasure. "Who was this man and what else did he say?" Karayans voice dripped with venom.

"I…I…I…" he began to say then passed out.

"Wake him," Karayan hissed.

With the prisoner awoken once more, Karayan continued. "I grow tired of your lies."

"I speak the truth," Garrien mumbled.

Karayan motioned toward another guard who held a large wooden mallet. Garrien never screamed, instead, he simply bit off his tongue and begun to choke on the flabby muscle. Blood ran from his mouth mixed with vomit and both eyes pooled with tears.

"This is only the beginning," Karayan said, dropping the limp leg to the ground and returned to his throne, "Make him kneel before me."

"Yes, my King."

Long sobs echoed through the palace as Garrien was placed on his knees, the lower portion of each leg bent forward so he could see his own feet.

"Once again, who was this stranger?"

"He came into—" the words where slurred.

A left-handed fist hit his head with a sickening smack as if someone dropped a cantaloupe from the ceiling. The beating continued for quite some time before Karayan motioned it to stop.

"You've already been warned about disrespecting the King," the guard screamed at him, spittle splattered across his face. Convinced the man had learned his lesson he lifted him back to his knees

"My King," he said, in between the sobs. Blood ran from his busted nose and stained his shirt a dull pink. Over the next few hours, he told what happened over the last few days.

With this newfound information he sat back in his chair and studied Garrien, he had finally got the truth.

"My King, what shall we do with him?"

"Feed him to the hounds," Karayan said.

"Yes, my King." With a guard holding each arm and another on his legs he was brought to the edge of a deep hole. Swung to and fro to build momentum then tossed in. The grunts and snarls drowned out the screams.

After the servants had cleaned the mess and left, Karayan searched the roster. Only one name was unknown.

Chapter 7

Unaffected by the laws of physics on Icearaus, Midnight covered leagues in minutes. His muscles rippled under his glossy smooth pure black coat with each movement. The ground cracked under his weight and each step sounded like thunder. The rider leaned forward placing his head next to the horse's ear. Closing his eyes he whispered, coaxing the beast onward. The response was immediate. Both rider and mount were one, each understanding the urgency. Each hoof dug deep into the ground and kicked up large swatches of dirt slinging them high as if launched by a catapult. Behind him, his robe whipped like a flag in a windstorm.

Midnight was from the Realm of Shettearah—Land of Animals —and his most trusted companion. Summoned with a thought he would answer the call and offer his life if needed, Elwrick would do the same. In fact, it was Midnight's quick reactions which saved Elwrick during the Great War or he would have perished along with the others. Those who knew them felt there was a bond stronger than a mother and her child. Letting his hand slide down the thick neck of the mount he took the reins. "What have I begun?" he whispered. "What if I fail?"

"Neigh," the horse let out a deep animalistic snort throwing his head backward as if he approved of his master's action.

His other means of travel was a portal back to his own world, The Realm of Light. The process though was painfully slow as his cells and fibers adjusted; a process which could take weeks depending on how long he visited Icearaus. A mortal could only stay in moderation before death would occur. He was no mortal though and his body functioned quite different. Regardless, he was forced to stay until the transformation was complete.

The sky turned a deathly gray as the silhouette of Gods Perch neared. The land before it was barren and broken, nothing grew except for small clusters of Gnarled Viper Vines speckled with finger long thorns. Elwrick could not remember that last time he had been here but nothing had changed.

Elwrick dismounted and met Midnight's gaze, a glint of sadness remained. "I can't take you with me," he whispered. The horse let out a crying whine as if he understood but it didn't lessen the pain. "Until next time my old friend," and with a word the horse shimmered in a golden glow then faded from existence. From the outcropping of rocks that created a balcony, he looked out over the swamp, the great De'Jan Mul' Anor… waited.

To reach the swamp you first had to travel the Ghu'lane, a wide, jagged set of stairs that was carved directly into the side of Gods Perch. Tracing the rocky face it wound midway down before coming to a large landing. There was evidence here of recent fires and a wooden sign labeled—*beware, enter at your own risk*—had been ripped from its post and discarded. From here, it was much more perilous as the second flights of stairs were uneven, half broken, or covered in a thick slimy moss, the last few of which vanished into a thick layer of mist that hung just above the surface.

De'Jan Mul' Anor was as dismal as it was foreboding. Winding trails of mud snaked their way through waist-high Splinter Web Grass that reached out to him, to rip the clothing off his body and the flesh from his bones. As he traveled giant pools of stagnant water devoured the trail forcing him to backtrack and find a more suitable route. Farther in, large clumps of trees sprouted up through the blackish water exposing their gnarled and twisted roots which were entwined into massive balls. A fetid stink made his nose wrinkle.

Each step was a constant battle between Elwrick who wished to keep moving and the ground which tried to hold him prisoner. A grotesque slurping sound moaned with each step. As he passed his prints were quickly devoured by stagnant water and muck which filtered up through the ground hiding the evidence of his passing.

With nightfall came the true horrors of the Anor. For things lived here that had yet to be named. In the gloom, something screamed… something died.

The end of his staff glowed as he wandered aimlessly through the night. Swarms of Gnats, Mosquitoes, Black Flies and Biting Midgets too small to see electrified the sky with the buzz of a million wings, the promise of an easy meal had arrived. Massing in force they came but were quickly defeated. The light sucked the life from them leaving only a dried-out husk.

Farther in, he felt the weight of a thousand eyes upon him, searching for a weakness, or an advantage. Somewhere, a loud splash offered a warning. The eerie creek and moan of a tree as it swayed in the water. Everything was magnified at night.

Locating a semi-dry patch he jabbed his staff into the ground and sat. The other end glowed bright yellow like a distresses beacon on a dark and stormy night. His plan was simple, let them find him. He knew the reptilians sent out patrols and it shouldn't take long to be discovered as long as he was in the right part of the swamp. They were known to alter their location quite often.

What would he say? What could he say when they found him. The probability was great he would not be remembered. Their leader, a great warrior named Hulradeeh Augeesdorees was already old and the Great War did little to lessen the effects. The last time they shook hands he felt it would be their last. No, he convinced himself. He would have to place his trust in a new generation. A generation born with a burning hatred for the very people he was going to ask them to help.

Another cry somewhere in the darkness caught his attention. It was not a quick kill like the last and the lingering screams echoed across the mirror-like waters.

With his mind drifting he never saw the bright colored dart but felt its sting. Grabbing at the projectile his fingers instantly went numb. Whatever the dart was coated with had to be magical as blood-based poisons were ineffective against him. It coursed through him and the effects where immediate. The ground blurred with each step and large black spots invaded his vision. His lower lip hung loosely as he tried to concoct a spell and a long string of saliva hung from his chin. His tongue flopped out the side of his mouth and water ran from his eyes. Staggering to one side he would have fallen into the muck if it was not for the hands that grabbed him.

Elwrick never completely blacked out and the ground below him passed quite rapidly as he was dragged across the swamp. *Am I dead, can't be, I still have thoughts*, he groaned while his head hung as if the bones in his neck had been removed? Eventually, he was thrust to the ground and lie there in a puddle.

Elwrick attempted to move, to grasp anything, something, even the ground but nothing functioned like it should. The realization set in he would just have to wait for the elixir to dissipate. Before him, an enormous root-ball rose up out of the muck and a doorway opened.

Inside, the stairs wound down into utter darkness as the reptiles needed no light, they had the gift of Thermal Vision, an ability which transferred heat sources into signals which allowed them to see in complete darkness as clear as a surface dweller on a bright day. Like them, Elwrick needed no light as well.

The stairs wound in a spiral pattern downward for many flights before it leveled off at another door, a guard was positioned on either side. After the door the ground was dry and felt of sand as they wound their way through multiple tunnels, ascending and descending more stairs they arrived at a wide, tall tunnel which seemed to be the main artery through their complex.

Many reptiles emerged from smaller tunnels to watch as Elwrick was marched past, the barbed tip of a spear inches from his back. Word must have spread quickly a prisoner was captured. At the end, a door was opened and a guard stood at either side, sword in hand, ready for anything the surface dweller may be planning.

The room was large, maybe twenty feet across and twice as tall. Directly in the center sat a single chair. Elwrick clearly understood its purpose by the leather bindings that hung loose. Still groggy he found himself tightly fastened at each joint. A second reptile checked the work, undoing one strap he felt was to loose and redoing it to his own satisfaction, then joined the other and they left.

Time passed slowly and the effects of the dart waned.

Elwrick understood the hostility, after all, it was the surface dwellers that chased them from their desert home reaping huge financial gains in trade for their skins. Hunted to near extinction they were forced to flee and relocated here where their struggles continued. Many of their young perished in the constant moist climate to disease or were killed by the unnamed beasts that lurked on the surface.

Fully aware now he could have easily freed himself by simply vanishing leaving them to find an empty chair. All this would have accomplished though was an increased hatred for man at the thought they had once again been infiltrated. His coming here was not to cause further conflict, but one of diplomacy, to offer a shred of hope in the diminishing world, and to recruit aid.

Time passed slowly and it seemed he sat for days when four reptiles entered. One wore a simple gray robe with a gold medallion loosely around her neck while the others preferred the more natural look. They were different from his escorts. Shorter, leaner, and much older, their bright green scales revealing a hint of gray. Ignoring him they examined the items which were recovered. One held up his staff for the others to see then whispered something in an unknown dialect and quickly left.

Elwrick waited patiently as they went through each item, a golden brooch with a picture inside that dangled from a silver chain, a small bag of coins, a pouch with four feathers from an unknown bird, and a few other trinkets. With the inspection complete the robed lizard approached, "Wizard, why are you here?" She asked in the common tongue.

Elwrick thought a moment. He wanted to tell her everything but now was not the time. He had to make sure they had not already been touched by the hand of corruption. "In search of aid… and to bring counsel," he said.

From his observation, the others did not speak common as she translated his words to the others. Many minutes passed while they conversed before she returned. "The others think you're a spy and should be executed."

"I am no spy," Elwrick demanded, his eyes narrowed and his face flushed red. His patience had grown quite thin. He had never been accused of such an atrocity in all his life and he was not going to now, regardless of the situation.

The reptile took a step back then screamed, "then the scout of a hunting party. Surface dwellers don't walk into the Anor without reason!" she snarled.

"I told you my reasons."

"And you lie," she shot back bearing white serrated teeth. "Do you think we can't see the fires burning up on the perch?" She glanced at the others and then back to Elwrick. "If you are no spy or scout, and what you say is true. What counsel do you bring us?"

"I must speak with Hulradeeh Augeesdorees," Elwrick said, but not in the common tongue. The words came in Draconian, an ancient dialect few understood.

Her eyes widened to that of saucers and her mouth gaped open. From somewhere within the folds of her robe she produced a crude dagger, the blade was chipped and nicked. "Where did you hear that name... surface dweller?" Her words held a sharp edge. "Tell me... tell me now or I'll cut your throat." Her eyes could boil water.

A painful silence filled the room before Elwrick spoke. His words were cold and calculated as he continued in Draconian. "I am no surface dweller and refuse to be treated as such. Your actions hold consequences you do not fully understand. Every minute I am delayed is time the enemy grows stronger. I have played your games long enough." Directly before their eyes, the clasps on his hands and feet unlatched and he freed himself.

Behind him, the twang of a bowstring could be heard. The arrow sped towards its target shattering moments before impact from an invisible shield. The bow in the guard's hand erupted into flames and leaped from his hands falling to ash. Chanting a few words he doubled in height and light spewed forth from his body flooding the room with a golden glow. "I'm not here to harm or destroy you." His voice shook the entire cavern.

Cowering in fear from this unknown evil they fell to their knees. "Take what you may but please spare the hatchlings," they pleaded. The guard had other plans and freed his sword only to find himself frozen. They had never seen such powerful magic and understood.

Elwrick shrunk to his normal size, and the light dissipated.

Moments later the door banged open and the reptile that left with the staff returned followed by another. "Elwrick," he said in the Draconian. His arms wide open as if to swallow him in a hug, "my old friend."

Hulradeeh was showing his age. His faded scales were ashen gray and the yellow underbelly had long since turned the color of new snow. His snout seemed shorter than he remembered and the missing teeth created large gaps in his smiling maw. Years of trying to keep a dying race alive had left a permanent mark in his dark black eyes, the left one of which was a cloudy gray. "How long has it been?"

"Far too long," Elwrick said, gripping him in a tight embrace that almost squeezed the air from his old companion.

"And Midnight?"

"Ornery as ever," he chuckled.

A long moment passed as they looked at each other. Water welled up in the old lizard's eyes and the memories of their past came crashing back in a flood of tears, "I'm sorry."

"Don't be," Elwrick said. "There's no shame in crying. You have been through much and this shows you have not grown hard and life still remains." Elwrick placed a hand against the white scaly chest and felt a slow heartbeat.

Having regained his composure he smiled. "When news reached my ear a wizard in white had been captured I just knew it was you," Hulradeeh said. "Then when I saw the staff, my suspicions were confirmed, and I came as quick as my tired legs could run."

"Your arrival could not have been more precise," Elwrick said.

"Come… come," Hulradeeh motioned for Elwrick to follow. "Let's see if we can't find more suitable sleeping arrangements."

"I won't be staying," Elwrick said. "In fact, I must leave as soon as I am finished here."

"Sounds urgent," Hulradeeh said as he led them to a chamber more suited for surface dwellers. "The last time you came in this manner a war was on our doorstep. Let's hope the news is not the same," Hulradeeh said as he leaned back in a chair resting his chin on a hand. His gaze was solely focused on Elwrick.

Elwrick glanced at the four reptiles who had accompanied them, then towards Hulradeeh. "A sickness spreads across Icearaus," his words carried a slight trace of anxiety. "Not one that you can see… or smell." Elwrick paced the room and stopped just before Hulradeeh, "or touch."

"And what sickness is that? the robed lizard asked.

"Another bearer has been born—"

"*EEEK,*" the reptile hissed. "That is a concern."

"Yes," Elwrick said, "A major concern and one we must address. You see, She is not the filthy creature you all would have her to be, but a woman carrying a child from the Creator and she needs our aid, aid which must be provided."

"What," the robed lizard screamed.

"We," Hulradeeh hissed and shot up out of the chair knocking it over. "Besides you, I care nothing for the surface dwellers, or their problems."

"I understand," Elwrick agreed. "After all, who knows more than you about the pain they have inflicted upon your people. But they do so because of the sickness."

"And what sickness is that?" His jaw clenched.

"A sickness of lies, and hate, and warmongering against all who oppose him. If you do not bow to him, adapt to his ways then you are labeled a traitor, a blasphemer. Public executions are quite common for people who refuse his perverted ways. Over time and torture, he's raped the people of their free will and his lies have become truth and law. We must unravel the lies and reveal the truth. Only then will your people thrive once more."

"And who is this man?"

"Karayan."

"King Karayan?" The robed lizard gasped.

"Yes, but he is far from a King," Elwrick said. He spent the next while telling them what has occurred up till now.

"This is all very interesting but tell me this, why should we help those who would not help us? Hunted us for our hides and put us on display, slaughtered the woman and hatchling so our numbers would dwindle. No… I believe these troubles that you speak of are theirs, and theirs alone."

Elwrick shoulders slumped, "make no mistake. When he has no one left to destroy, to abuse, to torture, he will come here. Nothing that lives will go unaffected by his touch. You will either fight him, or bow to him. There is no middle ground."

Hulradeeh shook his head in disbelief at what he heard. He was getting thrown into the midst of another war whether he wanted it or not.

"Would you not like to return to the land where you once thrived? To feel the heat upon your bellies again?" Elwrick asked.

"We have adjusted well to our new environment," he snarled.

"Your numbers dwindle without the vile touch of Karayan. Less than half hatch and of those many more succumb to death by the Anor. This land was never meant to be civilized. It was left for those uncivilized. In time all Karayan must do is wait and your race will be gone without him having to lift one finger." Elwrick knew the words hurt his friend, he could see it in the old reptile's eyes. "I cannot force you to help, just tell you the facts and you must make that judgment for yourself." Elwrick took a cup from the table and swallowed the contents, his voice had gone hoarse. "I feel now though if he is not stopped it may be too late for all of Icearaus."

"And what of the Elves, are they so willing to spill their blood?"

"No," Elwrick replied, hanging his head. "Ever since the death of the elven girl, they have gone into seclusion, sworn off all contact with man. I fear anybody who seeks their aid will not fare well."

"And you thought you would fare much better here?"

"I did," Elwrick answered.

"Our friendship is strong, Elwrick. But I cannot, and will not send my young warriors off to die. That is a price I cannot have hanging over me," Hulradeeh said.

"Is that why you think I've come? To watch the last of your race die, to send your warriors to face a battle I know they cannot win? Is that all you think of me? Do you think I have not witnessed my own share of destruction? My wife and children were destroyed in the Great War. The war we fought side by side together. Do you think I don't understand extinction, do you not realize I am the last of my kind?"

Hulradeeh had no response.

"I offer hope," Elwrick pleaded.

"Hope, what do you know of hope?" Hulradeeh's facial scales turned a bright shade of red, a shade Elwrick never dreamed possible. "Hope was lost decades ago when we were driven from our desert home. Where were you then? Living up in some ivory tower away from all the pain, misery, and suffering?"

"And don't forget training and learning, and observing," Elwrick added to the list Hulradeeh started. "Do you really think it does not trouble me? Do you believe I love to sit and watch mankind be destroyed?" Anger flared in his voice.

"So what do you propose, I just send out the last of my warriors to fight a madman?" Hulradeeh asked.

"No, I only need one."

"One? How can you fight this man with only one?"

"Because we're not going to fight him." Elwrick raised an eyebrow, "we're going to save the person who can."

Hulradeeh's face went pale. "Impossible," he said. "There has not been a bearer born in a hundred years, if not longer."

"Wrong," Elwrick said, leaning on the table. "There have been many born. They are no longer known as bearers, but as diseased creatures and hunted down and destroyed, sound familiar."

"If one must go, I will," Hulradeeh said.

"An honorable notion," Elwrick responded. "And I am sure even with your age you would be more than a formidable opponent. But I require the resources of a female."

"That I cannot offer," Hulradeeh said. "Our females are needed here, even the death of one is so grave it could lead to our extinction."

"Then let me go… father?" A massive reptile said as she emerged from the darkened hallway into the lighted room.

She was larger than any Elwrick had ever seen nearing the eight-foot mark. Bright green scales on her back faded to a burnt orange before turning a screaming yellow on the underbelly. A long well-defined jawline led to an extended snout with white protruding teeth showing signs of an obvious overbite. As she moved, the scales flexed and stretched as powerful muscles propelled the giant, and a long tail kept the creature perfectly balanced. As she moved a sword on each hip swung in perfect rhythm and across her back the handle of a two-handed sword was visible. Opposite the handle, a quiver was attached by a large strap slung across her chest and a bow was locked into her left hand. By all standards a pure killing machine.

"Augeessareth, shouldn't you be training the new recruits instead of eavesdropping upon your elder's conversations?"

"Father, when I heard the man who fought alongside you during the Great War now stood in our very labyrinth, I had no choice but to come greet him personally. And now I hear I may have a chance to follow in your footsteps."

"I won't hear any of this nonsense," Hulradeeh snarled. "You belong here, at my side raising the hatchlings."

Augeessareth crossed the room with her head turned down. When she reached the other side there was anger in her voice. "Why do you wish to keep me locked down here? From the very moment I hatched, I had a weapon in my hand. While my sisters played with toys, I held a sword. While they learned to cook, I trained with a bow. Even you said how amazed you were at how quickly I learned and felt a piece of you in me that none of your other hatchlings received."

"And look what it's done to me. Is this how you want to end up? A broken shell of something that could have been great? Do you think that's how I want my only remaining hatchling to end up? I won't allow it," Hulradeeh said. "There is too much at stake. We have hatchlings that need caring."

"Please forgive me…father," she whispered. "But I fear you have grown quite senile in your waning years and your judgment has become cloudy. I do not wish to continue living in this mud-hole," she waved her arms wide. "If I can help so others can once again feel the warmth of the sun upon their backs, I offer my services to Elwrick."

"I can't stop you, I am too old and broken. But if this is how you wish the family to end, the greatest dynasty to ever grace the reptilian race to be remembered, then you will have to do it without my blessing."

"That's why I must go," she said. "Because there's too much at stake if I don't. Our dynasty will end regardless, every egg I have laid has yet to hatch except for a few and they've died of disease before they reached their first hatchday. Think now how you wish to be remembered even if our race dies. Do you wish now to be remembered as a coward who died in a mud hole or on the field of battle, with honor?"

She felt as if her heart was being ripped from her chest as she watched a lone tear run down her father's cheek but turned away to face Elwrick. "It is an honor to meet you. Hulradeeh has spoken of you in the past and always with the highest regards. He has told stories of you and him fighting side by side against an unspeakable horror, and now I will take up that honor and fight beside you as well."

"The honor is all mine," Elwrick responded with a bow of respect. "But I am sorry as you will not be fighting beside me. I have other pressing matters which also must be addressed for this mission to be completed."

"Augeessareth, please don't do this, I beg you." He slumped in the chair.

"Have you not heard a word this man said? Do your ears fail you now more than your eyes?" Augeessareth hissed. "Do you think I don't fear this man Elwrick speaks of? What I fear more though is the possibility of knowing that my future hatchlings will not grow old. Or worse, grow old in a cage only to be harvested for their skins like cattle for their meat."

Elwrick tried to comfort Hulradeeh, "I am more than honored to accept your daughter into this highly secretive mission where only a select few will be chosen. If she fights anything like she argues then it is the enemy who should be shaking in their boots, not you."

"Why a female?" Hulradeeh demanded, his voice haggard. "If something goes wrong, which in all likelihood it will that is one less to create hatchlings."

"Because of Averie."

"Averie?" Hulradeeh had a puzzled look on his face.

"That is the bearer's name," Elwrick paused. "She has been abused and mistreated by men ever since it was discovered she was a bearer. As a woman, she can relate and Averie may open to her. And that's why I believe she will survive where others had failed. It will be in the best interest of Icearaus for a woman to escort her to the portal."

"Where is she now?" Augeessareth asked.

"I don't know, but I assume free of Lynn Brook," he said.

"You left her alone, out there?" Augeessareth snarled.

"No, I recruited another man to free her, one with more than enough experience I believe."

"Who is this man?" Augeessareth asked. "Can he be trusted?"

"His name is Pegan Rhoe, and I believe if anyone could save her, he can."

"How do I find this Averie? The land is vast," she asked.

Elwrick walked towards Augeessareth who grew more menacing with every step. "Kneel please, I need to touch your head and my arms will not grow that long." As she knelt Elwrick placed a hand firmly on her skull. Chanting words his hand glowed in a twinkling green then he gently pulled back. A green sliver of light left his hand and began to penetrate into the scaly membrane. By the time the spell was over the green light dissipated. "That is a maternity spell," he said. "Like a mother with a child in the womb you will always feel her presence, follow your instincts and it will lead you right to her."

Attempting to pull her towards him she never moved. "Relax," he whispered. This time she allowed herself to be pulled downwards. He kissed the end of her large snout, "and neither will you tire, run with Godspeed."

She could feel the spell working. Creeping into her veins like an icy chill it slowly warmed until she felt sick. Gagging, she tried to vomit, to eject this unknown entity. Throwing herself down she curled into a ball.

"What have you done?" Hulradeeh asked, a squeak of worry in his voice.

"Shhhh," Elwrick whispered. "It will subside in time and she will be left with a feeling none of us can imagine." Elwrick knelt beside her, stroking her coarse scales and reassuring her she would be fine.

From icy cold to pain, and now pleasure, she let the feeling embraced her. The joy of being a mother again to not five or ten but one. A very special one. A bearer.

"I must go. . . Now!" Augeessareth said. "I can feel her. Frightened, cold, wet. She's deep within the Ash."

Elwricks face went suddenly pale; the words hit him like a blast of icy cold water. The rescue had been a success, but for how much longer until her departure was discovered. He knew Karayan and the motivation behind him. No cost was too great or life so precious that he would allow the bearer to reach the portal.

"Are you okay?" Hulradeeh asked Elwrick.

"She just told me the words I longed to hear," Elwrick said. With her escape things had now been set in motion none of them could imagine.

"Augeessareth," Elwrick called to her. "You are to be her guardian, her protector. She must reach that portal alive. But I must warn you, do not challenge Pegan Rhoe. He is a dangerous man, more dangerous than you can ever imagine."

Augeessareth knelt, "I take this oath before you now, no harm will befall this woman," she said. "As long as air still fills my lungs and blood pumps through these veins I will fight for her."

With their goodbyes and good lucks said she broke from the chamber and traversed the tunnels at a breakneck speed. Others had no choice but to leap out of the way or get trampled. Gods Perch was still a good hour away when she reached the surface. Leaping twenty, sometimes thirty yards at a time it only took minutes to reach and in four long bounds, Gods Perch was behind her and the flatlands waited.

Hulradeeh looked half drunk and hollowed eyed when he glanced at Elwrick, "you just sent my only daughter to her death."

"No," Elwrick replied. "I sent your daughter to save the world."

Hulradeeh wept in low sobs.

"What I take I return as well," and he handed his old friend his staff. "Place it in the center of your labyrinth where all can see it and it will forever glow with the radiance of the sun. When you are sick, tired, or cold come to it and let its healing properties radiate through you. Move the eggs to it and never again will one not hatch."

Hulradeeh took the staff in both hands. "I will see it done."

"Hulradeeh," Elwrick called out to him. "This is a good thing, you should be very proud of your daughter right now."

"I am a very proud father right now," he said. "But the pain still weighs heavy on my heart. Nobody, man or reptile likes to watch their daughter head into war."

Elwrick nodded in agreement and the thought of his own children flooded his mind and they embraced.

Chapter 8

Not counting the throne room, the dungeon was the largest. The floor's construction was a single piece of black basalt while the walls were made from rectangular red granite blocks with gold veins that sparkled in the torchlight. In each corner a fluted pedestal supported a large, saucer-shaped bowl loaded with glowing coals. One complete side consisted of nothing but giant bird cages. One cage was raised by a thick chain which ran through a hook in the ceiling and to a winch fixed to the wall. Growing from the cage a bone-thin arm hung limp. The rotten gray skin dangled like stringy moss on a branch. Scattered around the room where multiple chairs adorned with clasps, ropes, and chains and a few tables with levers designed to stretch the body. Long whips with metal barbed hooks, gnarled clubs, cutting instruments and a small pear-shaped item designed to expand after being placed inside a body cavity hung neatly on hooks.

Near the back, Karayan stood behind a wooden desk. In his left hand, he held a thick book while his right was clenched in a fist. Beside him Lilith stood, her small frame looked childish next to his. Except for the occasional drip of water or moan from a man that dangled upside down, the room was deathly silent.

The door banged open and Kalliphae entered. He was a short man, thin around the waist but gifted with wide, bold, shoulders and bore a stern look. The color of his hair often reminded people of a setting sun and it hung in thick curls women often dreamed of owning. His thin eyebrows were often overlooked as your vision was drawn to his wide ocean-blue eyes. Crossing the room he moved with a pompous gait and a sneer on his thin lips.

His eyes bathed in Lilith's radiance as he addressed the King," good evening my King," he offered a quick bow then moved to stand beside Lilith, "and you as well."

"Same to you," she lied. She hated the arrogant bastard and everything he stood for. Kalliphae was the warden and in charge of every rank of the military. He was not always the warden though as the prior one had an untimely accident which led to his eventual death—a knife in the back while you sleep will usually cause that. And it so happened on that day he was there to step in and fill the void. Rumors circulated that he may have been the Kings illegitimate son, but any who spoke the rumor vanished, or had an accident of their own. Regardless of who his real father was, he was still the best swordsman in all of Lynn Brook and any who challenged him for the coveted position usually meet their fate at the end of a sword. Because of his authoritative position, nothing happened without his knowledge. When word reached his ear two guards had committed treason against the King, it was only natural for him to be present during their questioning.

"Where are they?" Karayan sneered.

"On their way... my King," he answered. "My guards located Berian quick enough, but Merwyn was harder to find. His capture didn't come till he tried to leave the city on official business."

"Official business?" Karayan asked.

"That's what he said... Sir," Kalliphae answered. "It seems you were sending him off on a quest to colonize the wilds. Designate a new location for a palace to be built and paid him twenty gold in advance, five of which he gave to his wife as he planned to be gone for some time."

"And how did you find this out?" Karayan asked.

"Unable to locate him, I had his wife brought here for questioning," Kalliphae nodded then smiled towards Lilith, the same way a dog looks at their master for a treat when they did a good deed.

The click of steel-toed boots gave warning someone approached. He was young, cleanly shaven with satin eyes and blond eyebrows that matched his hair which was pulled back then tied. His prominent jaw and cheekbones overshadowed a small, flat nose.

"Berian Poovey… rookie," Kalliphae whispered.

Moments later another man entered. He was older and his hardened face was wrinkled with years of experience. He had a bushy dark mustache that covered his upper lip, oil black hair that coiled well past the shoulders, piercing green eyes, thick-jawed and reeked with arrogance.

"Merwyn Brickell, Master at Arms." Kalliphae glanced at Karayan.

Standing before Karayan they both snapped to attention, rigid as stone their chest pushed out. Arms glued to their side and fingers curled inward making a fist. The evening was rather cool but the warm stagnant air in the room caused heavy, thick beads of sweat to grow on their heads.

Karayans gaze shifted between them, and without warning or provocation, slammed the book down on the table. "Do either of you know what this book is?"

Berian studied the dense item, "It resembles the guard shack log book… my King."

"What about you?" Karayan hissed to Merwyn.

He nodded, "Indeed, it is the logbook… Sir."

"Correct," Karayan said. Interlocking his fingers he stretched out his arms painfully slow till each knuckle popped while Kalliphae opened the book to a marked page. "And do you know why you're here?"

"No sir," Merwyn answered, his gaze flashed towards Berian.

"I have summoned you here because it seems you both worked the gatehouse the night a treasonous crime was committed."

"Treasonous?" Berian asked painfully slow. "The last time I worked the gatehouse was the night of the storm. We didn't do anything wrong, at least nothing I can see."

Karayans stare was icy cold; his jaw tightened as he jerked the kid by the collar and slammed his face into the book. "Can you see it now?" He rubbed the kid's face all over the page till the snot marks looked like snail trails and the page tore from the book. Angered even more, he slapped the man twice then threw him on the ground and kicked him.

"Now answer me this." His face twisted into a scowl and the veins in his neck bulged. He wanted to kill one or both of them on the spot. "After the gate was secured, did you let a man inside?"

Berian thought for a moment before he answered, "I...I... did let a man inside," his lips trembled. "I take full responsibility for my actions. The storm though was bad, wicked nasty and lightning was licking at our feet." He glanced at Merwyn for support. "It was so torrential, even the Royal Guards ceased their round and took shelter for a time." Berian lowered his head in shame, "I could not have it on my conscious to let him die at the gate."

"How noble of you," Karayan snarled. "But what you should have done was denied him entry. Now, the cost will be substantial while the city is searched to locate him, and the woman he kidnapped."

Incredible, Merwyn thought. *This could not get any better. The kid just openly admitted to treason.*

"He's not in the city. Later that night he left with his sister to Fairdenn. Merwyn advised me we have to let the crazies out and it didn't need to be logged... that he would take care of it in the morning."

Merwyn's face went pale as the blood drained to his feet and he all but collapsed.

King Karayan's face turned blood red and his eyes widened. Deep wrinkles creased his forehead and the smell of anger permeated the air.

Kalliphae backed away when Karayan faced him.

"Send word to every civilized town or city about the escape. I want them captured not tomorrow, or the next, but today," he screamed.

"Sir, It's already been done, two days ago in fact right after we discovered her missing. I had a feeling there would be trouble. I also sent word to the barbarians and the rovers. By now every town, city, or village should have been notified. Nowhere will they find a safe haven."

"You lying bastard," Merwyn screamed. The veins in his neck looked like worms and his eyes narrowed. With a closed fist he knocked the kid to the ground then kicked him in the back and head until he heard bones breaking. Merwyn's mouth curled into a wicked smile as he pulled back the stunned boys head by the hair and placed his blade against the meaty part of the throat. "Don't implement me into your lies now prepare to die you filthy swine," he growled and slid the blade from ear to ear leaving a grizzly wound. Blood gulped from the wound like a tipped over wine bottle missing the cork.

"Excellent," Karayan said as he clapped his hands, "saves me from having to get bloody."

"Sir," Merwyn said, having snapped back to attention. "I am sorry you had to witness this but we cannot allow liars to infiltrate the ranks of the honor guard."

"I could not agree more," Karayan said, his arms folded across his chest. "But you see…" he scratched his chin, "you're just as guilty as the man you murdered, even more so."

"I did it in your honor, to protect the reputation of the guard."

"You did it to silence a witness and line your own pockets."

"What?" Merwyn said. "That's a lie! The one who did this treasonous act lays dead and now you accuse me."

Karayan nodded at Kalliphae, "bring her in,"

Moments later Merwyn's face flushed pale when his wife walked through the doorway. Her dress was savagely ripped while her face was heavily deformed. She walked slowly as if every muscle had been bruised.

"You didn't say you beat her?" Lilith hissed.

"It's none of your concern" he fired back. "Regardless, it had to be done to get to the truth."

"What have you done to her?" Merwyn said.

"Nothing she didn't enjoy," Kalliphae winked his direction.

"Your wife will live," Karayan said. "It's unfortunate she had to experience life's uglier moments but it will make her a much stronger woman. Over time she will heal and put this dreadful memory behind her. The only law she has broken was to marry a traitor which is not a crime punishable by death."

"You whore," Merwyn screamed. The squeal of his sword echoed as it broke free from its sheath. He lunged towards her, blade aimed straight at her heart. Her scream filled their ears, but the blade missed flesh as Kalliphae was the quicker and deflected the blade.

Surprised, he struck at Kalliphae in a series of blows meant to remove the head, all of which were easily parried.

The warden countered with a vicious series that left Merwyn on his knees… screaming. Both hands lay on the floor, one still gripping the sword. A large pool of blood began to form.

"Cauterize the wounds before he dies," Karayan ordered. Merwyn struggled against the bindings that held him fast while Karayan searched through a tray of wicked-looking slicing instruments. Finding a thin blade for skinning he circled the prisoner.

Merwyn tried to follow Karayans movements but lost sight.

Directly behind him, Karayan raised his hand and delivered a thundering blow which almost knocked the chair over. Grabbing a handful of hair he jerked the head backward and stared straight down into Merwyn's face and spit. "I've known you since you were a boy. Since you hung on your mother's breast and you… you aid the enemy for a mere twenty gold. I would have given you double that if you would have come to me and told me of the attempted intrusion."

"Go to Hell," Merwyn spit back.

Lilith readied a gag.

"We won't need that," Karayan said. A razor-thin smile formed on his emotionless face. "I want all of Icearaus to hear him scream."

"Sir… I hate to interrupt—"

"Then don't," Karayan snapped.

Kalliphae wiped the last free drops of blood from his sword. "We're wasting valuable time. While you torture him, the bearer slips farther from our grasp. No word has reached us yet of her capture and the longer we wait, the colder the trail grows. If you wish to kill him I recommend the traitors mark and return him to the people. Then we can get on with the business of tracking her down."

Karayan thought for a moment then agreed. Once again his warden was right. "Bring me the eye gouger," he growled, "and then hold his head firmly."

Karayan's tongue hung from his mouth in glee as he worked the spoon-shaped tool just below the eye. Once inserted, the eye socket worked as a guide that allowed him to circle the eye, and when he'd made a complete revolution, he twisted the handle which popped the eye free emitting a grotesque slurping sound, but left it dangling by the nerve.

Screams tore at the stone walls and spilled out into the street through the small windows left purposely open so all could hear.

The chair rocked and Kalliphae had to reposition himself to steady the hysterical man.

"Spit in my face," Karayan said. Then with an evil, enjoyable smile, he went to work on the other eye.

Merwyn's screams had gone hoarse, and he choked on the blood that ran from the empty sockets filling his mouth.

"Bring me the iron," Karayan asked Lilith.

The rod was about three feet long and on one end was a wooden handle to keep the wielder from being burned. The other end was a flat plate with thick, well-defined letters protruding from its surface. The end glowed bright red as it had spent hours resting on a bed of coals.

Karayan held the rod up to examine the fine craftsmanship. Each letter in the word had been constructed with precision. The smell of hot metal filled the air.

Kalliphae held the head back while Karayan positioned the rod perfectly then pressed it hard against the forehead. The stink of burning flesh filled their nostrils and the hiss of steel cooling as it was quenched with blood filled their ears. Rocking the iron back and forth he made sure the writing was perfectly clear. Removing the iron the words "TRAITOR" permanently remained. "From this point on," Karayan whispered into the ear of the screaming man, "you will walk the streets a blind traitor."

Cast out from the palace he was left to fend for himself on the streets, which usually meant a slow and painful death.

Karayan addressed Kalliphae, "send a letter to Emperor Tak-Thukmand. I wish to have his army occupy the Majestic Forest; no one is to pass without my approval."

"Sir, it's already been done. By now I suspect the forest is flooded with bloodthirsty barbarians all looking for a chance to earn a name. Nothing will get through there... nothing." He bowed.

Karayan smiled. Once again his Warden was on top of his game.

"And for the rovers, I offered a King's pardon for all who are involved with her capture and return, much more valuable than any amount of gold."

Karayan liked the idea and patted the warden's shoulder, "you did excellent, and I think a promotion is in order."

"Yes, sir." Kalliphae bowed again and turned to leave.

"Kalliphae," Karayan called him back. "Send word to the Brotherhood I wish a meeting with Arlin Brack."

"Yes, my lord," he said as he bowed.

Back in his private chamber Karayan watched from his window as a mob formed around Merwyn. It was late evening and his hair frolicked in the breeze that filtered through the open window and lights begun to burn across Lynn Brook. I'm coming for you, he whispered to the night air. The chanting sound of traitor reached his ears as the kicking and hitting begun, Merwyn would be lucky to survive the night.

"So it's true?" Lilith asked.

"Yes. I'm afraid so," he replied, still watching the spectacle unfold on the street.

"So she has escaped the city?"

"That is true," Karayan said as he left the window to stand before her.

"You can feel her presence though, right? Detect her location?" Lilith asked.

"Only a presence," Karayan said. "A gift given to me by my Master, but I cannot discern her location, only one can do that."

"Elwrick," Lilith said. "That filthy creature still lives? I thought they were all killed during the Great War."

"All but him," Karayan answered then gripped her by the shoulders. "I have a plan to bring her back." He kissed her cheek and walked out.

Chapter 9

The Ash Mountains were foreign to Averie and filled with great sights… and greater fears. They traveled till the sky turned dark and continued through the night till the sky lightened. They traveled the next day as well only stopping when food or rest was required. On their travels, they passed jagged peaks with crowns of stone that touched the clouds and steep ravines thick with a swirling haze which obscured the bottoms. As the sky darkened a bright moon lit their way and a stiff breeze brought to life otherwise dead shadows.

Averie slumped slightly to one side on the mount. The rugged terrain had taken its toll, and she looked to fall at each turn.

Pegan guided the mule through a maze of thick trees and dense foliage. "We're almost there," he whispered to Averie and patted the mule.

She looked at him with pleading eyes as if begging him to stop.

Owooooo…

Startled, Averie bolted upright almost throwing herself from the mule.

"Easy," Pegan said. "It's only a wolf howling," he reassured her, but deep down, he knew it was more, something different in the howl, the type of sound an animal makes when it picks up the trail of something it's hunting.

The moon was high when they finally emerged at a small clearing no bigger than a house. A small stream trickled along one edge while a large ring of stone sat in the center. The skeletal remains of a long dead fire remained. "We've traveled a great distance from Lynn Brook. We should be safe for now."

Pegan patted the mule on the neck then loosened the reins. A thick layer of sweat coated his hide, and each breath glowed heavy in the moonlight. A long pink tongue hung to one side of its open mouth and long strings of froth dripped from its chin.

"You've been here before?" she whispered.

"Days ago, on my way to Lynn Brook to be exact," he answered. "But I built it years ago and to this day it remains."

"And nobody knows about it?"

"There are a few, but I have not seen them in a very long time."

In the moonlight, their gaze met, and he realized over the last few days he had neglected his charge by keeping such a brutal pace and traveling such rugged terrain. She looked ragged, as if she were dragged behind the mule, not ridden it. Dried blood coated her chin and heavy bags sagged under her eyes. She slumped to the left and her breath came in wheezing gasps.

With great care, he helped her from the mount then allowed the beast to roam free. A short while later he created a glorious fire with flames that leaped and danced. The light drove the darkness back to the edge of the glade and coated the entire area with an unusual warmth.

From the pack, he removed two large taters, salted meat, an onion and a few more vegetables he acquired and placed them in a pot to simmer.

The aroma was delicious and Averie was forced to wipe away drool on more than one occasion. Three helpings later she laid with her head resting on a pack starring at the stars. "What happens if we fail?" she asked… "What if we don't make it to the island?"

Pegan stirred his bowl, "Don't talk like that," he answered. "To speak in that manner only predicts our failure. We must remain positive."

Farther below the wolf howled again.

She glanced at Pegan, "will it attack us in our sleep?"

"I don't believe so," he glanced back. "They're nocturnal, it won't enter the light."

Averie fell into a deep thought, "where are we headed?" Her face twisted as she coughed. More blood seeped from her mouth.

"To Minx—"

"Minx," she grumbled. "That town is nothing but criminals. You might as well deliver me straight to Karayan and save the time running."

"Have you ever been there?"

"Well… no, but I've heard stories," she answered.

"They're just stories," Pegan said in between bites. "Minx has many fine people and most would give the shirt off their backs if you asked. There are some who are less than desirable but they keep to themselves. Because of its reputation, I feel it is the best place to get you help. And, it just so happens I know a healer there who owes me a huge favor."

She shot him a concerned stare.

"I fear my first assessment of your ribs may have been wrong, or they're getting worse. You keep coughing up blood and that tells me something internal is being damaged. It won't be much longer until a vital organ gets punctured. If that happens… well, I won't say, to talk about it predicts the future."

She wiped the blood away with her sleeve.

"Sleep now. We leave at first light," Pegan motioned for her to lay by the fire.

The crackle of the fire and its warmth eased her mind, and almost instantly, she was sound asleep.

Pegan though never slept. Instead, he stood at the edge of the glade, the bright eyes far below watched back. "What do you want?" he whispered.

She woke to a warm hand tapping on her shoulder and a salmon-colored sky. The air was crisp, cool, and left everything covered in a thick dampness. She tried to rise but the pain in her side throbbed with a new vengeance. Doubling over she hugged herself. A fresh trickle of blood leaked from her mouth and painted her chin a light shade of burgundy. "I'm sorry," she cried out through labored breaths.

I've decided to take the main route across" Pegan said. "Your ribs can't take the rugged terrain that lies ahead, so we will go straight north to the main pass over the mountain. It's not far, half a day's travel at most and is less rugged. We'll make better time but be more vulnerable. A necessity I fear we must risk," Pegan explained.

The sun was high when they arrived at the path Pegan described. It was wide and easily navigated and the hours passed quickly. As the evening approached Averie slumped in the seat and a long string of coagulated blood hung from the corner of her mouth and she had a distant, glossy stare. "I need to see your ribs again," Pegan asked. "I want to make sure our pace has not caused more damage."

The bruise had doubled in size and turned an angry blue outlined by tarnished pink. After he rubbed his hands a few times, he placed a palm against the skin. He could feel the heat radiating from the wound. A new sense of urgency fell upon his face.

"It's bad, I can tell by your face," she said. "Am I gonna—" Something caught her eye farther down the mountain and she fell silent.

Pegan looked past her, "What did you see?" He continued to scan the trail.

"I don't know," she said. "Looked like a bear but walked like a man and it moved fast, and in this direction. Really though it could have been anything or nothing, probably my imagination I would guess."

"Let's not delay," Pegan said as he took the reins to the mule. The trail was not straight but had many switchbacks with many clearings which allowed them a bird's-eye view of below.

Near the top, they finally got a glimpse of what Averie saw hours earlier. Four men worked their way up the mountainside and seemed no longer to care if they were spotted.

"This way," one yelled out to the others, "up this trail."

"Move your arses we're getting close," another answered.

Owooooo, the wolf bayed to the sky and dragged his master up the trail.

Pegan knew there was no way to outrun them, at least not with Averie and altered their course to a clearing which he knew offered the best opportunity to defend her. It was small and ringed with a band of heavy trees except for one side where a rock wall had collapsed offering a safe place for Averie to hide while he dealt with the would-be trackers.

—*I can smell the filthy creature*—Pegan heard one scream. They were close now, within two hundred yards of them when Pegan lifted Averie from the mule and told her to remain behind a jumble of boulders which hid her entirely.

Pegan leaned against the boulder, arms crossed and watched them burst through the tree line like a tsunami on the bank of a river. A sigh of relief escaped his lungs These were not the Royal Guardsman, but a party of rovers. Upon their approach, they fanned out surrounding Pegan and the intended prize.

"Give up the girl… and you live," one grumbled. His long gray ragged beard wiggled with each word.

All four were large, but he was the biggest. Draped in a bearskin he carried a massive two-handed blade in his right hand and in his left a rope fastened to the collar of the largest wolf Pegan had ever seen.

Mangy gray hair grew in wild clumps and a thick froth dripped from the gaping maw in long stringy trails. One eye had clouded over while the other sparkled clear blue. It snarled and growled, snapped and yanked on the rope begging to be released.

Pegan pursed his lips and reached for his weapons, "I got a better idea," he licked his lips. "You pretend you never found us, and I'll let all four of you live… including the beast." He stepped from the rock in their direction.

"Kill him, and bring me the creature," the leader laughed, his deep voice had a sharp edge.

"Take me," Averie screamed as she stepped from behind the boulder. The words caught Pegan by surprise and he glanced in her direction. "He's done nothing to you, leave him be," she said.

"Too late, he's dead," the smallest one said as he slid a wicked looking curved blade from its sheath. His darkened eyes squinted, and he screamed a battle cry of a man fit to rage. It was obvious he came with the desire to make a name for himself and would not be satisfied till blood was spilled. He charged forward and completed a series of basic maneuvers with his sword. The blade whizzed past but then made an abrupt turn then reversed back the other direction to surprise the victim. Not finding flesh his other hand joined the first on the pommel and with all his force he closed both eyes and stepped forward swinging the blade as if to split a log.

Pegan easily avoided the inexperienced attack and watched the blade bury deep into the ground then stepped on the spine rendering it useless.

The rover opened his eyes just in time to see a flash of steel flicker past and died without a scream. Both daggers were lightning quick and sliced through bone and muscle in a crisscross pattern severing the head clean from its body. A kick to the torso flung the dead meat back towards the pack pelting them in red droplets of rain.

Any chance of resolving this peacefully vanished. More blood would be spilled this day. Both men came from different angles and with much more experience, they feed off one another. As one worked high the other low, switching their routine often they kept Pegan from mounting an offense.

"Get her, bring her here," the Wolf Master laughed and released his pet. The rope trailed like a kite string and with only one good eye barreled into the trio trying to get at the bearer. One rover was knocked to the ground while the other managed to leap out of the way just in time. Pegan leaped straight up landing on the boulder now looking down on his adversaries.

Averie screamed and ran for the safety of the trees, but was no match for the wolf's quickness, and it over-took her. Leaping high it slammed into her back knocking her down. Averie flailed her limbs trying to fight off the beast, but it latched onto her arm and shook violently. The Wolf Master set to chase after his pet while trying to remove the large sword slung across his back.

All in one motion Pegan leaped down and parried the attack with one blade while the other buried deep in the rovers eye piercing the brain. The mouth jerked open to scream but death was instant and he crumbled in a heap of death. Ignoring the other he chased after the wolf master.

"NOOOO!" Pegan screamed. There was nothing he could do. The wolf had almost dragged her into the forest and the goon was already upon her. She kicked and screamed but was easily overpowered. Time slowed as he watched the sword rise. Each nick, every crack was a taunting reminder of his failed quest. The dried blood a memory of all who have fallen at his feet. His lungs burned while his muscles strained to get there. Unless time stopped, he would not get there in time. He had one chance left and flipped his dagger in the air, catching it by the blade, he reached back to throw it when the twang of a bowstring caught his ear and the burst of wind brushed his neck.

The Wolf Master jerked and twitched as if he had begun some demonic ritual then slumped to his knees, the sword slipping from his dying grasp. A pencil-thin shaft fitted with yellow feathers protruded from his neck. As he fell, the shaft snapped resulting in a loud crack. Wrapped in a frenzy of blood-lust the wolf never saw his master fall and continued to drag Averie until another arrow penetrated one ear and exploded out the other scattering brains all over Pegan.

The remaining rover ran for the safety of the trees and vanished.

Pegan ignored the danger and ran to Averie, she was pinned beneath the corpse of the wolf. With all his strength he heaved the creature to the side and rolled Averie up next to the beast. She had faded into unconsciousness and her breathing was labored. Kneeling, he made himself as small as possible and waited. He knew at any moment another arrow would slice them both to ribbons. He was ready though, to sacrifice himself to save her.

His eyes blurred as he scanned the tree line. Nothing moved and his ears hurt with silence.

A quick shadow off to the right, something was there, lingering, taunting, and playing a game of cat and mouse. He decided to make the next move and stood, placing both weapons across his chest he screamed, "Come out and fight me like a man."

Pegan stepped back as the enemy emerged. "Oh no!" he whispered. There would be no way he could carry Averie and fight this creature. Having made the decision he stepped over the wolf and met it half-way across the clearing. Their eyes clashed in a shower of sparks, him with his daggers, and her with a bow.

Licking the air with a large pink tongue as if tasting them for dinner it spoke, a slight hiss to her voice "Pegan... Pegan Rhoe?"

"You're a bit far from the Anor?" he asked, puzzled by her sudden calmness.

"Yes," she answered, and then unnocked her arrow.

"How did you track me? I took an ancient pass."

"I have been tracking you for days," she said. "I was not sure if I would ever catch you. Elwrick placed a spell on me so I will always feel Averie's location, that's how I found you. He called it a maternity spell, I'm a mother again."

Pegan eyed her suspiciously, Elwrick said nothing about having a reptile accompany them. "How do you know Elwrick?"

Behind them, Averie groaned.

Augeessareth brushed past Pegan and went to Averie, "she's injured, and grows cold."

"Her ribs are damaged, possibly broken. We're headed to Minx. I have a friend there who can heal people," Pegan advised her.

"Minx, that's not a good idea. Karayan knows she's escaped, people will look for her where ever we go."

"I agree," Pegan said. "But Minx is a rogue town. Many there don't follow Karayan or his ways and we need to get Averie medical help. Besides, he owes me a favor."

"Pegan?" Averie cried out.

"Shhhh," Augeessareth whispered, "save your strength child."

When they touched Pegan could see an instant bond grow.

"I am Augeessareth," she whispered. "Elwrick sent me to aid you, and to protect you."

"Auge... Auggews..." Averie tried but the words didn't come.

"Auge... I can't do it, I just can't." Pegan's face blushed red and he walked away.

"It's fine," she replied as the corners of her mouth curled upward and she sputtered like a half clogged faucet, "call me Saress."

Pegan was not sure, but he felt this was the first time he'd ever been laughed at by a lizard. "We need to talk, tell me what you know."

Time passed quickly as Saress told him about Elwrick and what he said while he told her about the rescue. When they had finished, he knew she was not here by accident.

"Saress," Pegan turned serious. "I need to know right now, without a doubt. Are you with me, regardless how bad things get?"

Saress looked at Pegan with a deadly gaze, "I swore an oath to Elwrick to protect her with my life, and follow you, to the end."

With a dagger, he sliced his palm. She did likewise, and they grabbed each other, "bound with blood, till the end," he said.

Saress nodded.

"We need to get her up and on the mule, the healer is less than a day away."

Chapter 10

ven with Midnight's blazing speed, it still took Elwrick the better part of three days to reach the Wruust Pass. In hindsight, he realized it would have been quicker to ascend the Perch, round The Whispering Woods, and then navigate the Plains of Gedeon instead of challenging the Nymph—even though the former was twice as long—

The Wruust Pass, also known as the trader's route was the only way to access Timber Hall which resided deep within the confines of the Frozen Tundra. Separated from the south by a jagged line of mountains that resemble the skeletal remains of a once forgot beast, which was spewed forth from the ground. The locals called them the Iron Jaw as they hung over the pass looking to devour weary travelers. They extended all the way from the Esk Ocean to the Bay of Tranquility with thrusting spires of naked granite that pierced the sky and bottomless ravines that coughed swirls of fog.

The year was still early and snow had yet to fall making the pass quite easy to navigate, that is, until he crested the summit. From there the wind would increase while the temperatures plummeted. Even during the hottest months, snow remained. There were no roads, only long poles sticking up through the icy crust to help would be travelers from getting lost and dying in such an inhospitable environment.

From the top, Elwrick viewed the vast openness. As far as the eye could see frozen ponds and icy lakes speckled the flatlands each ringed in ice which gave the land a sickly, scab infested appearance.

Onward he charged into an icy blast of cold wind driven from the Esk Ocean. His beard grew white and his whole body shivered. He fought for warmth as he wrapped his cloak tight and pulled the cowl down low. All around the plains wicked moans carried on the wind brought life to the Tundra and made it sound as if the land was dying.

The barbarians of the north were a savage bunch and knowledge of their brutality was world renown. They had chosen a different life than those in the south and were often rejected. Because of this, a burning hatred grew only quenched by their need for trade. Few, if any would have come with the purpose of diplomacy but Elwrick understood the need to have a Northern representative. A quest he intended to fulfill.

The snow just kissed Midnight's belly when Timber Hall came into view. It was a massive city built upon a hill that spiraled upward like a conical seashell. At the very top was where the Emperor could be found looking down upon his trusted servants. As he neared it became painfully obvious something was desperately wrong. With the onset of darkness, lanterns should have been burning in every window while The Rusty Horseshoe—Timber Halls only Tavern—should have been brisk with business, yet the town lay under a veil of silence and the only light came through the cracks of secured shutters.

Elwrick walked Midnight down the center of the road at a slow gait and observed the many houses and trade shops. Most sat empty, cold, and thick boards covered every window. With the hour growing late Elwrick decided to get a room for the night and discuss with Emperor Tak-Thukmand in the morning about what plagued Timber Hall, and perhaps an agreement could be reached. Bidding farewell to his trusted friend, he entered the establishment.

With all the shutters drawn the tavern looked more like a crypt and he was surprised to discover he wasn't alone. A few older men with gray hair and thinning bodies sat scattered about as if tossed by the wind while two younger boys, not quite old enough to drink, sat at the bar engulfed in a heated debate.

Of the many lanterns, only a couple burned, turned down to where the flame fought for life and the hearth sat cold. Elwricks nose twitched. The thick stagnant air reeked with the scent of stale ale, cooked meat, and lost hope. Two women walked the floor draped in simple furs offering their surfaces for a fraction of the cost. Something or someone had driven the life from the very town and Elwrick planned to find out who, or what.

Elwrick sat near the back where he could observe the patrons.

"Welcome to The Rusty Horseshoe," the bartender said as he approached. "Jasper Grub, cook, cleaner, owner, and operator at your service," he announced. A large smile stretched from ear to ear exposing all six of his teeth. With one hand he held firm to a bottle while the other shot straight out to greet him. He was a balding middle-aged man, bone thin and a large nasty scar raked across his face. He spoke with wheezing gasps through a crooked mouth, "and you are?"

"A representative of the south, sent here to see what troubles Timber Hall." Elwrick shook his hand. He felt it would be better to approach the Emperor if he had an idea of the problem.

Jasper let his eyes drink up the stranger, "A dignitary?"

"You could say that," he adjusted his robe. "Word reached my ear Timber Hall was in a state of depression and I had to see for myself. I always heard this was a bustling city but fear whatever has plagued it, may spread south. Better to stop it here, don't you think?"

Jasper let out a laugh which drew the attention of everyone, "the south is the problem."

Elwrick cocked his head sideways, confused.

"Have you been living under a rock these last few days? It seems the diseased creature King Karayan held escaped with the aid of another and now the entire world is out searching. I would be too if it wasn't for my gimp leg."

"Oh," Elwrick said. "But how does this effect Timber Hall? You're a world away it seems, I simply figured there was another problem."

"Nope," Jasper sat across from him. "Business is so bad I had to let most of my employees go and my girls are about to starve. Emperor Tak-Thukmand has taken every qualified man and headed south. King Karayan's offered a king's favor as a reward if she's brought in alive, but only twenty gold for her corpse."

"Kings favor?" He cocked his head slightly.

"Surely you've heard of it?"

"Enlighten me," Elwrick said.

"It's the greatest reward available. You get to be King for a day, fill his shoes and he becomes your servant. Anything you want…anything. Women… gold… sit in his throne. The world is yours for a day."

"Interesting, but I have no desire to die," Elwrick said. "Well, since I came this far I might as well stay for the night and have a bite to eat before I travel back to East Haven. I take it you still have a few rooms available?"

"You can have your pick of the lot," Jasper said.

The sizzle of steak echoed through the hushed environment as Elwrick's attention was drawn to the boys. Their conversation had grown quite heated, and they now stood to face each other.

—*"I tell you what,"* the taller blond haired boy argued. *"We'll go out there and steal that weapon. And when we do, we'll kill the man who helped that creature escape and claim the reward for our own… and split it right down the middle."*

"He must'n been tough, I mean… helping her escape and all," the other replied.

"He's a regular guy, just like us. No reason we can't take a shot at that reward. And besides, once we own that weapon we'll have the advantage."

"What about his son? He would rip us to chunks, gnaw on our bones he would."

"After all the excitement has died down, you know, in a few days we'll go out there and watch. When that big oaf goes hunting we'll slip in and take it. Nutten the old man can do. We'll be back in town before the big goon returns," the elder said—

"Who's those two?" Elwrick whispered.

"The Kahla boys, bad news they are," Jasper answered. "They tried to join the hunt, but the Emperor turned them down. Said they lacked experience… and intelligence. All they've talked about the last few days is stealing an imaginary weapon from an old man and collecting the reward."

"And you allow thieves in your establishment? Talk of hurting an old man."

"Ain't stealing from me, none of my business, know-how," Jasper answered. He set the plate of food on the table followed by a large mug filled with ale, the white foam ran down the sides and a large key. "You know, that's the problems with you southerners, always meddling where you don't belong."

"Not meddling, protecting. Someday that may be you in his shoes, and you'll be thankful if someone stepped up to help."

Jasper thought for a moment, he had never looked at it in that aspect. "I'll talk with them, set them straight if it bothers you that much."

Elwrick lay on the bed lost in thought when a knock on the door brought him back to reality. It was still early as the light had yet to find the window. The soft rapping on the door came once more. Elwrick looked through the small peephole to see a young woman standing there, a troubled look on her face.

"Come in," Elwrick said as he opened the door.

She looked in either direction as if making sure none noticed her then darted in and quickly closed the door. "Please help them," she said. "I will do whatever you want." She began to get undressed as if she knew.

"Wait," he stopped her, and pulled her shirt back down, "what are you talking about?"

"The old man and his son those boys talked about hurting, they're my family."

"And your father allows you to work here, in this profession?"

"I don't work here because I choose too, I work here as punishment, and to keep them from being killed by the Emperor."

Elwrick took a heavy breath and sat her on the bed, "I think you best tell me everything if I am to aid you."

"It's a long story," she said as tears dripped from her cheeks.

He brushed them away, "now tell me everything."

Her face went red with anger. "My brother tried out for the Emperor's elite force, only the best of the best gets accepted and he was. It was a marvelous time in the house and everything was good. That is until he saw the evil that truly existed inside the emperor and my brother tried to implement change, he suggested improvements to raise the moral. The emperor was furious and accused him of trying to overthrow his rule and removed him from the academy and banished him, and my family from Timber Hall never to return under the penalty of pain of death. The night we left guards came and I was taken as well and forced to serve the emperor until the age of forty as punishment to them. Eventually, he grew tired of me and sold me to Jasper and now I'm forced to continue my trade here."

Elwrick rubbed his chin deep in thought, "How would you like to go home?"

"I would love to but I don't see how that's possible. My home was razed to the ground and I have no idea where they were banished to."

"I don't know either, but I know someone who does, wait here."

Elwrick worked his way back down to the bar where the boys still sat arguing. Jasper must have turned in for the night as he was nowhere to be found and all other men had left as well. Elwrick casually walked up to them and stopped, "I didn't think that old man was ever going to go to bed."

"What?" One said.

"Listen, I'm here as well to get that weapon and with the three of us. I don't see a problem. I didn't wanna say anything until he was gone. Don't wanna have any chance of the old man catching word of our coming."

The boys smiled. They're waiting looked as if it was about to pay off.

"Follow me," Elwrick said and led them up to the room.

Seeing the young woman standing there, they both smiled thinking they are going to have some fun, until they discovered neither could move.

Elwricks demeanor changed. "Listen to me and listen well, neither of you will hurt the old man, or his son. In fact," he pointed to the older one, "You will draw me a map of where to find them or I will skin you both alive right here in this very room."

The eldest suddenly found only his hand could move, and a quill was placed between his fingers.

"It would behoove you to do as instructed," Elwrick said. Using his finger he pointed to the kid and made a slicing motion and watched the boy's face twist in pain. "It's a magical knife, one you can't see, but the damage is all too real."

He could feel the dampness of blood ooze between his toes.

The kid drew the map as instructed.

Elwrick placed his thumb against the kid's forehead, "with this mark I will always be able to track you, wherever you go. If this map is false or leads me astray I will hunt you down and you will live for years as a prisoner in my dungeon as a skinless servant."

The kid quickly scribbled a few changes.

Elwrick released them from the spell then put them in a drunken stupor and watched them pass out in a heap on the floor. "They'll be asleep for days and wake with a terrible hangover, completely unaware this conversation ever occurred."

Outside, Elwrick called to Midnight who gladly accepted the new passenger, and they rode off into the darkness.

Chapter 11

They traveled the remainder of that night and well into the next when they arrived at the edge of a large clearing a few leagues south of Minx. Near the far edge, a dainty shack surrounded by large oak, elm and willow trees only visible by the single window which glowed like a goblins eye in the dark and dense gray smoke drifted from the chimney. A short distance away was a large barn with the doors tightly secured and beside it a pasture where a small chestnut horse fed.

"Wait here," Pegan whispered. "I'll make sure it's safe."

"How long do we wait?" Saress asked.

Pegan thought for a minute and pointed at the moon visible through the trees. The majority of it lay hidden behind the house. "See the moon, if it clears the house and I've not yet returned then it's a trap. Flee north to the Majestic Forest then west to Talons Peak."

Saress's eyes flashed yellow and she studied the area intensely, "from what I can see the glade is vacant save for a few mice near the barn."

Pegan looked at her with wonder on his face and then remember the gift all reptilians had. "I'll make sure he's alone."

To the regular eye he would have gone unnoticed but to Saress, he looked like a walking beacon as he moved from shadow to shadow.

Tap... tap... tap... he rapped on the door with his knuckles.

"I don't want or need any company. Go away."

Pegan chuckled when he heard the croak of Jairo's voice. "Jairo, it's me... Pegan," he whispered.

The door cracked only slightly open, then closed again to allow a chain to be unclasped, then opened all the way. "Pegan my boy, come in come in," he said. His wizened old face bore many scars of experience and his droopy eyes made him appear to be sleepwalking. Small wisps of silver hair snuck out from under a dirty brown cap and his bone-thin body leaned with a slight hunch. "So what pleasure do I have finding you at my doorstep tonight?" he asked. Saliva ran from his lower lip dripping onto his chin as he spoke.

"Shhhh," he whispered. "No one should know I'm here." He looked down the narrow road to make sure nobody was coming. Voices carried great distances in the still of the night.

"Okay... okay," he replied.

The house seemed unchanged since his last visit. To one side a small cooking and eating area where pots and pans hung, utensils dangled by hooks on the wall, a small round table with two chairs rested on a bear hide and a river rock hearth complete with a slow burning fire made the area seem quite lovely. The main living area held a three seated davenport, wooden chest bound with steel, night stand with a partially burned candle, while a few pictures decorated the walls. From there two other rooms could be seen. One appeared to be his private chamber complete with bed and chest of drawers. The other was clearly the examination room with its stainless steel table and cart that remained littered with vials, needles, bottles, tubes, cutting instruments, bandages, and a multitude of other strange things he couldn't pronounce, even if he read the name.

"We'll... I'm still waiting?" Jairo asked.

Pegan rubbed his chin and shuffled his feet, "I have a friend whose injured her ribs and has very little money. Well, I owe her a favor and since you still owe me. I hoped we could strike an agreement."

"You animal," he laughed, "get a little rough with the ol' girl?"

No, nothing like that."

"Sit... sit," he slid a chair out from under the table then retrieved two cups from a cupboard.

"Her father is abusive and beat her senseless. She ran to me and I went and had a talk with him, and, well it turned ugly."

"My word, did you kill him?" Jairo asked. He pulled the pot from the fire and filled the glasses. Steam rose and permeated the room with a pleasant spice scent.

"I really don't know if he died or not. After I threw him down the stairs, I never went and checked."

"Good, he deserves it." Jairo filled the glasses. The steam fogged up his thin, wire frame glasses. "Well... I can't examine her if she ain't here."

"She's outside, waiting with a friend."

With an old cloth, he wiped the steam free and laid the spectacles on the table. "You made her wait outside in the woods. Not a good idea," he said. "I have seen strange folk lingering around these parts as of late. While just in town today there was a pack of barbarians from the north. All the way down here, can you believe that, smacking people around, asking questions, threatening their life?"

"What kind of Questions?"

"Looking for a man named Blair. I guess he helped one of them diseased creatures escape. If you ask me he's put all of Icearaus in danger."

Pegan realized Jairo could not be trusted but Averie still needed aid, and with him thinking they searched for a man who didn't exist. He may still lend aid to her. "I have seen them as well," Pegan lied, "stopped by my place the day before yesterday."

Jairo took another sip, "well go get her before the woodland creatures do." He watched him go to the door then studied the parchment the barbarians passed out and read what the capture was worth. Before Pegan returned, he folded the note and placed it in a pocket.

Pegan introduced Jairo when they returned.

Saress studied him with hungry eyes.

A look of disgust crossed his face as Pegan led her by the hand to the examination room. Her movements were slow and her face twisted with pain at every step. Fresh blood trickled down her stained chin.

Jairo lifted the robe to assess the damage, "your father did quite the number on you."

"You mean the keep—"

"Can you heal her?" Pegan intervened.

Jairo had an anxious stare and lost look.

Pegan could see the man was deep in thought, then, as if he came to a resolution his eyes shot open wide as saucers and his mouth curled upward. In the dim light, his face reminded Pegan of a bullfrog.

"I believe I can. In fact, I think I have the solution right here." He snatched a glass bottle from the cart. "But, I will need some fresh water from the well and put it on the fire, it will need to be heated. While you're doing that, I'll begin a complete examination."

Saress's eyes narrowed to the point they looked closed, "I'm not leaving her alone."

"Hmmm," Jairo groaned.

"I'll get the water, you stay here," Pegan whispered to Saress.

Jairo watched Pegan for quite some time through the window working the well pump. He knew as soon as he saw the creature Pegan was the man they searched for. He also knew the reward for turning her in. They had both gone back a long way but if word reached the King he aided her, his life would be forfeited in the most painful of ways. Then there was the gold, he could live forever on what the King offered.

"You going to start the examination or daydream until she dies of old age?" Saress hissed.

Pegan had the pail filled when a crash came from the room and the window shattered into a thousand shards. He froze and for a brief moment, his world came to an end. Then, without thinking, the pail sailed through the air and he bolted for the house.

The examination room appeared to have just gone through a war. The table was knocked over and the cart was crushed under the weight of Saress. Glass lay broken and scattered, liquids steamed from the floor, tubes lay like worms and bandages floated in the air like confetti. Jairo held a small sword stretched outward while Saress positioned herself between Jairo and Averie, a sword in her hand as well.

"She tried to kill her right after you left," Jairo croaked through a stiff jaw.

"You lie," Saress hissed.

Pegan agreed with Saress. "Hand me the blade, Jairo? We both know you're not the fighting kind." Pegan reached out to take the blade. It was only his quick reflexes that saved his hand from being sliced to the bone. As the blade whizzed by Pegan grabbed the wrist twisting it till the fingers released and the blade fell to the ground.

Averie snatched the weapon and held it straight towards Jairo. "Stay back," she growled in an animalistic tone.

Pegan pushed Jairo back, "Why? Why did you try to kill my friend?"

"You lied to me," Jairo said. "She's the creature that escaped and you aided her."

"She's not a creature but a woman carrying a gift from the Creator," Pegan said. "You need to listen to me, you're being lied to—"

"She's an animal, look at her," Jairo screamed, he'd heard nothing Pegan said. His actions driven by a lust-filled reward. "Now, help me tie her down and we can get the guards to come take her away."

"No," Pegan said. "I won't tie her down, or let you get the guards."

"Don't you understand? We'll split the reward three ways, we'll never work again. I'm not sure what that reptile would do with the gold, but I'm willing to split it three ways. And since you used an alias none will know you helped. Think hard about your actions and what turning this thing in would mean for your future…our future."

"No—"

"The choice is yours," Jairo snarled. His movements were fast for an old man and took Pegan by surprise as he snatched a scalpel off the floor and lunged for the frightened woman.

Saress though had been expecting the attack and her movements proved the faster and the scalpel fell to the floor, Jairo's hand still holding the handle."

"*AHHH,*" he screamed, then leaped through the busted window like a rabid animal and disappeared into the darkness.

"He's gonna get help, we should leave now," Averie pleaded.

Saress was quick to follow out the door almost taking it off the hinges. Her eyes blinked yellow and she focused on the red shimmer that ran.

Unaware she could see him he paused to draw a breath.

With expert precision, the arrow screamed into the night and drove deep between the shoulder blades exploding out through the chest taking most of the heart with it.

"*AAAGHHHH.*" A scream cut through the darkness followed by a *thump* as the body hit the dirt.

Pegan never saw the death, only heard it through the shattered window.

A short while later Saress returned holding a bloodied arrow, "I discarded the body behind a fallen tree. Within a few days, the bugs should have devoured most of it destroying the evidence of our passing."

Rummaging through the scattered supplies Pegan found a bottle —labeled pain reducer—and had Averie take a few. Next, he wrapped her side up tight in a large bandage.

Averie laid on the davenport sipping hot tea wrapped in a blanket while Pegan stoked the fire. Saress barred the front door and kept watch out the window for any movement.

"I'm sorry, I thought…" Pegan slammed his fist against the stone mantel and his eyes watered. "Look what I cost us, three days and for what. It could have been her life. I truly believed in him, he was my friend for many years."

"I don't blame you," Saress patted his shoulder. "Your intentions were honorable. Unfortunately, we still don't know what to do with her injuries."

"I think he owns a wagon," Pegan said. "I'll look in the morning and see if it's in the barn. She can ride in that as we go through the Majestic."

The pills Pegan gave Averie took effect and her head slumped and she slept like a baby. Saress slept below her on the floor, a faithful companion while Pegan kept watch out the window.

The morning came with bright sun and warm air, it appeared the storm finally passed. Outside the window, birds sang, and the air was thick with the scent of pine

Saress looked at Pegan. Thick black bags sagged under his eyes and his face looked exhausted. "You look terrible, did you sleep at all?"

Pegan shook his head no.

"Where do we go from here?" Averie said as she yawned, sleepiness still hung thick in her eyes.

"We stay another night," Saress said, "Pegan needs to rest."

"I'll be fine."

"No…" she hissed. "You need some rest to make sound decisions. Otherwise, you may lead us straight to our deaths. One more night won't kill us and Averie's ribs could use the rest as well."

Chapter 12

he sun peaked over the Iron Jaw Mountains and all the land sparkled like diamonds. The sky turned a light shade of lavender and the wind had a chilling bite.

"It's beautiful," she said with a quivering jaw.

Without having been asked Elwrick removed his thick cloak and wrapped her tightly in it. "According to this map," Elwrick glanced at the parchment that flapped like a flag, "where still a few hours away, can't have you freezing before we arrive."

Along the way Elwrick learned of her father—Juvall Raestmond—and that he was the great, great grandson of a man named Ghomik —a mighty warrior that never knew fear—and the rumors about the weapon is true, she had seen it herself. The weapon was passed down from father to son until it came to Raestmond's hand but he was not the killing type and spent his days dreaming of constructing great buildings, towers and keeps of monumental proportions. At one time he even designed plans for a building he named The World of Icearaus. It was going to be for all to explore and hold exotic artifacts since the beginning of time. Unfortunately, it never came to fruition as funds could never be secured. He learned about Thathra and how he looked out of place among the family due to his sheer size, and of her mother and what a beautiful woman she was, and how she longed to see her.

The map led them to a tall bluff where far below Elwrick viewed what looked to be a small dwelling. A narrow trail of packed snow wound its way down to the base where a small man chopped wood.

As he neared he could see the house was positioned so precisely that snow seemed to avoid it like an enemy. Constructed of logs cut with painstaking precision, not one gap was visible in the fitment and two small windows looked outward like eyes that never slept. The roof was high in the center and slanted at such an angle to keep snow from gathering and constructed with planks then covered with fine branches woven together to make it waterproof.

The man finished his chopping chore and was in the process of gathering the wood upon their arrival. He was short, wide around the belly and a halo of graying hair circled his otherwise balding head. Engrossed in his work he never saw them arrive.

"Good day Mr. Raestmond," Elwrick said.

Surprised, the man stumbled backwards spilling his current load except for one thin piece which he swung backwards in an awkward uncoordinated motion.

"I mean you know harm," Elwrick said, "and I apologize if I frightened you."

"Who… who…who are you?" he stuttered, "and why are you here?" He kept both eyes fixed on the intruder as he worked his way back towards the house where his spectacles sat on the windowsill.

Tanara fumbled her way off the horse and ran to the man, arms stretched out wide she screamed like a banshee, "FATHER."

"To return a valuable asset you lost years ago, to bring you council, and offer you a proposition."

Tanara collided with her father causing both to tumble to the ground. A tear came to Elwricks eye. He would do the same given the chance to see his daughter's again.

Lying in the snow they held each other for what seemed like an eternity, then he spoke, "How?" he asked, "the Emperor swore he would—"

"That man," she cut him off, "he came yesterday and saved me." Tears froze to her cheeks.

Raestmond looked at Elwrick puzzled then placed the wire-thin spectacles on his face. "Bajesus," he hollered, "you're a wizard." He drew back with a closed fist in defense.

"Father, he's a good man."

"No, no," Elwrick said modestly, "you give me more credit than I deserve." He climbed down from Midnight.

Raestmond studied the robed man. "I think we all best go inside."

The house was elegant but simple and utilized every square inch. The wooden floor was perfectly level and rugs lay in front of each piece of hand-crafted furniture. At the far end of the dwelling, a large hearth made from river rock held a warming fire and two fluffy high-back chairs rested within the heats reach. A large pot hung on a metal hook overlooking the fire and steam filled the room with a fresh scent. A small table with two chairs rested in the middle of the room and against the wall, a large tub for washing dishes sat empty. A second door led to another room where two beds were visibly divided by a small table.

"My name is Elwrick," he said, "and the misses did a very nice job decorating, Tanara has told me all about her."

"Where is mother? I would so love to see her. To tell her how much I've missed her."

Raestmond lost all expression, and he seemed hollow, suddenly devoid of all life. "Your mother passed on about six months ago. After the Emperor took you she just stopped living. She became ill, and I tried to help her. Her condition worsened and one morning she never woke."

Tanara crumbled as if every bone in her body turned to rubber and she wailed in long painful sobs.

Raestmond fell to his knees and hugged her, and they remained that way for hours.

It was close to the evening when she finally came to grips with her mother's passing and Raestmond led them out back to where an intricately carved tombstone broke through the snow. More time passed and the sky darkened by the time she said her final goodbyes.

Raestmond dished up food from the pot and they all sat in silence for some duration.

"And my brother… is he… dead also?"

"It was hard on him at first and he became distant, spoke very little and one day he left, without a word. I figured to never see him again, but he returned with a dead animal slung over his shoulder and said he finally discovered his calling in life, to become a hunter and a gatherer. He spends his days out roaming the tundra helping lost travelers or killing wild animals for their hides to keep us warm and put food on the table. I don't expect him home until late tonight.

"Sounds like a fine young man," Elwrick said.

Raestmond looked at Elwrick through glossy eyes, "The best." He took another bite, "I have nothing to give you in return. No reward I can offer equals what you have given me."

"I'm not asking for a reward," Elwrick smiled. "Only to lend me your ear and hear the tale I have to tell."

"I can do that."

At the hearth, they gathered.

Elwrick left no detail forgotten and told them about Averie, Pegan and Saress, the escape, and what needed to be done. He concluded with, "I wish to recruit Thathra as well."

Raestmond thought for a long while. "No," he said. "I've lost so much already and now you wish to rob me of my son, I'm sorry, but the answer is no."

Elwrick looked at Tanara first, then Raestmond. "No words can heal the loss of a loved one, or offer comfort for the grieving," Elwrick said. He placed an arm around the shoulder of Raestmond. "Sorrow will not bring her back, I'm sorry. Let her live in your memory but don't let it cloud your judgment. Someday you will walk side by side again with her, for now, rejoice in the memories," Elwrick whispered.

"And what do you know of loss or tragedy?" Raestmond hissed.

Elwrick rubbed his chin, taking some time to remember his own pain. The pain of what happened centuries ago suddenly felt like yesterday. "I watched my own wife die, torn limb from limb by a demon named Xannoruch. I should have died that night but I was left to endure. Both daughters died as well, victims of an onslaught from creatures men were never meant to encounter. My son, I still don't know as he was dragged into the darkest chasms that belched smoke, and ash, and fire. I only pray he died and did not become bound as a slave to their demented desires." His eyes drooped then he quickly recovered, "that's what keeps me driving on, driving towards a final goal. To rid the world of the filth not meant to thrive here."

I'm so sorry," Tanara whispered.

Elwrick drew a deep breath as a large solitary tear ran down his cheek and he slumped to one side as if he'd fallen asleep.

"Hello," a man said as he entered. "I saw the horse from quite some distance, we don't get many visitors this far out." He was large and towered over his father by a good two feet and at least as many wide. Long blond hair hung limp beside a stern rugged face and his muscular body flexed with anticipation under the wintery garb.

Tanara ran to him, and him to her and in the main living area, they crashed together.

"I've missed you so much," he whispered.

Tanara sobbed tears of joy seeing her brother again and tried to speak but only choked on the words.

Elwrick came to his feet then stretched out a hand, "I'm Elwrick, and been waiting to meet you for some time now."

Thathra eyes him suspiciously, and then took his hand in a firm grasp, "I'm Thathra."

Elwrick studied Thathra's movements. He had the strength of a warrior and the finesse of an artist. It was crude, but there, waiting to be refined.

"And why would you want me?" Thathra asked with raised eyebrows.

"Perhaps we should sit," Elwrick said. This was the first time he viewed the deep hazel eyes that floated in a sea of white marble.

"Elwrick wishes to recruit you, I told him no, but you're a grown man and should decide for yourself," Raestmond spoke softly, unsure what answer his son might give.

"Recruit me for what? I've already been banished from the barbarian tribes."

"To save a woman, a woman we don't know," Elwrick briefly explained.

Thathra's gaze locked on to something invisible, "I cannot go, I'm sorry," Thathra said. "Now if you will excuse me I got animals to skin before they spoil."

"What is stopping you?" Elwrick asked as Thathra walk away.

"My father is old and has lost so much already," Thathra said as he turned back. "I finally get to spend time with my sister and now you wish me to leave."

"Your father is old," Elwrick said. "But he is a responsible man. One who understands right and wrong, which understands reason and sees a purpose bigger than life."

"And if I die?" Thathra growled, "then what?"

"Then your father will understand you did the best you could to make Icearaus just a little better for all. Instead of just sitting and watching others suffer, you tried to bring peace into their lives." Elwrick's calm demeanor faded, replaced by something more assertive.

Raestmond took Elwricks arm, "And what is to become of us when he's gone. The Emperor will discover her escape and come looking. She will be punished all the more and me... I'll be tortured before I am killed."

Elwrick produced a key from his robe and placed it in Raestmond's hand, "take your daughter but travel lightly and head south to Rain Wood. You will find a house there. My own personal abode when I choose to reside in this realm. You will be protected there as powerful wards have been placed upon the structure. All your needs will be provided, but don't be surprised if I show up at random times."

The room fell quiet, and it was Raestmond who broke it. "I think you should go," he said to Thathra.

Something Elwrick said sunk deep into Raestmond and his position changed. Hearing this brought a smile to Elwricks face.

"Is that your wish?" Thathra asked, placing both arms on his father's hunched shoulders.

"Remember," Elwrick said. "This will not be a walk through some fantasy land. There are creatures, motivated by an evil none of you can imagine that would like only to feast on your flesh and suck the marrow from your bones. The dangers are real."

"How much time do I got to decide?" Thathra asked.

"Only minutes," Elwrick answered. "People already risk their lives to save her, and every minute we delay is time they may need your help."

Thathra turned back towards his father, "If that's your will, then I will see it done."

"You're becoming your own man," Raestmond said. He went to the other room and returned carrying a large wooden box. "Wherever your travels take you, just remember I will always be there." Opening the lid he removed the largest battle axe Elwrick had ever seen.

At over five feet long the wooden shaft was clad in metal and the lower half wrapped in a crossing pattern of leather straps. The axe was double bladed and curving sharply upward before swinging out wide and curving in at the middle then swinging back out at the end. The top of the shaft had a long steel spike and the steel sparkled like diamonds.

"I sat many long hours dreaming of the day I would pass this on to my son as my father did, and his father before him," Raestmond said.

Running his finger down the long blade Raestmond motioned for his son to take it. With a mighty grip that large blade that looked so large in Raestmond's hand now looked like a toy in Thathra's.

"I have one concern?" Raestmond asked. "My boy has never been past the Wruust Pass. How will he find his way?"

"I will be with him till we locate the others," Elwrick said. "Then Pegan will lead him the rest of the way."

"So you won't be there?" Raestmond asked. A look of disappointment filled his eyes.

"No," Elwrick said as he watched Thathra gather supplies. "I got other pressing matters which must be met long before she reaches the isle, or all this will be for not."

Elwrick handed Raestmond a pouch. "When you get to Rain Wood, buy something nice for the both of you, you deserve it."

They said their final goodbyes, hugged and kissed each other, then walked away.

Chapter 13

The hours slowly passed and they walked in silence, each deep in thought at what the future might hold. Through the dense swirling air and snow that fell in thick blankets, the Iron Jaw Mountains rose up like an eerie fortress. It was early fall yet winter had already arrived to the Frozen Tundra.

Thathra paused at the base and looked back. His home had vanished hours ago and their footprints were quickly fading. Their passing would go undetected and only a memory would remain, eventually, he knew, those too would fade and he wondered if he would ever see his family again.

Elwrick joined him, "magnificent structure," he said, "they run from coast to coast with only one pass."

Thathra shook his head. "No, there's another. A secret only the barbarians know. It follows the Esk Ocean and is said to drop down into a great forest. Those who have seen it say trees grow as far as the eye can see and their tops touch the clouds. It's where most of the wood comes from along with the majority of our furs."

Elwrick scratched his chin, "that's how the Emperor passed without being observed," he whispered.

"The Emperor?" Thathra asked confused.

"Yes," Elwrick said, "he too searches for the same woman, but not to aid but in reward."

"This poses quite the problem," Thathra kicked at a chunk of ice.

"Barbarians are skilled trackers and have many trained hounds. If they know her scent, they will track her to the end of the world, to Hell and back if needed. They will never stop hunting her."

"We'll... then I guess we should not delay," Elwrick said then started up the path.

The trail was steep but easily navigated and before the sky darkened they reached the summit. Once there, a world he never knew filled his vision and brought tears to his eyes.

"More than you imagined?" Elwrick asked.

"I didn't...." His eyes drift from east to west. "This is folly," he mumbled. "Not in a hundred years will we find them. The land is too vast."

"She's less than two days from here as the hawk flies," Elwrick reassured the young barbarian. "Remember, I can sense her location."

"And what about Karayan? You said he can as well."

He can, but only her presence, not her location. He knows she survives, that is all. Only I have the ability to follow her trail, a gift given by the Creator."

"And how does Karayan feel her presence?"

"Gifts offered by a dark and sinister being who I wish not to discuss. To even speak his name causes ill will and discontent."

"So you can lead us to her?"

"Almost," Elwrick answered. "The longer she stays at the same location the stronger the bond builds. When she moves, I can only follow her trail. As we speak though the feeling strengthens which tells me they have stopped, either willingly, or unwillingly. Without a doubt though, I can say they are somewhere in the Ash Mountains."

Thathra pulled his axe free and ran his thumb down the length of the long blade. Taking his time he examined each nick and scratch. "If you ask me we're going about this all wrong."

"What do you mean?" Elwrick asked cocking his head sideways.

"While his soldiers search for the bearer he'll be alone, vulnerable, weak. With your help, I can enter the palace and slay him. This would allow the bearer safe passage to wherever she needs to go."

Elwrick released a hearty laugh then slapped Thathra on the shoulder. "I like the way you think, but it won't work." Elwrick's face grew serious, his features chiseled. "We cannot kill Karayan, not me, not you, not anyone, only the child can. Karayan is a mortal man made of blood and bone and tissue, just as you. The difference though is he's been gifted with unnatural abilities. He never ages', wounds heal before a drop of blood touches the ground. He can't get sick, or ill, and is immune to disease and poison. Even the ravages of time…"

Thathra's eyes widened, "a minor detail you forgot to mention."

Elwrick drew a deep sigh. "Details that don't concern you, but since you have grown curious, it's best to tell you so you understand the evil you face."

"Hundreds of years ago it was an honor to be a bearer. Grand ceremonies were held whenever a bearer was discovered and the world rejoiced. Great halls were constructed and when their child returned, they lived in a great city named Skyn. The city was beautiful with vast gardens, enormous libraries, and magnificent fountains. People came from all over to hear their tales and learn. It was a wonderful time indeed, and the world rejoiced."

"All that changed though not long after Karayan returned. Something went wrong and nobody knows exactly what. Suddenly, bearers vanished without a trace and it seemed like all the world suddenly filled with chaos."

"Karayan was a child from a bearer?"

"Yes."

"Are all children from bearers immortal?"

"No," Elwrick said. "None are immortal, they succumb to the ravages of time just like everyone else."

But how did he become immortal?" Thathra asked.

Elwrick looked up at the sky and the falling snow. "From what I've been able to decipher he has been granted his unnatural abilities from the underworld. A place no human should ever dwell as its construction was not meant for man, but for the demons who challenged the Creator during the world's construction."

"He sold his soul to the devil?" Thathra asked.

"Again, you ask questions for which I do not have the answer, but what I do know is the fetus he steals from the bearer is sacrificed, but I don't know to what, or whom. The Dark Master has many agents and any one of them is capable of granting long life."

"I don't understand," Thathra said. "A man just doesn't wake up one morning and decide to sell his soul to the demons of Hell, something else went wrong, someone led him astray, possibly a demon disguised as someone tricked him."

Elwrick released a sigh, "I don't believe so. The Dark Master or any of his agents for that matter will not just arrive unannounced. They will only come if someone actively goes searching for them. Karayan was looking for something and what that is I believe holds the key to his existence."

"But to do this alone would have been a huge undertaking," Thathra said.

"He never did it alone. He offered huge rewards to all who turned in the bearer. He took great strides to convince the people that bearers are diseased filthy creatures and they are the cause of all the sickness in the world. Everything that is bad was because of them."

"And the people believed him?" Thathra asked.

"At first people refused to believe it but all those that opposed him were either bought off or killed. As generations passed more and more people fell to his lies and now it's a crime to conceal a bearer."

"Unbelievable," Thathra said. "Just when you think you heard everything you get slapped in the face. You would think the people would rebel against this tyrant?"

"He has massed enormous armies and keeps the people at bay through fear or bribery. Everything he does has one goal in mind."

"To destroy the bearer and sacrifice the child to appease some something?" Thathra asked.

"Yes," Elwrick answered.

"If he is this all powerful being, how come he doesn't track down the bearer himself and slaughter all who help her?" Thathra asked.

"Because the bearer is pure of mind, body, soul and free of the corruption and innocent at heart. When the Creator decides Icearaus needs a new steward, a female is selected that is pure. It is this purity which protects her from him. This is why someone else watches her, and another kills her. It is this corruption which destroys us as new bearers cannot be selected as all those born already have corruption within their heart.

"My word," Thathra's eyes sank, "what kind of sick world do we live in?"

"You live in an exquisite world. The world Karayan has created was never meant to be. He has turned this into a forsaken world where even the Creator has turned away. It is only now he has given me permission to intervene in a final effort to save it before it's destroyed. This world can be saved though and returned to its glory. And to think, you will be part of it."

"So what gift does the child have that can stop Karayan?"

Elwrick's face said it all before he answered, "I don't know, the Creator has never informed me. It is not my part to know so I don't ask. I only know the bearer has to reach the portal for this world to find salvation.

"So what is your part then?" Thathra asked.

"I hold the book of portals," Elwrick answered. "When the bearer reaches the Isle of Aramoor, I perform the ritual to open the portal. Now, with all that being said we must continue on, the hour grows late and our friends may be in peril."

Without the hindrance of snow, Midnight found he was able to support them both and rode at a blistering pace and the leagues clicked away in minutes. They rode through the night guided by a bright moon and dancing stars. The Lonely Mountain came and went and they passed many people who roamed the plains just outside Lynn Brook, swords drawn, torches held high. Still, they traveled through a glade and briefly paused at a well-hidden campsite then quickly departed. The sky was a shade of plum as they reached the base of the Ash.

"If I know Pegan he would have taken this trail," Elwrick said. A cool, crisp breeze filtered down through the trees carrying with it the scent of decay. The path was easy to follow as their noses did most of the guiding. Upon their arrival, Thathra covered his nose to keep from gagging as the smell was overwhelming.

Near the edge of the glade, a body jerked and twisted as if having a seizure. The mouth was fixed open and both eyes had long since been plucked leaving darkened cavities. The skin bubbled like boiling water and a large festering wound leaked a dark fluid. Just then, to their surprise, the skin could no longer contain the feast and the abdomen burst open spilling large piles of maggots out the side.

Near the body, a large wolf missing part of its head was covered with flies and the hide was torn and ripped.

Thathra turned away as Elwrick flip the body over to retrieve the broken arrow. The bright yellow feathers now stained red. "Saress was here," he said.

"The reptile?" Thathra asked.

"Yes, she was here."

"Are you sure?"

"Positive, the fletching is unique to the Anor. Normally they retrieve all evidence of their passing but it's plausible she left the arrow as a marker for someone to follow, possibly us."

"Should we wait a bit?" Thathra asked, "in case it's a trap?"

"There's nothing here to fear unless you fear death, then it's all around us," Elwrick answered. Near the far end of a clearing by a large boulder, they discovered two more bodies. One had been stabbed in the eye while the other was headless.

Thathra followed the footprints with his eyes which snaked its way higher into the mountains then disappeared over the ridge.

As night fell on the Ash, Thathra could barely make out the path, yet Elwrick moved with renewed vigor. At times he led them astray yet to Thathras amazement they would arrive farther up the trail. The moon was high and every star sparkled like ice when Elwrick halted at the edge of a large clearing. Before them, a small house was visible. Gray wisps of smoke floated from a chimney and a yellow glow filtered through shuttered windows. "She's inside that house, but who is with her I don't know," Elwrick said. "We must exercise caution."

Pegan removed the steel poker from the holder and shuffled the wood around in the hearth. "We can't stay here much longer. In fact, we've been here too long already."

"We leave tomorrow then, before first light," Saress responded.

"Which way?" Averie asked through struggled gasps. The rest had helped and her health improved but the pain was still visible in her eyes.

"North, up through the Majestic's then cut down through Valley Forge. That would be the quickest route." Pegan sat back in the rocker and peered out the small opening in the blinds. "It seems luck has finally rolled our way. A thick fog has moved in and should help conceal us."

"That's weird," Saress glanced out another window. "There was no fog the last time I looked."

Knock… knock…knock… a rapping sound came through the door. Pegan leaped to his feet and both daggers found his hands. "Take Averie in the back," he whispered, "while I dispatch the unwanted visitor."

Using his dagger, Pegan moved the blind back enough that whoever stood at the door would be visible. To his spite though, the fog thickened and only an outline of the unwanted guest was visible. Then another shape formed and it was much, much larger.

Tap… tap… tap… the sound came again. The handle turned, but the lock held.

Concerned, Pegan backed away and joined Saress leaving only a slight crack in the door from which to see who entered. "There's two, one my size while the other is a monster."

Tap…tap… tap… the noise repeated, and the knob jiggled.

"Maybe they'll leave if no one answer's," Averie whispered.

"Very unlikely, these men are here for a reason," Pegan answered.

Click. The sound of the lock unlatching echoed through the room.

"They must be thieves," Averie whispered. "How else could they pick the lock so easily?"

"Shhhh," Pegan whispered lifting a finger to his lips. "There are things in this world deadlier than thieves and locks are only a mere inconvenience."

A low growling moan filled the room as the door slowly swung inward. The cool outside air rushed in exhausting the flame leaving only embers to glow. Pegan's knuckles faded white as he gripped the blades. With one foot on the door, he waited to gain the element of surprise. Whoever came through that door first would die.

Saress nocked an arrow, whoever followed would die next.

As the outline of the intruder emerged Pegan sprang into action but was knocked backward by a flash of bright light. Both daggers fell from his grasp as he clawed at his eyes trying to subdue the intense burning.

Saress stepped out and released the arrow but it burst into flames and ashes flew across the room as if in a hurricane. Before her, two magical swords appeared and moved with frightening speed backing her up against the wall.

Averie screamed as if she'd been set on fire as a pulsating purple hue formed inches from her skin. It moved as she did and followed like a second layer of skin but caused no harm or pain. "What kind of evil is this?" she cried out.

Pegan slipped a blade free from his boot and charged at the darkened shape but was quickly lifted off his feet and thrown against the wall crashing down upon the davenport.

Saress drew her sword and swung at the blades but hers passed straight through without harm while the two magical swords easily knocked hers aside then pinned her against the wall. She gulped her final breath as she felt the blade press against her throat.

"The house is empty except for him, and the two in the back room." Saress heard a voice say.

Both swords faded then vanished in a shower of silver sparks while the purple hue that surrounded Averie faded to a light green, amber, yellow, then vanished.

Pegan felt himself being hoisted to his feet and placed in a chair. His eyes were still slammed shut as the burning continued. Relief finally came as he felt a cool cloth being draped over his eyes.

"Keep that in place for a few minutes. The burning will subside shortly, the effects are not permanent."

He recognized the voice, it was Elwrick.

"Elwrick," Saress hollered as she looked through the doorway. "Averie, come quick, there's someone I want you to meet," Saress called to her.

Averie did as she was told and glanced out the door at the two strangers.

"Come… sit, let me look you over," Elwrick said and took her by the hand and escorted her to the davenport.

"Elwrick," Pegan called out, there was obvious anger in his voice. "Why did you attack?"

"I had no choice, you would be too dangerous otherwise. And besides, it was not a true attack, only something to disable you long enough to assess who held Averie."

While Elwrick assessed Averie, Saress moved towards the large man who was busy relighting the fire. "Long way from home, barbarian?"

Saress spoke.

"Aye," he said, "Elwrick brought me."

"This is Thathra," Elwrick said. "He's our northern representative."

"Emperor Tak-Thukmand let him come, very unusual," Saress said.

"Well, not really," Elwrick said as he finished examining Averie. "Emperor Tak-Thukmand is already on his way here with every able-bodied man hunting you. It seems he's struck a deal with Karayan to capture Averie and do whatever he wishes to with the rest."

Pagan's mouth fell open and his eyes were as large as saucers when he heard the new revelation.

"You got bigger problems than him though," Elwrick said as he finished his examination. "The bearer is gravely injured. As we speak she sits on the verge of death."

"Her ribs?" Pegan asked.

"You know of her injury?"

"I have seen the bruises. With each day it grows larger. The Keeper did this to her before I arrived."

"You're a healer?" Saress eagerly said. "Can't you do something?"

Elwrick shook his head, "I'm sorry, truly I am but I cannot help. Mortal hands caused these wounds, so it must be cured by mortal hands. There are laws, and rules in place I cannot break. What I can do though is give advice and there's only one place that has a healer skilled enough who may help."

"Rhunsiire," Pegan whispered through pursed lips.

"Yes," Elwrick said. "But speak no word of this mission as there are some who would rather see it fail."

"There must be another way?" Pegan begged. "I was planning to go through the woods, hug the rim of Nye Lake, we can make it to the portal."

"You won't make it," Thathra said. "The woods are infested with barbarians. Even if you could sneak through their dogs would pick up the bearers scent before long. They will track what you cannot see."

"No," Elwrick said, "Fate has chosen your path."

"How far is Rhunsiire?" Averie asked.

"In your condition, five days, if we see no enemies," Pegan said.

Elwrick had a concerned look on his face, "Pegan, the portal can only be opened on the night of a new moon as it reaches its apex, she must be at the island by then."

"And if we fail to reach it by then?" Saress asked.

"We'll have to wait till another new moon, a full thirty days," Elwrick answered. "Now that you are all together I shall take my leave back to my realm to prepare the process. There is much work left to do before the portal can be opened," Elwrick said.

Thathra stood at the door and watched Elwrick fade taking the fog with him, "he's a strange one."

"But has a good heart and his mind is in the right place. It would be best to follow his advice," Saress advised.

"I would not be so sure," Pegan said as he passed Thathra and walked outside and trained his vision to the north.

Thathra followed, "did you not hear what Elwrick said, she'll die if we continue, we must go to this place you said."

"What I know is you have yet to get blood on your hands," Pegan yelled as he walked inside.

Thathra followed.

"We're leaving now, not tonight, not tomorrow, now," Saress hissed. "You're the leader, I accept that but I refuse to accept that you are willing to kill Averie because you fear the place you mentioned."

"You don't understand—"

"No, you don't understand. If you take her north, it will be you two because you'll have to kill me," Saress said, her hand slide down to the sword that rested on her hip.

"And me." Thathra slid the axe free from the straps that held it in place across his back.

Pegan let his eyes shoot between them for a few awkward moments before he spoke. "Okay, but I will have to draw you a map from there, as there's a good possibility I won't be joining you."

"You underestimate us. If there's trouble do you believe we will abandon you?" Saress asked.

"You underestimate what we are about to enter. Now I must get the mule ready to go," Pegan said as he left the building.

With everything packed and Averie in place they departed.

Chapter 14

The rover had no choice but to answer the questions. His fingers were already numb and a searing pain climbed up through his forearms. The bindings were purposely cinched tight and a mangy dog was so close each time it barked saliva splattered onto his face.

"Unless you wish to be eaten alive by Fang, I suggest the next words out of your filthy sewer best have the answer to my question. Where are they?" Brilgord demanded.

"I already told you I don't know," the rover begged from his knees looking up at the large burly man. "We stumbled upon them by accident. There was more though than just him and the filthy creature. Some other thing I had never seen before was there as well, looked like a large lizard, and slaughtered all but me. I fought tooth and nail and somehow escaped—"

"Ran like a coward more likely," Brilgord snapped back. Anger infused the man as he ran a mighty hand through his thick beard and let his eyes scan the surrounding mountainous terrain. Thick lush trees faded to a ring of bone white snow that crested the jagged peaks while bottomless ravines hissed steam as if the mountain were alive. Any attempt to find them in the unfamiliar terrain would be all but impossible. "Take us to where you encountered them and you may just earn your freedom."

"It's a long way from here, a few days at least."

"I didn't ask you how far it was. I said to take us there, now." With a mighty grip, he lifted the rover to his feet. "And if you try to run…" the barbarian glanced down at Fang.

"Sunrise will be in a few hours," Pegan said. "We'll travel till then and stop to eat." The trail they followed kept them hid in the shadows of an enormous sheer wall while far below the mirrored surface of Nye Lake sparkled. The air had a cool crispness to it and the land had not yet warmed enough to burn off the dampness from the night. Along their journey, Thathra told them of his past and of Emperor Tak-Thukmand. How the barbarians were excellent trackers, and how even if they left no trace of their passing, dogs could track them by scent alone. Saress used her thermal vision to keep track of any movement behind them, and sometimes when the land was cast in dark shadows, she would scout ahead. The Barbarians or any other enemies never revealed themselves and besides a few wild animals, they saw nothing. As the day lingered on they stopped to eat and rest but otherwise kept a steady pace.

"The sweet smell of death, I love it," Brilgord said as he whiffed in the scent of decay. A sickening smile widened upon his hardened face. "Looks like your boys bit off more than they could chew," he continued as he walked across the clearing.

"Took the head right off this sorry sap," another barbarian said.

Behind them, a dog growled and pawed at the ground.

"Her scents been located, shall we release the prisoner?" A much younger barbarian asked. The excitement in his voice was hard to hide, quite probably his first real encounter.

"Sure, and besides, the dogs need the practice, make sure they haven't got rusty in these waning days," Brilgord said.

The rover watched nervously as the bindings were cut.

"You're free to go," Brilgord said. "Hurry, before I change my mind."

As the rover fled into the dense brush Fang and the other dogs were released. "Get him, boy," Brilgord hollered.

Even in the shadows of the trees out of sight, they knew what was happening through the snarling, growling and screams. Each dog returned holding a different piece of the body, their faces glowed red with fresh blood. "Now let's go after the real prize." Brilgord patted Fang.

The sky was painted a crimson gold by a fading sun when they reached a small dell on the banks of Nye Pond. Directly across the water, the gleaming tips of the Silver Mountains towered above the Rocky Crag and far beyond The Great Divide waited. While it was still light, they cooked pheasants Thathra trapped and fish Pegan caught. As the land darkened the fire was stomped out to conceal their location and Saress slipped into the darkness. She often took the night watch as her vision allowed her to see well beyond what theirs were capable of.

Pegan woke to a stiff nudge. Thick, black, angry clouds obscured the moon and stars leaving the land cast in a blackness so dark Pegan could barely make out who woke him. Saress motioned for him to follow. Up a small trail in silence, he went taking great care not to fall on the jagged, sharp rocks which lay scattered. She took him to a small plateau that overlooked their camp and offered a view of the direction they came.

"I didn't see a need to wake the others just yet until I discussed with you what I observed. The barbarians have picked up our trail. I could sense them earlier but to be sure I backtracked many miles till I came upon them," she said.

"How many?" Pegan asked, a concerned look on his face.

"Nine and five dogs."

"Fourteen," Pegan replied. His hair danced on a cool breeze from the east.

"Can we outrun them?"

"No. At their speed, I would guess they will be upon us within a day if not sooner."

Pegan drew a deep sigh and rubbed the stubble that grew on his chin.

"We knew they were coming, it was only a matter of time," Saress whispered, her voice carried on the wind.

Pegan looked down at Averie, "So innocent," he finally said after a few moments. Saress could just make out the slight trace of a tear as it ran down his cheek just before he started down the trail.

"So what would you advise for our next move?" Saress questioned him as she followed.

"Half a day from here is a gorge. Rock on both sides and slightly narrows into a choke point that will give us an advantage, but we need to leave soon," Pegan said.

"Let's wake them now," Saress suggested.

Each worked in silence as the makeshift camp was dismantled and any traces erased.

"What now?" Averie asked, her eyes welled up but tears never came.

"We don't have a choice, we must keep moving for another half day," Pegan said.

Traveling proved to be much more tedious in the darkness as Pegan led them farther south. The trail traced the edge of Nye Pond for a short while then abruptly veered east up the side of a steep cliff. The path was invisible in the darkness and anyone who might be watching would get the impression they were floating. As the sky lightened to a dull gray Saress brought the mule to a stop next to a babbling brook.

Thathra stood on the edge of the bluff. From here he could follow the trail all the way back down to where they camped. They had not traveled far in distance but climbed more than a few thousand feet. "Look, down there," Thathra pointed to small black dots combing the landscape.

Pegan joined Thathra, "they've traveled faster than I expected."

Averie slid from the mule landing on her knees next to the stream. She splashed water on her face and took long wheezing gasps of air. Her eyes grew weary, and she seemed lost in a strange fogginess or stupor.

"We can't keep this pace," Saress said, kneeling next to Averie.

"I think you underestimated our foes," Thathra said. His eyes were fixed on the black dots that discovered this new path and were making the climb. "They'll be here shortly. How far is Rhunsiire?"

"Two days to the Tlumn River, then one more to Rhunsiire," Pegan said.

"That's no good," Thathra argued. Large beads of sweat formed on his brow which he swiped away with a large hairy hand. "We can't outrun them, especially in her condition."

"We need to keep moving," Pegan pleaded a sense of urgency in his voice.

"To where?" Thathra voice rose. "They'll track us to the edge of the land, and even further if they must."

"We don't have a choice, we must try," Pegan snapped, his hardened gaze fixated on the barbarian. "We can't defend ourselves from here, it is to open, they will surround us."

Saress placed Averie on the mule and they started to leave.

Thathra turned back towards the berm that separated the bluff, from the trail. "You three keep going, I will hold them as long as I can." His axe slid free from the bindings. "I refuse to run anymore. Like criminals were chased and hunted. I would rather die as a warrior." Thathra wiped the spittle from his chin, "than to live as a coward."

"I as well grow weary of this game of cat and mouse," Saress said as she slipped her bow free and nocked an arrow. "It ends right here, right now. Take Averie and go. If we survive, I will track you to Rhunsiire," Saress tried to tell Pegan, but all she spoke to was a shadow as Pegan already faded from sight and advanced towards the enemy.

With her keen vision, Saress was the first to see the solitary barbarian leave the safety of the trees and climb into view. He was a large man but slightly smaller than Thathra. With a mighty fist, he pounded on his hairy chest and let out a thunderous howl. Upon his head, he wore a small metal helmet resembling a bowl with two horns protruding from either side. As the war cry finished what came next astonished her. The man showed no fear as he leaned forward and charged directly at them. A large wooden shield in one hand and a wicked looking axe in the other.

Thathra adjusted his stance and readied himself for the impact.

Saress had a better plan, and it included this madman never making it close enough to strike. She pulled back the string on her bow until the rosewood limbs creaked with tension. On the verge of snapping she released. The twang of a vibrating string ripped through the air and Thathra's hair fluttered as the arrow came within inches of hitting the back of his head. Her aim was deadly accurate, and the impact was fierce. The helmet ripped open as the arrow pressed through driving completely into the torso before exiting out through the back snapping the spine. The barbarian died instantly but at full stride, the momentum carried him forward landing with a loud crash at Thathras feet. Blood pumped from the open wound leaving the corpse lying in a pool of steaming blood.

An unnerving silence filled the air and nothing moved.

"Why do they wait?" Saress whispered.

"A simple mind game," Thathra said. "It's common for barbarians to only send out one at first, usually younger and less experienced to expose the enemy. Often, this pause in battle will leave the enemy frazzled destroying their morale."

Many long painful minutes past and neither side moved.

With Pegan advancing upon the enemy undetected, Saress knew Averies survival now fell upon her shoulders. "When the fighting starts make sure you stay behind us," Saress whispered to Averie who took a defensive position behind the beast. In one hand she waived the small sword she gained earlier.

Far off to the right and just out of view a horn sounded, low and throaty, like a thousand horses charging. The blower let the last few notes linger off his tongue.

Saress flexed her muscles then drew another arrow from her quiver and waited.

As the first horn ended another began. This one was to the left and not as deep. More of raspy scrape like sandpaper being dragged over rough stone. Unlike the first, this horn master did not let the last note linger but instead chose an abrupt end to his blast.

Pegan knelt in the shadows less than twenty feet behind the group of barbarians. There were five in total and three were accompanied by large dogs. To his amazement, the hound masters whipped and beat their dogs into a wild frenzy that left them snarling, growling and on the verge of attacking each other.

A veil of worry engulfed Thathra's face and he went pale, uninjured, he stumbled backward and would have fallen if it was not for Saress who caught him. "The Horns of the Ancient Harp," his voice cracked.

"The what?" she asked.

"The Horns of the Ancient Harp are given as honorary items to those who showed courage against insurmountable odds. It's believed the horns are imbued with magical properties which provided strength, speed, and agility to the party."

"We have something better than those horns," Saress said. She had to find something to restore his moral. "We have hope."

"Hope…" Thathra looked at her with glossy eyes, "What good is hope against insurmountable odds? What good is hope—"

Saress struck him hard across the face with the back of her hand, "Hope is stronger than the darkest magic, and with it, the impossible can be achieved," she whispered.

Erupting over the berm they were caught by surprise at the sheer speed of the dogs. Their paws dug deep into the dirt kicking up large plumes of dust and they ran at random which made them a much harder target. Snarling as they came, large swatches of gray foam dripped from their snapping maws and hung in long glistening strings.

Saress aimed, fired, but the creature darted past unscathed. The arrow impacted a boulder erupting in a shower of sparks.

Readjusted for its swiftness she fired again but this time where she expected the dog to be and the bone-shattering impact was horrendous. Launched backward the dog performed a complete flip then crashed to the ground dead. The arrow shattered numerous ribs and tore a fist-sized hole through both lungs.

With the hounds closing her bow became useless, and she tossed it aside in favor of the large two-handed sword.

If the dogs had any fear, it was not visible as they crashed down upon them like a hammer upon an anvil.

The lead dog made straight for Thathra and just before impact launched through the air catapulted by powerful rear legs. Snapping its jaw it went for the throat but Thathra easily avoided the clumsy attack and followed with an upward swing of his axe. The heart, lungs, and guts spilled out as the underbelly of the hound were flayed open killing it instantly.

Pegan monitored the five before him and when they made their move, he made his. With one giant leap, he landed on the barbarians back. One hand jerked the massive head to the side exposing the thick bulging vein that ran down the neck while the other hand buried the blade until it hit bone. Quickly he jerked the head the other way snapping the neck. Satisfied, he kicked the corpse forward causing it to crash into the remaining four who still did not understand exactly what the hell just happened.

Saress screamed an angry hiss that drowned out the snarl of the rabid dogs. With both hands, she gripped her sword and prepared for battle. Two dogs circled her looking for a weakness while another focused his attention on Thathra.

The pair which solely focused on Saress must have been trained together as the next attack seemed coordinated. One dog leaped at her throat while the other charged in low in an attempt to tackle the much larger prey. As the first dog passed the large two-handed sword fell with blinding speed. Like the blade of a guillotine, it easily cut through tendon, flesh, and bone severing the head. She was not quick enough though on the backswing and the other dog latched hard onto her leg with a grip of iron. The impact was bone shattering and they both tumbled to the ground. As the dog bit down harder scales ripped exposing the soft meat which now lay unprotected. The dog adjusted its grip and latched on harder. Blood sprayed like a fountain painting the dogs face a ghastly green.

Thathra spun as the dog circled, each looking for a weakness.

Lightning quick the dog lunged at the wrist that held the weapon.

Thathra spun then countered but the weapon found only air.

The hearty laugh of the barbarian echoed through the trees as he observed the much smaller man who squatted only ten feet away. "Kill him," The barbarian barked. "And bring me his head as a trophy."

"Gladly," one replied as they fanned out to engage this new foe.

Saress felt dizzy and she all but blacked out from a pain words could not describe. The creature shook, gnawed and chewed on her leg as if it had not eaten in months and the taste of her green blood only excited it more.

Averie released a howl fueled by rage having seen her friend taken down by the hound. She had to do something, anything, so she did the only thing she could think of and ignored the words she had been told and lunged at the dog. She had never killed a thing in her life, yet the blade fell as if it was guided by an experienced warrior and easily slipped between the ribs, passed the lung and pierced the heart.

Even in death the jaws remained locked onto her leg and Saress had no choice but to use both hands to pry the jaw open snapping the bone to free herself from the carcass.

Neither Thathra nor his opponent had mounted a successful attack on the other. They continued to circle one another searching for a weakness or a mistake.

Pegan had no worries. The men were massive and one hit from their weapons would prove fatal, but after studying them for just a short time he realized just how clunky they were.

A wicked grin by a mangy barbarian was all the evidence Pegan needed to know there was no turning back, which was not an option anyway. He remained squatted, ready to spring like a cat as they approached. Each held a large, wicked looking axe except for one who chose a thick club, the end ringed in a layer of knobby steel.

The first barbarian, an older looking one with leathery, wrinkled skin struck first. Swinging his blade in an awkward untrained fashion he left himself exposed to a counter-attack but Pegan saw through the ruse. Instead, he did the opposite of what they expected. Like a cat with built up tension, he performed a flip and twist over the shocked barbarian and landed a few feet before the one who had barked the orders.

Their eyes clashed in a painful stare and the barbarian knew he was staring death in the face.

With lightning-quick thrusts, Pegan planted each dagger clear to the hilt on either side of the heavyset man puncturing both lungs. Hoarse scream of pain followed by gurgling, frothy, spewing blood was all the evidence Pegan needed to assure his aim was true.

The attack was so sudden the remaining three barely had their weapons up in enough time to mount a defense.

Having heard his master's scream, the hound abandoned Thathra to lend aid.

Saress retrieved her bow and fired but the arrow trailed off into the woods.

Thathra screamed a war cry of his own then lowered his head and charged after the hound. Saress tried to follow but her severely damaged leg slowed her progress and all she could do is watch as Thathra disappeared over the berm.

His eyes narrowed with anger as he observed Pegan engulfed in combat. One barbarian already lay dead while another grasped at his chest trying to plug the steady flow of blood from somewhere underneath his hide skin armor. Still, at full stride, he let his momentum carry him into the chaos landing with a knee on the skull of the wounded man. The bone was no match for the weight and it popped like a pimple scattering brains. His momentum never slowed, and he rolled into the feet of another barbarian sending him crashing to the ground.

Limping over the berm she arrived as if it had been planned that way. Both barbarians had their backs to her and so engrossed in the fight they were easy targets. Taking aim she planted an arrow right between the shoulder blades. The impact sent the barbarian fumbling forward and to his knees. Grasping at the arrow which protruded from his chest he ripped it free which only diminished his chance of survival.

Averie hid behind the mule as she watched the four men emerge from the woods. One held up a large crossbow and fired it in her direction. Either his aim was off or she was not the intended target as the bolt buried deep into the mules head killing it instantly. Careening to one side the mule collapsed pinning her legs beneath it.

Clawing at the beast she tried to free herself but the men were already upon her and she had no other choice but to grab her blade in defense.

Both Thathra and the one he had knocked flat climbed back to their feet at the same time. He was a younger barbarian and inexperienced. His commander lay dead along with most of his brothers. In a panic to save his own skin, he turned to flee with Thathra matching him step for step.

"Get back to Averie," Pegan commanded all the while dodging a man who swung his axe as if he had gone insane.

How could she make such a fatal mistake? She was better than that and she knew it. In her blind rage, she forgot her duty, to protect Averie at all costs.

With both daggers, Pegan blocked an overhand swing which provided the opportunity to kick the attacker's kneecap folding it backward snapping the bone. Unable to support his large structure on one leg he toppled over dropping his weapon and grabbing the broken limb. Pegan's move was instant as the blade swiped sideways severing the throat.

The dog whimpered at the sight of his dead master then turned to Pegan, a growl on his lips and anger in his eyes. In a lust filled rage, he leaped at the assassin only to receive a dagger to his throat.

Saress cleared the berm only to find Averie in trouble. Faster than light she nocked an arrow and pulled the string taut. She never aimed, never had time.

"Hold this," the barbarian said as he handed another his broad axe. Moments later he produced a large rope from his back and unraveled it. When he had a length of it undone, he began barking orders once more. "Hold her down so I can get this rope around her neck," his hands feverishly working a noose into the rope.

"Were supposed to bring the filthy thing back alive," his companion said.

"And we will, but I don't wanna touch the wretched thing."

Oblivious to Saress's the other three believed their companions had dealt with the others.

The arrow's flight was impossibly accurate and sliced through the throat severing both arteries in a single pass. Blood sprayed into the air coating both his companions and Averie.

With both hands, he tried to plug the gaping wound but quickly faded and with one last gurgle he stumbled backwards, dead before he hit the ground.

Surprised, the other three bolted for cover.

Saress had another arrow nocked and was about to strike when a crash from behind sent her leaping forward out of harm's way. Twisting in midair she landed only to see another barbarian crash through the timber like a giant bear. Directly behind him Thathra was in pursuit and was just out of striking distance. His blade cocked back, his arms loaded with tension, waiting for just the right moment to strike. Startled, the barbarian hesitated to determine a new path around the giant lizard. That was all the help Thathra needed and with a mighty swing the blade buried into the barbarians back.

Hit from behind Saress stumbled forward and fell to her knees. Her left arm went limp and her bow dropped to the ground. Disoriented, she struggled to rise and fell twice more before staying upright. Instantly her sword leaped to her right hand and she turned to face her attacker.

The barbarian knelt behind the mule and was loading another bolt into the weapon.

A strange weariness fell upon her and her mind clouded, along with her vision. She tried to move but her feet grew heavy and she stumbled once more. The next impact would prove fatal. Saress closed her eyes and pointed her head towards the sky. What began as barely audible turned into a loud series of hisses and reptilian barks that echoed through the clearing.

The noise was deafening and suffocated all sound on the bluff. Farther below a flock of birds took to flight.

The distraction caused by Saress allowed Pegan the diversion he needed and allowed him to move undetected. Observing his friend take a hit sent a burning rage he had not felt in a very long time. Skills once forgotten returned, and once more he was the killer he spent years perfecting. The hunted became the hunter.

The impact she waited for never came. As she opened her eyes she was mesmerized by the glint of flying steel. Pegan had returned and was dissecting his opponent. Just as an artist uses a brush to create a masterpiece he guided both daggers in a series of thrust, jabs, and slices that left his opponent lying in pieces.

The other two barbarians circled Pegan looking for an opportunity to strike unaware Thathra was heading at them in full stride. Sailing through the air with a knee thrust out he crashed into the closest slamming him into the other knocking both to the ground.

Clawing at each other for leverage, the barbarians tried to find their footing in the pool of blood they are laying in, only to find Thathra now hovered over them. Lifting his axe the closest one died in a single swing.

His companion though having observed the treatment wanted no part of it and leaped to his feet then bolted for safety.

"Help Saress," Pegan yelled in an animalistic tone that Thathra could barely understand. "I'm going after the other."

"Wait..." Thathra called out. "He won't go far. To return alone without the subject would be considered an act of cowardice, a crime worthy of death."

Pegan drew in a deep sigh and slowly let it out. All around him lay the bodies of those who tried to kill them. They overcame insurmountable odds but at a heavy cost. Averie still lies trapped under a dead mule and showed no signs of life while Saress remained on her knees across the bluff. A bolt still stuck in her shoulder that leaked green blood while a large section of scales was missing from her leg.

Pegan freed Averie then went to Saress, a dying gray film grew over the lizard's eyes and she remained motionless. Her breathing slowed to the point her chest barely moved, and she looked on the cusp of death.

"She's been poisoned," Thathra said.

"Poisoned, with what?" Pegan asked.

"Atropa Belladonna plant, it's common among the barbarian archers. I know of no cure."

Averie coughed then grabbed at her chest. A trickle of blood leaked from the corner of her mouth.

"Averie... Averie..." Pegan yelled into the air and pulled her in tight against him. Her limp body looked like a rag against his.

"Lay her down here," Thathra removed his thick hide coat and placed it on the ground. Adjusting the coat to fit around her he bound it tightly with the rope. "This will keep her warm and help prevent the ribs from moving anymore. It's not perfect but will help."

With Averie bundled Pegan focused on Saress, "Deadly Night Shade," he whispered.

"What?" Thathra asked.

"Atropa belladonna," Pegan said. "The plant is more commonly known as Deadly Night Shade, and it so happens I know the cure. We need the leaves off of a Maranhem Jaborandi bush."

"Where do we find those?"

"A good days travel south," Pegan answered. "Normally this poison works slow but with its sudden onset, I would say there is something else involved. I can't say for sure though but if what you say is true, by the next sunrise we will have found the cure."

The trail was narrow and not well defined and in many places proved quite difficult. Farther up into the mountains they went before turning east. The new path was wider and more traveled but only for a short distance then they turned south again on what appeared to be no trail at all.

As mid-afternoon arrived so did the rain. Pushed sideways by blustering winds their pace slowed. Saress could no longer walk on her own and had to be guided. The wound grew ugly and long, bright red lines snaked out like vines while her eyes had completely clouded over. With Saress's condition growing worse each minute they decided to battle the weather and trudge onward, each taking turns carrying Averie who woke but was in no condition to walk. As darkness arrived Pegan located a suitable spot protected from the weather and a small camp was made.

"We'll rest here for a spell then continue on," Pegan said.

Eventually, the rains ended and the sky cleared. Bright stars twinkled in the heavens and the moon glowed brightly. The added light made travel easier and by morning Pegan stood by a large bush picking leaves. Carefully he crushed just the right amount into a cup with boiled water and with Thathra's aid after it cooled he poured the contents down Saress's throat.

Thathra proved once again he was the hunter and killed a hardy bunch of rabbits which released a mouth-watering scent when cooked.

Averie barely ate even when ordered to eat more. She too appeared on the verge of death. Her eyes had lost their spark and she seemed weaker than normal.

"Will the concoction work?" Thathra asked.

"Only time will tell," Pegan answered. He stoked the fire then moved close letting his clothes dry in its warmth.

They sat the remainder of the day in silence watching, waiting, for the one who fled from them but he never came. As evening approached weariness overtook them both, and each faded into a silent slumber.

They woke to a dull thud hitting the ground.

Pegan jumped to his feet, and both daggers leaped to his hands. Thathra was not quite as oriented and stumbled over backward as he tried to rise. Before them lay the barbarian that fled. Bound and gagged he wiggled and squirmed in a feeble attempt to free himself. Above him, Saress stood a look of disgust on her face. The sun was high and the air warm.

"I caught this one less than fifty yards from the camp. As you both slept he was creeping up, it's a good thing one of us was keeping watch," Saress chuckled.

Pegan didn't have an answer, he just stood there shaking his head in disbelief. "Sorry, I… was exhausted."

"How?" Thathra looked puzzled then remembered the cure. "The leaves, they must have worked."

Saress scratched her chin, "leaves?"

Pegan took a few minutes to explain the poison and the cure.

"Well, you three looked exhausted so I so no need to wake you."

"Thank you," they all agreed.

"While you all rested, I questioned him and it seems they picked up our trail from the rover that escaped our first encounter," she said. "So what do we do with him? It's against my honor to kill a bound man."

Thathra glanced towards Saress then shot Pegan a dirty look. "He would show us no mercy so I shall afford him none." The axe blade glistened in the sunlight.

"Not that way," Pegan said.

"You let one escape and look what it led to. If he would have been killed, this fight would have never happened," Thathra demanded. "I will make it painless."

Pegan knew Thathra was right. That whole fight was because of the one who got away. What if he lets this one leave and he's captured by someone else and informs them of our location?

Averie buried her face in the arms of Saress as Pegan nodded his approval. She didn't need to see it happen as the sound of meat slicing and bone snapping was gruesome.

They traveled the rest of that day and none spoke of the incident. They knew it was for the best but none would admit it. Thathra spent his time examining the horns he recovered from the barbarian Saress captured. As night fell upon them once more Pegan made the decision to keep moving. "We're almost there, I promise," he said. The weariness in their eyes begged for a break. Before the moon reached its summit, he turned their direction east and led them out of the Ash Mountains towards Rhunsiire.

Chapter 15

Averie sat on a fallen tree that extended partway over the slow-moving waters of Tlumn River. It took three days to reach and along the way they saw few and of those none showed any interest. The sky was clear, the air crisp, and the ground remained damp from the recent storm.

Pegan stood in silence, his mind deep in thought as he watched Thathra gut breakfast.

"It might not be that bad," Thathra said as he held the rabbit up by the hind legs and peeled away the hide.

Pegan never answered. His focus diverted from the rabbit to Averie, her toes just touching the water. Under the dirt and grime, he saw beauty, like a diamond buried in a chunk of coal just waiting to be discovered. Saress though was making the best of the situation and floated past flat on her back, the tail of a fish hung from her mouth. "She sure loves the water."

Thathra tossed the rabbit into the pot of boiling water then sat beside Pegan. "She's a lizard, part alligator if you ask me," he chuckled.

They both followed Saress with their eyes as she used her powerful tail to propel herself upstream then began the process of drifting back down once more.

"They don't make many like her," Pegan sighed, "abandoned her own to save the life of a race that wishes to see her extinct." He looked off into the distance. "She would give her life to save Averie's, and yours." His gaze fell upon the barbarian. "You abandoned your family and killed your brothers to save a woman only weeks ago you would have made a slave."

"Those were not my brother's, never were, never will be," Thathra argued. He could see Pegan had a thought on his mind. "What are you getting at? We've all made sacrifices."

"Except me," Pegan snarled. "I'm a loner, a rover, I've yet to make a sacrifice. You represent the north, Saress, the reptiles. Where do I belong, what is my purpose?" Pegan grew angry.

Thathra's head slumped, "I can't answer that," he groaned. "But I don't believe Elwrick would have chosen you without a purpose. You may not know it yet, but I guarantee there's a reason." Thathra stirred the pot, "get up here you two," he hollered, "breakfast is ready."

As they ate, the worry on Pegans face remained.

"We've faced death already once," Thathra said. "And from the look on your face, it seems we may face it again. Tell us what lurks in those woods so that we may be prepared for any enemy we encounter."

Pegan drew a heavy breath, "I know only bits and pieces."

Thathra leaned forward.

"Did you all know the last bearer was an elf?" Pegan asked.

"No," they answered.

"Yes," Pegan continued. "The last bearer was an elf. They threw a grand party and it was a time of celebration. Every town across Icearaus sent a representative and each was greeted with open arms upon arrival."

"Were you there?" Averie asked.

"Yes," Pegan responded. "But I was much younger and more naïve."

"Continue," Thathra said.

Pegan took up where he left off. "The party continued throughout the night and in the morning the bearer set out. Five of her closest friends went as well to see her off and wish her the best. As the days past her friends never returned so search parties were dispatched. Eventually, they made a horrific discovery, her companions were dead. Hacked and slashed with such ferocity and anger none were recognizable and the bearer had vanished."

"Is it possible she fled?" Saress asked.

"No," Pegan answered. "Days later an abandoned horse entered the Whispering Woods. Upon its back was tied a large satchel. It is rumored within that satchel was a king's ransom of gold coins and a pair of eyes. Those eyes belonged to the bearer."

Thathra stood in disgust, "who would do such a cruel and shameful thing?"

"My guess would be whoever rode that horse," Pegan said.

"And who was that?" Averie asked.

"That's the question, no one knows," Pegan shook his head. "Since then the elves have sworn off all contact with man, declared their borders closed and all who enter are considered criminals." Pegan took a bite. "It's said that those who have entered, none have returned, and we expect to fare better, I think not," Pegan chuckled. "No, I got a bad feeling we'll meet the same fate as those before us."

"Fate has determined our path and brought us here," Thathra said. "With the injury to Averies ribs and I don't think Saress has full use of her shoulder yet, even though she would argue otherwise, I don't see another option. Possibly, once they hear our tale they'll offer aid"

"Remember the words of Elwrick—*do not mention this to anybody as there are those who would rather see this fail than succeed*" Pegan snapped. "Let's be on our way," he said, "the pain of not knowing is worse than death itself."

It was near noon when they set out. The water was clear and icy cold and even though the rocky bottom was visible, it was much deeper than expected. As the water reached her chin Averie froze with fear. The only thing she feared more than Karayan was drowning. Saress felt right at home though and with one arm plucked her from the water and carried her across.

Once across, Pegan adjusted his weapons then looked back the direction they came. It seemed a world away.

The Whispering Woods was like nothing Averie imagined. The trees were old, and the bark was thick and gnarly. Huge roots sprouted from the ground like giant worms coiling around the trunks and anchoring the towering behemoths to the forest floor. Their lengthy limbs created a latticework canopy while dense, broad leaves blocked all but the hardiest of rays casting the land into a premature darkness. Long strands of stringy moss hung like webs while the air was thick with an earthy scent. "How will we find our way?" Averie asked. "The forest is so dense we cannot see more than ten feet."

Pegan remained silent as he led them farther in. He moved as if guided by an unnatural instinct and only stopped once, to survey his surroundings then they were back on the move.

Saress switched to thermal vision only to discover they were surrounded by an uncountable number of elves. "They're all around us," she whispered.

"And they have been ever since we crossed the river," Pegan answered.

A good distance later they arrived at the edge of a large clearing. The trees thinned and the canopy cleared allowing the land to brighten. A wide, well-defined trail edged with orbs of glowing lights greeted them. "This is the road that leads to Rhunsiire. It used to go all the way to the river's edge," Pegan said.

"Why do they wait to attack?" Saress asked. She tried to keep her voice low, but it carried like a ravens cry.

"They're watching us, to determine how much of a threat we pose," Pegan answered. "Regardless, we won't find aid unless we reach the city and that will be impossible without a fight. I believe our best option is to walk out and greet them with open arms. To show any aggression would only lead to our slaughter."

They all agreed then walked out into the clearing, arms raised in surrender. "We come in peace," Pegan yelled.

Across the way, an elf materialized from the shadows. He was tall yet slender and covered from neck to foot in light green armor with dark accents that matched the wooded environment. His long black hair was pulled back revealing a furrowed, menacing face with high cheekbones and hazel eyes that burned with hatred. A longbow was slung over one shoulder while a long thin blade hung at his waist. He moved like the wind and with a blur his blade hissed free and found Pegans throat. All around them they came, each identically dressed and equipped. Within seconds they each had a sword at their throat except Averie who was surrounded by spears, none dared to get close.

"You've entered the Realm of the Whispering Woods, unannounced, and uninvited," The elf said who held Pegan hostage.

Even though there was no chance of escape, elves continued to come until those in the rear had no view of the trespassers.

"We come in search of aid," Pegan said. "My friends have been gravely injured."

Whatever Pegan said worked as the elf lowered his blade and slid it back into the scabbard. "Separate and search them, take all but their clothes," the elf said. "Lady Alenia can decide their fate as they have surrendered willingly."

With the search finished and stripped of their belongings, bindings were placed upon their wrist and thick black cloth bags covered their heads.

—*What shall we do with sickly one*—Pegan heard an elf ask.

—*Take her straight to the ironbark caverns*—Pegan would remember that name if he ever escaped.

A lone tear ran down her cheek as she watched her friends led away bound and blinded.

"Walk," one spat at her.

She too was then led away at spear point.

In the secluded, windowless environment time lost all meaning and hours passed, possibly days before the door opened.

"Turn around," the elf snarled.

Bound and blindfolded he was forced to walk backwards. Occasionally, he was told when to step up or down but otherwise, they traveled in silence. This went on for some time until he was spun around in a circle until he dreamed of vomiting then guided up a spiral set of stairs. Having reached the top he was spun a few more times to disorient him further then brought to his knees by a hard object swung at great speed which contacted the back of his legs.

An embarrassing squeal escaped his lungs as the blind was ripped free catching his hair in the process. Pegan kept his eyes firmly closed. It was only after a few minutes did he slowly let them open to adjust. It was a skill he learned years ago as to not be blinded when coming out of complete darkness.

Instinctively, he took immediate notice of his surroundings. The room was round and extremely large only held in check by dark wood walls. Crystal clear ceramic tiles laced with veins of blue and pink covered the floor and gleamed with a mirror-like reflection. Across the room was a large ornate white granite table. The edging around the table glowed pink from rune words chiseled into the surface and a single golden fluted pillar candle-holder held a milky white candle which flame seemed to light the entire room. Even though the environment was not well furnished, it reeked of royalty.

Behind the desk, a slender elf dressed in a white silk gown with black trimmings stood. Her skin was like freshly poured buttermilk and deep thick hair the color of chocolate faded to a dazzling silver as it cascaded past her shoulders. It had been decades since he'd last seen the elf queen, yet her beauty remains as if she has been untouched by the ravages of time. Out of respect, he bowed his head.

"I am Lady Alenia," she said. "And you are?"

Pegan looked up at her and then remembered Elwricks advice before he spoke. "I am Blair, Blair Sherwood from Minx," he answered. Her deep silver eyes told him she knew he was lying.

"Well… Mr. Sherwood," she said after making her way back to the desk. "Would you be so kind as to tell me why you have entered the Realm of the Whispering Woods?"

"I have come in need of aid for my traveling companions," Pegan responded to the question. "Two of them have injuries beyond my skills."

"I must say," she rested against the table and crossed her arms. "In all my years I have never seen such a strange fellowship." Her voice played like a symphony. Each word was in perfect harmony and her mouth acted as the conductor. "Where would such a strange group be traveling?"

Pegan carefully considered his answers before replying. "Were we are headed is my own business."

She studied him like a science experiment. "Your business was your own. But ever since you felt the need to enter into my realm it has become my business." Her voice lost the smoothness it once had. "Regardless of your intentions which matter not, the only reason we are having this conversation is so you can explain this." She held up Fel Strike for him to see. "I wish to know how it came to be in your possession."

"Where are my friends?" Pegan asked.

Lady Alenia never moved, instead, she let her eyes drift to the elf who stood behind him, then nodded. The signal had been given and the elf never hesitated as he let loose a series of blows to the back of Pegan's head with a small wooden club which split the scalp. A thin trail of blood trickled down his face.

"Enough," she commanded, then motioned for the elf to stop. "Shall we try this again? How did you acquire this item?" She showed him the dagger.

"Release my companions, they have no part in this," Pegan snapped back with a hateful rage.

Casually, she strolled across the room to stand before him. Pegan flinched as she reached down and took his chin. The way she changed he expected it to be hard as stone but was pleasantly surprised to find it softer than rose petals. Using two fingers, she lifted his head till their eyes meet. "Let me put your troubled heart at ease," she smiled. "Your companions are alive, for now. I could not take a chance on the sick one though contaminating the elven population and she had to be exterminated." She released her fingers and watched his head droop, "Shall we continue?"

The thought of her dying drove a dagger of hate straight through his heart and all care in the world now meant nothing. He had taken an oath to protect her and he failed. He had no choice but to die himself because there was no way he could face Elwrick. With all his built up rage he screamed, "YOU LIE!" His arms tensed to the point of explosion and the dull throbbing wound on his skull faded.

"Try as you may," she said. "The bindings are magical and as you struggle, they only get tighter."

His anger turned to nausea and everything in his stomach splattered on the floor.

"Look, he's getting sick, shall I fetch the healer?" The elf released a hearty laugh.

In his blind rage, he felt no pain, no pity. His actions were instantaneous as he leaped to his feet and kicked the closest elf squarely in the chest sending him tumbling backwards through the open doorway. A crashing sound could be heard as he tumbled down the stairs. Ducking a swing he kicked the elf directly on the knee shattering the cap. The gruesome sound of bone snapping echoed through the room as the elf collapsed in a fit of screams. Footsteps alerted Pegan to the door and the first one through received a foot to the face shattering the nose. Blood sailed through the air painting the wall while the elf fell to his knees both hands covering his face. It took four more elves to subdue him, but not before he was kicked, punched, and hit an uncountable number of times.

"Bring in the chair," Lady Alenia screamed.

Hit directly in the stomach any air that remained in his chest was forced out in a loud whoosh. Gasping, he tried to breathe but each time he was kicked again and again. Dizziness overcame him and he fell forward, his head splashed down in the vomit he spewed earlier. He tried to keep his mouth shut as the elf pushed his face deeper into the frothy mess.

"Lick it up," the elf yelled.

Pegan refused at first, that is, until Lady Alenia arrived at his side with a long silver needle and slowly began to thrust it into his armpit. Shocked with pain his tongue thrust outward as if he was dying of thirst and licked at the vomit like a dog on a fresh water bowl.

As the chair arrived Pegan was jerked to his feet and thrust into it. By design, it was not intended to be used by a man in bindings. Forced back in the chair his shoulders were drawn forward causing him to bend at the waist. Unseen hands gripped his shoulder and with a sudden jolt, he was slammed back against the rest. The final motion created a grotesque popping noise as both shoulders dislocated. Leather straps were then wrapped around every appendage and the bag was placed back over his head. Refusing to give them the dignity of hearing him scream he felt the blood drip from his chin as he spat out a chunk of his tongue then faded into unconsciousness.

The room was longer than it was wide and lit by a lantern that hung by a rusty hook screwed into the wall high above her head. Besides the door, there were no other exits. Time had no meaning as she could no longer watch it pass. Was she there for only minutes, hours, or days? She couldn't tell.

She rose with a groan then walked the perimeter of her confinement. The wooden walls were smooth and seemed to be one solid piece. Not even with her fingernail could she find a place where boards were mated. The growing pain in her stomach was a stark reminder to the last meal she ate.

The door banged open with the force of a hurricane. Surprised, she stumbled backward tripping over her own feet and fell straight back landing hard on the wooden floor. Fighting hard to regain the air that was knocked free she choked up blood that coated her chin a dull red.

Kicking and screaming she tried to defend herself from the two elves that entered but she was quickly overpowered. Bound at the wrist she was forced to walk at a rapid pace that left her winded. They followed the same route for some distance when a large archway created by woven tree limbs became visible.

A firm hand on her shoulder jerked her around to where she faced her escorts. His deep silver eyes and long white hair sparkled in the shadows of the canopy. A long sword swung on his left hip and a long spear filled his right hand.

"Keep your eyes focused on the ground," he said. "If you look away or attempt anything my hand will be forced to end your life."

Averie nodded. Without question, she believed every word the elf said.

"Good, now walk," the elf snarled.

The path was wide and led directly under the archway. Even with her eyes down, she caught slight glimpses of the town. Giant trees grew on each side of the path. Straight ahead, narrow steps hug the circumference of each tree working their way higher and higher, until they vanish from view. Moss of different shades hung like curtains from lowers limbs, keeping the rest of the forest shrouded in darkness. At random spots, doors could be seen cut into the trunks and many windows glowed brightly with yellow light. High above the forest floor, wooden bridges supported by thick ropes created floating city streets. Upon the bridges, she observed elves of every shape and size going about their business. Often times they would pause just for a moment to look at her then continue on their way.

Averie was brought to a halt at the edge of a large clearing. In the center was a large, circular, wooden platform accessed by a series of wide steps. Directly in the center, a stump rose up about a foot above the floor. One of her escorts left them to converse with another who stood at a large rack loaded with weapons just off the platform.

Thousands of small round lights hung from the trees, bridges, or magically floated on the breeze. They provided just enough light for her to see but not bright enough to be blinding. High above her, more bridges spiderwebbed the sky and each was filled with row upon row of elves. In the shadows, she could not see their faces, only the silhouettes of their bodies.

Beyond that platform was another. Smaller but higher, it looked down upon the first. Loaded with elves, she didn't see the two figures forced to kneel.

After a short conversation, the elf waved the other forward and she was escorted up onto the platform where the elf rejoined them. As she drew closer she could see the deep chasms gracefully carved into the block by a thin, sharp blade. It was at this moment she realized what was about to take place. She was to be killed and all the elves had come to witness the event.

The thought to flee caused her muscles to flex and each elf tightened their grip until dark bruises formed on each arm. In an attempt to resist, she drove her legs forward into the platform but was no match for their strength. Slammed down upon the stump she was held face down staring straight into a woven basket. Around her neck, the cool touch of steel sent a shiver up her spine as a clamping device was pounded into the stump preventing her head from lifting.

From here she could see the other platform better. Thathra and Saress were there. Forced to kneel, they had no choice but to watch the spectacle as well. "He's not here," the words slipped from her dry throat. "That bastard, he's not here," she screamed to her companions. This was all a game, a setup. He's out there laughing somewhere as were about to die, the thought flashed through her mind.

Pegan woke to the smell of burning sulfur. His eyes watered and his nose bled.

"Good, you're awake. I was quite surprised they didn't kill you right on the spot," Lady Alenia said as she examined Fel Strike once more. "Perhaps now we can continue our discussion." She let out a giggle that reminded Pegan of a devious child. "Who are you? And how did you get this?" She held up the dagger. Her words burned with the intensity of Hellfire.

"Go to Hell," he mumbled. What did he care? Why should he care? They came in peace, seeking aid, but found only torment and misery. He decided long ago to deny her the satisfaction of breaking his will. If she wanted information, she would have to pry it out of him, a task she would find rather difficult. Pegan was no stranger to pain. Years of training had taught him to ignore it, and how to give it. Averie was dead, the mission was a failure. He hoped Elwrick would return to seek vengeance upon the elves. Make all the trees wither and die, something, anything, he didn't care.

"Courage when all is lost and hope has faded, I love that in a man," she said, "but let's see how much courage remains after you meet Rimdruziahl."

Pegan's eyes narrowed as he studied her words.

She walked across the room to a small door built knee high into the wall. Releasing a small latch, the door slid open and she rapped twice on the side then stepped back. Moments later two pink tentacles covered in a clear slime poked through the opening. Wherever they touched a sticky residue remained. Both tentacles traced the edge of the opening until it dripped with this pungent smelling slime then more tentacles emerged.

"I have discovered a different way to interrogate," she let out a deep sigh. "One that doesn't end with me covered in blood and often proves to get the prisoner talking long before it even begins."

The Elf Queen faded as his vision focused on the numerous tentacles that whipped and lashed from the opening.

"What kind of monstrosity is that?" Pegan screamed.

"Shall I send it back?" She offered a wicked glance. "Answer the questions."

Pegan turned his head in denial.

"Very well," she said, "you had your chance. Continue, my pet."

In horror, Pegan watched as each tentacle gripped the frame of the doorway and pulled the large pulsating bulbous body through the opening. The creature was the color of pink bubble gum with black splotches and floated level with the Queen's face. From the top, thin stalks grew until they reached the length of a man's arm. At the end of each stalk was one large eye. Underneath, the tentacles whipped and thrashed inches from the floor.

"Rimdruziahl," she called to the thing, "I wish to know who he is, and how he got this." She held up the weapon for all six of its different colored eyes to gaze upon. "And any other information he has somehow forgotten."

Pegan's eyes widened as he watched the creature float in his direction. Thick globs of slime percolated from its body then hung in long pungent strings that left a glistening trail. As it arrived, Pegan saw each tentacle was not smooth, but covered with thousands of minuscule suction cups.

He shivered from its touch, something living shouldn't be this cold. Each tentacle went to work caressing and massaging his body in different locations. One discovered his face and prodded at the ear while another worked under his shirt and explored the navel. A third entered up through the cuff of his trousers and spiraled up his leg. As it moved, he could feel the peristaltic waves as it worked higher towards his torso before thinning out and pushing its way towards the rectum. His body quivered as a fourth tentacle became pencil thin and entered up through his nasal cavity.

Even if Pegan wanted to scream, it would have been impossible as a tentacle emerged out through his mouth then curled back up and entered the skull by sliding underneath an eye.

Each eyestalk lengthened until they were hair thin and the eyes moved about studying its victim. As each tentacle pushed deeper into each orifice, his entire body twisted and jerked as if something inside him was alive and fighting to get out.

"I tire of this delay. Rimdruziahl, retrieve the information I desire," Lady Alenia screamed.

Each eye focused with a renewed determination and each tentacle begun to pulsate with waves of energy. Unable to resist the strength of the creature, bones shattered, muscles tore, and ligaments ripped, causing them to snap and curl into small balls.

Pegan felt as if his head suddenly exploded as the tentacle which entered through his ear become hair thin and burrowed like a parasitic worm into his temporal lobes. Each eye of the creature blinked with such speed they appeared to flash as the beast tapped into Pegan's memory and relived his whole life. From birth till now, there were no secrets Lady Alenia wouldn't know.

Sweat dripped from her face as she clawed at the block. What nails had grown back where ripped from her fingers and her muscles tensed. If it was her arm that held her captive, she would have chewed it off to escape. "You bastard," she yelled at the elf who stood at a rack which held numerous swords and axes. He seemed to either not hear, or care as he picked up one blade then quickly put it back and chose another. "I hope you die, Pegan Rhoe," she screamed. Her voice was hoarse and scratchy.

Saress wanted to help her but there was no aid she could give. The magical bindings held tight and each time she tried to break free they only tightened more biting into the scales. Green blood dripped from where the metal edge already broke through.

If Thathra felt any remorse or anger, he refused to let it show. Finding just enough movement he looked towards Saress. "The failure of this mission rests on our shoulders, not Pegan's," he said. "He told us, no, begged us not to come here and we refused to listen. Who knows what the hell has become of him as they drug him from that cell."

Saress had no response, she knew he was right.

"So this is how it all ends," Thathra whispered. "I suppose we're next."

Satisfied with his choice, the executioner walked from the rack and positioned himself making sure he didn't block the view from the gathering spectators.

Her eyes swelled and refused to cry. She knew it would be painless but didn't care. A cryptic silence filled the air as everybody waited in anticipation. Even the bugs stopped to observe. She would die, but her friends may still have a chance. "Free yourselves, run," she whispered but doubted Saress heard anything beyond a whimper.

Where the executioner stood all she could see was his feet, his stance widened. With all the strength left in her lungs, she screamed to Saress, "I love you." Averie watched as one large tear leaked from the lizard's eye and ran down her scaly face and dripped from her chin.

Closing her eyes she found internal peace. A relaxing sense flowed over her and she was suddenly calm. She was no longer there. She was a little girl again running down the street playing with her best friend Serenity. Laughing and giggling they picked flowers and fed mischievously acquired apples to passing horses. The fruit stand owner, Mr. D. accepted the girl's smiles as payment.

At night the smell of dinner cooking on the open fire, her mother yelling to wash her hands, and her father coming home from work, everything was perfect. They would sit and talk for hours, about their day, what they saw, and what they did. All that changed though the day she became diseased. She tried to block it from her mind, but couldn't. It flowed through her veins like an icy chill, a painful reminder. She alone was responsible for her mother's death who could not accept the fact of what her daughter had become, and flung herself from the highest cliff she could climb, a fall which would guarantee death. Word spread and the people of Lynn Brook despised her. Every muscle tensed as the terror returned. Maybe she deserved to die. How much filth and hatred had she spread? How many people would die because of her? In the darkest recesses of her mind, she could hear the whistle of the blade as it fell.

The dull thud of steel hitting a block of wood echoed through the clearing.

Her companions were led away but never blindfolded.

"Did you see that?" Thathra asked Saress who he believed was walking behind him. When no answer came, he glanced back to find she was being led off in a different direction.

Pegan lay on the floor next to the chair. His chest heaved with uncontrollable spasms and he choked on long- winded gasps like a fish thrown on the bank of a river. Mucus leaked from his nose and a razor-thin trail of blood came from each ear.

Before he succumbed to the creature he pleaded for death but the beast refused. Begged Lady Alenia to take his life yet she never obliged. Fought to make it stop and it wouldn't. His body, a broken pile of bones and torn tendons, lay in ruins.

—*Pegan*—the words sounded familiar but they meant nothing to him. Lost in the darkest, the deepest recesses of a tormented hell every fiber of his being cried out.

—*Pegan*—the noise came again. Somehow, he associated those words with the one who had inflicted the pain. Crying louder, he tried to roll away from whatever or whoever spoke, but his body lacked all strength.

The messenger rapped twice on the door then waited.

"Enter," he heard the voice say. Lady Alenia was on both knees looking down at a man who appeared to be on the cusp of death.

"Get Gleia… quick," she said.

"Yes, my lady." The messenger bolted from the room.

"Pegan, help is on the way, hold on," she said. A mask of worry blanketed her face. She placed a hand on his shoulder. It had grown icy cold, and he shuddered at the touch.

"How long did he resist?" Gleia asked when she entered. Her voice was intoxicating.

"Over two hours before Rimdruziahl could break into his mind."

"Impossible," she said, shaking her head in disbelief, then laid a hand on Pegans forehead and frowned. Unlike Lady Alenia, she could feel the tremors coursing through his body. "We need to get him to the ward, we might still have time."

Chapter 16

Something was terribly wrong. A tenday passed and Elwrick sensed Averie had not departed the Whispering Woods. In fact, there had been no movement at all. *She is not dead.* He would have felt her life forces leave this realm and journey towards the next. A hundred different thoughts raced through his mind and none ended pleasantly.

The book was prepared and the process started. The portal could only be opened on the night of a new moon which thankfully is still a few weeks away. They could reach the Isle in plenty of time as long as they met no resistance along the way, but they had to leave now. If they failed, there would not be another for thirty days which posed a new set of problems. For one, her pregnancy would be farther along hindering her travels and two, the added time in this realm would allow Karayan to spread word of her escape and hire more bounty hunters. No, they couldn't wait. As of now time and speed were their advantage but any delay and it would become their undoing.

Lady Alenia stood hesitantly at the plain wooden door. She had not been here for decades but the path remained clear as if she walked it yesterday. Drawing a deep breath, she let the fresh scent of the Chocolate Cosmos fill her lungs. They were her favorite without question. Not because of the vibrant green leaves or the deep reddish brown flowers but the scent. Chocolate always brought a smile to her face, so she was not surprised when Elwrick planted them.

Slipping silently inside the room, her hand lingered on the cold wrought iron handle as the door slowly closed. What would she say? Rage and anger turned to fear. There were many nights she sat alone, repeating the words she longed to say and now she had the chance. What if she looked like a fool and the words never came? Or worse, came out wrong. The questions hounded her ever since that dreadful night. With her eyes closed, she leaned her head against the door. If she only knew the answers, hopefully, this night they would come.

The room was large and adorned with many windows, each had the curtains drawn tight. A golden lantern hung on each of the otherwise bare walls, and the flickering light exposed an impeccably polished hardwood floor. In the center, a circular dais of white marble impregnated with rich blue veins was accessible by three stairs carved into the stone. A thick multi-colored runner lined with golden tassels led to a thick, intricately hand-carved pedestal fitted with an onyx abacus. A simple glass bowl rimmed with gold seemed to grow from its surface. The silver liquid inside sparkled with a mirror-like finish.

Her arms never swung as she climbed the stairs then circled the pedestal, studying the device like it was an unknown species. After all these decades why had she come now? Fighting back the urge to leave, to run away and never come back she took a long gaze into the bowl. Inside, she saw anger, frustration, and then fear on the teary-eyed face of a woman she barely recognized. She was not the woman now she was then. Older, more experienced, yet in some aspects more naïve.

She turned away, the image was too painful. A shiver danced up her spine. She had used the scrying bowl a thousand times. The words to activate it etched into her mind. Even if she never said them again for another lifetime, she would never forget. She had come this far, too much was at stake to stop now. Swallowing her pride she glanced down at the woman in the bowl, "forgive me," she whispered.

Lady Alenia closed her eyes, her breathing slowed. With each breath she relaxed, anxiety melted away. Physically, she remained rigid at the pedestal but mentally she was free. Free from the boundaries of the physical realm. Time and space meant nothing as she fell deeper into the trance. Light as a feather her eyes reopened. They were no longer the piercing blue but clouded in gray. She gazed into the bowl, not intently but in a gentle manner allowing her eyes to relax until they closed. With her index finger, she stirred the bowl in a slow, counter-clockwise motion.

Then, with a heavenly voice she chanted,

> Goddess Silver, moon and night,
> Grant to me the second sight.
> Through the bowl of what may be,
> Let my inner wisdom see.

As the words finished the liquid rippled with anticipation as if it came alive and a thick steam rose from the surface. As it cleared, her reflection no longer danced upon the surface. Something new took shape. A mere outline at first, thin black lines twisted and wiggled as if withering in pain before the shape of a horse formed. Enormous hoofs powered by muscular legs propelled the creature. Around its mouth thick white froth formed and the pink nostrils flared wide. Upon the steed rode a man in pure white, his robe lashed at the wind, his face locked in concentration. Urging the beast on, he leaned forward as if chased by death.

Placing her hands on the pedestal, she leaned forward until her face is only inches from the silvery substance, then she spoke with a soft, vibrant voice.

The Freihn Sea was unnaturally violent this day and angry waves sounded like thunder as they crashed upon the shore then crawled inland for some distance before the sea called them home. The sky was clouded and the land was cast in lengthy shadows. The air was warm and smelled clean, in the distance, white lightning flashed across the sky.

Rhunsiire was less than an hour away and it was there he hoped to discover the reason for their delay, even if it meant facing his greatest fears.

—*Elwrick*—

The voice was barely audible. For a moment he swore he heard his name called. He glanced back as he rode making sure he wasn't followed, his eyes scanned the hills, nothing. "Nerves, just nerves," he whispered.

—*Elwrick*—

It came again, penetrating deep into his mind. Someone was not calling to him but through him. The voice echoed as if spoken in a cave. The more he tried to block it, the more it hung upon him like cheap cologne.

—*Elwrick*—

The voice came again, stronger and more determined.

His resistance had grown strong over the years, or had she grown weaker? Could it be too strong? The possibility crossed her mind as she bit her lip. A trickle of blood ran down her chin. The response she longed for never came. She would need to find another way.

With a bladed hand, she thrust it into the silvery liquid and latched hold of the steed. A mental war erupted as their minds clashed. Midnight was immune to the harsh realities of this world but his mind was still susceptible to attack. The beast stumbled but recovered, reared, leaped through the air as if jumping hurdles, then fell down.

Elwrick held on for dear life as his mount seemed to be going through seizures.

The battle was hard fought, but she won and took control. Midnight seemed completely unaware of Elwrick, his gaze fixed on something nobody could see.

Elwricks knuckle's turned white as his fingers curled inward. There was only one who had the knowledge to stop his mount, to reach into his mind. Only one person would even have the audacity to try... Lady Alenia. The name sounded foreign as it rolled off his tongue. How long has it been? How many nights had he wished to hear her voice, to feel her touch, days, weeks, months, years? Longer, in fact, it had been decades.

Elwrick let his mind wander to when they met. She was there the night his wife died, as the demon ripped her to pieces. He should have died as well. His magic was exhausted and with no defenses, the demon moved in close enough to strike when she arrived. Materializing from the darkness wielding powerful magic, she drove a sword of frost that sliced through the demon as if it were made of paper. More elves arrived and drove them back. It was not him who saved

Icearaus, it was her, along with the elves.

Broken, and on his knees, he crawled like a child to his wife and gathered the pieces and tried to reassemble her. His white robe torn, ripped, and stained red with blood Lady Alenia understood his pain and comforted him. She held him as he cried, let his pain become her pain and she cried. It was because of her he found the courage to go on living, to crash down the cave from which the demons spawned thus ending the Great War of their time.

Years later as peace returned he became a name among the elves and spent many nights walking through Rhunsiire, a welcome guest. He was there the night she married, there the day her daughter was born, there the day her husband died.

Pain turned to anger and she became distant, confused. Placing the blame solely on his shoulders, she wanted someone to pay for her suffering. Fit with rage, she cast him away never to return. From a distance though he watched and wondered if she would ever recover. Over time she had accepted her husband's death but the next blow she should have never of witnessed, the death of her daughter.

She lashed out at mankind and the elves moved deeper into the Whispering Woods. Most believed they went the way of the dwarves who simply vanished without a trace, but Elwrick knew better. Even with the turmoil and hate, he never lost hope in the Elf Queen and someday, he hoped she would return to her former glory.

"My Lady, it's been an elf's age since I have last heard your lovely voice," Elwrick answered. Even though she was leagues away her words carried a sweet scent. They were an aphrodisiac to his mind. An image formed deep within his mind. Her tall slender body draped in a silky gown, her fair skin and natural lips which needed no make-up. Long black eyelashes like spider legs. How she gracefully danced around her chamber dress billowing behind her. "So what pleasure do I have in inviting your company this evening, my Lady?"

The answer came back cold and callous. "You knew, you knew all along and you never told me." The pedestal rocked as she slammed her fist against it. "Why… tell me why?"

Elwrick felt her sorrow encrusted voice attack him. She knew, somehow she had gotten the information from Pegan. "To protect you, my lady," he whispered back.

"Protect me from what?" she snapped back.

"From yourself. I knew what you would have become if I told you the truth.

She studied the bowl, then his words that came through. He spoke the truth. She was barely herself now, and who knows what she would have been capable of then. "I think… I think there's more to this story and if you wish my aid, it's time you told me everything."

There was a long pause and for a moment she thought the connection had been severed when the voice returned. "I know Averie lives, what about the others?"

Now it was her turn to wait. She hated having to inform him of Pegans condition. "They're fine except Pegan, Rimdruziahl—"

"How could you?" he screamed back at her. He knew the capabilities of the creature. The way it could tap into the mind and re-live the life of the host from birth till then. The destruction the monster was capable of doing to the body was atrocious.

"Me," she snarled back. "It was you who told him to speak nothing of this mission. Had he told me, Rimdruziahl would not have been necessary."

"But he lives?"

"Yes."

"Then you already know everything. It would be a waste of my time to tell you otherwise."

"No," She growled. "I only know what I learned from Rimdruziahl. I wish to know why he killed Meriel, yet saves Averie."

Elwrick waited until her anger diminished. He could sense the tears that ran down her face. How he longed to hold her, to pull her tight against him and let her know it would be alright. "The evil he has done we cannot undo," Elwrick whispered. "And there is evil yet that walks this land we cannot prevent. Heed my words," Elwrick grew angry. "You now know who killed Meriel. He held the blade, but Karayan guided his hand. You channel your anger in the wrong direction, blaming Pegan. Nothing can bring her back, no amount of magic, or suffering, or hatred, nothing. Now is the time for you to put that anger behind you. Let it go, realize she is in a better place. Where she is now, there is no pain, or suffering, or hatred… Only love."

Through the mental connection, Elwrick felt her pain. Each tremble, sob, and tear that flowed was like a dagger thrust into his heart.

"The best thing you can do now is help. If you kill the bearer you are no better than Pegan. Meriel died a martyr. She did what no other woman could do. Upon her death, she changed the future of our world, your world. If it was not for her and the magic that flowed through her into him, the world was doomed. Focus your anger on the man who has relentlessly stalked bearers, slaughtering them before they understood the reality of their heritage. The man who convinced the citizens of Icearaus that a bearer was not a bringer of the future, but instead a carrier of disease. It hurts me more than you can ever imagine seeing what was done to her. I was there, in that room as Pegan carried out his instructions. Rest assured though, she never suffered. I took the pain for her."

"You were there?" she asked through gagging sobs.

"Yes, I stood right there and held her hand. Told her it would be okay and not to worry. She was going to another place and I gave my word that someday you both will meet again. Each cut, each slice, I took, so she didn't suffer."

"I'm sorry," she said. There was nothing else she could say. "I didn't know. You should have told me."

"I would have, but I knew you would have tracked Pegan to the end of the world and slaughtered him without knowing the truth. Your mind was not your own at that time. You fell to your anger and no matter what I said, you would have killed him. I had a hunch Pegan would play a larger role in the future of Icearaus so I kept an eye on him. Saw how the magic she released into him as she died changed him. I knew someday I would call upon him," Elwrick said.

"When they are ready, I will send them on their way. Please don't come here," she whispered. She did not want him to see her broken at this moment.

The air was thick with smoke and smelled of burnt meat. All around campfires burned and tents were erected. Near the far end, a canopy of hides and furs kept Emperor Tak-Thukmand cloaked in shadows. He was unusually short for a man of power but held a savagery in his mysterious deep green eyes. Not one of a rabid animal but more of a calculated coldness. Black bushy hair and matching beard hid most of his face while a short broadsword hung at his hip. Dressed in forest garb, a thick steel plate covered his chest.

A wide path had been cleared and on either side barbarians stood like columns. They'd been expecting his arrival for days.

King Karayan spurred his horse and started down the trail, followed by a dozen elite soldiers.

At the far end of the path, Emperor Tuk-Thukmand waited. His makeshift throne carved from a giant stump perched upon a raised dais of stone which allowed him to look down upon his troops.

King Karayan passed in silence, his head on a swivel as he examined them as much as they watched him. Most had never seen the man, but it only took his name to send them cowering in fear. "Hold this," he tossed the reins to a slave and dismounted.

Emperor Tak-Thuk'mands untrusting eyes followed King Karayans every movement. There was carelessness in his walk and no weapon swung at his hip, which made him all that much more dangerous. Unpredictability was a dangerous weapon, one he used many times. Never reveal you're true intentions until you are ready to put them into action.

Emperor Tak-Thukmand stood as King Karayan reached the last step, "Greetings, my King," he said, then bowed.

"Where is she?" he asked. His voice was like sandpaper.

"There were… complications—"

"I didn't ask you about complications, I asked you about her location," he snarled, then grabbed a fist full of hair and lifted the emperor's head till their eyes met. "I hired you for results, not excuses." He removed a heavy glove and slapped the emperor hard across the face. Blood dripped from his chin as the lip was torn open. "Where is she?" he asked again.

"It appears she had help," Emperor Tak-Thukmand choked on the words. "My men tracked her down and all of them were killed, including the dogs. This man who you say helped her escape is no ordinary hunter, but a highly trained killer."

Karayan slapped him again. The weight of his hand knocked the emperor to his knees. A splattering of blood decorated the throne. "Did I not inform you of this? That's why I specified if you find them to attack from a ranged vantage point. Do not try to capture her until he has been dealt with. Did you read the whole message, or can you even read you ignorant fool?"

"There's more," Emperor Tak-Thukmand pleaded. "I went to the scene and discovered tracks of a creature I had never seen. I recovered an arrow with unknown fletching for you to examine. Otherwise, I left the scene undisturbed with the thought they may return. Did not wish to give away vital information."

"Let me have it," he said.

A slave retrieved the arrow from a wooden chest next to the throne and handed it to Karayan.

Holding the arrow up to the light, the yellow feathers glistened bright as if they had just been plucked that morning. "Gilded Flicker feathers. Only found in the Anor," he said. "Nothing makes an arrow fly truer. Looks like there is more here at stake than I first thought." With one hand he snapped the shaft in half and threw it on the ground.

"I also believe there may have been another, possibly a rogue barbarian. We discovered wounds created by a large axe, one I don't believe any regular sized man could wield," the emperor added.

"So what you're saying is you cannot even control your own men. Maybe I should take charge of this ragged band of untrained trash. Whip them into shape and create a formidable fighting force—"

"It would benefit you not to embarrass me in front of my troops," there was a challenge to his words. A short wide sword occupied his hand.

Karayan let out a hearty laugh, "put that thing away. If I wanted to kill you, you would already be dead, and not a thing you could do to stop me. For now, though, you still serve a purpose."

"And what might that be?"

Karayan ignored the question and removed a small parchment from his robe and unfurled it. "Point where the altercation took place."

Tak-Thukmand studied the map closely, then pointed with a short, stout, hairy finger to a heavily forested area near a large bluff, "here."

"You sly devil," Karayan whispered. "I see what he's doing." His eyes followed the jagged outline of the Ash Mountains. "Tak-Thukmand," Karayan called to him. "Look here," he pointed to the map. "Do you see what I see?"

The Emperor nodded. "He plans to travel around the horn of the Ash Mountains and traverse the Broken Crag."

"Exactly! Take a small force, maybe thirty, and set up here," Karayan pointed at a ridge, "Any more than that will be obvious." Set no fires and stay hidden in the shadows." King Karayan scratched an x on the parchment. "There is a choke point at that spot. They will be left out in the open, vulnerable, easy targets for bowmen. Remember. I want the girl alive, the others do with as you please."

"As you wish," he responded. "I will take a group of my best archers and spearmen. They will become pin cushions long before they ever see us."

"Don't get cocky," Karayan said. "They already killed some of your best men and besides, there are trolls that inhabit that area. You may try and make peace with them or simply stay out of their way. They are formidable though and you don't want to fight them."

"We'll befriend them."

"Do as you wish, but don't fail me again. I will meet with you again in a tenday, if not sooner. Now I must take my leave as I have other obligations which must be met," King Karayan mounted his steed then turned back towards Emperor Tak-Thukmand, "it would be wise for you to have the bearer within your grasp when I return," then rode away.

Chapter 17

The first thing Averie heard was the sound or lack thereof. Both eyes crawled open only to discover darkness, no walls, no floors, no ceiling… only darkness. From somewhere a breeze came causing goosebumps to speckle her naked form. She believed heaven was a place of eternal light, everlasting joy, and beauty beyond words. This was far from heaven.

A sense of dread crept into her bones like an icy chill. She shuttered as a shiver climbed up her spine like a stalking spider. She must have gone to the other place, the one rarely mentioned. *What will become of me? Offered to a demon as a slave? To have its malice, its cruelty, and its hatred for all things living unleashed upon my soul? She quaked with fear.*

A low, rumbling moan that sounded more like a growl escaped her throat as she reached for her neck to feel the gaping wound she knew was there. Although her skin was cold, she knew she was alive because of the rhythmic sound of her still beating heart.

"Easy now," a woman said. "You're not supposed to be awake yet."

Averie stiffened with fear and her eyes slammed shut like steel shutters. She chose not to resist as she felt her arm being lowered then a warm blanket chased away the shivers.

"Where am I?" She wanted to scream, but the words came as a whisper.

"The city of Rhunsiire if you must know," she answered with a giggle, but more precisely, the house of Lady Alenia."

Averie sighed when she felt a warm cloth wipe the sweat away that percolated on her head.

"Lady Alenia ordered the rest of your treatment to be here, under my care. We can't have you creating anymore… disturbances."

"Disturbance?" she whispered. "I'm dead. My head was severed. I heard the blade fall."

"No. Word reached the weapons master that your destruction was not to occur and you were to be immediately transferred to the medical ward under the strict care of Gleia. What you believe occurred has only been constructed within your mind. Unfortunately, the entire way here you fought like a rabid animal and had to be sedated to prevent injury to us or to yourself. Upon your arrival, you attacked one of your companions and almost killed him. If it was not for Saress, your attempt would have proved successful."

"You lie," she said. "I would never attack any of my companions."

"Try to rest," she said, "you've been through a great deal."

Averie felt the soft palm of a hand press gently against her head and her mind eased into a world of peaceful dreams, her whole body relaxed and her breathing slowed.

The snap of a curtain echoed through the room as a gust of wind ripped through the open window. Pegan lay flat on his back, his vision focused on an enormous block of wood carved into the shape of a flying angel. From its wings sprouted seven thick beams polished to a glossy shine that arched downward supporting the alabaster colored ceiling.

From where he lay, he could see the room was heptagon shaped with a neatly made bed at each wall, except the seventh, which held an intricately carved wooden door with a smaller window designed to allow someone to observe inside. Above each bed was a stained glass window which painted the room in an array of abstract colors.

Pegan had never felt so alone. Averie was dead, and what befell his companions he didn't know.

Swinging one leg over first, then the other, he tried to stand but his legs felt boneless and he collapsed, ripping the blanket free from the bed as he went. A loud groan escaped his lungs as he found the floor. Everything around him blurred and his body felt as if he had been disassembled and put back together by a blind man.

Dazed, he tried to crawl away from the large green scaly feet with black nails that filled his blurred vision.

Saress carefully lifted her fallen companion and placed him back on the bed. "You're not supposed to be out of bed yet, doctors' orders."

He recognized the voice, "Saress, is that you?" His face cringed in pain as he spoke.

"Yes—"

"Thank the Lord," Pegan fought every word. "I thought they were going to feed me to a dragon."

—*He tried to rise but fell*— he heard Saress say, but to whom? His eyes fired open but his vision was fuzzy and nothing came as it should.

"Oh dear, we can't have that now, he's nowhere near ready," Gleia said, then pricked his finger with a small needle and watched as the broken man faded back into unconsciousness.

Averie woke to find she lay upon the soft mattress of a rather large bed. A thick blanket was pulled just above her bosom. Her arms uncovered at her side. The room was plain except for a large round window framed with vines and grapes that caught her attention. Propped open with a stick, the scent of fresh flowers carried on the gentle breeze tickled her senses. Across the room, a door stood partially open and singing could be heard. The words were foreign, but the voice was beautiful.

"Saress?" she whispered.

The singing stopped and a woman entered. "Good morning," she said with a smile. "I am Amra, and, welcome to Rhunsiire."

Averie's vision drank up the woman. She was gorgeous, tall, slender and fair skinned. A long gown the color of autumn leaves hung loosely from her shoulders and long hair the color of straw cascaded well past her shoulders. Her icy green eyes screamed with passion and rode on delicate cheekbones.

"How long was I asleep? And where are my companions?" she asked. The words came easy. The pain in her side that haunted her for weeks was gone.

"They're all here."

"Can I see them?"

"Not till after your meeting with Lady Alenia. As her daughter, I was given the task to care for you. While you slept, measurements were taken and a dress—the prettiest one I have ever seen—was tailor-made just for you. Before you can try it on though, you need to bathe."

"Why did she do that?" Averie asked. She had yet to meet her.

"I think she has something planned, but her lips are sealed. She won't reveal anything of her intentions."

Averie tried to rise but her legs trembled.

"Careful," Amra said. "Gleia just finished your treatment. If you were to hurt yourself already, she would kill me."

Her second attempt proved successful and she maintained her balance, but turned a blush red as the sheet her shoulders once carried fluttered to the floor.

"You're fine," Amra assured her, "I am the only one here." Amra took Averie by the hand and led her towards the open door. "I've prepared the tub."

At the door Averie halted, her nails digging deep into the wooden frame. The room had a surgical feeling to it. There were no windows and the pure white marble floors climbed all the way to the ceiling. A vanity against the far wall was filled with neatly folded fluffy white towels. Sitting on top of the vanity is a picture of a beautiful elf girl. Her eyes though were drawn to the enormous porcelain tub. Chipped in a few places, it was scrupulously clean and sparkled in a brilliant white. Steam drifted from the mirror smooth surface of the water.

"Where are my companions?" Averie said in a rush.

"Don't be frightened," Amra said.

"I can't help it." It was common knowledge around Lynn Brook that one of Karayans favorite punishments for rebellious individuals was public boiling.

"Please don't be. As one woman to another, I won't let any harm come to you."

Wooden steps on the back side allowed Averie access. As she sunk lower a tingling sensation trickled up her spine. Behind her, Amra sat on a three-legged stool, her hands diligently working through the filthy clumps of matted hair.

The smell of sweet lavender soap lay heavy on the steamy air.

Averie had finally found peace, or it had found her. Either by accident, intentionally, or by the power of some unforeseen God, she rested. A heavy sigh escaped her throat as she closed her eyes and drifted off to some faraway place, far from the pain, the suffering, the hatred.

"I do love the scent of lavender," Amra whispered. "Don't you?"

Averie never answered, her mind drifted in and out of reality.

"What's it like…you know, being a bearer. Do you feel different?" Amra asked.

"What does it feel like?" Averie pondered the question. "I would not wish this curse upon anybody, even my worst enemy."

Amra retrieved the picture from the vanity. Her head slumped and tears ran as she looked at the image. "She was my sister, Meriel. She sat in this very tub and I did her hair the same as I do yours…" She placed the picture back on the vanity with a trembling hand knocking the towels to the floor. "I'm sorry," she said, then rushed from the room closing the door behind her.

Averie climbed from the tub and picked up the towels. After she had dried and neatly folded them she left the room to find Amra sitting on the bed, her face buried in her hands. Long wailing sobs could be heard. Averie sat beside her, tried to comfort her but any words she said, she knew wouldn't help so she just let her cry, and held her.

Pegan fought with the sheets that held him down as he watched her enter. He searched for something to grab, anything, he needed a weapon but there was nothing, nothing he could use. As she neared he screamed. Not the kind you would expect from a man but that of a wounded animal who watched death approach.

Lady Alenia slowed when she saw Pegans face go pasty, his eyes widened and his chest heaved in wild, panicked, gasps. "I have hurt you, and for that, I am truly sorry."

Pegan was rigid as if suddenly turned to stone.

"Blinded by hatred I have caused more harm than good. No words can undo the torment I have inflicted upon you… and your companions. I came here to apologize and ask for forgiveness."

Pegan snarled in her direction as if he suddenly morphed into a rabid dog.

"I would also like to inform you that the bearer has been taken away to heal, both physically and mentally. She has some problems—"

"What did you do to her?" Pegan hissed through clenched teeth.

"No harm has befallen her, in fact, she has healed nicely and probably soaking in a tub having her hair done as we speak."

"I want to see her," Pegan said.

"She's inaccessible at the moment."

"Ssshe's gone?" Pegan stuttered.

"Not forever, she needs time alone, to gather her thoughts. After our discussion, we both felt it was for the best."

"You lie," Pegan screamed. A tear ran down his cheek. She couldn't break him physically so what game was she playing now.

The door burst open and Saress entered, a bewildered look on her face.

"Kill her, kill her now while you have the chance," Pegan screamed. A rabid madness filled his eyes.

"Why?" Saress asked.

"She killed—"

"She's done no such thing," Saress answered. She knew exactly what he was thinking. "I've talked to Averie myself. She's fine… the baby is fine as well. I just left her not thirty minutes ago. She wants to see you, to cry on your shoulder and tell you how sorry she is for what she's done."

"Sorry for what?" Pegan's eyes darted from the lizard back to the elf.

"She can tell you when she's ready, but not before then. Get some rest," Lady Alenia said. "Gleia did a magnificent job healing you but you're still not ready."

Lady Alenia followed Saress to the door then turned back. "You're free to roam, but I suggest you don't go looking for Averie."

Pegan's eyes looked at his clothes that hung on a hook against the far wall. He hadn't noticed them earlier. "Where are my weapons?"

"In safe keeping… for now," she paused. "I've discovered much about you, things you probably forgot, things you wish you'd forgotten. You are a very dangerous man Pegan Rhoe, too dangerous to have your weapons until I am sure you are ready. Besides, while you are here protection will be provided."

The next day Pegan woke to hunger pangs. No longer could he rest and set out on a quest for food. He didn't know how long it had been since he ate, but his body seemed frail and his clothes fit loosely. He walked for hours passing buildings of all shapes and sizes. All built high up in the trees and connected by streets made of rope. Some wide, others narrow but the elves had no concerns as they crossed. Throughout the day elves went about their business paying him no mind as every other city did.

The evening grew late when the smell of food lured him from his current direction, across a slender rope bridge, down a spiral staircase to a wide opening in the side of a large building which spanned a great distance across multiple trees. As he neared, the sound of laughter and cheer mixed with the clanging of glass carried the promise of a hearty meal and fine wine.

The enormous room was similar to what one would expect in any given town. Tables of every shape and size were abundant. A band played on a raised platform and to the right is a long bar lined with elves each holding a drink. To the left, another door led to a kitchen where many elves worked with a smile on their face. The food and drink in this bar appear to be free as there is no place to pay and no one seems worried about collecting money. The elves truly did look out for one another and nobody went hungry regardless of their station.

Cheers erupted from a table near the back and the crowd parted allowing an elf to walk out, head hung low, an embarrassed look on his face.

"What's going on back there?" Pegan asked an elf at the bar.

The elf downed the last of his drink which was quickly refilled by a woman wearing a flower infused dress. "An arm wrestling tournament, you want in on the action. The line starts back there." He pointed to the far wall.

"I think I'll just watch," Pegan answered. It took a few minutes and a few pushes and nudges but he eventually arrived at the table only to discover Thathra was taking them down quicker than the seat could be filled.

"Next," Thathra hollered out.

A big elf sat down and adjusted his position then their hands locked. The judge started the match and the elves face flushed with energy and sweat dripped from his chin as if he stood in a furnace.

Thathra though looked bored and never once strained as he forced the arm back till the knuckles slammed into the tomato smashing it flat signifying the match had ended. Without a word, the defeated elf walked through the parted crowd to pats on the back and comments like better luck next time.

"Do I have to wait in line as well?" Pegan asked.

Thathra looked baffled for just a moment, then leaped to his feet knocking the chair over and then took his friend in a bear hug which lifted Pegan clear off his feet.

The crowd knew the competition had come to an end and begun to disperse.

Food was brought and for a while none spoke as Pegan ate. It was only when he slid the plate back did Thathra finally strike up a conversation, "You look good, well, at least as expected considering the incident."

Pegan smiled and leaned back in the chair. "It was nothing, never even hurt."

"Yeah, sure," Thathra said with a chuckle. "That's not what Saress said when you were lying on the floor screaming like a newborn hatchling."

"And what would she know?"

"I know for a fact when they brought you to the ward she never left your side. She risked the wrath of Lady Alenia and refused to leave. It was only when Lady Alenia allowed her to go see Averie did she go."

Pegan's stare turned distant, "Is there any word of Averie yet?"

"No," Thathra said. "I've talked to Saress once over the last four days and she tells me Averie's doing fine and that she misses us, but knows the time ain't right."

"I feel weird," Pegan said. "Like a piece of me is missing without her—"

"You're a hard man to follow," Saress said as she entered the hall. "Been all over Rhunsiire, traced your steps for miles. Do you ever stop walking?"

Pegan looked baffled and then leaped to his feet. "Saress," he hollered.

The trio left the hall and followed the stairs downward till they reached the ground.

"It's good to see you again," Pegan said to Saress.

"And you as well."

"How's Averie?" Pegan asked with excitement.

"She's doing fantastic, and the first signs of her pregnancy are evident."

"You understand with this delay we'll never make it to the island in time," Pegan said.

Saress looked concerned. "I understand. But she's now healed and this was for the better. Trust me. We'll just have to wait till the next new moon."

Thathra looked concerned, "will she still be able to go through the portal?"

"According to Lady Alenia who talked with Elwrick, she'll be fine. Elwrick knows about the delay and will make adjustments."

Thathra drew a sigh as if luck had finally turned in their favor.

"Regardless, tomorrow evening there is to be a celebration. A going away party for Averie and we're all invited as guests of honor."

Pegan had no words to describe how he felt so he simply hugged the big lizard.

"Great," Saress said. "Now I have to wash again, I got your smell all over me."

A tear trickled down her cheek as she looked at the dress in the mirror. It fit perfect in every way, even around the small bump which had become quite obvious. Looking straight into the mirror, then turning sideways and looked again, she could see no flaws in the material. The rose-colored skirt highlighted the black bodice which matched perfectly with the fluffy wristbands. Dense, dark brown hair rolled down past her shoulders. She had begun to regain her weight and appeared quite healthy.

Lady Alenia stood beside her at the mirror, "you look ravishing. You know, you're going to drive them wild."

Drawing a sigh she let her head hang, "I can't go," she whispered. "I can't face the man I tried to kill days prior."

Lady Alenia wiped the tear away then used one finger to lift Averies head till their eyes met. "You must go, your longing is not to remain here."

Averie walked to the large window that overlooked the festival grounds, "it's not that…"

"I already know what you're going to say," Lady Alenia said. She joined Averie at the window. Far below elves looked almost like ants as they went about their tasks. "I sense there is more going on inside your heart than just the fear of the unknown?" She asked.

"Yes," Averie answered. "I am worried I won't be able to pass through, what if the feelings grow and they become too strong? I have only known him a short time. Way too short for me to have these feelings. It's just," she wiped another tear away. "Nobody has ever cared for me the way he has."

Lady Alenia leaned against the wall. The words Averie spoke brought back her memories of Elwrick. She understood exactly what was going through Averie's mind. She also chose not to reveal what she discovered buried deep in the subconscious parts of Pegan's brain. "In the end, I trust you will do what is right. Now, wash your face, we only have a few more hours before the festival.

The glade was magnificent. Each tree was trimmed back allowing them a picturesque view of the moon and a million twinkling stars. The grass was meticulously manicured and not one leaf tarnished the ground. One entire side was covered with tables placed end to end and row upon row of high-backed chairs stood like sentries. At the far end, there was a large, crescent-shaped raised platform where an elven band played. The music was chocolate to the ears.

At the other end grew a tree larger than any dreamed possible. Wide stairs spiraled up like a candy cane a good hundred feet before ending at an arched door. Beside the door, a circular window watched them like a giant eye.

"Welcome… welcome," an elf said as he approached. "They call me Ruven, Ruven Dorharice, Grand Master of Ceremonies and Monarch of the Elven Council." He was older and remnants of silver still remained in his mostly gray hair. Deep grooves lined his rugged face yet his eyes still burned with the vigor of youth. From neck to toe he wore a simple green robe decorated with golden thread. Extending a hand, Thathra tried to accept but the elf pushed it aside and firmly grasp hold of Pegan's.

Pegan felt strange as if his mind was suddenly violated, but the feeling was brief. All elves contained magic so any ill-will towards him quickly diminished. Thathra though gleamed with anger towards the disrespect.

"Follow me," he gestured with a quick nod. He led them across the vast space to a smaller table, separate from all the others. It was lined with food of every sort, breads and butters, salted and pulled pork, giant bowls of rice, and cakes. Multiple rows of bottles all filled another table with drinks of every kind. "And specifically for you," he looked to Saress, raw meats and game which had been freshly caught, some still twitched.

With the banners hung and lanterns lit, all of Rhunsiire attended the festivities. The band was in full song, and many elves began to dance. The younger generation chose to perform more modern dance moves which consisted of leaping through the air while performing flips and twists. The elders chose to dance more slowly, arm in arm with their partners. Children darted about chasing fireflies and for a moment, the entire world felt right.

Somewhere from within the glade, a bell chimed, the band stopped, and every elf found a seat. Ruven took to the stage holding a giant trumpet with both hands. The glade fell quiet as a tomb. He looked out over the audience. His chest rose as his lungs filled with air and he began to play. The sound was magical.

Embarrassed, Pegan turned away. He couldn't allow the others to see him in this condition. Both eyes glistened with moisture as Lady Alenia and Avery descended the stairs. They could have been sisters.

"Close your mouth," Saress whispered to Thathra.

Averie moved with the grace of a queen.

As her feet found the ground, she looked at Lady Alenia with a smile. She smiled back and offered a nod of approval.

Averie darted towards them bypassing Thathra and Pegan and leaped into the open arms of Saress who stood mesmerized. No way was this the same woman that was taken from them days earlier.

Food, drink, and laughter flowed deep into the night.

The cloaked stranger arrived long before the crack of dawn. Her movements were cautious as she crept her way through the darkened room, careful to avoid waking those who slept. Saress though was not sleeping and her eyes followed the intruder whose heat made them glow like a lantern.

"We need to talk," she whispered to Pegan.

Moments later he rose and followed her. At the door, he looked back to make sure none stirred, then vanished into the darkness.

Saress followed to the door and from there only with her eyes. She would not leave Averie alone again.

They traveled a few hundred yards then sat on a bench carved from a stone wall. Once there she pulled back the cowl. "I needed to speak with you… alone," Lady Alenia whispered.

Pegan's eyes narrowed as he looked past her. Farther down the trail, something moved "You seem bothered by something? Or someone" he said.

"Shhhh," she whispered. "Keep your voice down. In the still of the night, voices carry farther than you realize and can reach those who should not be listening."

An eerie breeze drifted past.

She looked around to make sure they were alone. "Rumors grow of an uprising. Elves are not happy they say. Some believe I have forsaken them in favor of man."

"Why would they think that?" Pegan asked. "We've done nothing to harm you or your people."

"It's not that simple," she sighed and took his hand. Warmth radiated from her skin. "I don't know how, but details of your past have surfaced and they are screaming for your execution."

"Who are they?" he asked, "and would it help if I talked with them?"

"Rumor is there are only a few, but one of them is a well-respected elder, who holds much sway within the elven community."

"Ruven," Pegan whispered.

She gave him a confused glance.

"Today at the festival, he purposely grabbed my hand and I felt strange as if someone just read my mind, but brushed it off knowing all elves hold some form of magic."

"Strange," she said. "He has no telepathy abilities, but it does concern me greatly if what you say is true. Regardless, there is to be a council meeting today before your departure to decide if you should be allowed to leave with your companions, or make you stay and stand trial for your crimes."

"And what do you think?"

Lady Alenia looked up towards the sky. Her eyes sparkled in the dim light. "I think you should all leave, now, before the council has a chance to stop you. I have ordered my forces to allow you safe passage from the Whispering Woods by whichever means you choose."

Pegan scrubbed his chin.

"There is something else. My son, Lorandrial, will be joining you to represent the elven community.

"No," Pegan sighed. "I will not take the life of another in my hand."

"I knew you would disagree, so while you celebrated, I spoke with Elwrick and he agreed it was a wise decision."

"You talked with him? How? Is he here?" Pegan fired the questions.

"No, he is not here. We communicated through a scrying bowl."

Pegan felt sick with the thought he may lead another to their death and tried to alter her decision. "And what of this uprising turns out to be true? Then would your son not better be served at your side?"

"Too many questions and not enough time to answer them, but rest assured, any attempt to overthrow me will be dealt with swiftly. I worry more for Averie becoming a victim of somebody's injustice."

Pegan watched farther down the path as the thing he thought he saw move, moved again. Its movements were calculated and not one sound was made. One hand eased to his dagger. If there was to be an uprising, it very well could start right now.

Lady Alenia noticed Pegans sudden change. In the still of the night, her elven ears heard sounds Pegan's couldn't. "Lorandrial, come here," she whispered, waving her arms at the same time. "I felt it was best to have him remain at a distance until I informed you of the change."

Pegan stood to greet the man. He was a hand taller and appeared quite gangly. Dirty blond hair framed his boyish face and his dark green leather armor looked custom made, except for silver, leaf shaped pauldrons which were obviously an afterthought. A longbow slung over his left shoulder appeared to long for use and the ornate sword hanging on each hip looked suitable for display, but neither seemed suitable for combat.

"Lorandrial... Pegan Rhoe," she introduced them both. She could see the look of uncertainty plastered on Pegan's face. "He looks young, I know," she said with a giggle. "Elves age different from you. Rest assured, he's had twice your lifetime worth of experience with a blade."

"We should wake the others and head out while it's still dark," Lorandrial suggested.

Lady Alenia hugged him, "until your return, my son."

Chapter 18

Jorandrial stood at the water's edge, his vision focused back towards Rhunsiire. The orange sun painted the land a vibrant peach and long shadows created by the dense trees kept him cloaked in shadows, a disturbed smile creased his otherwise smooth face. There was to be a hearing to decide Pegan's fate, that much was true. His fabrication of the rest though had worked perfectly and he slipped right in without question. When the time was right, he would give the hearing and deal out the punishment as judge, jury... and executioner.

They traveled one full day and almost through the next until they arrived at the edge of a rocky cliff. Far below, a sea of golden sand rose and fell in swells as far as the eye could see while waves of heat caused the ground to shimmer unnaturally. Saguaro cactuses poked through the sand like deathly fingers while creosote bush grew like wild untamed patches of dense hair. Near the edge, a stifling heat tore at their faces and threatened to suck the breath from their lungs.

Thathra dropped his pack and wiped the sweat from his face. His fingers fumbled with the stopper on a large flask. After a long drawn-out swallow, he allowed some to spill onto his parched lips. "I think this may have been a mistake," he mumbled.

"I feel like we've entered a forge," Averie said. Her hair hung limp in long glistening strands. "Hopefully when the sun drops it'll cool down."

Pegan seemed to be lost in confusion as he dug through his pack.

With one hand Lorandrial blocked the sun. "I have crossed this arid, inhospitable wasteland only once and why Pegan chose to lead us in this direction is beyond me. The days are blistering hot and leaves you on the verge of insanity while the constant wind chaps the skin and pelts the body with sand thrown like darts. Then… night comes and the temperature plummets well below freezing. Either way, by day or by night, death always lurks."

Pegan shook his head in disbelief as he handed each a long strip of white cloth. "Wrap these around your head and only leave slits wide enough to see then tuck the rest into your tunics. It will keep the sun from cooking our brains." As they finished Pegan produced a large green jar. "When you're ready, place this salve on any exposed skin as well."

"What is it?" Thathra asked while he watched the salve turn Pegan's skin a light shade of green.

"Aloe Vera extract," Pegan said as he applied the second coat. "It was given to me by Gleia the night before we left. According to her it will protect our skin and we need to be diligent about applying it early every morning before the sun rises."

"How long will this take to cross?" Saress asked. She failed to mummify herself as she was naturally protected.

"Were technically just tracing the edge till we make it to the Rocky Crag, but to answer what you really want to know, we'll be in this environment for three, maybe four days at most."

Saress looked to the north. "Would it be better to work our way north some and follow the edge of the mountains?"

Pegan shook his head in disgust. "That whole region you pointed to is festered with nomads, wanderers, outcasts, renegades, and criminals, all looking to gain Karayan's favor. It's a double edged sword. Too close and we'll be spotted and chased to our deaths, but the other way presents its own challenges. If we lose our way and travel to far inland, the desert will be our final resting place."

"Great… just great," Lorandrial moaned.

Pegan led them to a series of uneven, jagged, basalt stones slick with wind-blown sand that traced the edge of the cliff.

"Stay near the face so the wind doesn't rip you free and fling you to your death," Pegan advised.

Travel was slow and each step was precisely picked for maximum footing. Pegan led the way followed by Averie, Saress—who kept hold of Averie—Thathra, and finally Lorandrial. As they made their descent into the valley below, the wind increased and began to toss Averie around like a kite with a broken string. Panicked, she clutched hard onto Pegans waist, which he didn't seem to mind.

The desert floor was substantially different than it appeared from above. The simmering sand shifted frequently hindering movement. The dunes that appeared as tiny hills from far are now giant mountains obstructing their views making it impossible to see far in any distance. As they crested each dune, the wind howled in dreadful, dying moans that forced them to walk backwards or risk having their eyes gouged out by blowing sand.

Ascending then descending, the pattern repeated itself deep into the night and all the while the temperature continued to drop until their breath glowed dense against a bright moon.

Averie's jaw chattered causing intense pain to her teeth and jaw while the minimal heat generated by her movements was quickly leached away by the bone chilling breeze that worked its way under, through, or around every piece of clothing. Her mind wandered and her friends faded then something happened she had not expected. In the distance, a cabin appeared through the howling sand which fell like blustering snow. Each window was lit with bright lights while a steady stream of grayish smoke drifted from the chimney. She could almost feel the warmth radiating from the fire as she approached.

Pegan reached the ridge of a razorback dune and looked back. The wind buffeted his body and his wraps flapped like a flag.

One... two... three... he counted the shadows at the bottom. "Where's Averie," Pegan screamed as he ran back down the dune.

"She's right—"

"Find her, now," Pegan growled. Anger flashed across his eyes.

Lethargic from the cold, Saress had become oblivious to those around her and was unaware Averie had wandered off alone. Her eyes flashed into the thermal spectrum, but being at the bottom of the ravine they proved useless. She raced to the top but lost all hope as she spun in a tight circle. There were simply to many dips and swells for her vision to be of any use.

A tear froze partway down her cheek and fell. Twice now she had made a mistake and left Averie alone. The one she swore upon her life to protect she abandoned. "I've failed us," she whispered, "and so I give up my life." She pulled a small blade free and pressed it against her chest.

Pegan knocked the blade away then slapped the lizard bloodying his hand. "She ain't dead, yet, use the instincts Elwrick gave you," he screamed.

Saress is cold-blooded creature and needs the sun to thrive. In this frigid environment, her body slowed and her mind almost entered a state of hibernation. Hearing the words she closed her eyes and concentrated. Instantly, the feeling swam through her veins like a salmon returning home to spawn. "This way," she mumbled pointing out into the darkness.

Averie was close, only one hill away, half undressed, and mumbling something incoherently. The wind whipped at her naked body and small blisters formed on the exposed skin.

Thathra arrived first and grabbed the deranged woman.

Out of her mind, she screamed like a banshee then bit his arm.

"You're going the wrong way," Thathra groaned.

"Can't you see it?" Averie screamed back through chattering teeth. "There's a house."

"There's no house," Thathra answered.

"Right there," she pointed towards the darkness. "The smoke from the chimney, there's a light burning." Tears froze to her eyelids.

Thathra carried Averie at a full sprint screaming something about needing a fire and now.

"There's nothing to burn," Pegan answered.

"Find something," Thathra screamed holding the woman tight to allow some of his body heat to penetrate her, "or she'll be dead by morning."

Pegan already knew the barbarian was much better at surviving in the elements and quickly went on a search for anything useful. Minutes later he returned with a handful of creosote bushes.

Thathra produced steel wool and laid it under the bushes. Satisfied, he struck a small steel rod against a gray stone and bright blue sparks fired off but the wind was too fierce and nothing ignited. Each attempt resulted in the same outcome.

"Let me try," Pegan said as he took the striker but the results were similar. "Light you damn thing," he screamed and this time the wood erupted.

"How did you do that?" Lorandrial asked.

"With this," he held up the striker.

"No, the fire erupted before the sparks even hit," Lorandrial eyed him suspiciously.

"Who cares how it started," Thathra said.

Pegan made many trips into the desert and collected hundreds of the bushes. Satisfied there would be enough to last the night he joined the others next to the flame.

The shivering ceased and Averie spoke somewhat understandably, "why am I half naked?" she asked.

"Because you were freezing to death," Thathra explained. "When the body gets too cold, blood vessels expand increasing blood flow creating a false warmth. The sudden rush of heat makes the person hot, extremely delusional, and often times they strip their clothes to cool. On the tundra we call it the naked death as most are found stripped of all their clothes and laid out as if reaching for something."

"Will there be any permanent damage?" Pegan asked.

Thathra examined her fingers, nose, and cheeks. "I don't believe so. The color is returning nicely but I'll monitor her through the night to be safe."

"Well thank you for the education," Lorandrial said. "But none of that will help us cross the desert. You said three days if we traveled non-stop. This delay will cost us."

"Her death would cost us more," Pegan fired back.

Saress walked to the top of the dune to survey their surroundings, "I can't see the mountains have we lost our way?"

"No," Pegan answered. "At night I travel by the stars," then pointed up.

When Saress looked up the sky stole her breath. This was the first time she had seen the sky so clear. Salmon pink and streaked with purples and blues while a million stars sparkled like diamonds.

Some shimmered while others blinked. A few were so bright she was surprised they didn't set the night on fire.

"See that big one there?" Pegan pointed up towards the heavens. "That's Cynosūra, the traveler's star. That's how I know we're on track." Over the next few hours, Pegan explained his knowledge of the stars and how to use them for travel.

Even though the morning was cool, they still wrapped themselves and applied the cream as recommended. At first travel was quick and they covered a great distance, but by noon the weather took a turn for the worse and the temperature rose quickly. Travel slowed and as far as the eye could see waves of burning heat floated from the sand.

It was nearing evening and the relentless heat finally claimed its first victim. She tried to call out, but her words came only as a jumbled mess and she swayed to and fro like a drunken sailor then collapsed to one knee then fell forward. Her face planted in the sand.

Saress screamed for help but the words only came as a frantic hiss which actually worked better as the horrendous screech caught everybody's attention. Pegan bolted to the location where Saress held Averie in her arms, Thathra was there too, a flask in hand.

"Sit her up," Pegan advised.

Thathra slowly poured some water down her throat and wiped the blood from her cracked lips.

"We need shade," Saress demanded. "If we don't get her out of the sun, she'll die." With her highly perceptive vision she could see Averie's body was drenched with heat.

Pegan studied their surroundings and located what appeared to be a pile of large boulders surrounding a thick cactus. "Over there," he pointed off in the distance. "We can find shade among those boulders."

The others offered to carry Averie but Saress refused. The sun had little effect on her.

To their surprise what they thought was a pile of rocks turned out to be a roof. Small stairs wide enough for a single person spiraled down into the darkness.

Pegan vanished down the hole only to return moments later, "it's empty."

The small dirt room offered little in the way of comforts but luckily it was deep enough to remain cool, even when the sun reached the hottest part of the evening.

"Who do you think built this," Thathra asked.

"Possibly a hermit," Pegan said. "Whoever it was knew this area well. These cactus roots will hold water for months."

With Thathra's aid, Pegan milked the roots refilling their flasks they had emptied.

They remained there until the sun sank and the land cooled. Refreshed, they traveled quickly and made good time until it turned too cold to continue. Along the way, he collected bushes again to start a fire. The next day when the heat turned relentless they built shade and waited. The next few days the process repeated itself. A fire was built for warmth at night, and shelter was located during the hottest part of the day. One the fifth day, Lorandrial protested. "Just admit to us now you're lost. You've led us in circles the past few days and we're nowhere near this place you call the Broken Crag. It probably doesn't exist anyway."

Pegan rubbed his scruffy chin, "Our pace slowed for the safety of all, but by tomorrow evening we'll have reached our destination."

Thathra shook his head, "We won't make it. We simply don't have the water."

Pegan moved in close to the fire as the air turned icy cold, "do you think I brought us here unknowingly? Just as you, I have kept track of our supplies. I knew long before you pulled out that flask there was little left. There is an oasis not far from here called the Ponds of Tranquility. If we leave with the sun, we'll be there before the ground warms."

"Should we leave now?" Saress asked.

"No," Pegan answered. "There are evil vile things in this land that go there at night to resupply their water for the day. To go there now would just provide them dinner as well. Let's get some rest, tomorrow will come soon enough."

Pegan roused the others while it was still dark and they set off at the first crack of light. Travel seemed easier today, perhaps because they knew the end was near or driven by an unforeseeable force none could explain.

They traveled only a few hours when Pegan led them down a

narrow parched trail which snaked between two colossal hills of sand impregnated with jagged pieces of shale and slate. In the distance were two black basalt spires that looked like toothpicks. Their location signaled the entrance to The Broken Crag.

"The ponds are just ahead," Pegan said. Their pace quickened as the sound of water carried on the wind reached their ears. A renewed sense of vigor flowed through their veins but turned icy cold when a thunderous boom like mountains colliding erupted close by.

"What was that?" Averie asked.

"My best guess would—"

Pegan was interrupted by a high pitched squeal.

The hair on Averie's neck stood erect. She had only heard something like that once before, and that was in school when the teacher drug her nails down the chalkboard.

Boom! The noise was deafening and sand and stone blown loose by the impact rumbled down both dunes.

"Run," Pegan yelled as he grabbed Averie's hand. To either side all hell broke loose as boulders, rock and stone tumbled downward gaining speed. Directly behind, massive chunks of shale and slate no longer supported followed releasing a brute, thundering roar as it rode a wave of smaller, stones, sand, and dirt.

They cleared the ravine as the first boulders collided with an ear-splitting concussion. Blasted by the force, they were flung forward like paper dolls in a wind storm. The sky darkened from a dense cloud of dust and debris. Then, for a moment, everything went silent.

Thathra coughed out a mouthful of sand and climbed to his feet. Saress did likewise. The rest lay scattered like twigs.

"Did you see that?" Thathra screamed as he helped Saress with their companions.

Crash! Another sudden bone-crunching boom shook the ground violently almost taking them from their feet.

As they passed what little remained of the dune, Averie screamed something indecipherable then backed away slamming into Saress.

Pegan froze, he had never seen a Sand Lurker grow to such a proportion.

The enormous crustacean was the size of a small house. The flat, sand-colored body looked like a pie but more elongated. All along the edges were the carapace met, large thick ripples formed as if the thing was pressed together. Eight spiked legs lifted the creature off the ground. Two tiny black eyes sunk back in bony sockets looked out between two massive claws.

"What is that thing?" Saress screamed at Pegan.

"A sand lurker," he shot back.

Concentrating solely on the giant wasp it had pinned to the ground by its silken silvery wing, the creature remained oblivious to the fact that strangers were watching the battle.

"Over there." Pegan pointed to a small pond behind the sand lurker. "We can circle around and come out behind it and refill our flasks unnoticed. Hopefully, they will keep fighting until we're finished."

The beast raised one massive claw supported by an appendage which appeared too small to support the weight. Snip… snip…. The claw snapped at the air then propelled itself towards the wasp.

Just before impact, the wasp rolled to the side avoiding instant death. Large cracks spider-webbed the ground where the wasp's head rested moments earlier.

The wasp screeched angrily before thrusting its black and yellow stripped torso upward slamming the dagger length stinger hard into the shell. Not only did it fail to penetrate the rock solid surface, the stinger broke covering both the wasp, and the lurker's underside in bluish venom.

At a brisk pace, Pegan led them around a smaller dune and came out on the back side of the oasis near the spring.

Help me…

Averie paused and cocked her head sideways, confused at the squeaky voice that just entered her mind.

Friend… help me… friend… friend…

As the voice came again, she knew without a doubt it was the wasp begging for help.

"Did you all hear that?" Averie asked. "The wasp just asked for help."

Pegan gripped Averie by the shoulders and their eyes met, "those two creatures are natural enemies, as they are with us."

"This is a risk we don't need," Thathra yelled as he pulled flasks from his pack.

The wasp's movement slowed and would soon find death.

Please… help… friend…

"It needs our help," Averie pleaded.

"That wasp would just as soon attack you the moment it's free," Pegan explained.

Thathra and Saress began to fill the flasks as Lorandrial stood back and watched.

Just in his peripheral vision, Pegan kept the elf in sight.

Averie shoved Pegan, "how do you know it will attack us?"

"Because we're enemies," Pegan fired back. There was anger in his voice that startled her but she refused to surrender.

"Why, because it's different," she screamed, "have you ever tried to talk with one? Are you going to kill Saress because she's different? What about me, I'm different?" Her eyes watered.

Pegan suddenly realized he has never been attacked by a wasp, but the lurker is different.

"I've been that wasp," she whispered. Her hand trembled as she slipped the small sword from the scabbard. "Help me… please."

Saress returned, alarm in her eyes at the sight of Averie holding the blade.

"We need to save that wasp," Pegan said.

"What," she hissed.

Pegan's daggers sprung to life as he called out to Thathra. Lorandrial moved close so he could hear the conversation. "Let's save the wasp."

Thathra stood there in silence, his mouth stuck wide open waiting for the right words that never came. Then, he said the one thing that came to mind as he slid the axe free, "I hope this thing taste better than it looks."

Saress nocked an arrow and climbed to the top of a dune. Lorandrial climbed a different dune and set the creature up in a cross-fire.

Saress fired first, but the creature turned and the arrow ricocheted off the hard shell causing orange sparks to erupt like a volcano.

The sudden turn left the creature exposed and a perfectly placed arrow by Lorandrial severed the tendon rendering the raised claw useless.

Thathra charged directly towards the creature while Pegan worked his way around the dune to attack from behind.

The sudden onslaught was successful as the Lurker released its hold on the wasp and skittered up the hill towards Saress.

A blustering buzz filled the air and dust blinded their sight as the wasp took to flight and quickly faded from view

Three more arrows left her bow, two bounced harmlessly aside while the third buried deep into the soft tissue of a leg. Too big to kill they had to somehow disable the creature.

Thathra swung his blade in a flurry of motion. One leg was knocked to the side while he ducked underneath another. Twisting in midair to gain momentum, he swung with all his might and the blade sliced cleanly through a leg which toppled over like a fallen tree.

The creature screamed a mind-numbing hiss through a circular mouth lined with serrated teeth before slamming its massive body to the ground in an attempt to crush the man under it.

Thathra rolled free just before the behemoth impacted the ground.

Suddenly, the thing leaped high into the air aimed directly at Saress. Seven legs kicked wildly as if balancing itself while one claw was drawn back waiting to be swung like a club.

Pegan rounded the dune to see the creature crash to the ground creating a mushroom cloud of dust. Saress backed away as a massive claw larger than a full grown man pounded the ground. Somehow, she avoided that attack but tumbled backwards down the dune losing her bow in the process.

The creature chased after her and vanished over the hill.

Pegan ran at full speed and leaped from the dune and landed on the hard shell. Both daggers slashed and jabbed in a flurry, but they were too small to divert its attention from Saress who was now pinned beneath it.

Thathra followed from behind and with a monumental swing, another leg fell free.

The lurker reared on its hind legs.

Unable to hold on, Pegan tumbled from its slick back.

Saress scampered out from under as the creature slammed down to crush her.

Lorandrial took another shot. The arrow ricochet off the creature's leg out of control and headed directly towards Pegan.

Observing the deflection Pegan rolled out of the missiles path just before impact.

Thathra circled around as Pegan regained his footing. "Go for the soft tissue on the legs," he yelled as he swung. A sickening crack echoed as the heavy blade was not slowed by the shell and another leg fell spraying yellow blood like a fountain.

Pegan used his agility and somehow managed to clamber up the lurker's claw and buried a dagger into one of its piercing black eyes.

The beast shook violently tossing Pegan like a rag.

Averie unexpectedly appeared. The small sword she normally carried on her left hip was now held firmly with both hands and she appeared ready for battle. However, before she could charge in, she was grabbed from behind and pulled back. The look in the lizard's eyes told her not to proceed any further.

Lorandrial had a clear shot as the creature rose on its hind legs. The placement was precise, and the arrow vanished down the gaping maw.

The creature hissed an evil cry and slammed himself to the ground once more. With its remaining legs, it kicked in a flurry of motion at the ground until camouflaged in a cloud of sand. When it cleared, the lurker was gone.

Pegan stood exhausted, hot, sweaty, and covered in dust as he looked out over the others who stood in awe at the thing they just defeated.

The next few hours they spent washing in the water and refilling the flasks.

"We should go," Pegan said. "The Broken Crag is only a few hours away."

Chapter 19

arayan sat on a plush, pillow-top chair on the balcony just off his private chamber and watched the rainfall. From here he could see clear across Lynn Brook to the rusty bars of the portico, a haunting reminder of her escape. Far below, life went on as usual, lights burned in every window of each house, men went to work, children to school. For most, her escape has long been forgotten. Others though, quickly remembered each time they wanted to go outside after dark but couldn't because of the new curfew which prohibited night time travel.

Movement far below caught his attention and he rose to get a better view. Leaning against the railing, he could see the strange man shimmered in the wet air as he passed through the lantern light of each house yet his movements lacked any sense of urgency. Could this possibly be the man he was expecting?

High above, lightning split the night sky in a blinding flash, wet air sizzled, a thunderous boom shook the core of Lynn Brook. When his vision returned, the stranger had vanished. Karayan looked towards the palace door. It was firmly closed and all six guards were still in place.

His vision shot back to the last place he saw the man, but no trace remained of anybody having passed, not even a footprint in the wet, soggy ground.

Was this all a dream? Was this really happening? The thoughts came quick. Or was this a mental mind game from some demonic demon playing games with his head? Karayan reached out with his hand and felt the cool water pool in his palm, this was no dream.

"Expecting someone?" The voice was more of a sinister cackle than actual words.

Karayan turned to face a man cloaked from head to toe. He was completely dry as if he arrived on a sunny day yet outside rain fell in waves. Karayan shook his head in amazement then walked in and closed the large glass door to the balcony. "You're a hard man to locate."

"When I choose to be," Arlin answered.

The door opened and Lilith entered, "Sir," she bowed. "I am here to report that Arlin has—"

"I am quite aware of his presence, now leave us," Karayan said.

"Yes… my King," she bowed.

"Do you always do as you're told?" Arlin asked. The words came with a passionate gesture.

She paused at the door to answer, "I understand authority."

A menacing chuckle erupted from him that made the fine hairs on her neck stand erect. "You confuse authority with brutality." His head slightly slanted and turned back, the whites of his eyes cutting through the shadows of his veil.

Karayan sidestepped the large desk which sat fashionably bare and darted towards Arlin, his white fisted knuckles glowed in the candlelight. "Nobody questions the loyalty of my servants," he growled.

Pulling back the veil the bald head glistened in the light. He seemed younger than their last meeting but he still wore a thin mustache which turned down towards the corners of his mouth leaving his chin an island of skin. Shorter than Karayan by a shoulder his muscles were ripe with tension. "I don't question her loyalty, I question the means by which she stays loyal, that's all."

"By my own choosing," she answered. "Now if you don't mind." She slammed the door as she left.

Arlin could sense a hint of truth in the lie.

Lilith however, chose not to leave but instead leaned against the door placing her ear against the wood. "*Aurel escalation*," she whispered and her ear melded into the door and her eyes flashed red. She could now hear every word as if she stood in the room.

"Well… now that you ran my trusted servant off, shall we discuss business, Mr. Arlin Brack," Karayan said, his thick muscular arms folded across his chest.

"And what business might that be, this letter was rather vague?" He tossed the parchment on the desk.

"Someone near to me has been abducted; I want her returned alive and unharmed."

Arlin massaged his chin. "Continue," he nodded. He had worked for Karayan many times since the death of his brother and never once had Karayan revealed the slightest concern for a missing woman, so this sudden change told him there was more to the story.

"A woman's been kidnapped. Her abductor seems to be a man of great skill, quick with a blade and deadly accurate."

"A woman... or a bearer?" Arlin questioned.

"What difference does it make?"

Arlin chuckled, "the price of my services. You see, the value of a woman is not worth the trouble, yet a bearer is priceless."

Karayan now understood Arlin had already been informed of the escape. "A bearer," he admitted, a deep sigh escaped his lips.

"The story grows more intriguing as we speak," Arlin said. "How exactly did she escape the keeper?"

"She had help, from your brother—"

"What did you say?" Arlin hissed through a locked jaw. "He's been dead for over twenty-five years, I put him in the ground."

"You put someone in the ground, but I do not believe it was your brother. I've seen the work Demetrius did, and it was the best." The squint in Arlin's eyes let Karayan know he hit a nerve. "I saw what was done to the keeper. No normal man did this."

A grin spread across his face, "I'll do it," Arlin said lacing his thin fingers together, "Not because I believe it was my brother, but because I cannot have you thinking someone's better than me."

"So you want nothing from me then?" Karayan asked.

Arlin smiled an ugly grin, "oh no... no... no... My services are never free, I want Lilith as my own. Give her to me and consider this task done." A disgusting smile formed on his face and the glint in his eye told Karayan he had already thought this over long before his arrival.

"You want my servant?" Karayan asked.

Arlin simply nodded an affirmation.

"You bring me the bearer, alive. And the head of her abductor… and you can have her," he said with a smile. He could always find another servant. She was special and he would hate to see her go, but the cost is worth the job.

"Then we have an agreement?" Arlin asked.

"Because of your delay, I was forced to hire out the forces of Tak-Thukmand. They have the Majestic's inundated, and a trap is set at the Crag. If it is your bother, he may try to slip through the Dugab Caverns."

"You wasted your time, resources, and money. The barbarians are brutal, yes, but not very smart and easily outwitted."

"They were the only option I had available," Karayan argued.

"You underestimate me," Arlin said. "You let fear blind your judgment."

"Find her," he hissed.

"Then we have an agreement?" Arlin repeated.

Karayan looked flustered, "yes, we have an agreement."

"Consider it done," Arlin said. "But first I must seek counsel in East Haven."

"East Haven, that's the opposite direction. While you're out gallivanting around trying to get with some old whore, your subjects slip farther from your grasp."

"I seek no whore, but a witch who will pinpoint their location. They could be right under you own nose and you would never know it."

A wide grin stretched across Lilith's face from ear to ear. Business was about to pick up.

"If you dislike my tactics, or wish to employ someone else the decision is yours," Arlin said.

Karayan snarled. "Do what you will, but I suggest you don't fail me."

Chapter 20

The opening looked more like the entrance to Hell than a crag. A gruesome spire at either side twisted in painful torturous shapes which appeared small against the jagged towering graphite stone walls with peaks that punctured the heavily clouded sky. A stiff wind howled through the opening giving the mountain an angry voice which displayed its current displeasure.

The climb was treacherous as the clay ground was broken and upheaved with large cracks and steep ledges, while glistening black razor-sharp shards and fragments from boulders lay scattered as if thrown from Heaven. Below the carnage, the hint of a long-abandoned staircase remained.

Travel was painstakingly slow as they carefully chose the safest route.

As night fell so did the rain adding to the terrains complexity. Lightning sparked the blackened sky and thunder boomed. The clay ground became slick as ice and each step threatened to send them tumbling to their deaths.

"We need shelter," Thathra hollered out over the relentless cry of the wind.

Pegan nodded in agreement and altered their course which brought on much grumbling from his companions. Now they were forced to navigate around impossibly large boulders, fallen trees, and other debris washed down from above which collected in huge conglomerations that thwarted their progress at every turn.

They traveled this way for what seemed like hours when they broke through into a small cut-out created from a dislodged boulder.

Averie shivered and her teeth chattered as she walked past, "can we have a fire?"

Pegan shook his head to her disappointment, "the wind is too strong here.

Within minutes of hearing the dire news, Thathra was hard at work using logs from fallen trees to construct a frame. Next, he wove branches and limbs carefully together and fixed those to the frame with strips of thin bark and then eventually covered that with finer branches creating a small, but impenetrable retreat complete with a door which could even be secured.

Pegan nodded his approval of the work and even lent aid when asked. "Magnificent," he said, "looks like tonight we'll sleep in comfort."

Within minutes, the fire Pegan built left them all stripping off their clothes.

Saress crouched on a boulder some distance away and watched them enter. She wanted to go as well and sit by Averie's side but right now more important matters persisted. Besides, she knew with Pegan there, no harm would befall Averie. She could sense a bond forming between them stronger than friendship. Satisfied Averie was safe, she pushed off with her powerful hind legs and sprung from rock to rock navigating the terrain working her way to what she believed was the rim.

Near the top, she crawled into a large crevice created between two boulders and watched. In the distance, she could see the faint heat traces of men. Laying her head on the stone, she closed her eyes for a moment and sensed subtle vibrations in the ground. Something was coming from the west, something large.

When her eyes opened, two enormous beast approached from the west The smaller of the two was her height, the color of mud and thick with muscles and bulging veins. Its hands and feet were disproportionately large while a small head rested on a torso with no neck and its piercing green eyes cut through the darkness.

The other one looked more human than monster except for the fact its skin looked like that of a shark and towered over the other.

He walked in long strides and carried a stalactite for a club.

The shorter one quickened its pace to keep up.

To her surprise, from the east a barbarian appeared not twenty yards away. Obviously, he had been expecting this unusual meeting.

—Emperor Tak-Thukmand studied the two things with disgust in his eyes. When they were close enough to spit on, he spoke, *"Welcome,"* he said with a grin. *"I am Emperor Tak-Thukmand and this is my second, Major Turik Tor-Enrogue."* He pointed to a big burly bastard covered with either fur or hair, none could tell the difference. In one mighty hand, the Major held a large axe and in the other a shield manufactured from a broken wagon wheel. *"And I am here under direct order from King Karayan."* He unrolled a parchment and read the writing. *"It seems he demands our unification to capture an escaped prisoner and bring punishment to her accomplices."*

The short one with no neck groaned, *"Me no like King, Ulgra bow to none."*

"Truly you can't be that ignorant, or stupid. The King gets what he wants, whether you like it or not," Tak-Thukmand said, and then rubbed his bearded chin. *"When I inform the King you refused to cooperate in such an important matter and because of it, the prisoner has possibly escaped beyond our reach…"*

Ulgra curled his fingers inward transforming his hands into massive clubs at the threat, *"me no help, King problems not mine."*

Emperor Tak-Thukmand had a disheveled look on his face as he turned towards the other, *"what about you, Hazgrag, King of the Stone Giants?"* He looked up at him. *"We all know what happens to those who refuse the King's orders. Do you wish to meet the same fate as this ignorant troll? Or are you willing to aid in the capture of a known criminal?"*

Hazgrag scratched his butt, *"me help,"* he grumbled.

"Fantastic," Tak-Thukmand said, *"at least you're not a coward and won't be forced to face the wrath of King Karayan. Now, gather up your men and place them at the top of each ridge and when they appear, let stones rain down upon them till their bones are crushed to powder."*

Emperor Tak-Thukmand faced Ulgra, *"you just remember this when your wife's skin is used to make curtains."*

Ulgra snarled and bared a carefully hidden set of fangs. The pounding of his feet could be heard long after he was gone from sight. Saress heard enough to know the crag was being watched. Without a sound, she backed from the crevice and bounded back down the hill.

Lorandrial screamed like a frightened girl as he looked towards the door only to be greeted by a large pair of yellow eyes with dagger-shaped pupils.

Pegan leaped to his feet as well until he realized it was only Saress sticking her head and one arm through the door.

Thathra was already in the process of apologizing about the blunder and assured her the situation would be rectified immediately. Within minutes, the opening doubled in size which allowed her to enter, but only if she squeezed in sideways and ducked her head in the process.

She gave Averie a hug and licked her cheek—a reptilian kiss—then sat by the fire to warm.

"What did you discover on your travels?" Pegan asked.

Saress shook her head negatively, "nothing good. The crag is being watched. In fact, we would have been spotted by now if it was not for this wonderful enclosure Thathra built."

"What are you talking about?" Pegan leaned forward giving her his complete undivided attention.

An hour passed while she told them of the strange meeting.

Pegan never said a word as he rose and walked to the door and looked south.

"Now what do you propose?" Lorandrial sneered. "You marched us through Hell only to discover your plan's a failure."

"We should turn back and try the Majestic's," Saress said. "If they are here, then it's possible we can sneak through undetected."

"Aye," Thathra agreed. "But it's a long way's back, and we have neither the endurance nor the supplies, we might not be as lucky this time."

Pegan listened to his companions recommendations. "No!" He finally said. His voice seemed distant and void of hope.

"You plan to fight them?" Thathra asked… surprised.

"No. That's a fight we can't win," Pegan said. "We're left with no other choice but to go through the Dugab Caverns."

"Those caverns are only a myth," Lorandrial said. "I think you should listen to your companions."

"They're no myth," Pegan argued. "I've been through them hundreds of times. They're located deep within the Silvers at the end of a long winding set of stairs. The only problem is we'll travel extremely close to the Lost Sanctuary."

Lorandrial spit on the ground in disgust. "Another fantasy created in your own mind. I have walked this world three times longer than you and we both know the Silvers are an impenetrable mountain range. I say we take a vote. Let me lead and we'll be there within a tenday, or you can continue to follow this deranged man and die of old age, or at the hands of the enemy long before having reached the goal."

Saress looked at Pegan, then Lorandrial, then back at Pegan and finally Averie.

Averie never hesitated, she walked straight to Pegan and took his hand, "whichever way you go, I will follow."

"That answers my question," Saress said.

"Mine too," Thathra agreed.

"We'll leave at first light," Pegan said to his companions then addressed Lorandrial whose face grew quite red. "You can go whichever direction you chose, but were taking the caves."

Lorandrial's face was bitter as if he just licked a lemon, "I'll see this through to the end, even if I disagree with the actions."

The morning arrived with the bluest skies Pegan had ever seen and the air was warm and carried a freshly washed scent. Insects revitalized by the sun were alive and buzzing with life and for just a moment, the entire world felt right.

Murderer... killer...

Pegan froze. The words pounded in his brain like a ten-pound mallet. He had not heard them in twenty-five years, ever since he returned the eyes to their rightful home.

Murderer... killer...

Pegan looked up the crag, then down. Did they know of his troubled past? What would they do when they discovered the truth? His companions had yet to emerge from the cocoon Thathra constructed. Maybe he should leave now, vanish without a trace forcing them to follow Lorandrial. Perhaps they would be better off.

Murderer… killer…

"What more do you want?" Pegan screamed into the air.

Saress never slowed as she rammed into the side of the shelter busting through sending timbers flying like slivers. An arrow already nocked clearly expecting to see a horde of barbarians and giants waiting.

Thathra followed through the gaping hole with Averie right on his heels.

Pegan knelt on the ground gripping his head as if to crush it between his palms.

"What do you want…" he just kept repeating.

Averie ran to him and gripped him in her arms, "Something's wrong," she cried out to the others. She could see the pain visible on his face.

Thathra arrived and lifted the distraught man to his feet.

"He's a coward or deranged" Lorandrial said as he stepped out, "obviously out of his dang mind."

Saress's movements were blinding fast as she grabbed the elf by his neck and lifted him free of the ground and shook him violently.

"Let him go… before you kill him," Averie screamed to Saress.

Saress let the elf go and collapsed herself taking Averie in her arms, "I'm sorry… I'm sorry…" she kept repeating, holding the woman uncomfortably tight. "It's just…"

Thathra brought Pegan around with a few well-placed slaps to the face. "What happened?" he asked.

"Voices," Pegan mumbled. "I started hearing voices…"

"That's a bad omen," Saress said. "I suggest we leave now, and in a hurry."

They traveled quickly and before the sky darkened they crossed the last of the Cursed Desert and arrived at the base of the Silver Mountains. The base was mostly rock with smaller sagebrush, while higher up large thick trees poked through the massive gray stone. White snow glistened near the peak which vanished into the darkening sky.

"We travel south from here and eventually turn west," Pegan said.

Days past and besides the usual animals they observed no one. A constant cool breeze flowed down the mountain while water and food were abundant.

Pegan knew what waited though and kept it to himself.

Dawn came early as Pegan altered their course and took them into the mountains. The faint path was no more than a game trail that slithered around large rocks, across a dry river bed, through a graveyard of dead trees, and finally vanished over the edge of a large rise. To the untrained eye, or the unaware traveler, it would have gone unnoticed. But to Pegan, it's an arrow straight to a long forgotten history.

They traveled the remainder of that day and the next when they entered a large flat glade ringed with dense trees and thick brush. "We'll camp here tonight," Pegan recommended. "Not only is it hidden from view, it also has a hot spring to bathe in."

Averie raised her eyebrows.

Pegan could tell Averie was baffled but refused to ask to not look ignorant, "the water is warmed from the fire under the ground."

Averie had experienced nothing like this before and was reluctant to enter, even after Pegan leaped in. Nervous, she sunk clear to her neck and let the warmth penetrate her body. Later, the smell of meat cooking drew her towards the fire and a well-deserved dinner.

"I'll take first watch," Lorandrial said. "Even though we have encountered no enemies, we should not so carelessly lower our guard."

The night was warm so Averie rolled her cloak into a tight pillow and laid flat on her back and listened. All around her wildlife was abundant, a wolf howled, an owl hooted, and crickets sang. In the heavens, between the wisps of gray clouds that drifted past she watched the stars twinkle. She wondered if that's where she was going, one of those distant stars. She hoped it would be beautiful, a world without hate, and suffering. One she would call home until her return.

Another day passed without incident, but on the third, they encountered a large ledge with narrow moss-covered steps cut into the side. Far below they could see the trail turned hard west and followed another ledge before disappearing into a patch of dense trees and thick with ferns. Not far from there, they encountered a sheer rock wall as far as the eye could see in either direction.

Saress surveyed the blockage. It was well over two hundred feet tall and worked smooth from time and weather, not one-foot hold could be found. "A dead end, now what?" she asked.

"We travel south. There is a hidden passage where the stones slightly shift that is not visible unless you look at it from the correct angle,"

Pegan said. He followed a non-existent path that traced the edge of the wall for a great distance that led to a well-camouflaged passage.

"How do you know this location?" Lorandrial asked.

"You've been here." Averie not so much asked a question but made a statement.

"Of course he has, otherwise he would have thought this a dead end like the rest of us. It would have taken days of searching to discover this passage and he brought us right to it."

"I have been here before," Pegan said. He leaned against the stone wall.

"And this is the correct way to the... whatever it is you said?" Thathra asked.

"The Dugab Caverns," Pegan answered. "In two more days, we'll be there. Hopefully our passing by the Lost Sanctuary will go uneventful."

Lorandrial chuckled, and then outright laughed.

"What's the Lost Sanctuary? And why do you dispute Pegan?" Averie asked.

"The Lost Sanctuary is a fantasy land that doesn't exist... never has," Lorandrial said. He walked around them in a circular motion. "They say it was a magical city where druids and wizards train, where great wonders are discovered, and people can talk with the Creator. I saw a map once but what it revealed was faint and offered no location. Someone simply created it in their mind."

"It does exist, albeit not in the condition you describe," Pegan argued.

"You talk as if you've been there," Lorandrial said.

"I have," Pegan responded. He watched a bird leave its nest and take to wing.

"How do you know all this? Thathra asked.

Pegan drew a deep breath and let it out through his nostrils. To keep himself credible among his followers he had no other choice but to reveal his past, at least some of it. "I know all this because I was raised in the Lost Sanctuary," Pegan confessed.

"What?" Lorandrial asked.

"You see," Pegan continued. "From what I was told, I was abandoned at birth and discovered in an alley. I was taken far from the cities and raised by another. A man named Rayne, Lord Rayne." Pegan hesitated, "he's the Grand Master of Assassins."

"Assassin," Averie whispered.

"I spent decades under his training. As others graduated I remained. I wanted to be the best, had to be the best, and after I accomplished that, there was nothing left so I went out on my own and killed for hire. I traveled the land working for those with the most coin, but lacked the courage to do their own dirty work. Eventually, I grew weary of the senseless killing."

Saress went to speak but Pegan stopped her with a raised hand.

"What you don't understand is taking an oath from the Brotherhood is for life, and if you want out, that is what you surrender. So in order to retire, I feigned my death and vanished like a shadow on a sunny day. I still don't understand how Elwrick located me."

Thathra stood there shaking his head.

"We need to get going," Pegan said.

For a trail that once appeared non-existent, the travel was actually quite easy and by the end of the day, the swaying grass of the flatlands broke before them. The sky turned a pinkish blue and a light breeze blew up from the south brought with it a hint of salt.

"Is the ocean near?" Saress asked.

"A day's travel south of here," Pegan responded. "We'll camp here. Should be safe enough as few know this location."

Averie let her eyes focus on the glowing embers in the darkness while the smell of cooked meat lay heavy on the evening air before she spoke, "why does it have to be me?" she asked all.

"I don't know," Saress answered. "That's just how it's always been."

Pegan sat down next to Averie and pulled her tight against him. He could feel the warmth radiate from her body, feel her muscles tense with anxiety. "Perhaps Elwrick can explain to you when we next meet him. I just know you were chosen because you're pure." He took her hand and stared straight into her eyes, then placed his hand on her belly. "I don't know when, but sometime in the future, the baby you carry will become the steward of Icearaus. When he returns, he will bring with him wonderful ideas. And don't forget, you will always be remembered through him."

"When I return... will you all be here waiting as well?" She asked. A small smile etched across her face.

"You don't know?" Saress spat in anger.

"Know what?" Averie cried. "I have a right to know."

"Of all the known bearer's, only the child has ever returned," Pegan answered with a tear in his eye.

"So I won't be coming back?" Averie asked.

"I'm afraid not," Saress said. "Your legacy though will live forever. Especially if the child you carry can defeat Karayan upon his return."

"And what of my son, when he comes back he will know nobody or nothing?"

"The day he returns, Elwrick will be there to greet him," Pegan said, "along with the rest of us."

They all agreed.

"Why have you kept this from me?"

"I'm sorry," Pegan said. "I just never felt the timing was right."

"So how long did you plan to wait?" Saress asked.

"I don't know," Pegan said. "I'm sorry."

"And Elwrick will be there?" Averie asked

"Yes, as will the rest of us," Pegan said again and then tossed a few more sticks on the fire as the evening air turned cold.

"Why doesn't he come here now and create the portal?" Averie asked. "He must want me to suffer a bit longer before I leave."

"The portal can only be opened on the Isle of Aramoor, and he can't do it alone. It takes the help of three others. For who they are I don't know," Pegan said.

"And you don't know what happens on the other side of that portal?" She asked.

"None of us do," Saress answered.

"Am I going to die?" she blatantly asked.

Nobody said you die, just none has ever returned. Besides, you may find it's more beautiful than you could have ever imagined and don't wanna return," Saress said.

Averie fell into the arms of Saress and her tears fell like rain.

"Get some sleep," Pegan whispered to Averie. "You got a lot of information thrown at you all at once, and I fear our fighting is not yet complete."

Saress glanced Pegan a nasty hateful glare that could have melted steel.

The pinkish blue sky faded to black and the night sky lit with a million tiny dots.

"Somewhere up there," Pegan paused, almost choking on his words, "is where she's going."

"Aye," Thathra agreed. "But only if we can get her to the portal. And like you said, I too believe our greatest tribulations are yet to come." Thathra patted Pegan's shoulder then walked alone into the darkness deep in thought, fighting some private demon of his own. Pegan sat alone watching the night sky. Far off in the distance a night bird called to its mate.

Chapter 21

The old woman appeared from thin air. Bent at the waist and draped in tattered rags, only her two bone-thin arms covered with pale skin that sagged like candle wax was visible. One hand with three crooked fingers held an unlit lantern by a rusty chain while the other grasped a twig-thin cane which bowed under her weight. Veiled in darkness, she was featureless except for her eyes which gleamed like those from a crazed animal caught in the moonlight.

Arlin shivered. He had been watching for the woman for many hours from the gated entrance. The night sky was cloudless and the moon was bright. From where he stood, he could see clear to the Silvers if he chose to, but his vision was focused in a different direction. His eyes followed the wide and easily navigated road down the treeless grassy knoll which afforded no places to hide. Across the fields and pastures all the way to East Haven with its twinkling lights he observed nothing, yet there she was, standing before him.

"The grave has already been dug, and the coffin opened," Arlin said.

She paused and held up the lantern to look at who spoke, then glanced up at the large sign that spanned the distance of the rickety, twisted, wrought iron, rust-infested gate—Field of Honor Cemetery. "How ironic," she cackled.

Arlin slowed his pace to walk beside the woman as they passed row after row of tombstones. Whenever they neared a unique one she would stop and read the epitaph. Each time, Arlin wanted to grab her by the neck and strangle her. They only had one chance to accomplish the summons and if it failed because of her delay, he promised himself he would do just that. "The ritual must start at the exact time the moon reaches its zenith," he said.

"As I am aware," she answered.

"We're still a good distance away and the time grows near. Perhaps you can finish your exploration of exciting and unusual headstones after the completion of the task," he suggested.

"Oh, I suppose you're right," she said. "But I could spend days talking with those buried beneath them. I find their tales so interesting."

Arlin suspected the woman was borderline crazy, now he was positive about the fact.

Near the back next to the fence a large mound was visible and the smell of freshly turned soil filled the air. Near the pile, two men sat on a crate talking about what to do with the money they'd soon receive. From their stark age differences, they could have been father and son. The older one rose when he saw the pair approach, "you got our payment?" he asked.

"I told you, I will pay you after her confirmation, but not before then."

Both men watched the hag evaluate their work.

The witch shook her head in disgust. "You fool's, you destroyed the skull in your excavation," she said in a raspy voice.

"No," The older gravedigger said. "The skull was not in the coffin."

"Does it matter?" Arlin answered. He moved to the grave and looked down at the stack of lifeless gray bones picked clean from insects. Around the hip bones, the belt remained and the pommels of each dagger glistened. "All we need are the bones is what you said?"

"I said we need a complete set of bones," she growled, exposing pointed teeth. "Is the head not a bone?"

"Can we use another?" Arlin asked.

"Yes," she answered, "but—"

Arlin slipped a dagger free and flicked it with blinding speed. The older man stumbled backward and tried to scream but nothing came as his voice box had been severed. Grasping at his throat, blood spurted through his fingers spraying his partner and painting his dirt-stained coveralls a ghastly rust color. Struggling to stand, he stumbled forward and fell into the hole. The younger one decided the money was not worth his life and fled into the darkness.

"Well that was exciting but all for naught," the witch said. "If you would have let me finish, you would have heard the skull must come from someone, or something that died at the same time or before the skeleton we wish to use."

Arlin drew a deep sigh. In a few more minutes the ritual had to begin and there was no time now to exhume another.

"Lucky for you I suspected your ignorance of the dark arts so I brought the shrunken head of a gargoyle from my private collection. This skull, captured from the underworld acts as a complete set, but the price is very high as they are all but impossible to acquire," she said. From within the folds of her garments, she produced the head and held it up for him to see. It's about the size of a grapefruit and shaped like a dog's head. Covered in brown leathery skin, the eye sockets were sunk deep back and two short horns sprouted from the top. The mouth held multiple rows of jagged teeth and two long fangs hung down past the lower jaw.

Arlin hesitated. He despised making deals with such creatures, but his need to discover the location of the bearer and those who aided her outweighed his concerns. "Name your price?" he answered.

She thought for a moment. A necessary delay knowing his desperation grew and waiting until the moon was only minutes away from the exact location required, would all but guarantee his acceptance of her fee. "One drop of your blood."

Arlin froze. He has heard stories about what could be done with a single drop of blood from a man who has given it away willingly, but that was to a demon, a creature from the underworld. She was not a demon but a creature of flesh and blood, the same as him.

"You must decide now," she said. "We have less than a minute to begin, any longer, and this summons will fail."

"Can my soul be possessed if I do agree?"

"No," she said with a greedy smile and a broken voice. "I cannot possess souls."

"I'll do it then," he said.

A blood chilling grin appeared on her face after hearing what she wanted to hear. "Shall we begin," she said. Moments later, the moon reached the exact location and she tossed the gargoyle head into the grave then opened a small, blood-red pouch and poured the white powdery contents into the hole. Satisfied, she looked to the sky and screamed a few words in a language that was more animalistic than human, then stepped back and waited.

Time almost seemed to come to a stop. "If this doesn't work you receive nothing, you hear me… nothing," Arlin hissed.

"Patience," she growled. "It takes time for the magic to work."

Suddenly, a black smoke blasted from the hole and the pungent smell of sulfur filled the air.

Arlin crept to the hole and peered in expecting to see the underworld, but what he saw frightened him even more. Each bone had come alive and wiggled and squirmed like giant maggots making their way towards another. As they came into contact, they fused together at the joints until a skeleton lay where only a pile of bones once rested.

The ground began to rumble. Limbs on nearby trees shook violently shedding their leaves and then curled into haunting shapes while the grass nearby wilted.

Arlin fled behind a nearby headstone and watched.

The sky darkened as ash and soot fell like rain, and the painful tormented screams of those trapped in Hell could be heard.

As the smoke cleared a skeleton stood. The gargoyle head had grown to full size and blazing purple eyes burned in the sockets. Its teeth gnashed and a long black forked tongue lashed out at the woman.

"Is it you who summoned me… hag?" The voice shrieked a god-awful noise.

"It is I who have summoned you oh great one, but in the service of another," she answered.

The demons head jerked in painful movements while his boney hand shot forth, palm straight out and fingers stretched wide.

Arlin felt strange as if he was no longer in control of his body and was forced to walk. Hesitant, his body jerked and twisted in grotesque movements as he lumbered from behind the stone towards the thing that claimed ownership of his body. Tears leaked from his eyes and he wanted to scream but his mouth failed.

At the hole, Arlin crumbled to the ground and looked up at the demon. Maggots crawled, squirmed, and wiggled all over the bones and fell in large piles.

"Why have you forced me from my home and brought me to this world?" The demon hissed.

"To find the answers to a question that haunts me," Arlin answered. His voice was barely audible and the words broken.

The demon shot a wicked glance at the witch then back to Arlin. "And did this witch tell you there's a price that must be paid?"

"Yes," Arlin said, he found the strength to stand.

"And it will be extracted at a time of my choosing?"

"Yes," Arlin said. "She also told me that the payment cannot include soul possession."

The demon let out a laugh that cracked nearby tombstones. "And why would I want your soul, I receive thousands each year." The skeleton waived a hand and a man appeared but he was semi-translucent. On his knees, he cried out in sheer terror. Both eyes were gouged out and on his forehead, the words TRAITOR glowed brightly. Each finger was broken and disfigured while long slashes across his back were evidence he had been whipped by something not from this world. "Here is my latest." The demon let out a wheezing laugh.

Arlin cringed at the sight.

"Ask your question," the demon hissed in a voice which almost sounded human. "I wish to stay in this pitiful world no longer."

Arlin thought for a moment. When he was sure what he wanted to ask, he looked straight into the demon's burning eyes, "where are the locations of those who save the bearer?" He figured this way if there was more than one he would discover the location of all.

The demon thought for a moment, looked towards the sky and his eyes flared. With one bony finger, he drew a flaming circle in the air. Within the circle, an image formed and Arlin was now looking down from high above. From here he could see there were five people, the bearer, a lizard from the Anor, a barbarian from the north, an elf from Rhunsiire, and then he saw him, older, but the features were still recognizable, his half-brother Demetrius. They all were sitting around a campfire at a spot he knew not two days from the Lost Sanctuary. The fire around the circle fluttered and died taking the image with it.

"I have shown you their location," the demon snarled. "In time, you will be contacted by one of my agents for payment when I decide what I want." As he finished speaking the skeleton burst into flames and fell to a pile of smoking ash.

The area turned deathly silent only broken by Arlin's heavy breathing.

"I don't know what the demon will want, it varies depending on its needs," the witch said, "but I take my payment upon services rendered." She produced a small test tube and a needle.

Arlin was hesitant to pay, but who knows what kind of hex this witch would invoke upon him if he refused, so he held his hand out. Her grip was vice-like as she pricked the end of one finger and squeezed until a single drop of blood fell into the tube.

"Payment in full," she said with a giggle

Arlin tried to ask her one final question, but she was gone.

Chapter 22

Normally Pegan was the first to rise. He would have a fire burning, breakfast cooking, and hot water ready for them to wash by the time the others woke but on this day, he rose last. His body ached and he felt as if he slept with his back arched across the giant root of a sycamore tree. All around him there was movement as his companions went about completing what needed to be done. A loud pop drew his attention to the pile of red-hot embers which sparkled against the morning sun while the smell of cooked meat weighed heavy on the cool air. High above, a flock of birds resembled a poofy cloud as they drifted past.

"You're awake," Averie said.

Pegan rubbed a bit of crust from his eyes and stretched till his arms neared dislocation, "I overslept. You should have woke me hours ago."

"You needed the rest," she answered. "What I did for you was no different from what you have done for us, besides, you looked exhausted." She brought him over a small bowl of food.

Pegan nodded, "no argument there."

"Where do we go next?" Thathra asked.

"We'll follow the plains for a day then drift back into the mountains and wait for darkness. Saress can use her vision to detect any patrols and hopefully our passing will go uneventful."

With breakfast consumed they set out. The grasslands were easily traveled and they put a good distance behind them. As dusk fell,

Pegan led them deep into the mountains where travel became much more grueling.

"Why did you bring us back into the mountains so soon?" Lorandrial complained after Pegan brought them to a halt next to a large horse sized boulder.

"The Lost Sanctuary is just over the next ridge. To be caught anywhere between here and there will not be favorable as the Brotherhood claims these lands as their own, and anyone who is caught passing is considered criminals and prosecuted by a biased jury."

"And if we get caught?" Thathra asked.

Pegans face went pale. "The baby she now carries will be aborted and she'll be forced to carry one of theirs. Lord Rayne will expect her to produce a male child every year until the ravages of time take her health, then she'll be discarded. It's common for the Brotherhood to keep women for breeding." Pegan pointed at Lorandrial and Thathra. "You both will spend months in the torture chamber while new techniques are perfected and Saress will be skinned alive and her hide made into armor." Pegan sighed, "I can't even imagine the things they will do to me when my identity is discovered."

Averie's face lost all expression and then she threw up. "We have to turn back. I won't take this risk," she said through a trembling lower lip.

"Easy now," Saress said. "We ain't been caught yet and we'll pass in the cover of night. We've come too far to turn back now. It's a risk were all taking."

An awkward silence filled the air only broken by Averies sobs of what the future might hold.

"Tell me more about this city?" Lorandrial changed the subject.

"The Lost Sanctuary was previously known as the City of Skyn. It was a great city where the bearer's child would live when they returned. It was where the knowledge was stored that they brought with them."

"What knowledge are you talking about?" Lorandrial asked.

"I don't know," Pegan said. "It's rumored of those who returned, that they brought with them the knowledge on how to build great things, wondrous inventions that stole your breath, cures for things we could only dream of, and marvelous machines that could do the work of a hundred men."

"And you believed all this nonsense?"

"Yes… yes I did," Pegan said. "This is also where the hammer stroke hit the hardest during the Great War. Demons crashed down upon this city like none other and when they were finished nothing remained."

"Why… why would they want to destroy such wonderful things?" Averie asked.

"Because knowledge is power, power the underworld wishes us not to have," Pegan answered.

Lorandrial shook his head in disbelief, "and you know this how?"

"I've read it in tomes, History of the Old World, History of the Great War. This is a history that will repeat itself unless we make a change and it starts with getting Averie to the Isle of Aramoor."

"I hate just sitting here doing nothing," Thathra said. "Let's just pass this place and put this trouble behind us."

"We still have a few hours until it's dark enough to pass unseen. I suggest we relax because the next few hours will be harrowing," Pegan advised.

They remained hidden until the sky turned black then continued on their way. Far below the summit, the skeletal remains of a great city came into view. Jutting up from the ground their broken outline slashed the horizon. Sporadic torches looked like matches in the darkness and the place held onto an eerie timeless feeling as if the world forgot it existed. Time slowed as they passed and it was only once the city was well behind them they each drew an easy breath.

During their travels it was apparent Saress was bothered by something and suddenly seemed filled with a strange hate, or anger. "Tell me…" Her eyes burned like the sun. "How many children did you sire against their will?"

The accusation hit Pegan like a mallet and he wasn't sure if Saress was truly being sincere with her statement. "None…. I killed, maimed, and tortured without remorse but never took a woman against her will."

Saress turned away, disbelief still on her face like grease from a left-over meal.

"I tell the truth," Pegan pleaded his arms flung wide.

"We should go," Averie said. "This place breeds anger even among friends, I can feel it gnawing at us standing here."

"I agree," Thathra said. As he turned to leave the click of a crossbow caught his attention.

"What have we here," A squeaky voice cackled.

All around them men formed from the darkness and soon they found themselves surrounded. Each man wore black leather armor and their faces were hidden behind blackened silk masks.

"If any of you move, you'll die before your next breath," another said. His voice was deep and throaty. He was dressed the same as the others except his face bore a blood-red mask.

Thathra studied the enemy but there were too many and they moved at a blistering pace. To attack now would only be suicidal.

Saress slumped, she let her anger blind her mind and allowed them to be snuck upon. She wished they would kill her first. She would not fight them if it meant her friends were guaranteed a free passage, but she knew better. There was nothing she could do but follow their directives.

"Search and bind them," the red-masked man barked.

Satisfied all weapons were seized they were each bound and led down the mountain at a frantic pace. "Quickly now," the man urged on his comrades.

Averie sighed as they entered the town. She had never seen such wanton destruction in all her life. Fine gray silt covered everything as if it had not been touched in decades. Stone buildings reduced to rubble were laid out as far as she could see and wooden beams lay burned and splintered as if picked up and thrown by a giant. The streets were littered with wood, glass, stone, twisted metal, and bone. The buildings still standing teetered on the verge of collapse while the deafening silence left a strange ringing in their ears.

They wound their way through town and eventually came to a building that was missing the southern half. Led through multiple rooms, they arrived at a thick door bound with knobby steel that lay flat on the floor. It looked strangely out of place as if it fell from Heaven and this was its final resting place. Two men materialized from the darkness while a third opened the door. Narrow rickety wooden steps partially lit by a single lantern spiraled down into the ground.

"Seems odd they would show us the entrance to their compound?" Thathra whispered to Pegan.

"Because more than likely, we won't survive to tell anybody," he whispered back. He had escorted many people down these stairs and not one re-emerged… alive.

Averie expected the place to be dark and damp with tree roots and worms poking through dirt walls but her eyes widened in amazement when they reached the bottom. The entrance hall was impeccable. An obsidian stone floor polished to a mirror-like finish went as far as she could see, while perlite walls sparkled in the amber light produced by gold-plated lanterns that hung on silver hooks.

Forced to walk single file, they wound their way deeper into the complex until they arrived at an enormous oak door polished till it glistened. The one with the red mask tapped on the door in a random series—obviously a code—then stepped back. Moments later, the door swung inward allowing them access.

The hair on Averie's neck stood erect like an angry cat. It was not the blood red tiles that lined the floors, wall, and ceiling, nor the man at the back that dangled from a rusty black chain impregnated with tiny barbs that dug into his flesh, or even the pregnant woman strapped in a chair, her dress splattered with blood and every finger fashionably broken. It was the man who sat behind a decorative, black walnut desk. The top which is covered in every type of cutting, or torturous instruments only a twisted mind could conceive. His feet propped up on the surface of the desk and leaning back in his chair, he casually swallowed the last bite of his apple. When their eyes met, his mouth curled upward into a sadistic smile and he licked his blackened lips.

Forced to stand before him in a row like products on display at the market, they waited. Only the harrowed sobs of the woman broke the silence.

The red-masked assassin approached the desk and bowed, "Lord Rayne, we caught them on the outskirts of town," he whispered. The lie was obvious in his smile, "no doubt looking to rob us."

"He lies," Thathra responded to the accusation. "We were a great distance from town when this band of thugs accosted us."

Lord Rayne smirked, "Master Murik, do you tell me the truth, the whole truth and nothing but the truth?" he asked.

"Yes," he responded, and then flashed Thathra a crooked smile.

Lord Rayne looked in their direction, the light from a candle glared off his piercing green eyes. "The court finds you all guilty of trespassing, and conspiracy to commit robbery, which are all punishable by death if I so choose?"

"That's not fair," Averie lashed out.

Of course, it was not fair, it was never meant to be. She was too naïve to understand the way of the Brotherhood, Pegan thought.

"Silence," Lord Rayne snarled, then methodically removed his feet from the table one leg at a time and stood.

He was taller than she expected and his prominent cheekbones and stiff jawline became visible.

"Or shall I add contempt of court to your growing list of charges?" Lord Rayne finished.

"Sir," Murik produced a long black baton. "The mouthy one is in the early stages of pregnancy, no doubt carrying the child of this criminal." He hit Pegan hard across the back of his knees driving him to the ground. "Shall I abort the child and have her carry mine?" He cracked a broken smile then begun to unfasten her dress.

Saress hissed in his direction and struggled against the bindings but they never gave.

Murik studied the lizard, "You'll make a fine pair of boots and matching gloves."

"My Lord," a third man called out as he approached. In one hand he carried a bloody ice pick, and in the other he swung an eyeball by the cord. "I have done every form of punishment upon her and yet she still refuses to confess. His brown tunic was splattered with blood.

"Perhaps we need another method." Lord Rayne snapped his fingers from having gained a renewed idea, then addressed Murik, "enough with her for now, we got plenty of time. Bring in the woman's boy."

Lord Rayne made his way to the woman then forced the boy to kneel before her so she could see the tears streaming down the child's face. "Look at him?" Lord Rayne screamed at the woman.

Averie almost fainted as she looked at the woman. Her face was swollen and bruised and one eye had been plucked.

She began to sob once more as Lord Rayne held a knife to the child. "Confess of your crimes now or I'll cut his throat?"

"You bastard," the hanging man screamed. "Leave the child alone."

Lord Rayne never hesitated as he spun and sliced the man's throat. Blood flowed like water over a dam painting his bared chest red.

From there it flowed down each leg and then dripped from each foot creating a large puddle.

"Are you willing to confess your guilt now?" He edged the bloody blade up against the skinny neck till a trickle of blood began.

The woman cried, "I'm sorry, I cannot confess, I am not the bearer."

"Then he dies," Lord Rayne said, his eyes locked onto her face.

"Wait," Averie screamed. She fell to her knees. "Let her go, she's not the bearer... I am."

Lord Rayne threw the child to the ground and faced Averie, "what did you say?" he asked, his voice almost sounded polite.

"I'm the bearer," she repeated. "Kill me not her, let this curse end now."

"I'm so proud of you," Saress said. "It takes courage to offer your life to save the life of another. Our tale ends here, but in the next life, you'll walk with your head held high. It's rumored in Heaven you're rewarded for your acts of kindness done here, your reward will be significant."

Lord Rayne sat back at his desk then addressed Master Murik, "get the woman and her child out of here. I grow tired of the sobbing and besides, I got more pressing matters that need to be addressed."

"Am I to be killed?" Averie asked.

Lord Rayne ignored the question as he studied each of them. Unable to tell by their looks he blatantly asked, "Which one of you knows Elwrick?"

Pegan knew torture would come to all if none spoke so to save the pain from his companions he confessed, "I was the one he first contacted, I was the one who killed the keeper, and I was the one who helped her escape. My companions should not be held accountable for my actions."

Lord Rayne finally answered Averie. "My dear, your death has not even been considered, yet. It seems your future is based solely on this man's ability." An evil smile returned to his face. "It seems we may be able to come to some sort of agreement to earn your release, along with your companions."

"I have a hard time making a deal with a man who would kill a boy in front of his tortured mother," Pegan said.

Lord Rayne suddenly seemed agitated. He moved with great

speed to stand before Averie, his bloody blade pressed against her belly, "I know what you carry and to be truthful, I couldn't care less whether it, or you live. My men might be upset as you're quite pretty. I know," he smiled and walked away then turned back. "I could have a tournament, a training tool if you would. He who wins a different challenge each day gets you for the night. A little extra incentive to make them train harder as the ones we have now are quite worn and dated. A fresh face would bring on a new level of motivation. That is, of course, after I have grown tired of you and the child has been disposed of. No one wishes to pleasure themselves on a woman carrying a wretched creature." Lord Rayne found his way back to his seat and plopped his feet back up on the desk.

Pegan knew there was no lie in this man's words, "what would you ask of me?" Pegan asked.

Lord Rayne laughed and slapped the desk, "Ain't it funny how a few simple words can completely change a man's attitude. Get you to do things you never dreamed possible." He motioned to a man hidden in the shadows, "Remove his bindings and provide our friend here with a seat, I don't strike deals with prisoners."

Pegan sat in the provided chair, aware of the guard on each side and the knife at his back.

"Do I know you?" Lord Rayne asked when their eyes met. "It seems I've met you somewhere."

"I don't believe so," Pegan answered. "You're rather…unforgettable."

"Hmmm," Lord Rayne responded. "No matter the difference I suppose. I will be as forthcoming with you as possible. You want your friends to live and be released, I can offer that. But in return, I want something only you can provide."

"And what might that be which I have that you cannot get?"

Lord Rayne rose and walked around for a moment, his hands behind his back he seemed deep in thought. "What I seek is a magical weapon only you can acquire. One that will bring me to the pinnacle of perfection, and with it my abilities will become so profound, none would even consider questioning me or the Brotherhood."

Pegan raised his eyebrows and his eyes opened wide.

"What I seek is Fel Strike, a dagger created in the bowels of the Silver Mountains by a long-deceased race of dwarves."

Pegan shook his head with what he just heard, "I know nothing of such a weapon so how can I possibly fulfill this request. You simply provide me with an agreement you know I cannot keep to justify holding these innocent people captive for no other reason than for your own pleasure, or torment."

Lord Rayne laughed hysterically, "I would not expect your insignificant little mind to understand. I know you cannot provide the weapon, but what you can provide is Elwrick."

"What?" Pegan had a bewildered look.

"You've told me yourself you were contacted by him, now all I wish is for you to bring him here and upon his arrival, your friends will be allowed to walk free."

"Unharmed?" Pegan asked.

"Completely," Lord Rayne answered. "But you must also understand time is of the essence. I cannot wait a lifetime for him. I will offer you fourteen days. If he has not shown by then, one companion will die each day until none are left except her. Then I will begin the tournaments."

Pegan tried not to smile, but he knew now he had a chance to save his friends. "I have a few demands of my own, four in all," Pegan said.

"I don't believe you are in a position to demand anything."

"Then I am prepared to die with my friends," Pegan said, he hoped his bluff worked.

Lord Rayne believed he was bluffing, but the risk was too high. He had waited too long for this opportunity so he was now forced to play the game. "What are your requests?" he asked.

"First, I need my weapons returned," Pegan said.

Lord Rayne nodded his approval.

"Second, they are to be fed and not mistreated."

Lord Rayne thought for a moment and then agreed.

"Third, I want an assassin's agreement."

Lord Rayne looked at his palm and all the scars from his long history of deal-making. Reluctant at first, he finally accepted it.

For the last request, Pegan leaned in close so only Lord Rayne could hear. "They get to keep their clothes." His mouth smiled up into a wicked grin that mimicked Lord Rayne's. He knew this last demand would startle Lord Rayne. How could a stranger know that prisoners were stripped naked, unless he had been here before.

"No," Lord Rayne hissed. "It is my policy to strip captives; it prevents them from hiding any weapons they may have gained."

"No," Pegan whispered. "It's to morally break and shame them. If you won't agree with my four demands then no deal." He backed away and stood beside them.

Lord Rayne drew a deep sigh, "You got fourteen days."

"You have not met my last demand."

"I met it with our agreement to let you leave," Lord Rayne argued.

With his weapons returned, Pegan slashed his palm and held it out. Droplets of blood splashed against the desk. Lord Rayne did likewise and then they clasped hands allowing their blood to touch.

Pegan kissed Averie and told her he would be back and no harm would befall her. Next, he kissed Saress on the snout and whispered the same.

"I know you will, I have faith in you," Saress whispered.

"Fourteen days, then one dies," Lord Rayne reminded him.

A tear found Averies cheek as she watched Pegan walk from the room.

"He won't forget us, have faith," Thathra whispered.

Averie shivered as Murik ran a hand down her back, "shall we strip them?" he asked.

Rayne looked at his bloody palm. "No, not till the fourteenth day. Then do with them as you will. Until then, put them in the dungeon."

The dungeon was like Hell compared to the surface. The air was stale and reeked with the fumes of urine and feces. Rats squealed and scurried, their claws scratched at the stone floor as they fought to find darkness as the guards passed with lit torches. The high-pitched squeak and clang of metal doors opening and closing sent shivers up Averie's spine as they approached their new home. The memory of a painful past returned.

Each cell was small, windowless, and constructed of solid granite with a small door made of hardened steel bars.

With the barbarian and the elf secured they now turned to Saress. "What should we do with that thing?" one assassin asked. "The door is much to small for her to fit through."

"She will if we cut her in half," a second assassin offered his opinion.

The assassin let out a hearty laugh, "I would love to, but, unfortunately, Lord Rayne says we have to keep them alive, for now."

The other assassin looked up and down the hall and noticed the big iron rings attached to the wall at multiple places used to hold prisoners for torture or entertainment. "I know what we'll do," he said and walked away but returned moments later dragging a bundle of chains and ropes. With his partners help, they soon had Saress shackled to the wall by her neck, arms, legs, and tail, while a thick rope was wrapped around her snout multiple times then securely tied with multiple knots.

Averie was purposely placed in last as the guard followed her inside the cell. He seemed to be in no hurry as he searched through a massive key ring till he found the one he wanted and unlocked a steel collar that hung from a chain fastened to the ceiling. "Don't move," he ordered, then placed the collar around her neck and clasped it shut and locked it. "Lord Rayne ordered extra security with you sweetheart," he said, and then eased his hands across her chest groping everything as he went.

Averie did all she could to keep from vomiting from the touch.

Satisfied they were all secured he walked away, paused, then backed up and spit a big glob on Saress then left laughing.

Chapter 23

Pegan eyed the three assassins who guarded the entrance. The thought to kill them crossed his mind, but he knew better. He could walk away and never look back guaranteeing himself freedom, but his companions would suffer tremendously for his actions. No, he had to wait but made a promise to himself. Before the ravages of time took his body and left him old and crippled, he would return and make memories worthy of songs.

For now, his plans were simple, but the execution would be extremely dangerous. He would have to travel the southern region of the Cursed Desert at a point nearly twice the distance of their earlier crossing, and much more unforgiving. From there, he would return to Rhunsiire and beg Lady Alenia—that is if the uprising had been squashed by now—to contact Elwrick and tell him of his failure. Elwrick was wise and knew more than Pegan ever gave him credit for, the wise old one would know what to do.

Besides the desert with its burning heat and lack of water, he had other problems to contend with. Mating season is in full swing for the sandworms which inhabited the region making them hungry, angry, and extremely territorial. Now a strange unwanted feeling told him he was also being followed.

Pegan casually walked as he crossed the compound and made his way to an enormous stone which looked to have been there since the beginning of time. Leaned sideways, it protruded from the ground like a giant tooth and do to its bent and twisted shape, it had thus been nicknamed decades ago The Devils Fang do to its blackened color and bent and twisted shape.

From here he viewed the Lost Sanctuary in its entirety. Immense piles of rubble someone once called home lay strewn and the slight trace of a long since destroyed perimeter wall remained visible. The once glorious ponds and fountains lay dry and if he listened closely, he could almost hear a weeping cry carried on the light breeze.

Pegan had not climbed The Devil's Fang to sight-see, or reminisce about the past. He climbed it to get a better look at who is following him, take note of where the assassins were stationed for observations, and the most direct route out of the Lost Sanctuary after his companions were freed. Something told him even if he did get Elwrick to come, a fight would still be required to escape.

From high above he could clearly spot his followers. There are four, and they seemed rather young and extremely inexperienced to be given such a difficult task, especially since he felt Lord Rayne knew his true identity. The ability to hide in shadows unseen is one of the first skills taught, but even now he could clearly see them fidgeting with their tunics, or playing with the end of a blade. Lord Rayne though never did anything without a purpose, a purpose Pegan felt he would discover later, probably at the end of a blade.

Alone, Pegan traveled at a swift pace and yet somehow he never grew weary. His muscles should have felt worn yet he felt rested and his breathing came not in heavy spasms, but light as if he was only on a brisk stroll and that was when he remembered the words of Elwrick so long ago…

—The dagger has magic and senses the needs of its owner, how it will affect you I cannot say.

Pegan stood at the edge of the mountains looking out over the shimmering sands. He could already feel the sweat percolate from every pore on his body and his tunic stuck to his chest and back. Behind him, he could hear his followers finally arrive. In his haste, he failed to hide his trail and thus they easily tracked him, albeit a good distance behind.

Pegan waited till the sky turned purple and the sun was below the horizon before he entered. His movements were purposely slow, each step meticulously calculated. He had no desire to disturb that which lurks below the surface.

Slow and steady he traveled through the night and when dawn broke, he found himself at the peak of a large razorback and studied his direction. He had not been here for decades and to lose his way now would prove hazardous to his health. Satisfied he was still on course he started down when he located a young vibrant green cactus. Not wanting to kill the plant he poked only a small hole into it and allowed enough water to flow filling his flasks. He had never seen such blue water come from a cactus. Quickly, he plugged the puncture with sand to make sure the cactus would survive when the words he feared most came…

Murderer… killer…

Pegan wiped the sweat from his face. Is it the cactus talking? Did he do the unthinkable and kill the defenseless innocent life form.

Murderer… killer… it came again… stronger.

"I have to survive," he whispered to the cactus as if he was talking to an old friend.

Murderer… killer…

Pegan remembered Saress and what she said… omen. Something bad is going to occur.

Placing the flask back in his satchel a wave of sand slid past—was this a warning from the eyes? Were they actually helping him? He tied the string on his satchel when another wave, much larger than the first passed. Instinctively, he leaped to his feet, each hand held a weapon.

"Give me your supplies," the assassin hissed, the low pulled cowl kept his face hidden in the shadows.

"You take my supplies and I'll die out here. You should have come more prepared," Pegan said pointing his blade at the wannabe assassin.

He cocked the bow and took aim. "I won't ask you again. Give me the satchel and you might survive, otherwise, I can personally guarantee you won't." He let out a cackling laugh.

Pegan had no choice and tossed the bag to the man who caught it with one hand. "You're not as dumb as you look," he said, then ran away.

A thousand thoughts raced through Pegan's mind as to what he should do when he felt the subtle yet distinct vibrations in the ground. What he should have done was curl up into a ball yet his curiosity got the better of him and he began to crawl up the side of the dune. What he witnessed at the top left him horrified.

A thunderous boom cracked and sand violently erupted as a sandworm breached the surface. The blinding quick assault surprised the assassin who had no chance to counter and fell into the open maw of the creature. Only his arms splayed arms kept him from being swallowed whole.

The thing looked like an overgrown earthworm at nearly twenty feet long and four feet around. Sandy brown skin harder than scale coated the body, and while one end was shaped like a fish's tail, the front has a circular mouth ringed in jagged, twisted, dagger length teeth. Its long body twisted and thrashed in mid-air as the mouth clamped down upon the victim with such force it cleaved the assassin in two. One half was instantly devoured, while the other sailed through the air leaving the entrails to flap like flags in the wind only to land a good distance away with a sickening splat.

Observing the horror, the others abandoned their mission and ran which Pegan instantly recognized as a fatal mistake. He had spent a great deal of time studying these creatures and knew how they functioned. Completely blind, they hunted by small, almost invisible fibers called feelers that covered every inch of their body and detects movement on the surface. If you walked slowly, it was possible to pass undetected, but a man running sent subtle vibrations that foretold their location, which made them easy prey.

The trio made it over the next dune then vanished from sight when the bloodbath began. He couldn't see the carnage but the screams, cries, flying sand, and thunderous booms told him the worms were having a feast.

Pegan remained motionless till the worms finished and moved on before he went back to find his satchel. To his dismay, his satchel is ripped in a thousand pieces, his flasks are empty and smashed to bits, his food is no longer edible, and the jar of protective salve is possibly floating in the stomach of one of those worms.

Pegan wanted to cry as he knew what lie ahead and to turn back was not an option. Adjusting his clothes to provide the best cover from the relentless sun, he wandered out into the blistering heat and shimmering sand… alone and unprepared.

The elf moved with blazing speed. Trees passed in a blur, limbs slashed at his face and his chest heaved in spasms as his lungs struggled to replace lost air. Even as he leaped from limb to limb, his feet moved in a flurry of motion as if he ran on the wind. He landed in a crouch and let his movement carry his slender form forward as he sprung to another tree. As he hit the ground he dived into a roll which carried him back to his feet then on to his destination… Gleia.

He bounded up the stairs three at a time until he came to a small landing with an irregularly shaped door. Under normal circumstances, he would have knocked first and waited, but these were not normal circumstances and burst right in.

Gleia leaped to her feet at the intrusion knocking her experiment to the floor. Glass shattered and a purple liquid hissed and steam rose as it spread. The scent of burnt wood instantly filled the air. "You imbecile!" she screamed and tossed a handful of rags on the spill.

The young elf covered his elongated ears to buffer the sound and tears filled his eyes.

"You better have a good reason for this."

It was only after he took a deep breath did he finally speak. "It's Pegan! He's on his way here and his condition is dire. He kept mumbling incoherently about a capture, assassins, Elwrick, Lady Alenia. There might have been something in there about the end of the world as well. I don't know for sure, he was so hard to understand."

Gleia ran to the door and looked to see if anyone followed. "Who else have you told?" she snapped.

"No one, I promise," the youngster pleaded. "Ryul told me to come straight here and not say a word."

She had known Ryul all her life. He is extremely wise and bore an air of authority. No wonder the youngster barged in. She would have done the same if he commanded that of her. "How long till they arrive?" she asked.

"Soon," he answered. "They were right behind me on the horse, but then I took to the trees and cross cut the forest to arrive here first to inform you."

"Watch outside and warn me if anyone comes," she said, and then gathered a combination of salve, bandages, vials, creams, lotions and a multitude of other things from a cabinet she might need for a man who spent time in the desert. With her arms loaded to the point of breaking, she headed back towards the desk where she laid everything out.

"Here they come," the elf advised.

Gleia gasped. Pegan was apple red and every piece of exposed skin was covered in large gray bubbly blisters that leaked a yellowish fluid. His upper lip had swollen till it touched his nose and both eyes lacked pupils. His lower lip was split from end to end and a blood dried crust covered his chin. Incoherently, he kept mumbling something but his swollen tongue blocked half his mouth.

"Help me strip his clothes," she ordered Ryul.

Pegan howled like a banshee as each piece was painfully removed taking with it long strips of skin exposing ugly patches of shiny pink flesh.

"I'm sorry… I'm sorry," Gleia kept repeating until she had a naked man laying on the table. "Now off to the ice tub."

Pegan fought like a madman, but he was no match for Ryuls strength and was eventually forced into the tub of cool water.

She could see the relief on Pegan's face, he finally began to relax.

Only now did she address the youngster, "get Lady Alenia now, but not a word to no-one he is here, do you understand me?" she said.

He nodded and left.

Gleia opened Pagan's eyes and waved a candle before them checking for a response, anything, just something to show he had not gone insane. "We may be too late," she said shaking her head negatively.

Lady Alenia entered in a rush, almost taking the door free of its hinges. Near the back Gleia leaned over a porcelain tub. Her hands working feverishly rubbing an ointment onto Pegan's arms. On her way, she grabbed a three-legged stool then sat beside the druid. "What happened to him? Is he going to make it? Is there anything I can do to help?" She fired off a line of questions.

"Only time will tell," Gleia answered. "Right now the most important thing is to get him cooled down, perhaps tomorrow we will know more." She grabbed a different tube of salve and spread the light yellow cream colored goop onto his face.

"What happened to him?" Lady Alenia questioned Ryul, "Did you not find him?"

"I don't know," he answered. "I was keeping watch as ordered and I saw this black dot appear in the distance. At first I thought it was nothing, but then it moved so I went to investigate. I didn't know it was Pegan until he fell into my arms."

"Was he alone?" Gleia asked. "There may be others out there who need our help."

"No," Ryul answered, "he was alone."

Pegan remained in the tub the remainder of the day and well into the night until his temperature dropped then they moved him to a bed. Gleia coated his entire body with a bluish salve except for his face which received a purple colored cream.

Lady Alenia sat at his side and held his hand as if he was her mate.

Two days would pass before the fever broke and he could put together a coherent enough sentence they understood.

"Can you tell us what happened?" Lady Alenia asked, she still held his hand while Gleia stood at the foot of the bed, still monitoring his condition.

The process was painstakingly slow but eventually, Pegan revealed to them everything that occurred since they left.

Lady Alenia was furious, "Ryul," she called out. "Ready your men. It's time we eradicate this scourge known as the Brotherhood."

"No," Pegan found the strength to scream. "They still hold my companions and if you attack, they'll surely be killed. I must speak with Elwrick first and then get them out safely."

Lady Alenia listened to his words and knew he was right. The Brotherhood could be dealt with at a later date, would be dealt with at a later date, that she made a promise. Unfortunately, Elwrick was there only days before Pegan's arrival and would not be able to return anytime soon, this left her with only one choice. She would have to send Pegan to him.

Chapter 24

few days later Pegan was summoned to a private meeting with Lady Alenia at her personal residence. His skin was still severely blistered and the mere thought of putting his clothes back on brought on a fear worse than another encounter with Rimdruziahl. Gleia though offered the perfect solution, a full-length robe made of cotton which felt soft and smooth against his skin and somehow held a strange, but invigorating cooling property. With Gleia at his side—she was the only one permitted at Pegan's request—they made their way across Rhunsiire.

"Why would she summon me here and not just come see me?" he asked.

"I don't know," she answered. "But I am pleased she honored your request to have me come because I would like some answers myself. You really are in no condition yet to be out of bed."

"Hmm," Pegan mumbled. "Possibly the uprising has something to do with it. Could the rebellious elves have discovered my return, and she feels I'm safer at her home than in the ward?"

She helped him up a few steps to a bench where he sat to rest. His breathing grew labored and his face tired. "No," she said, and then sat beside him. "The uprising turned out to be nothing more than a fabrication created in the mind of a sick individual and we've yet to discover the perpetrator. Lady Alenia has sworn when she does, they will pay significantly for their deceit."

"Strange, why would someone want to start a rumor like that?"

"That I can't answer," she sighed. "I'm sure Lady Alenia will discover the truth and when she does, I would want to be that elf. By the grace of the Creator, I have never seen her so angry in all my life."

"All twenty years of it?" Pegan laughed.

She laughed so hard she almost fell backwards off the bench. In truth, she was probably that times fifteen. "Twenty-five, thank you very much," she answered.

Lady Alenia met them at the door and ushered them both in. She gave Gleia a long hard hug, then offered Pegan a slight kiss on the cheek. "I'm glad you both could make it," she said. "There is something I feel you both should know and if I wait much longer, it might become detrimental to our situation."

Pegan could see the woman had a distraught look on her face as if dire news waited in the shadows.

"But why here if I may ask?" Gleia said. "Pegan really is in no condition to travel."

"I'm sorry and I apologize for any discomfort I may have caused, but it is imperative what I am about to say remain highly secretive. At this time I am unsure who I can trust, beyond you two and Elwrick," she said, and then made her way to the window and glanced out. "Therefore, I have placed a very powerful deafness spell upon my residence."

"Can I sit," Pegan asked. He could feel his knees growing weak and wished not to fall in the Queen's presence.

"We should all sit," she answered.

Lady Alenia took his hand in hers, and when she spoke her voice was drained of all emotion. "Tell me, what do you understand about the Ebreuphere?"

Pegan searched his mind but the name evaded him. "Nothing, never heard of it."

Gleia's eyes perked open and she sat up in her chair. Unlike Pegan, she had heard of it and knew it was something to do with a boundary, a boundary that separated good and evil, a boundary that fell once which allowed the demons from the underworld to spill forth into theirs.

"What about the Fabric of Odure?"

Pegan shook his head no.

"No, no, no, no," Gleia begged. She leaped from the chair and backed away till she was tight against the wall. She was only a small child when the boundary fell last and never participated in the war but she remembered the carnage as if it happened yesterday.

"Shhhh," Lady Alenia tried to calm her.

Gleia sat and tried to look strong but Pegan could see the fear which lived right behind the skin of her eyes. Lady Alenia had brought up something which terrified the elf.

"Let me explain. The Ebreuphere, also known as the Fabric of Odure is the barrier that was put in place by the Creator at the beginning of time, to separate our world from the underworld."

"You mean realms, like where Elwrick lives?"

"No," she responded. "Realms are kept within the same fabric of time and space, a parallel universe if you will."

Pegan looked confused.

"In order for you to understand, I have to go back to the beginning of time. Long before you and I, or Elwrick walked this land. The world was new and wonderful and he filled it with a race of beings he called angels. They were extremely powerful and could do wondrous things with magic, things our simple brains could never fathom."

She paused to fill three glasses of grape wine and handed them each one before continuing. "As time went on, these angles began to question the Creator and felt they could make things better. The Creator denied their request for change and they became angry."

She took a sip of wine and savored its flavor. "Ultimately, a war erupted in the Heavens between those who rebelled against the Creator, and those who agreed with the Creator. It was short lived from my understanding, only hours, but the results were horrific. This is where the Ebreuphere comes into play. The Creator had to come up with something to separate those who rebelled, so he created the underworld, more commonly known as Hell. And this barrier keeps them from entering our world."

"Okay," Pegan slowly said. "Then what are realms?"

Lady Alenia scratched her forehead then went to a basket across the room and grabbed an apple. "Picture this apple as the world.

Everything you see, trees, grass, the blue sky, the stars, they are all contained within this apple."

Pegan studied the apple trying to imagine that small red object with a long stem and green leaf as the world. "Okay," he agreed.

Next, she removed a small knife and carefully sliced the apple into ten different sections then spread them out so one just barely laid on top of the edge of the other. "Now," she giggled at her own marvel. "As you can see it's still the same world, just cut into layers." She pointed at one slice, "this here is Icearaus, the world as you know it." Then she pointed at another slice. "This here would be the Realm of Light where Elwrick is from. As you can see it's still the same world, just a different layer."

"I think I now understand," he said.

"Have you ever had an experience where you thought you saw something but nothing was there, just a faint glimpse, a passing sight sort of."

"Of course," Pegan said.

Lady Alenia smiled, "that's usually where the realms intersect. You are getting a brief glance into another realm."

"And Elwrick has the ability to go from layer to layer?"

"Yes, but you must remember he is not mortal like you and me, even Averie. We are bound to this realm except for brief periods and if you do go to a new realm, death usually occurs within hours. Our bodies were not meant for other realms. This is our world and we have to make it the best place possible. The Creator has given us all the tools to make that happen."

"I understand now, but I still don't understand why we had to have this meeting here."

Lady Alenia's face went somber, "a few days ago I felt a tear in the fabric, a million souls screamed out in anguish. A demon had come through the fabric."

"But you said that they cannot pass through the barrier," Pegan said.

"They can't on their own accord. They can only enter our realm if someone from here summons them. This person though must be well trained in the dark arts and strong. Not physically but mentally. There are many that say they can talk with the underworld but their frauds. Few truly exist that have this ability."

"So you're worried there might be another Great War?" Gleia asked.

"I don't believe so, this demon came through with another purpose, a purpose of gathering or giving information. I responded quickly to the location of the demon. It had all the signs, plants withered and dead, the rank smell of sulfur and decay, bones turned to ash. Unfortunately, I was too late. The demon had returned through the tear back to the underworld. This is a good thing because the tear was restored upon his return."

"What makes you think this demon was only looking for information, not possibly scouting to see if another war was possible?" Pegan asked.

"Because the encounter took place in a graveyard. The body had been exhumed and the bones turned to dust. That tells me the demon was looking for information about the body which was in that grave."

"So whose grave was it?" Gleia asked.

"Pegan's," she answered.

"Mine," Pegan looked startled. "My body was never in that grave."

Lady Alenia took his hand and their eyes met, "The body in the grave is just the conduit needed to connect with the underworld. The name on the headstone is what's significant. Make no mistake. For some unknown reason, whoever summoned that demon was looking for information about you."

Pegan's face drained of color.

"So we need to track down whoever did this and find out why?" Gleia asked.

"That's not so easy," Lady Alenia sighed. "I cannot find them unless they are caught performing the ritual, but I have my suspicions."

"And," Pegan said.

"A long-dead necromancer, but we'll discuss that later. Right now, we need to make sure Elwrick is warned the Brotherhood searches for him.

"But how will you do that?" Pegan asked.

"I plan to send you to the Realm of Light."

"Didn't you just say I'll die if I go there?"

"You can survive long enough for him to hear your tale and send you back."

Pegan knew it needed to be done, he just didn't like the penalty for failure. "When do we begin?" he asked.

"Now," she answered. "Gleia needs to prepare you for travel. In one hour meet me at the scrying chamber."

"He's nowhere near ready for realm traveling? Gleia advised.

"We have no other choice. Elwrick must be warned and informed of the Brotherhood's plan."

"He will be," she said. "But in time though," Gleia argued.

"I don't know what the intentions are of whoever summoned that demon, but I can feel a dark evil here at work. It's like a thick icy sludge that seeps through my veins."

Gleia knew Pegan was not ready for what he was about to endure, but she had no choice. The Elf Queen had spoken.

An hour later Gleia cracked open the door just enough so she could see if anybody approached. Her eyes strained as she stared into the darkness. It was not until she felt comfortable it was safe that they snuck from the ward. They hurried down the stairs, crossed the main road, then vanished into the trees. It seemed to take hours but in all actuality only minutes had passed when they came to a secluded room buried deep back in the woods. As she reached for the door it opened on its own and they entered. Across the room, Lady Alenia stood at the bowl.

"Bring Pegan here, quickly, the spell has already been initiated," she said.

The door closed behind them as they entered.

Upon his arrival at the bowl, she grabbed his right hand with a grip of steel, then slammed her bladed right hand down into the bowl.

Pegan released a blood-curdling scream as if he were being pulled in a million different directions all at once, followed by an intense searing pain that erupted through every fiber of his being. He tried to rip his hand free but her grip was firm and held fast. Their eyes met only for a moment then he collapsed to his knees.

She had only performed this once and the results were disastrous. To use her own body as a conduit to transfer someone to another realm broke every natural and biological rule. Lady Alenia focused on the bowl and screamed the words to start the process.

Gleia stumbled away till her back hit the wall.

Lady Alenia appeared crazed, all around her a vortex of fog swirled and different colored lights flashed. Her hair flew wild in the wind and her dress whipped and thrashed till the ends tattered.

The pupils in Pegan's eyes turned blood red and each vessel black. He tried to open his mouth to speak then everything went black. There was no pain, no smells, no sounds, and no air.

He stood alone in the blackness, a darkened void of lifelessness but there was light. He could see it far off in the distance. A million little pinpricks in the blackened velvet sky. Over time, the pricks of light grew until Pegan realized they were coming directly at him and fear set in. He tried to move and his heart raced yet he found himself immobilized. Bigger and bigger they grew and faster they came, crackling with energy and burning with intensity. Pegan screamed, but no sound came. He could feel the hairs on his arms and neck stand erect. Quicker and quicker they came until the light passed him in long broken beams that crackled and hissed with power. As quick as they came they were gone, and he found himself back in the darkness of a bland void but only for a split second and then he stood in a room. It was a strange structure that lacked any solid features. Glowing green lines outlined where the walls should have met the floor and ceiling while a blue outline formed where a door and window should have been.

For not having a light source the room was unnaturally bright. He tried to raise a hand to shield his eyes which burned like fire, but his movements are lethargic and couldn't complete the simple task.

In time the walls solidified, but still held a transparent quality and there were candles, millions of candles floating on a sea of nonexistent air. Their flames flickered just above the wick and no wax melted. Each time he blinked new objects would appear while those already there faded.

Soon a desk formed and a person sat on a simple stool. They were nothing like Pegan had ever seen before. Featureless and radiating like a million suns. On the desk, Pegan saw an impossibly large black, leather-bound book open on the table and there was gold writing on the pages. Rapt in its studies the person was unaware of his arrival.

Suddenly, it stood and darted around the room at a pace Pegan's mind could not comprehend. It's almost as if the thing moved with a simple thought. One second he was there, the next completely across the room leaving behind a shimmering residual image which took seconds to blend back in with the original form.

"Pegan... how did you come to be in my realm?" There was confusion in the voice.

Pegan heard the voice long before the thing approached, but here it was now, standing before him.

"Pegan, it's me, Elwrick."

Pegan heard the voice before and it was indeed that of Elwrick but he had never seen the man before look like this.

"Where am I?" Pegan asked. He had completely forgotten what had transpired for him to be sent here.

"In my home, in the study to be exact," Elwrick answered.

"Lady Alenia—"

"She sent you?" Elwrick cut him off.

"Yes," Pegan said.

"It must be dire for her to risk sending you, she understands the consequences of sending a mortal to another realm."

"Avvveriee... ttthere gooonnna—"

"Easy now," Elwrick interrupted him once more. He could tell by the way Pegan slurred his speech delirium had already begun to set in and the realm was already causing intense damage to his fibers. He would need another way to gather the information Lady Alenia wanted him to have.

Unable to communicate effectively, Elwrick had no other choice but to relive a section of Pegans past and find out what she wanted him to know. With a palm pressed firmly against the mortals head that's exactly what he did, and then he understood. Before he finished, he whispered a few words and the raw skin on Pegans body instantly grew back and all the blisters vanished.

"She's not dead yet," Elwrick said. He hoped that information would bring relief to Pegan's aching heart.

"Why do they want you?" Pegan somehow managed to get out through jumbled gasps.

"I don't know, but I believe it's a trap. Lord Rayne has no intentions of letting them go, even after this meeting he requires for their release." Elwrick scratched his chin, "either way I must send you back now before the damage becomes irreversible," he said. Back at the desk he scribbled a note on a small piece of parchment and tucked it into a pocket on the robe, "read this upon your return, show it to no one."

Unlike his arrival, he remembered nothing about the return. His whole body convulsed in tremors and he screamed out in fear. Blood ran from his nose and ears as he hugged the pedestal. Although he couldn't see, he could feel strange hands all over his body. They were warm and soft and transferred a feeling of security. Wooziness came upon him and he faded into a deep sleep.

When he woke the next day, he found himself in a familiar bed. The pain was gone but the words Elwrick said kept pounding in his head—*read the note*. He reached into the pocket and searched, but the parchment was gone. Panicked, he frantically searched again.

The door opened and Gleia and Lady Alenia entered.

Pegan sat up to greet them, "Good morning Ladies."

"See you're doing much better," Gleia said.

"Your skills as a healer are simply remarkable," Pegan answered.

She released a hearty laugh, "I can't take credit, you were in bad shape when we sent you to see Elwrick, and he performed the healing. I wish I had only a slight percentage of his skills."

"How can that be? Elwrick is prohibited from healing mortals, he told me that."

"I can't explain it either," Lady Alenia said. "We're both hoping you would give us some insight into his world."

"I remember little but what I can is vague. Bright lights everywhere, brighter than I have ever seen, like the sun. And he, he's different there," Pegan stumbled on the words. "Not like I remembered him. He glowed with an intense light also," Pegan continued. "He gave me a note but I can't seem to find it."

Gleia handed him the parchment, "it fell from your pocket when we carried you back here. I tried to read it but it's written in a strange language. Perhaps you can?"

Pegan took the note and studied the writing, it was clear and concise.

"Can you read it?" Lady Alenia asked.

"Yes," Pegan answered. "The words are clear. Except now I have a more serious problem."

"What does it say?" Gleia asked.

"Well... the note says on the third day after my return when the moon is at its apex to free my friends. I won't make it," Pegan said in a hopeless tone. "I have slept for one day so that only leaves me two to get back to the Lost Sanctuary, I don't have enough time but I need to try." Pegan climbed from the bed and got dressed.

Lady Alenia stopped him. "You need to just slow down a minute," then motioned for both of them to follow her. They went to a small circular room that was lined with bookshelves.

Pegan and Gleia patiently waited at the desk while she searched through row after row of books till she located a large, thick, leather-bound book and dropped it on the table. A resounding thud echoed through the room. Without a word she flipped through the pages till she found what she wanted and turned the book towards Pegan.

Pegan looked at the page and his eyes widened. It was the Lost Sanctuary before its destruction. The details were perfect. Every aspect of the city was there. He tried to touch the page, but she stopped him.

"The oil on your fingers will destroy the parchment," she said. "You're probably wondering why I have this."

"I am," Pegan said.

"Nobody knows this, not even Elwrick," she said. "But after the Great War, I recovered this and decided to keep it in secrecy until such a time the Lost Sanctuary can be restored and rightfully named once more the City of Skyn. Now, point to me the building in which the entrance to their hideout resides.

Pegan performed a cursory search of the page and pointed to a building, "there, that one."

She flipped through a few more pages then stopped at one that revealed the catacombs beneath that building. "Is this the hideout?" she asked.

A tear rolled down Pegan's cheek. Before his eyes is a highly detailed map of the Brotherhoods main hideout. "Yes," he answered. "And they'll be held here," he pointed to where the cells were.

"Fantastic," she said. Tomorrow, just before the moon is high, I will port you there through a dimension door." She pointed to a room at the far end of the hall. "I would offer help but I know you would refuse."

Pegan agreed with a nod, "I won't risk any more lives."

"I thought so," she respected his decision. "What you will find there I have no clue so step through prepared to fight," she said.

Pegan spent the rest of that day, and the next faced off to a hay dummy. Sweat poured from his pores as he hacked and slashed with a blinding speed that left all who observed questioning their own skills.

Chapter 25

ady Alenia's fingers burned as the smoldering, black, barbed chain dug into her flesh. Dangling over a large misshapen cauldron of boiling blood heated by stones that dripped lava, her nude body glistened with sweat. All around her in a wide circle, the most disgusting creatures she had ever seen circled performing a strange demonic dance that consisted of flips and twists. They reeked of filth and their torsos were covered with festering wounds that leaked yellowish pus. As they spun, large, glowing red welts and slashes appeared on their backs from some sadistic torture devised in the mind of a demented individual. Their legs were a whole different sight to behold. Shaped like a goats with thick massive black hooves while scraggly hair grew in ragged patches. Their faces were deliberately disfigured then reshaped to resemble a bat. Each long, crooked arm ended not in a hand, but a long jagged hook. As they danced, they took turns slashing at her. The wounds healed in seconds, but the intense burning pain never subsided.

Outside the ring Karayan walked, a sick smirk smeared across his face. Behind him she could see elves hanging by the hundreds, some by a single leg, others a hand, yet they were all in different stages of being skinned alive. She cringed to watch as the last piece of skin hit the ground and then to her astonishment, it all instantly grew back and the process began anew. In the great distance, she could see blue, yellow, and red flames licking at the fiery sky while ash fell like rain.

She woke in a fit of ear piercing screams and frantically searched her body for wounds. Her breath quickened and her pulse raced. Blankets where strewn across the room and a perfect darkened outline of her body stained the mattress. Her gown was translucent from sweat and her hair remained plastered to the sides of her face.

Hysterically, she searched the room and found a long silvery colored robe and fled. Fled to the one place she believed comfort could be found… the scrying chamber.

A faint steam drifted from the bowls silvery surface. Once here, she drew a long breath in hopes to gather her thoughts and control her fears. When she was ready, she chanted the words but never completed the process. A warm hand on her shoulder caused a shiver to race up her spine. She wanted to turn and face the man she knew stood behind her, take him in her arms and never let go, but she refused the temptations. They had been seeing each other a lot more recently and the feeling she felt inside could not be explained. They were not the same. What she felt would never come to pass.

Elwrick refused to let the moment pass. "I felt your terror, your pain and was here waiting. I knew you would come," Elwrick said, then wrapped his arms around her trembling frame.

She could feel the anxiety that flowed through her veins being leached away. He alone was taking her fears, her pain.

When the shivering stopped, he picked her up and cradled her in his arms. On their journey back to her home they never spoke. It was only after he sat her in a plush, high backed chair did she speak.

She confessed about the dreams and how Karayan was there, smiling and enjoy himself. The tear in the fabric, the demon at the grave, and when she finished… she wept once more.

Elwrick listened with great emotion, evaluating each and every word. The dark circles around her eyes proved this was not the first night she's had them. "I don't believe what you're experiencing are mere dreams, but you're being afforded a slight glimpse into the future," he said.

She glanced up at him through moist eyes, "how can that be?" she asked. "Is the Creator sending us a subtle message that Averie will not survive and Karayan's plans will come to fruition?"

"Cause I've had them too," he said, then kissed her forehead.

Afterward, he walked across the room and opened the window, the air had grown quite stagnant, and the room smelled like a sweathouse. From here he could see all of Rhunsiire and the surrounding woods. It was beautiful the way the sun lit the tree-tops almost giving them a soft, cotton ball appearance. "I don't fully understand it either, but I fear we are being warned of an evil far greater than you or I ever imagined possible."

Lady Alenia joined him at the window and stood there looking out for some time deep in thought at the words he'd spoken. She knew he was wise, but this new revelation drove a dagger of fear deep into her chest piercing her heart.

Elwrick finally broke the silence, "Karayan's plan has never been a world ruled by demons, he only wishes to retain immortality, which can only be accomplished if he continues to sacrifice the bearer's child." He reached down and took her hand and squeezed it tightly. "After my first dream, similar to the one you experienced, I spent countless hours researching Karayan, trying to find a way to penetrate the protection spell placed upon his mind. Having failed, I fell to my knees and prayed, no, I begged the Creator to help me. In my mind, I had a vision, and what I saw frightened me more than anything I could have ever imagined.

"What did the Creator reveal?" Lady Alenia asked.

"I discovered Karayan is a mere puppet to something much more sinister which hides in the shadows and we are but pawns playing a dangerous game of chess and he's about to call checkmate."

"I don't understand," she sighed. "Are you saying there's another person, someone more powerful than Karayan who wants to rule?"

Elwrick sighed, "I don't know what it is," he admitted. "The Creator never revealed it to me in the vision. But from what I was able to decipher, this thing, this entity, has direct contact with the underworld, possibly an agent of the Dark Master."

He led her by the hand to a table where they both sat. "It's extremely difficult to explain but I will try. What you must understand is this thing, this entity, now needs Karayan out of the way to further its goal, which I believe is Hell on Icearaus. This is why the dreams have been sent to us, however, since Karayan is blessed with immortality, this cannot be accomplished as long as he continues to destroy the child. What we failed to understand is that this blessing is valid in Hell, just as it is on Icearaus. If this thing initiated its plan now and recreates Hell on Icearaus, there's a possibility Karayan could challenge the Dark Master and become the Master of Hell as Karayan cannot die. It's something this entity will not allow which makes me believe even more he's a dark agent who's been here for decades hiding in the shadows biding his time, till the time was right to strike, which it must feel is now."

"Oh! my world," Lady Alenia said. "Now I understand. This thing, this entity is basically playing us as well. If we give the bearer to Karayan, we continue to live under his suppression. If we aid the bearer, that would results in Karayans death and ultimately the destruction of Icearaus."

"Yes," Elwrick said. "In my mind, I believed I was doing the right thing, but now I realize how ignorant I really am to the truth. I alone have caused the destruction of Icearaus unless we surrender the bearer."

"Are you suggesting we surrender Averie?"

"Absolutely not," Elwrick snapped. "I would rather die a thousand times at the hands of a demon than to know I sent an innocent young woman to suffer at the hands of Karayan."

For some reason Lady Alenia no longer felt fear, she felt anger at having been played for so many years. "So what is our next move?" she asked.

"First, we speak nothing of this. If the elves believe we've already lost, then we have. Second, we do what we must to get Averie to the portal and accept the consequences of our actions and we'll deal then with this new threat when the time comes. Speaking of that, when did Pegan leave for the Lost Sanctuary?"

"He hasn't left yet," she answered. "He's still resting. Tonight, just before the appointed time he will leave."

"That does not bode well for their escape," Elwrick explained. "I cannot stall Lord Rayne for days. He needs to be there the same time as me, and ready for the fight of his life."

"He will be," she said, and then explained their plan.

Elwrick smiled. "Excellent plan, I suspect there will be few inside the catacombs as they'll be out expecting his return."

"And what of you?" she asked. "Will you be killed on sight?"

Elwrick shook his head. "No, Lord Rayne wants Fel Strike."

"What makes you believe he will just not have a band of goons waiting to kill you and take the weapon from your corpse."

"Simple," he answered with a smile. "He will want to make sure I have the weapon. If he kills me and discovers it's not on my body but at my home in the Realm of Light, his chance of getting the weapon will be forever lost."

"You always have the answer to everything," she sighed.

He laughed, "I just wish I had the answer for this new threat."

She sighed, "me too."

"I do have the answer though for your dreams," he said. From his robe, he produced a small clear bag full of plant stems with prickly leaves and handed it to her, "take this before you sleep tonight. Place two leaves in a cup of boiling water, let it simmer till all the color has drained from the leaves. Allow it to cool till it's drinkable but not cold. That will keep the dreams at bay."

She placed the bag on the nightstand. "I was led to believe you were only a spiritual guide who could only bless us with your wisdom," she said.

"It's true, I cannot assist when the damage is done by another mortal. These dreams you're having, the same dreams as me are not coming from a mortal man though." He pointed towards the heavens with a single finger.

Lord Rayne leaned against the doorway and watched the sun drop from the sky through a partially collapsed window. Pencil thin beams of light thick with dust sparkled like diamonds as they sliced through the darkness, while his silken black cloak danced on a stiff breeze that carried the scent of pine down from the Silvers.

"You risk much for an item you only believe to exist," Lauden said from across the room. He blended in so well with his surroundings it seemed as if the wall spoke.

"It does exist, and now I finally have a means to acquire it," Lord Rayne fired back.

"Who's to say this man won't return with a sizeable force, lay waste to the compound, and rescue the bearer. It's quite obvious from what

I've seen, the elves and the reptilians—which I might add are both formidable opponents—are working to rescue her."

Lord Rayne never answered, instead, his vision remained focused to the east.

"If you ask me, we should put this whole fiasco behind us and kill the prisoners.

"I didn't ask you… did I," Lord Rayne spat in anger.

"It just a simple weapon," the man pleaded. "The risk doesn't match the reward." Using two fingers he fondled the hairs of a thin, handlebar mustache. "All this delay does is provide an opportunity for the hideout to be discovered and the Brotherhood infiltrated."

"Demetrius will do as he's told like a good dog and retrieve Elwrick. Elwrick will come as it seems he has much invested in seeing this woman reach freedom. Demetrius will return as well to finish what he started, whatever that may be."

"You make many assumptions."

"I have spent years studying people and what motivates them to do things they otherwise would not. We see it in ourselves such as greed, or in Karayan's case… immortality."

So what motivates this man you believe to be Demetrius? As I see he has nothing to gain and only his life to lose by finding Elwrick then returning."

"I don't know," Lord Rayne answered back with a snide tone. "I saw something, something different in his eyes as if he found a renewed sense of purpose for his miserable existence. A revised hope, a fleeting thought his task can be accomplished."

Lauden let out a sinister laugh. "You're positive the man who stood before you is Demetrius, the one and only, no other?"

"As positive as water runs downhill," he snapped back. "To verify my beliefs, I sent four men to follow him. If it is Demetrius, they will not return."

"So you sacrificed four to verify your beliefs."

"What are four men when I could claim ownership of Fel Strike?" Lord Rayne started down the stairs then stopped. "Make sure you have every man at the ready. Demetrius is both cunning and deadly, he'll be back seeking revenge."

"We'll be ready," Lauden said as he crossed the room and stood in the doorway. "If he returns, he won't get within five hundred yards of here without being noticed, regardless of his skills. Truth be told, I'm more worried about Elwrick. I know nothing about him or his demeanor, what have you learned? Does he use magic? Can he cast spells? What weapons does he carry?"

Lord Rayne searched his memory, "everything I understand about Elwrick has come from reading old tomes but from my understanding, you won't have a problem knowing it's him."

Lauden nodded his approval.

"Oh," Lord Rayne paused and turned back. "I needn't have to tell you if you see Demetrius kill him on sight. As for Elwrick, make sure he finds his way to my private chamber, unharmed. Once he's there wait for my word about the prisoners."

"You don't intend on releasing them?"

Lord Rayne laughed then vanished into the shadows of the underground.

Another man dropped through a hole in the ceiling and landed without a sound, "I'm with you Lauden, this is a dangerous game he plays."

Karayan is a man of his word so it was no surprise, that even with the fierce northern wind and bone-drenching rain, he appeared. Like an apparition at first, a solitary shadow emerging from the distant tree line searching for a soul to steal. Behind him, a large grouping of men followed, their steel armor shined as a bolt of lightning tore through the sky followed by an angry crack of thunder. Unwavering, they moved like a death squad.

Underneath a makeshift cover of hides, limbs, and brush, Emperor Tak-Thukmand sat on a temporary throne built upon a raised dais of stone. From a throne carved from a solid stump, he waited and watched the King's approach.

Karayan never altered his course, which was a straight line from where he had come from and directly to the man who waited. All those in his path either moved or were trampled, Karayan couldn't care less.

"I trust you have the girl in your possession?" Karayan asked from his mount. The tat... tat... tat... of rain pounded against his thick black cloak.

"No sir, she has—"

"Then why are you sitting here and not out searching?" Karayan screamed but quickly regained his demeanor. Carefully removing each glove, one at a time he tucked them under the saddle then gracefully swung one leg over and slid to the ground.

Emperor Tak-Thukmand stood when King Karayan climbed the stairs. His finger nervously twitched the shaft of his axe.

"Do you think because of this rain the diseased creature will also take to hiding?" Karayan asked.

"Absolutely not," Emperor Tak-Thukmand said, he waved a hand through the air and looked towards the sky. "She moves like the wind through a forest, we chase a dream we can never catch. Therefore, I have personally devised a plan which will deliver her right to my hands… and then to yours."

Karayan's face glowed like hot coals and the decision to kill the man right where he stood was only quenched by the desire to hear his plan. "And exactly what might that be?" he asked and then crossed his arms and waited for the man to answer.

Emperor Tak-Thukmand released a tight-lipped laugh, "First, watching the Crag was a waste of time and resources, so I recruited the giants who were more than willing to help and second, we should send men to every port and wait, eventually they will have to arrive at one of them. Once there, your men can snatch the woman while mine handle her escorts."

Karayan shook his head in utter disbelief, "do you think I'm stupid… what about ignorant… maybe both?" he asked. "Is that what you believe?"

"No Sir," he answered. "But there has to be a better way. Right now we chase a ghost, a deadly ghost at that."

It was only now Karayan realized how right Arlin was about how stupid the barbarians really were and was quite excited he had not solely put his trust in them. "How do you know she's headed to a port?" Karayan asked.

Tak-Thukmand responded brashly, it was now his turn to question the man. "Do you think I'm stupid? That I can't read. Oh, I know your lies," He said with a crooked smile. "The secrets you keep hidden away for none to see. I know about the old tomes, how you tried to destroy them but your ignorance has blinded you and a few survived. I know the truth behind the bearer and her intended purpose, not this story you've forced everyone to believe. I choose to say nothing as it benefits me just as much as you to keep it secret."

Karayan's face looked worried at first, as if he'd been caught doing something wrong then the corners of his mouth slowly curled up into a smile. "So you mean to blackmail me then?"

"Never, well, not intentionally but that must seem how it appears," he snapped back. "As long as I remain in power of the north, to do with as I will your secret is safe," he chuckled.

"For some reason, I feel as if I should fall to my knees and beg for mercy, but yet, somehow, I just don't see that happening," Karayan replied to the simplistic threat.

The Emperor, feeling he now had the upper hand, released a hearty laugh mocking the now inferior Karayan, as if the facade had been revealed.

Karayan laughed back then moved in till their noses all but touched.

Uncomfortable, the emperor backed away.

"What you read is why the barbarians will always remain only one notch above animals. You read something and only take from it the parts which fit your agenda and disregard the most important facts. If you would have studied the whole book and not selected pages you would have discovered that the boat is linked to the bearer. Whichever port she chooses, the boat will arrive. I have men waiting at every port east of the Silvers ready to snatch her up the second she's spotted. Hence why I believe she is headed west where there are ancient ports so desolate few know their locations." He let out a laugh then slapped his leg. "In reality, this is my fault, I should have known better than to send an army to search for her when a few men would have sufficed. That meddlesome Elwrick probably saw the mass movement and warned her in a different direction."

"So really, the blame lies with you," the Emperor said.

Karayan sighed, "There's another reason for my visit I have yet to reveal," Karayan advised the emperor. "You see…" Karayan removed a foot long dagger and begun to clean under his fingernails with the point. "The underworld grows restless waiting for a soul I have yet to deliver. Since I cannot provide the child's, yours will have to do for now."

The Emperor backpedaled and his hand grasped for his axe.

The attack was explosive and took the Emperor clear off the dais. Together, they busted through the furs that made up the back wall and landed with a splash.

The Emperor raked at Karayan's smooth face with rough nails but to his shock, the wounds healed instantly. So instead he struck Karayan hard across the face with a closed fist covered with a glove made of metal plates. The blow was horrific and should have shattered bone and left Karayan unconsciousness.

Karayan laughed at the assault then leaned forward till it appeared they became one then whispered, "I think you'll discover you made a huge mistake in attacking me. What you should have done was fallen to your knees and begged for forgiveness." Karayan's smile never faltered as he pushed the blade in slow as if wanting to prolong death. Inch by inch the blade vanished into the flesh severing bone as if it was warm bread until a thin trail of blood leaked from each corner of his victim's mouth. Next, he began a sawing motion as if cutting a piece of lumber. Up and down he worked the blade skillfully guiding it around the chest until a circular pattern was created.

Karayan drew gasps from the gathering horde when he reappeared. In one hand he held the blood covered dagger and in the other the beating heart of their now dead Emperor.

The barbarians are a brutal relentless force but what happened next even left them in shock.

Karayan held the heart up high for them all to see, then took a bite of the muscle. What remained he squeezed down with a mighty fist pulverizing the heart while blood squirted through his fingers.

More gasps followed as members of his Royal Guards recovered the corpse and tossed it at Karayan's feet. As if still alive and suffering it twisted into contorted knots and other grotesque positions.

Karayan raised a hand to silence the crowd. "Emperor Tak-Thukmand has failed. Not only has he failed me, he has failed you. His tactics had grown antiquated and his mental state tarnished. No longer could I allow a man in power that questioned my authority. Just as you do not accept that amongst yourself, I would not accept it from him."

The crowd went wild screaming and chanting King Karayans name. None here would have the gall to question him."

Karayan raised a hand to silence them. "Therefore, I now offer the position to his second… Emperor Haumlell' De' Janaro."

The sound was deafening as the cheers erupted, almost as if they were glad Emperor Tak-Thukmand was removed.

Not all were happy though, and a few raised their hands in protest, threw down their weapons they walked away refusing to follow him.

Emperor Haumlell' De' Janaro took to the dais. He was a large man thick with muscles. A dense beard covered most of his face and two tiny eyes hid behind bushy eyebrows. Taller than most his height almost equaled that of King Karayans.

Knelling, he bowed before King Karayan and took the required oath which ended with him offering his life if he failed to appease the King's demands.

At the base, the body continued to twist, wiggle, and convulse.

"King Karayan," A barbarian called out from the crowd. "How long until he dies?"

King Karayan saw an opportunity he had missed, "He was dead before he hit the ground. What you see here signifies the torment that is being performed upon his body. The convulsions will last until the body rots, but the torment upon his soul will last forever. That is the punishment for those who disobey me."

A loud *OOHHH* could be heard throughout the crowd.

Karayan positioned Emperor Haumlell' De' Janaro so the crowd could see him better, "Tell me," Karayan smiled, "As Emperor, what is your first command?"

Haumlell thought for a moment then stood tall. "I cannot stand cowardice and weakness, so my first command as your new emperor is to hunt down the swine that left and slay them like the pigs they are. We cannot have a bad seed planted in our garden."

Karayan clapped and patted him on the back.

The crowd went wild.

"Next, we will return home to our families and small parties will be formed to track down this filth that so easily avoided Tak-Thukmand. No longer will we sit and wait for her to come to us. We will take the

fight to her," he yelled.

The crowd roared.

Karayan smiled. He began the process of expanding his loyal army and only one man had to die.

The black rusty bars looked frail compared to the mighty fist the curled around them. Thathra wedged one foot against the wall and flexed his corded muscles. Sweat glistened like grease as it ran down his bare chest. Releasing a hearty grunt, he heaved with all his might yet the bars never flexed. The process repeated until the last of his strength fled his body and he collapsed to the floor, exhausted.

Strapped to the wall Saress had a perfect view of the botched escape attempt. "Save your strength till Pegan's return," Saress said. She had worked her massive jaw stretching the rope just enough so she could talk but not enough to make it obvious in the dim light.

"How is it possible these rusty old bars still hold so much strength?" he asked her.

"He ain't coming back," Lorandrial argued. "I could see it in his eyes when he walked out. He abandoned everything once, he'll do it again." Lorandrial wiped the sweat from his face. The air here was stagnant and thick with heat. From somewhere down the hall the crack of a whip cut through the darkness followed by the crying sobs of a tortured soul. "If I was a betting man, I would say we're stuck here till we rot. We don't even know how long it's been. For all we know today could be the day one of us dies."

"Well, I don't look good as boots so I refuse to give up hope. As long as my heart pumps blood and my lungs process air, we have a fighting chance, and it would do you wise to think the same," Saress snapped. Having grown angry she changed the subject, "are you doing okay Averie?"

"My legs burn, my back pains and I'm so tired of standing. I only wish to lie down and sleep."

"Pegan should be here any day now to free us." Saress felt bad for the woman but there was nothing she could do, the chains that held her were thick and impregnated with tiny barbs that drilled their way into her scales with each movement.

"Hope," Lorandrial laughed. "Are you blind to our situation? What hope do you believe we have? You speak as if we're on equal ground. We're out-numbered, weaponless, oh, and locked in a stinking cage." Lorandrial's rant continued. "And if you're so tired, lie down and go to sleep."

Saress hissed an angry growl towards Lorandrial, "she can't you ignorant fool. Unlike us, they put a collar around her neck as added security and she's forced to stand."

"Sorry, I didn't know," Lorandrial answered sarcastically.

"Well if you weren't so cocky you would understand," Thathra said, "not all of us—"

"Silence," a guard yelled from down the hall. The jingle of keys echoed off the hard stone walls as he approached.

"Maybe we're being released?" Averie tried to whisper but her voice carried clear to the end of the hall.

"Not today sweetheart," he said, and then let out a laugh that sounded like a cat hacking up a fur ball.

Averie almost vomited as she watched him approach. Lumbering down the hall like a massive slug, his shoulders bounced from wall to wall while bulbous rolls of fat hung down over a weapons belt loaded with every type of conceivable device designed to cause an extreme amount of pain and suffering. When he stopped, his belly rolled like a wave starting at one side of his body and continuing until it reached the other then wiggled a few times before coming to a saggy rest. Long trails of glistening grease from a recent meal ran down his chest and cascaded over the rolls like a shallow stream staining his dirty trousers. Depending on how he turned, his eyes changed from gray to silver and when he spoke his breath could wilt a flower.

"The master ordered a change in your diet and informed me to serve it. This way if there's any complaint I can personally address them now." As he laughed the long flab of skin which hung from his neck reminded Averie of an old tom turkey she once had for a pet.

Behind him, a small boy carried a large wooden pail and a handful of wooden bowls. He was barefooted, stood in silence and his head bowed.

"Give them each one scoop, except for her. I'll feed her personally."

He waited till the others were served then snatched the bucket from the child.

Averie turned away as the man unbutton his trousers and relieved himself in the bucket then stirred the concoction until he was satisfied it was thoroughly mixed. Sweat dripped from his chin and saliva ran from the corner of his mouth.

Forcing back her head by the hair he plugged her nose till she had no choice but to gasp for air and when she did he poured the contents down her throat spilling most of it down her shirt then rubbing it all over her face with his hand. Afterward, he placed the bucket on her head then banged it a few times with the ladle.

"You bastard," Saress screamed as he finished.

"I didn't know boots could talk," he chuckled.

"When I get free, these boots are gonna stomp all over you." She frantically yanked on the chains but they never budged.

The Jail Master stood just out of reach of a deadly claw. *"Tisk… tisk…"* he said. "I simply hate being threatened. It appears it's time for you to have a little accident. A deadly accident," he grinned.

"It takes a real man to kill an unarmed, defenseless person," Thathra yelled. "Let her free and then we'll see just how tough you really are."

The Jail Master turned towards Thathra, "you still had six days before one of you died. But with comments like that, I believe two will die today." He looked at Lorandrial, "You got anything to say, wanna make it three?"

Lorandrial remained quiet and backed away from the bars.

The Jail Master waited a minute. "No… good. Your two companions could learn a lot from you."

Saress growled a low rumbling noise that sounded like an earthquake deep underground.

The Jail Master slid a blade free, "time to skin you like the lizard you are."

"Please no," Averie screamed. She couldn't see what was happening but the vision that formed in her mind was horrific. Frantically, she swung her head trying to remove the bucket.

"Shut up," he yelled and banged a wooden nightstick against the bars.

"What are you doing?" A voice lashed out from the darkness.

"Having some fun with our guests," he answered.

Lord Rayne moved into the light. "And why does she have that bucket over her head?" He slapped the Jail Master hard across the face."

He didn't have an answer.

"If she dies from suffocation, you'll find yourself in this same cell," Lord Rayne said. Then he slapped him one more time. "Now, remove that bucket and get her cleaned up.

"Clean her up," he snarled back at Lord Rayne. "What are you, growing soft in your old age?"

The movement was almost magical and none saw the blade but there it was, pressed against the fat of the Jail Masters neck. "You see this," he held up his palm so the scab was visible. "I took an oath, an assassin's oath that they'll be cared for until the allotted time has expired. What good is a man if he can't keep his word?" He flicked the blade slicing open part of the fatty cheek. "Now get her cleaned up before I finish flaying your face open."

"Yes sir," he answered.

Lord Rayne looked at Saress and the way she was shackled to the wall, shaking his head in disgust as he left.

Saress drew a deep breath and relaxed. The man almost sounded humane.

Chapter 26

Elwrick sat on a flat stone and looked down upon the bustling City of Skyn, or what remained of it. He had not been here in a very, very long time and it all looked so foreign to him. All around the city he could see the movement of people, fading in and out of the shadows like apparitions on patrol. From here it was obvious, the Brotherhood was clearly expecting his arrival. In less than fifteen minutes Pegan would arrive, the time had come, the call for action was now. Biding Midnight farewell he started down the path.

Part-way down it became painfully clear he was being followed and minutes later he found himself surrounded by a dozen or more well-armed men all dressed in obsidian black garb with matching veils that covered their faces. One though stood out from the rest, he bore a blood red veil to conceal his identity.

"Bind him." The one wearing the red veil snarled.

Elwrick lifted a hand in protest; he could not allow himself to be detained. He knew the Brotherhood had shackles imbued with dark magic to drain his abilities and render him harmless. "If he tries everyone dies, everyone except you." He pointed a crooked finger directly at the one who spoke. "You'll be spared and forced to crawl back on your belly like vermin to tell Lord Rayne your companions are dead, and how you're the one responsible for this failed meeting."

The one in the mask hesitated, "then the bearer dies as well, along with her companions."

"There'll be more," Elwrick said with a wicked smile. "But here's the real question, are you willing to accept the punishment for costing Lord Rayne a chance to get what he craves." His hands began to shimmer a faint red as if he was about to cast a devastating spell.

There was a long awkward silence between them, only broken by the sound of crickets then he motioned for his comrades to lower their weapons. "Forgive me, no need to get hasty and cause unnecessary destruction," he said then dipped into a low bow. "I seem to have forgotten my place. Lord Rayne has been expecting you for some time now and I am to make sure you arrive… safely."

The flash of light was so bright it blinded all in the room and lit the hallway clear to the opposite end. The wind created by the sudden burst extinguished every torch and made a loud whooshing sound as it passed by their cells. Pegan stepped through and mentally marked the location of each guard.

Startled by the flash, one guard stumbled backwards over a wooden table smashing it flat while the other let out a snarled groan as he smashed face first into the stone wall trying to run out the door.

Pegan attacked the dazed man first in a flurry of swipes that left him bleeding from an uncountable number of wounds. The next two swipes sliced the throat while a third would have connected had the head already not been severed.

Pegan heard the hiss of steel as the blade was jerked free of its sheath. A warning which told him the man already recovered from his tumble.

In complete darkness, the assassin felt he had the upper hand and lunged.

Pegan leaped to the side narrowly avoiding the attack but tripped over a broken table leg and crashed against the wall.

"What in the world just happened?" A guard yelled from the far end of the hall. The torch he carried cast the room in gray shadows.

Pegan watched as a wicked grin formed on his adversaries face.

"You're dead now," the guard hissed towards Pegan who squatted in a defensive posture. "We have an intruder. It might be Demetrius," he hollered down the hall. "He's killed Fredrick, but I got him cornered, get in here." Both hands gripped an angry-looking sword.

Pegan had to act now as he knew the rules of engagement. If this man was to reach the prisoners before Pegan arrived, their throats would be cut. Throwing a chunk of wood at the assassin, the diversion worked and allowed Pegan just enough room to slip through the doorway at a full sprint and meet the assassin just before he arrived at the cells.

With his sword already out, he began a series of thrust and lunges.

Pegan easily parried the attack then went on the offense landing a series of jabs, thrusts, and swipes which left the man butchered.

"Here comes another one," Saress screamed. She yanked and jerked on the chains but they held fast.

The man froze, he knew that very instant he was dead.

Pegan had a lust filled hate that burned deep in his eyes.

Turning to run, Pegan quickly caught him and drove a dagger between the shoulder blades at an angle which he knew would puncture the heart as it exploded out through the chest. He hated killing a man that way as he preferred to look them in the face as they died but time would rob him of the satisfaction.

As the last body fell, Saress called out to him for aid.

"I need to get the keys from the Jail Master, I'll be back."

"Don't leave me," Averie cried out in a terrified voice.

"You're an assassin, pick these damn locks!" Lorandrial screamed.

"I can't, their pick-proof."

"Smash them with your daggers," Thathra pleaded.

"It won't work," he answered. "They're made of tungsten. Averie would have her baby and we would all die of old age long before I even made a scratch."

Saress groaned, "We'll go get the dang keys and stop wasting time talking to us."

Elwrick was amazed by the elegant taste Lord Rayne displayed. The room was reasonably large and fashionably decorated. Elegant tapestries hung by golden rods that depicted rare battle scenes while blue laced agate walls mesmerized the senses. The way the veins interlaced made the wall almost appear to swirl. A wooden bookshelf hand-rubbed to a high gleam spanned the entire back wall. Not one empty spot was visible and before it sat stacks of books piled waist high that gave off a threatening lean. To the left of the bookshelf, the smoldering remains of a hearth fire glowed red in the dim light produced by a few well-placed candles. Large white porcelain vases clogged with flowers lined the right wall and the scent of lilacs filled the air. Near the bookshelf, Lord Rayne sat at an ornately carved mahogany table that held down a large woven rug with tassels on each end. The rim of the high back chair was barely visible behind his balding head. Besides the vile beast at the desk, the room almost had a homey feel.

Lord Rayne studied Elwrick, while Elwrick studied the stone walls. "Blue laced agate," Lord Rayne said.

"What?" Elwrick asked.

"I caught your gaze staring at the walls," Lord Rayne said. "They're blue laced agate. Unnatural to this environment, I had them delivered from beyond the Wilds. I chose them specifically because it's believed they have a calming effect that relieves stress by fostering peace and tranquility."

Elwrick studied the walls a moment longer to see something in them he had not noticed before, but nothing struck him as unusual. "I find it rather ironic?" Elwrick said.

"What might that be?" Lord Rayne responded. He leaned back in the chair and placed his feet on the desk.

"That a man who practices kidnappings, torture, rape, and even murder for no better reason than personal gain, would line his library with stone designed to represent peace. I figured brimstone would suit you better."

Lord Rayne released a snide chuckle then gracefully came to his feet. "Come, sit a while. We have much to discuss." He motioned for a young slave girl to bring over a chair.

Elwrick neared the desk, "I'll remain standing if you don't mind."

"Suit yourself." Lord Rayne said. Adjusting himself in the chair he waited a few moments then their eyes meet in a clash of superiority. "Do you understand why I have summoned you here today, to my private chamber no outsider has ever seen?"

Elwrick pondered the question. One wrong word could lead to the death of the prisoners, yet now was the prime opportunity to stall. "No," he answered. "But I'm sure you will fill me in on all the gory details."

Lord Rayne released a laugh that echoed through the room, it was deep and throaty, the laugh of a man who smelled victory. "Before we begin, let me explain I know your true identity… and I can prove it."

"My identity is no secret," Elwrick said.

"I must explain from the beginning, therefore you cannot deny the claim I make," Lord Rayne said then went to a tapestry which was much larger than all the others which depicted the victory of a hard-fought battle. On his way, he produced a long pointer and extended it to full length, the end of which was bright white making it visible in the darkened environment. "Do you know what this tapestry depicts?" He pointed the thin rod at the image.

Elwrick watched every detail of his movements. Not understanding yet where Lord Rayne was taking this, so he played along. Besides, this history lesson worked in his favor. Pegan should be here by now and the rescue well within progress. "Can't say I do," Elwrick said as he studied the tapestry.

"Well, it's possible the light is bad from there, come closer." Lord Rayne not so much asked but ordered.

Elwrick took up a position near Lord Rayne but still far enough away he could defend himself in a sudden attack. "Sorry, not a clue," he said, shaking his head side to side.

"Are you positive," Lord Rayne asked.

"Quite positive," he answered.

"Look here," he pointed towards a spot on the tapestry. "Tell me what you see?"

Elwrick studied the splotch, "It looks possibly like a man standing on a ledge in the early stages of casting a spell. I could be wrong though as this tapestry appears ancient."

"It appears to be the final battle of a war where victory is all but achieved," Lord Rayne corrected him. "It's easy to spot from the dead scattered all around."

The light from a candle caused dancing shadows to skate up the side of his head as tendons and muscles moved with each word spoken.

"Now that you mention it, your assumption is plausible," Elwrick nodded in agreement.

"Good… good… at least we can agree on that," Lord Rayne said. "If that was a man, who do you think that man is?"

Elwrick inspected the image closer, "don't know," he grinned. "It could be anybody or nobody. Could be a stain. After all, this tapestry is archaic in nature."

"It's not a stain," Lord Rayne corrected him. "He clearly has arms, a head… and… and wearing a white robe with gold thread." He turned from the tapestry to face Elwrick, his movements were methodical and well reserved, a crooked smile formed on his pale face.

"Are you implying I'm that wizard?" Elwrick asked.

"Very much so," Lord Rayne said. He moved back to his desk without a sound and sat.

Elwrick stood at the tapestry and took a second glance.

"Try as you may but it won't change. The simple fact remains you are the only wizard who survived the Great War."

"Even if I am, you still have not explained why you brought me here?"

"Simple, the reason I brought you here is that you were given something at the end of that war which I want. But I could not simply come out and demand it as I had to prove you were the one it was made for. Now that I have accomplished that feat without deniability—"

"What of the prisoners? It is my understanding they were to be released upon my arrival.

"After I have which I desire, we will then negotiate their release."

"That was not part of the agreement."

Lord Rayne leaned back in the chair and observed Elwrick as he crossed the room making his way back towards the desk. "The agreement has been altered."

Pegan glanced through the gap created by the partially open door. The room was exactly as he remembered from years past. Plain, drab, and besides the wide rough cut wooden table, no other furniture was visible. Three chairs sat empty while the fourth was occupied by the Jail Master. Before him on the table was a massive bowl overloaded with greasy chicken legs. To his left, a woman covered from head to toe with a long white dress stood. She watched his every move through slits cut in the headpiece and used a soft cloth to wipe away the grease that dripped from his chin. Another woman dressed similar stood to his right and fanned him with a large white feather. Reaching back, he grabbed the girl with the feather and pulled her down to him, kissed her where her lips would have been, then shoved her away with such force she tumbled to the ground.

Pegan could care less if the Jail Master perished, but he had to be careful with the two slaves. Depending on how long they had been held captive, it was quite possible they would fight him or attempt to warn others of the intrusion. Regardless of their intentions, Pegan's hand was now forced as the Jail Master stood over the fallen slave and begun to unbuckle his weapons belt.

Pegan pulled his cowl down so only his mouth was visible and pushed the door open and casually strolled in as if he was expected. The Jail Master glanced his direction but seemed to show no interest as he turned back towards the woman who tried to crawl away.

"Come here wench," the fat slob snarled. "Papa has something for you."

She cried out in pain as he stepped on her ankle to prevent her from moving. "Now lift up your robe and I'll make it easy on you," he snarled.

Pegan knew better than to kill him. The key ring had numerous false keys designed to jam and break off thus making it all but impossible to open the locks and only the Jail Master knew which keys those were.

Completely engulfed with his sexual desires, the Jail Master forgot Pegan had entered.

Pegan didn't need to sneak, instead, he casually walked up and kicked him hard behind the knees. They buckled as the man crashed to the ground hard landing on both knees. Pegans next motion was so quick the Jail Master wasn't sure exactly what happened, until he discovered his inability to stand. The tendon at each ankle dangled like rubber bands. Pegan released a smirk as the man began to beg for his life and eagerly handed over the keys.

Both slaves bolted for the door. Pegan wanted to go after them, but knew he needed to free his companions first.

Pegan twisted the fat meaty ear on the bloated head until he complied with his orders and began to crawl on his hands and knees like a dog to the cells.

"Which key opens this cell?" Pegan asked quite nicely.

"I would rather lick a dog's behind than help you," he growled back, looking up at Pegan.

Pegan smiled, the Jail Master screamed, a nipple hit the floor. "Don't make me ask again."

The process repeated itself with Pegan slowly dismembering the man until all the cells had been opened and the only lock that remained was the collar around Averies neck.

"Which key is it?" Saress screamed then slapped him across the face leaving four long gashes clear to the bone.

"I already told you, Lord Rayne took it from me for added security," he sniveled as snot ran from both nostrils.

Pegan removed another long layer of skin off the bottom of the Jail Masters feet.

'I'm not lying," he screamed, cried, and begged.

Saress snapped and latched onto the Jail Master by the neck and lifted him clear off the ground. With his feet dangling their faces were only inches apart. "Now you listen—"

There was no need for her to continue as his neck could not hold the weight of his unsupported body and the head popped free. The bloated body fell like a hose spraying them all in a blood thicker than mud.

"Good job," Lorandrial said. "You just killed our only source of information."

Thathra shot him a nasty look. He knew why she did it, her frustrations, her anger had got the best of her. She lost control at the sight of seeing Averie hooked to a chain and there was nothing she could do about it. "Leave her alone," he said.

"Hand me the keys," Lorandrial demanded. "I'll figure this out."

Pegan sighed, "If we use the wrong key it will break and we'll never get her free."

"I think the Jail Master is full of it," Lorandrial said as he snagged the keys and shoved one into the keyhole and begun to twist until it snapped.

Saress gasped in horror.

Averie begun to cry, she knew now there was no hope.

Pegan studied the lock then released a sigh of relief. Lucky for them, the key was not inserted all the way, and he managed to free the broken piece.

"We're done," Lorandrial said. "There is no way we'll find it, and Saress killed the man who knew."

Thathra's eyes followed the chain up to the ceiling where it was latched to a large eyebolt. It was wedged in between two pieces of granite and held there by a strange type of mortar. "I have an idea," Thathra said. He dragged the fat dead man into the cell and had Averie stand on it allowing quite a bit of slack on the chain. He gripped it with both hands then swung himself upside down to where his feet were placed on each side of the bolt. Bending his knees he pulled with all his strength. The bolt wanted to break free but he lacked the strength.

Saress was too big to fit inside, so she rolled onto her back and snaked her tail up between Thathra then coiled it around the chain. At the count of three, he pulled while she pushed on the bars with her hind legs and with a loud crash dust exploded from the cell as the bolt ripped free taking a good section of the ceiling with it.

From there, Pegan led them down a different hall, down a second set of stairs, across a small rope bridge, back up a set of stairs so narrow Saress had to squeeze sideways, then to a wide hallway and finally a secluded room. Catching the two men inside unprepared, Pegan quickly dispatched one while Saress used her tail like a whip and caught the other across the head snapping his neck.

"I didn't know you could fight with your tail," Pegan said.

Saress smiled, "every part of my body is a weapon."

Elwrick stood in silence for some time before he spoke. "Stop speaking in riddles and wasting my time, what exactly is it you want?"

Lord Rayne laughed, "Straight and to the point, I like that in a man."

Elwrick crossed his arms as if waiting for an answer.

Lord Rayne suddenly became serious, "Fel Strike... I want Fel Strike, and I want it now."

"Fel Strike," Elwrick chuckled... "Fel Strike," he repeated the name once more. "I don't believe I can really help you there, I don't know of, nor, have I ever owned a weapon named Fel Strike." Elwrick leaned on the desk, "obviously living here, underground, in the dark, your mind has played an evil trick on you."

"Enough with the antics," Lord Rayne looked directly into Elwrick's eyes "I know for a fact, without question, the dwarves of the Silver Mountains created for you a special dagger named Fel Strike, and I want it... or your friends die right now."

"I can assure you I possess no such weapon," Elwrick spoke cautiously."

Lord Rayne removed a large tome from the desk drawer and slammed it down on the table. "Don't take me for a fool," he snapped. "For years I heard rumors of a dagger blessed with magical properties but I could never find the evidence until recently. Throughout my search I have read every book in this library searching, searching for an answer to the missing puzzle piece that eluded me. That is until I finally cracked this strange passage in this particular tome. Here, let me read it to you in its native tongue."

"My time is rather valuable and I care little for these fairy tales you read," Elwrick interjected.

Lord Rayne listened carefully, then continued, "bear with me a moment," and he opened the book to a pre-marked page and begun to read."

[—Og það bar til árið tíu níutíu og tvö eftir
Mikill stríð er Dwarven her, Led
frá General Dur'snag Grudgemore veitti
sköpun Fel Verkfall. Að svikin í eldheitur
ofnum of Gul-Zun Del'Amoor varðveittur og sýndur
sem Elwrick, yfirborð dweller sem leiddi
þá til sigurs—]

Elwrick knew exactly what the words meant, but wanted to test Lord Rayne, to make sure he understood as well. "What exactly am I supposed to make out of that conglomeration of words, they mean little if anything to me," Elwrick said.

"I knew you would never understand so I will translate for you."

[... And so it came to pass in the year Ten-Ninety

*two after the Great War the dwarven army, Led
by General Dur'snag Grudgemore authorized the
creation of Fel Strike. To be forged in the fiery ovens
of Gul-Zun Del'Amoor and presented to Elwrick,
the surface dweller who led us to victory…]*

Elwrick stood motionless as he watched Lord Rayne close the book. If he was not blinded by ignorance and actually knew half of what he studied, he would have realized Fel Strike was already in his grasp, yet, he simply let it walk right out the door. "So you believe I hold some exotic dagger tainted with magical properties because an ancient tome says so?"

"Well then," Lord Rayne answered. "If you do not possess or cannot acquire said item, then I see no need to further our discussion. I will just keep searching. You're free to go as I personally invited you here. The prisoners though will not be afforded that luxury," Lord Rayne said.

"That was not the agreement," Elwrick said. "I was informed if I had this meeting they would be allowed to leave unharmed."

"You were informed wrong," Lord Rayne said. "Now I may consider releasing them to whomever can produce the weapon, but unfortunately, the cost to keep them alive now outweighs the reward and it probably would be best just to forget this whole ordeal. They've already been found guilty of trespassing, guess it's time to carry out the sentence."

"I can't give you something I don't possess."

"Then our meeting has come to an end. Goodbye Mr. Elwrick."

That must have been the signal as eight shadowy figures materialized from the darkness and came at him from different angles.

Elwrick knew this was a setup even if he did have Fel Strike, and thus had a spell already prepared. Whispering a few words under his breath, a light green hue formed around his body and grew brighter as he spoke. As they reached him, the green hue erupts into a blinding explosion of colors that leave all eight reeling backwards. Sparks shatter the darkness and the flame of every candle burst to life in the shape of a dragon's head, which snaps at the fleeing assassins who are sure the world his ending. After the flaming heads died away and their vision returned, they discovered the wizard was gone. In his place instead was a charred floor that leaked wisps of gray smoke.

"Send the message to have the others killed… now!" Lord Rayne slipped from the back of the room into a secret passage closing the door behind him.

From the vantage point near the center of the ceiling, a wide smirk stretched across Elwricks face. He's not the only one who understood darkness and how to use it to his advantage. After they filtered out, Elwrick descended to the floor and grabbed the tome Lord Rayne read from, then his form shimmered gold and he was gone.

Digging through the piles of weapons, they eventually located their gear and were about to leave when Saress brought them to a halt, "people are coming," she whispered nocking an arrow.

The door crashed open with a loud bang as it slammed against the wall.

Saress let the arrow fly. At such a short distance it blew clear through the first man who dropped instantly and buried to the fletching in the next.

Pegan acted on instincts and opened the door to a small closet and not so gently pushed Averie inside. He could hear her yelling at him but his attention was drawn to a much more serious situation. Six men flooded into the room.

"Find the girl and kill her," one wearing a red mask yelled.

Hearing the words Averie shut up as to not draw attention to her location.

Pegan stood firm at the door, guarding something he treasured more valuable than life.

Saress found one corner while Thathra moved towards the opposite, their backs against the wall as to not be surrounded. Lorandrial took up a position next to Pegan and what ensued next was complete chaos.

The clang of steel echoed back down the hall as Saress parried the attack then returned with a series of mighty blows. The assassin had under-estimated her strength and the blade was knocked free from his hands and bounced across the stone floor out of reach, but he quickly drew another.

Thathra was not as generous and never even allowed the assassin to attack before he began a series of swing blows designed to keep the much more agile man at bay.

They all knew Pegan was the greatest threat and three had him successfully backed against the door. Unable to mount an attack, he spent his entire time defending access to Averie.

The assassin on Lorandrial was blistering fast and slipped through his defenses landing a strike.

Lorandrial screamed and fell to his knees gripping the large slice across his wrist.

The assassin pulled off his mask. He wanted the victim to see his killer, to see the evil grin of victory.

Saress could see Pegan was in trouble and in an acrobatic spin she extended her tail wide taking the feet out from under two of his attackers.

Surprised, the third looked to see what in the world just happened.

Pegan saw the distraction and made the most of it driving the dagger deep into the side of the man's neck. The way his mouth shot open, it appeared as though he was going to scream but no words came as he slid off the blade… dead.

The assassin who stood above Lorandrial laughed ready to strike the deadly blow. He would have succeeded if it was not for Thathra who abandoned his own assassin temporarily and charged in a different direction. Swing his blade fast and hard as he moved, the blade cut through the neck bone effortlessly lopping the head off the would be killer. Lorandrial would live for now.

Blood from the assassins racing heart pumped with such velocity it sprayed straight up painting the ceiling then dripped like rain.

By now the two who were knocked to the floor had recovered but were having a much harder time controlling Pegan.

Saress let her momentum from the spin carry her too far and the assassin she fought found the opening and buried his blade deep into her calf muscle.

She howled a painful, piercing cry. Enraged, her arm fired straight out grabbing the man by his groin, and jerking him towards her open maw. No screams could be heard as the jaw clamped down upon his face crushing his skull.

Neither assassin saw what happen and was caught off guard when Saress somehow managed to nock another arrow. At such a close distance, the arrow blew through the chest of the first assassin, and buried to the fletching in the second.

Thathra began a series of blows the assassin was unable to counter and eventually turned and fled back down the hall.

Alone and surrounded by enemies, the final assassin fell to his knees to surrender, but Thathra was in no mood to show mercy and ended his life in one fatal blow.

Saress hobbled to the door, "one escaped, we need to get him."

"He's long gone by now. We need to move, and quickly," Pegan advised.

As they left, the sound of running feet told them more approached.

Pegan hurried them down another hall, then up another flight of stairs which led to a large room. Beyond it, they entered another hall which they followed for some distance then entered another room which Pegan slammed the door shut and snapped a key off in the lock. "That should delay them and buy us some time," Pegan said.

Averie began the process of wrapping a cloth around Saress's wound when she looked at where Pegan led them, and she almost fainted. All around her the walls seemed to close in suffocating the life out of her. She grabbed her chest and stumbled backwards and begun to hyperventilate.

Saress turned in a complete circle taking in the room. Every torture device one could have ever imagined must have been created right here. There are braziers with glowing coals that emitted a dim, malign glow and burnt iron pokers still coated with charred flesh hanging on rusty hooks. There were chairs covered in metal spikes designed to puncture but not kill, while others were adorned with leather straps to secure the victim while unnamed tortures were performed. Near the back, a single table sat against the far wall with rollers on each end wrapped with ropes designed to stretch the person till ligaments tore and bones dislocated. Everywhere you looked, manacles lined the walls. Numerous carts set on small rollers littered the room, each covered in instruments designed to slash or poke. One cart still held a complete set of teeth. A metal cage hung from heavy chains over a pool of acid which reeked of sulfur and a device used to remove a head was stained blood red. What frightened Saress the most though was the fact every item here, looked used.

"Where are we?" Lorandrial asked. His face had gone flush.

"The torture room," Pegan answered.

"I thought the room where we met Lord Rayne was the torture room?" Thathra asked.

"No, that was simply the interrogation room. If you confess there to your crimes, then you're not brought here. Often times though, the techniques there make this room obsolete."

"Judging from the way this room looks I would beg to differ," Saress said.

Averie finally finished wrapping Saress's leg and was now tending to Lorandrial.

"More importantly, is there any other way out?" Thathra asked.

Pegan moved to an unused section of the wall and tapped on the stone, "the secret door is here, we just need to find the mechanism. They change it quite often to prevent this very thing."

Spreading out they pulled on this, yanking on that, pushing on other things, and finally resorted to kicking everything in sight. Nothing moved or opened.

Thathra stopped moving to examine the area more closely and picked up a design flaw none of them recognized. A design flaw only a skilled builder would have recognized. Following a jagged crack, he worked his way to a stone pillar in the center of the room where a skeleton hung. "The lever is on this pillar," he said.

Methodically, they began to search every inch of the pillar when Averie pressed on a small bolt head that protruded no more than a few centimeters and the door slid silently open. So quiet in fact, none even heard it open. It was only when Saress looked back did she actually see the opening.

Averie screamed with joy.

With the light from an acquired torch, Pegan led the way as they entered the corridor.

Thathra entered last and cut the thin wire which activated the mechanism allowing the door to slam shut. "When they do get in, they can't follow us now," he said.

After multiple turns they climbed a spiral staircase before coming to a small landing, the exit blocked by a thick metal portcullis. Built into the wall next to it was a small wheel that when turned, the gate crept upward. With everybody through except Pegan, Thathra and Saress stood under the gate using brute strength to hold it open until Pegan had passed then stepping out letting it slam to the ground.

Chapter 27

Startled by the sudden intrusion, a flock of birds which nested in the rafters of the dilapidated structure took to flight leaving behind a birds worth of feathers fluttering in the air.

"I wish we could fly," Averie grumbled as she watched them fade into the cloudless sky. She hunched slightly forward and her face looked worn.

"Aye," Thathra agreed. "It would make things a lot easier."

Pegan stood at the end of the room which was shaped more like a long hallway. Down each side broken statues lined the walls and rubble marred the tile floor. The high arched ceiling was broken through in many places and in one area a large section of the wall had completely collapsed almost blocking the exit.

"You look horrible," Saress said to Averie. It was apparent the heavy chain was wearing her down. "We need to remove it soon, before it kills her," Saress demanded.

Thathra sent Lorandrial up to the entrance and ordered him to keep watch while Saress and he worked on the chain, looking for a way to possibly remove it.

Picking the lock was impossible. That was Pegans expertise and he already informed them it couldn't be done, so instead he focused his attention on where the chain fastened to the collar. Examining it like a fine piece of jewelry, he discovered the chain itself was hardened along with the collar but the steel rivets where it fastened proved to be the weak link in the design, and then it made sense. If the rivets were hardened, it would have been impossible to smash them flat, so this is where they focused their effort.

Having discovered the weak link, another problem soon reared its ugly head. The only way to gain access to the head of the rivets was to remove the head of the person wearing the collar, and that was not an option. "We can't risk chopping at it," Thathra said. "One mistake and it would prove fatal."

Saress agreed then wrapped the chain around Averie's waist making it into a belt. "At least it won't dangle anymore."

Lorandrial leaned against the wall and complained, "That many birds leaving at once are bound to draw someone's attention. What little chance we had to slip away unnoticed they took with them."

"Slip away unnoticed." Pegan laughed at Lorandrial as he glanced out the opening. The street was clear in both directions except for a few dust devils that stirred in the slight breeze. "Every assassin in the Brotherhood knows exactly where that secret passage ends. Why they're not here already has me far more concerned than those birds."

Having finished their examination, Thathra, Saress, and Averie joined them at the entrance.

"How far away are the caves?" Saress asked.

"A good day's travel from here, and that's if we don't have to fight," Pegan answered. He scanned the road and crumbled ruins searching for any sign of movement.

"Can we sneak through the rubble unseen?" Averie asked.

Pegan sighed, "I like the way you think but it won't work. Between here and the mountains is an area known as the Sacred Gardens. At one time it was adorned with intricate fountains, colorful flowers, and all manner of vegetation, but now it remains only a circular, barren wasteland of nothingness. It will take a good hour to cross and we'll be easily spotted, surrounded, and eventually decimated."

Thathra looked back the way they had come, "we can't stay here either," Thathra said. "Besides the obvious reasons of not being able to retreat if things go bad, fighting in such close quarters we risk slicing each other to ribbons."

"If we can't make it to the caves, and we can't stay here, where do we go?" Saress asked.

Lorandrial sighed. "Here we go again, running for our lives. Why is it every time we listen to you we end up inches from death? If you would have just followed me—"

Saress shot Lorandrial an icy glare to silence the elf.

"See that building across the way," Pegan pointed to a half-collapsed structure. "There's a passage that leads to the other side of the Lost Sanctuary. It's used quite frequently to travel without being seen. My best guess is they probably think we've already reached it and are currently scouring every inch as it has many off-shoots, rooms, and places for us to hide."

"Then we should probably get going now before they realize we're not in it and come searching," Saress said.

"Yes," Pegan agreed. "We'll go to that building over there." He pointed to one in the opposite direction. "They won't expect us to go in that direction as it leads away from the mountains, but once it gets dark, we'll circle the town using Saress's vision to guide us."

Saress glanced out the doorway, "I think it would be best if we go one at a time to draw as little attention as possible."

Thathra nodded in agreement.

"I'll go first," she said. "I run the fastest. After I make sure the building's clear, I'll signal for you to come."

"Don't delay," Pegan said.

Without a word, she shot from the opening like a bullet and arrived without incident.

Their hearts raced as they waited. The pain of not knowing was excruciating. She could be lying there wounded and in need of aid or even worse… dead and they wouldn't even know. It seemed like hours passed when she finally appeared through a partially blocked window waving her arm for them to come.

"One at a time," Pegan said but Lorandrial had already blown by him and was in full sprint on his way towards the building. They each held their breath until he vanished through the door. Moments later he appeared next to Saress.

"Go," Pegan directed Thathra.

Moments later he too was safely there.

"Run like the devil's on your heels," Pegan said. "I'll be right behind you."

Averie stepped out but hesitated to make sure Pegan followed when she felt the impact. It was hard and directly in her abdomen knocking her backwards. Stumbling as if drunk she screamed in agonizing pain. As she spun to retreat back into the opening, she was hit again. The impact was fierce and launched her into Pegan's arms.

Pegan's mouth fired open as if his worst nightmare had just come true and then he screamed but no words came. The bastards had been there all along waiting and hiding, he should have known better. Perhaps Lorandrial was right, maybe he wasn't fit to lead.

Pegan lowered her to the ground.

She gasped in hurried breaths, "I'm sorry," she said. Her face turned pale and lost all expression.

Pegan looked around panicked and twitched nervously.

"I'm sorry," she whispered again "I should have—"

"Shhhh," Pegan said. He placed a finger against her lips to silence her. "Save your strength, you're going to be okay." He could see a large red ring beginning to form around the broken shaft that protruded from her chest.

Averie moved her lips as if talking but no words came and then, in silence, her eyes closed and her chest ceased to rise. A peaceful expression came to her face, almost doll-like.

After a silent prayer, he slipped his cloak free and placed it over her. Seeing her lying there he became woozy and fell hard against the wall and slid down until his knees touched his chest. A thick heavy tear rolled down his cheek. He had never known love as it brought on weakness. Often, he had used that same love to interrogate someone by hurting their spouse. "Damn you," he raised a fist to the sky and yelled. Was this all an evil trick, a way to punish him for all his wrongs he's done? He looked down at the lifeless lump with misty eyes. It seemed like an eternity before he pulled the cloak back, to look at her face one last time.

He had no explanation why, but in their short time together he had grown to love her. Yet he never told her once. He spent many nights awake wondering if he would have the strength to let her leave without breaking down. Now, none of that mattered. There would be no trip to the portal, no sobbing goodbye's, no new steward, all because of him.

Out of instinct, Pegan went for his dagger as he heard the scuffle of footsteps approach then he let his hand slip free. There was no need to fight anymore. Every reason he had to fight lay dead before him on the ground. A shadow fell upon them as he knelt over the body in a protective position. He waited to feel the bite of a blade, instead, he felt a comforting hand.

"She's dead," Pegan said, choking on the words.

Saress had never seen Pegan act or look this way. He seemed confused, lost... broken. "How?" she whispered.

Sitting by the body, he pulled his legs up tightly to his chest and buried his face. The sobs came pouring through in muffled gasps. "She paused to make sure I followed and in that split second she was hit with a bolt." He struggled with the words. "When she spun she got hit again in the back."

Saress picked up the shaft, anger burned on her face as she snapped it many times then threw it down and crushed the pieces with her foot.

She refused to talk to a cloak, so she pulled it back and said her final goodbye's then kissed Averie's forehead. "We cannot complete the mission," Saress choked on the words. "But I refuse to let her death go in vain. Every last one of the Brotherhood dies today, or I'll join her in death! There can be no other outcome."

Pegan looked into her eyes and what he saw frightened him. There was an anger, no, a hatred, a burning hatred to kill all things that wore black.

Thathra returned to see what the delay was but when he saw the covered body, he knew better to not ask.

"One last battle so grand they'll write songs about us," Pegan said. Then with her aid, he climbed to his feet and adjusted his belt.

Lorandrial barely made it back to the safety of the opening as a bolt whizzed by just inches from his head.

"Every arrow will be spent, every sword broken, before today ends," Thathra yelled in his deepest barbarian tone. "Give us the strength to overcome these odds, grant us the stamina to endure, and the skill to survive this day," he prayed to his God.

The plan was simple. Saress and Lorandrial would deal with the archers while Pegan and Thathra handled those on the ground bold enough to attack.

"For Averie," Saress yelled while Thathra blew his horn with all his might.

With everything set and the belief none of them was going home, they would fight like maniacs. Pegan darted from the opening then went straight into a roll. The motion was too quick for the archer and he had no chance of success as the bolt buried into the ground several paces behind him. Knowing Pegan had no means to attack, he remained in his position and cocked his bow for another shot.

Saress stepped out and with her vision located the sniper and let an arrow fly. The shot was no less than perfect as it passed through the assassins head scattering bone, blood, and brains against the wall behind him.

"For Averie," Pegan cheered as he watched the man crumble.

They never tried to hide and remained directly in the street waiting for the attack.

Darting in and out of the shadows, the Brotherhood seized the opportunity and moved in from all directions. They climbed over, under, around and even through the rubble to get at them.

Saress looked towards Lorandrial with a grin, "don't die with unspent arrows."

The twang of repeated bowstring sounded more like musical instruments in a duel than a war while assassins fell like flies. Their aim was meticulous except for the rare occasion when they missed and sparks lit the sky as steel tips found stone. Behind them, more enemies approached.

"We can't win," Pegan said to Thathra who stood beside him.

"No, we can't," Thathra replied. His massive hand dwarfed Pegans shoulder as he pulled him close, "but they'll feel my wraith before it's over." His face held the smile of a man who had gone insane with anger.

"One final charge for Averie," they yelled in unison and took the fight to the assassins.

The Brotherhood had not expected the sudden charge and halted their advance while a few retreated.

Pegan arrived first and crashed into them without fear. His movements were reckless yet precise and his first victim—confused by the sudden change of events—allowed his weapon to be knocked away and died without a scream. Next, Pegan began an attack placing both blades at different angles and spinning in a clockwise, corkscrew motion. He paused, spun counter-clockwise, paused, then spun again clockwise.

The strange attack was something they had never seen and frantically climbed over one another trying to get out of the way. Those who failed fell dead at Pegans feet, sliced to ribbons. Screams of pain and agony that could curdle blood filled the air as a trail of corpses dotted Pegan's path.

Thathra was not as quick but held a different advantage. His axe was long and sharp and prevented any from being able to mount any serious assault. The first who tried leaped in but quickly retreated as the blade whizzed by only inches from his face.

More worried about the blade than his location, the assassin backed away for another attempt but ended up in the direct path of Pegan, or more precisely his blades and died having never seen his killer.

All around them pools of blood formed like large lakes and ran like rivers as it was spilled faster than the ground could drink it up.

From another angle, a few more assassins arrived but died. Thathra sliced left, then right, then left again cleaving the man in three distinct pieces while the last swing took the head off a second unsuspecting assassin.

Somehow in all the chaos, Pegan heard the click and twang of a bolt being released and he knew it was destined for him. He jumped straight up and performed an acrobatic back-flip. Upside down in midair, he watched the bolt pass where he stood only moments before. "Archer," he yelled as he landed.

Saress scanned the surrounding area till she found the man high upon a pile of rubble. She drew the string taut then delivered the arrow but missed as the man ducked behind cover to reload his bow.

Completely unaware that an arrow just missed his head, the archer rose to fire but was hit directly in the chest. Screams told her he still lived but would never fight again.

All around them dust-choked their nostrils and the ring of steel and screams of men dying filled the air. A few assassins abandoned the fight to aid their fallen comrades.

With his last arrow spent, Lorandrial abandoned his bow for his sword and engaged the enemy.

Pegan exploited every weakness of his current target and sliced with surgical precision taking the fingers off his latest victim.

Determined not to surrender, he continued to fight with bloody nubs.

Pegan admired the man's determination but then buried his dagger to the pommel in the man's eye then twisted the blade. The attack effectively ended the man's career.

Thathra was not having as much luck and the pile of bodies around him was only about half that of Pegan's.

Saress fired her last arrow which ended the life of another then jerked her two-handed blade free. With the blade in one hand and her claws extended like daggers, she charged into the battle.

Lorandrial screamed with rage and his eyes squinted red against the sun. His long slender blade dripped with blood and all around him lay dead men except for one who crawled around looking for his hand in the bloody mess.

Saress crashed into a waiting group and swung her blade with all the fury of a hell-bent mother.

Seeing her coming they scattered, but one wasn't quick enough and was caught by her claw as it raked past removing his face. Another died as her tail snapped to one side catching him across the head effectively shattering the skull.

The sound of war tore through the city letting all know exactly where the battle was taking place, and by the screams of pain, who was winning.

As they fought, the sight of more assassins coming to aid drained what little hope remained. Covered in blood, dust, and other bodily fluids, they soon realized the end was nearing. The time had come for one final charge to end it all, which would never come.

Pegan jerked backwards and screamed in pain as his left hand became useless. His dagger fell to the dirt and his fingers tingled, a bolt had torn through his shoulder. All around him time seemed to slow, and he knew when he saw an assassin emerge from the shadows, blade held high, without a doubt, his time here on Icearaus was about to end.

Saress threw her short sword killing the one who was just about to deliver the killing blow to Pegan and then charged in his direction to lend aid.

Wounded, Pegan was still a formidable foe and fought like a rabid animal with only one arm.

Severely outnumbered, Lorandrial had his back to a wall and was unable to mount even the slightest attack.

Thathra stumbled and nearly dropped his axe as he grabbed his leg. An intense pain erupted up his spine and he crumbled to his knees. A loud groan escaped his lungs. His mind blocked out everything around him and his only concern at that moment was to get the shaft out of his thigh.

Seizing the opportunity, the assassin landed a kick to the side of the barbarian's head leaving him to lie flat on his back.

Even now, wounded, and partially dazed, Thathra continued to fight off his would-be attackers. He kicked, squirmed, wiggled, and blocked with his axe, but was unable to regain his footing.

The archer smiled as his unsuspecting victim was oblivious to his presence and loaded a bolt.

Having heard the click, Thathra rolled out of the way just before the bolt impacted where his head had been seconds earlier.

"No," Pegan screamed as he saw the archer try to destroy Thathra. The next words out of his mouth almost sounded demonic and the archer screamed the most ungodly noise you could ever imagine and fell to his knees clawing at his face as both eyes began to dissolve.

Saress leaped through the air and landed next to Thathra, to aid him back upon his feet. As they fought, a head rolled by as Pegan snarled something unintelligible, and then kicked the dead assassin clear.

Saress looked at him with fear in her eyes, she was still not sure exactly what she saw, but it was something no mortal was capable of.

Pinned to the ground, Lorandrial was in the process of being restrained. It was obvious they had plans to extend their suffering if at all possible.

Somehow finding the horn, Thathra blew it again and prayed to his God for strength but was hit from behind with something hard and collapsed to the ground.

Pegan tried to maintain his balance but suddenly fell like a cleaved tree. Around his ankle was a cord which was weighted on each end and thrown effectively binding his legs together. On the ground and with only one hand, he was surrounded by a group who was kicking every perceivable inch of his bruised and battered body.

Saress looked around the battlefield at the bodies strewn like trash on a windy day. Lorandrial was down, Pegan was severely wounded and would probably die any moment, Thathra was tangled up in a net, and here she remained, unwounded but surrounded, she just wondered if her hide would become belts, boots, or gloves.

In the distance a blackened cloud worked its way towards them, moving against the wind it came quick and with purpose. The land darkened as if a massive cloud had just blotted out the sun and an annoying hum filled the air.

"What is that noise?" Saress hissed while her sword parried the dagger of an assassin.

"Don't take me as a fool, to get me to look away so you can strike me dead," the assassin snarled as he came in low and quick to take the legs out from under her, which she blocked by instinct, never taking her eyes off the strange cloud.

The wind increased and the noise grew in intensity till they found themselves no longer able to fight. With no other choice, weapons were abandoned and ears covered.

Blinded by dust and other flying objects ripped free by the wind, debris now swirled in a massive vortex. Screams filled the air as assassins dropped to the ground. Their bodies' swelled and large ugly pus filled blisters formed on their chest, arms, and legs. Eyes bled and mouths were forced open by tongues that swelled so rapidly their mouths could no longer contain them, and bubbling green ooze seeped out between their rotting teeth.

"Elwrick," an assassin screamed into the sky just before he collapsed dead. It had to be him, no mortal man had the power to summon such a devastating storm.

All around them things darted with such speed it left their vision blurred and they only wondered when their time would come but it never did.

When the cloud dissipated and the dust cleared, every assassin lay dead but what shocked her more was the fact not one member of her party had been affected.

Pegan climbed to his feet and stood on tired legs, mouth agape. Words could not describe what just occurred and had he not witnessed it, he probably wouldn't have believed it.

Moments later, a large wasp landed before them on legs no thicker than spaghetti. It looked similar to the wasp they had saved due to Averie's demand, but larger and the outer exoskeleton was a different shade of green. Along the abdomen, there are black, honeycomb-shaped markings with yellow spots. The lower halves of each of the six legs were covered in a fine light brown hair as was the torso giving the appearance it wore a fur coat. Two antennas sprouted forth from the top of the head and at the end where you would expect an orb was instead a huge puffy ball of fur that matched that on the torso. Each one of the four eyes glowed blue and down the sides of the abdomen was a red light that pulsated with each heartbeat. The end of each leg instead of having a pointed claw had an articulating hand with four fingers. In one hand it held an assassin by the scruff of his neck.

Saress gasped, then released a sigh. The man that thing carried was no other than Lord Rayne.

The Wasp… thing… creature threw down its captive and aggressively jabbed a long silver hypodermic-like stinger from its abdomen directly into his back. Moments later the stinger was removed then he was tossed aside like a used rag.

Pegan lowered his weapons accepting defeat as the creature approached.

"I heard the call from the one who saved my daughter, the debt has been repaid," it said in a high-pitched voice then took to flight. Each of its four silver wings flapped slowly at first to not create a dust storm.

The sound sent shivers down Pegan's spine. He stood dumbfounded as he watched it fly away to catch up with the darkened swarm that hovered off in the distance.

"Even in death she saved us," Saress said.

"Yes… yes she did," Pegan agreed nodding his head.

Pegan never hesitated and went straight to Lord Rayne who withered in pain. Large beads of sweat dripped down his face.

"Kill him," Saress hissed, her eye's narrowed.

"Kill me, kill me now," he demanded through a jaw that was locked open.

Pegan rolled the assassin over until he found what he was looking for, a black shiny key. "I won't take Averie back with the collar around her neck."

"Kill me," Lord Rayne hissed.

Pegan thought for a minute and watched the man squirm. The pain was obviously immense. "No," Pegan said. "Suffer the same as you have made us suffer."

Lorandrial searched through the bodies till he found his weapons, "I suggest you find your weapons, another attack may come before we know it."

The noise of battle once filled the air but now there was only silence except for a crying moan from the light breeze.

As much as Pegan didn't want to admit, the advice Lorandrial gave was probably sound, and they all did likewise.

Back at the building, they stood around the corpse of the woman they all came to love and watched Pegan slide the key into the collar. They all held their breath till they heard the audible click of the mechanism snapping open.

"Give it here," Saress demanded. To their amazement, she walked back to Lord Rayne and latched it around his neck and securely fastened the mechanism. "How do you like it?" She said as she looked directly into his eyes, and then slammed his face down into the dirt.

"We'll take the body back to the elven people for burial. Lady Alenia adopted her as her own, she deserves a proper burial," Lorandrial said.

"How do I tell Elwrick?" Pegan said. "He entrusted me, and I failed him." Pegan pulled back the cloak to take one last look at her, stroking her long hair he kissed her forehead as a sign of respect. "Bury her in my cloak, that's all I ask." His words came not as a request, but as an order.

"I can do that," Lorandrial said, as he pulled the cloak back over her face.

"Wait!" Saress screamed. To their surprise, she ripped the cloak free.

Pegan studied Saress. There was a glint in her eye as if Averie would become a quick meal.

Reluctantly, Pegan tried to cover her again but Saress ripped the material free from his hands and threw it towards the street.

"She's not dead," Saress screamed.

"She's lifeless and not breathing. I would say that's pretty much dead. I know it hurts, I wanted to take her place, to be lying there instead but I can't," Pegan choked on the words.

"She's not dead, damn it," Saress snarled. There was a hiss in her voice that only came when she became extremely agitated.

Knocking the others out of the way to get a better look, almost how a grieving mother would react before placing their child in the ground.

"Saress," Pegan softly said. "There's nothing we can do, we need to let go. I hurt just as much as you, please." He recovered his cloak and tried once more to cover Averie.

Saress grabbed the cloak and tossed it aside then drew her sword. "She ain't dead, and if you cover her again, I will *KILL* you."

Thathra stepped between the two and led Pegan away, "let her grieve, she may be a reptile, but she still has feelings."

Saress picked Averie up and cradled the woman in her arms. She gently stroked her hair and smiled a mother's smile. "We need to go… now" she said, then walked from the room towards the street.

Lorandrial glanced at Pegan. "Don't say a word, she needs time to grieve."

Pegan offered to carry Averie as they neared the edge of town but collapsed. His face had gone pale, and he became disoriented. Thathra lifted Pegan back to his feet and tried to lend aid but he was no better off, and the pair leaned on each other for support. They slowly made their way out of the city and encountered no enemies in doing so, which was a blessing because none of them was in any condition to fight.

Pegan led them to a nearby glade surrounded by dense vegetation and a latticework of branches. The ground was covered in a soft blanket of grass and a small stream trickled along one edge. To the north there was a large pile of stones that provided shelter from the wind. Lorandrial built a roaring fire and as the sky darkened they all huddled around the flames.

Hours later Pegan moved closer to the reptile. "Saress?" he asked. He looked down at the lifeless body she cradled, watched her stroke the hair. "How do you know she's not dead?"

"Because I can see things you cannot," she said. "Her body is not losing heat. She is not going cold as a corpse should. That cold stone floor where she laid would have leached every ounce of heat from her body in minutes, yet somehow she remains warm."

"Thathra... Lorandrial," Pegan yelled their names.

Before he finished the two stood beside him. "We need to examine the wounds," Pegan said. "But remember, she's still a lady so we need to remain respectful." They used his cloak to keep her covered while pulling up her dress to examine the wound. To their shock, the tip of the bolt no more broke the skin than a scratch that was not even deep enough to draw blood. The wound on the back was even less, not even a bruise was visible.

"Impossible," Pegan said. "I saw it happen, heard the impact. It was a direct hit, and there was blood. Look, he pointed to the big red stain on the dress. No one could survive two hits like that."

Thathra looked baffled.

Pegan looked more like an apparition than a man as he moved closer to the fire. "It doesn't make any sense," he said with a painful face.

Lorandrial lowered the dress then rubbed his fingers almost as if it had left a strange residue. Sniffing his hands he looked back at the material and ran it through his fingers one more time. "My word," he said and then began to examine the impact area. "Well this explains it," he said.

"What?" They all turned towards him.

"The material is different from what you believe. It's not regular cloth but Spiderweb silk weave cloth."

Saress looked dumbfounded.

"Spiderweb silk weave cloth is a material constructed from the silken thread of the Birch Spider that inhabits the Imperial caves. It is extremely rare and priceless. So rare in fact it takes over a hundred years of collecting to make a single dress. Such a rare item is often only given to Elven Queens," Lorandrial said.

"How does it work?" Pegan asked.

"I truly don't know, but the thread is woven in layers and when complete it's lighter than silk yet harder than dragon scale."

"Then why is she laying there limp?" Thathra asked.

Pegan slammed a fist against the stones lining the fire and walked away into the darkness and sat alone.

They all watched him go, but only Saress followed and sat beside him for a long while.

"I think you should follow Lorandrial," Pegan said. "At this time I don't think I'm worthy to lead us anymore."

"What?" Saress asked.

"I've made to many mistakes, and now, I almost made another had it not been for you. I know what happened but yet I'm too blind to see it." Pegan licked his dry lips. "And now my body is broken. I can't fight, hell, I can barely walk. I'm a simple burden now, go on without me. I will tell you how to get through the caves."

"Teach me," She said, "tell me what happened so I can learn as well."

"Tetrodotoxin," Pegan said. "Those bolts were coated with tetrodotoxin, mummy poison."

"What?" Saress asked.

"It a neurotoxin… a poison," Pegan said. "It's found in the sex organs of the puffer fish that live along the shoreline south of here. When used properly, it makes those inflicted with it go into a coma so severe that they appear dead to the normal eye. Luckily, you don't have normal eyes."

"So their intent was to have us think she was dead and leave her?" Saress asked.

"Or put us into such a rage that we would fight to the death and then they would come claim her."

"A groan at the fire drew their attention and they looked just in time to see Thathra fall backward."

"Well, I guess it must have finally hit him," she said but Pegan was already leaning against her shoulder, completely unconscious.

Chapter 28

Far to the east beyond The Shadowed Mountains and deep within the Wilds stood an eerie dilapidated shack in the center of a knoll which appeared like a balding head breaching the stagnant waters of an unnamed bog.

Upheaved by massive roots, the structure appeared twisted and leaned to one side as if being swallowed by the spongy ground. The door hung cock-eyed by a single rusty hinge and massive claw marks scared the rotten plank siding, as if a giant cat tried to slash its way in. Every window was fractured and what few shingles remained flapped like clapping hands as the wind drifted past releasing a tormented cry. Around the shack, a yellow haze rose and the pungent smell of decay lingered and all vegetation within its reach lay dead.

Lucinda darted around the shack ignoring the high-pitched squeal of rickety floorboards which threatened to fail at any moment. In one hand she carried a large glass beaker half full of blood, and in the other a small eye-dropper which she used to place a single drop in each corner of the shack. The blood sizzled on contact and a faint whiff of red smoke plumed.

Her blackened lips curled into a smile almost cracking her pale skin, this was the first sign everything was in place.

She looked out the window at the night sky. Thin wisps of faint clouds that looked like apparitions drifted by obscuring the moon and brought to life ghastly shadows that danced against the back wall.

Her body trembled at the thought of what she was about to do and considered leaving now. The only harm she had caused so far where the three dead men which lie just outside the door. Nobody would miss them anyway. *In the eyes of the citizens, they were criminals, she had done a good thing*, she thought.

She had never delved this deep into the dark arts, never once considered it before, but the need outweighed the risk. She shivered as a cold, tingling sensation raced up her spine. What she attempted tonight would ensure the survival of her species.

The moonlight licking at the edge of the window frame confirmed the time grew short. There was much she still needed to accomplish before the light reached the summoner's circle. She needed to hurry, to let herself sink into the euphoria of what might be would cost her what should have been if she failed to time it perfectly. Back on task, she opened a large satchel that lay on a rickety bench and removed four small rodents by their tails. Unmerciful, she jabbed each one with what resembled a rusty fishhook and hung one in each corner by a string made of goat sinew. The rodents wiggled, squirmed and squealed but she worried not about them drawing unwanted attention as she didn't expect company, at least none who would care.

Directly in the center of the shack, she examined the summoner's circle going over every last detail exactly as the book described. She had no choice but to work from memory as she could not risk the theft of the book being discovered. Her plan was simple, each night as King Karayan slept, she would sneak into the library and read the words until the process was so ingrained in her mind, she was incapable of forgetting.

The floor was blasted away leaving a jagged edge that jutted out like serrated teeth exposing the dead ground. It was there she constructed the circle. It was six feet in diameter and constructed from human bones interlaced together. Three heads—freshly killed that morning—were placed on pikes with purple streamers and raised exactly six feet above the ground. Each eye was plucked and positioned on the floor where they gazed into the circle.

Moonlight crept through the window like an evil phantasm searching for a lost soul and landed precisely on the circle. The time to act was now, delay was not an option.

In the center of the circle, she dumped the entrails of her victims then went to the bench and unfolded the obsidian colored cloth which concealed the ceremonial weapon. Carefully, as if peeling away layers of skin, she spread out the cloth until the double-edged, razor-sharp basalt dagger lay exposed. The handle was carved from a human thigh bone and the pommel mimicked a grasping hand.

The weapon felt cold in her hand, not a freezing, painful cold, but a good cold, like a cool mist on a hot summer day.

Back at the circle, she extended her left arm over the pit with her palm turned up. Next, she positioned the dagger till it reflected a thin beam of light onto the entrails. It was only now that words appeared on the blade. She studied each word reading them in her mind, one wrong pronunciation and the spell would be ruined. With all doubt removed, she read the sentence out loud in a commanding voice. As the last word escaped her mouth, she slashed the blade across her palm. The cut was so fine nothing happened. She waited in silence, not the slightest hint of pain visible on her face. Her lips curled back into a snarl exposing rotted teeth and her eyes faded to white. Her palm filled with blood until it reached the gaps between her fingers then flowed like a waterfall onto the entrails.

She understood enough blood was spent when the blade cracked in many places then crumbled. As the last chunk fell, she tossed the handle into the circle and watched the bones burst into flames. On the bench next to the cloth, a book materialized. The correct page was easy to locate as it only held two. On the left side, she placed her bloody palm leaving a perfect imprint. The book's bloodlust was satisfied so on the right page, it revealed the hidden words in the form of writing the color of blood.

Time is crucial. She began to chant the phrase and when the last word slipped off her tongue, the entire page glowed electric blue and the words radiated a dazzling silver. The conjuration was complete.

She was ecstatic, the spell worked exactly as the book described it would if performed properly. Now, she simply waited.

Unlike demons which wanted to be here, liches despised the world and wished nothing but ill will towards man. Because of this, a lich required a much more delicate process and power way beyond her capabilities, but she discovered a way to circumvent her inabilities.

Regardless, there was still no guarantee she could lure one here to the Realm of Mortals.

As the light of the moon drifted off the circle and nothing happened, she sulked with defeat. With neither the time nor energy to try again, she would return to the library and research once more, honing her skills even sharper for next time when all hell suddenly broke loose.

An unpleasant green fog billowed from the circle smothering the room, while ash fell like rain and the smell of rotten eggs tainted with decaying flesh crossed her senses. Backed up to the door she had two choices, stick her head out for fresh air, or risk suffocation. The shack rumbled and shook but somehow remained upright while inside the sound of entrails being devoured crossed her ears.

As the fog dissipated, a translucent shape solidified within the circle. It was about the size of a normal man and wore a tattered black robe. The skin visible under the robe looked desiccated and stretched to the point of tearing, while the head was completely skeletal except for a thin shred of shriveled black skin, which only remained because it was pressed between the skull and the heavy steel crown that held a glowing blue gem. Silver eyes that burned with a fiery hatred filled the blackened sockets and his bony fingers wore many rings, each a unique design. Around his neck, there was a chain of yellowed bone and each link was carefully inscribed with runes. A large purple pendant that pulsated with a strange energy dangled from the chain and a shroud of whirling mist that induced fear circled his entirety.

"Speak forth your reason to rip me from my realm?" The lich hissed. A long forked tongue lashed out and fire flared up through the jagged hole which left the edge smoldering.

Lucinda reeled back from the blast of heat as he released his anger. "What is your name?" she demanded.

The lich responded with another blast of flame. The charred ceiling dripped hot embers that fluttered like snow.

"WHAT IS YOUR NAME?" She demanded as she circled the magnificent beast taking it all in. She could feel the power dripping off the bones.

"Phlorax… from the Realm of Agathys, the Thirty-Third Plane of Tartarus," the lich responded. "And who might you be?" He was astonished at how this mortal had learned such a powerful spell normally reserved for those who dwelled in the underworld. The easiest way to discover her source of power was to learn her true name.

"Lucinda," she responded. If the spell was done properly, the creature was bound to the circle and could cause her no harm, unless she ventured to close which she cautiously remained just out of reach.

"And why have you called me?" Phlorax snarled while he held a palm up towards the sky and watched a small flame leap from finger to finger.

"I summoned you…" She knew liches were twisted evil defiled creatures that should never be trusted, but she lacked the magic to gain what she wanted, so a trade would need to be arranged. She only hoped what she had to offer would be enough to satisfy the liches hate. "I have acquired something that I know would suit you extremely well back on Agathys," she said.

"And what do you possess that I can't gain on my own?" His voice hissed like steel being quenched and both eyes flared brightly.

"Man blood," she said. "I have it here, upon my body."

"You waste my valuable time with man blood," Phlorax said.

She could see the anger form on the skeletal head and fire shot from his mouth which singed her hair.

"I could get man blood by the gallons," he snarled and his tongue lashed out towards her. "I may yet strike you dead where you stand for your insolen—"

"You are correct, you can get man blood by the gallons," she interrupted him, "but willingly and from none other than the elusive Arlin Brack."

From under her robe, she removed a small golden chain and from it a small vial dangled which contained a single drop of blood. She twirled the vial as if stirring a cauldron until the clear sides turned a bright red.

Phlorax calmed greatly having seen the blood.

"There is great power contained within this small tube for those who know how to extract it… properly," she said.

"Give it to me… now," Phlorax demanded. He reached out with an open hand.

She waited till his fingers neared then jerked it away teasing the undead monster. "Do you honestly believe I would give this to you without wanting something in return?"

The lich remained quiet, his eyes focused on the frail, yet very powerful woman. Her ugly disfigured face was quite beautiful in his eyes and she carried a fog of mystery while emitting a strange aura that stunk of quality.

"What is it you desire, perhaps a familiar to keep you company?"

She listened to his words intently and knew there was nothing a lich could grant that she was interested in. "I don't need company as I can get all that I desire." Right before his eyes, her form changed as she became a man. Tall dark, and handsome, he was corded with muscles. "I could have any woman I desire," she said with a deep and masculine voice. When she changed again, she was a beautiful woman with long blond hair with fair skin and the most dazzling eyes that sparkled in the moonlight. "Or any man of my choosing." The voice was soft and warm.

The lich released a wicked laugh that shook the entire structure. "The ability to change appearance is but a minor spell, easily detected and simply prevented." His eyes focused on her and she could almost feel her skin begin to crawl.

Her arms stretched and her fingers lengthened until they scrapped the ground and both feet enlarged till they busted through their shoes. Massive warts that sprouted long black hairs that wiggled like worms formed all over her body and her skin turned a sickly black as if she had died days earlier. Her body screamed with pain yet her mouth never moved.

She panicked, and by the way his eyes flared she knew he sensed it. He took control of her and now she was a puppet in his hands. Had she pressed too far? Would she be destroyed? Or worse, dragged back to his realm and forced into an eternal life of slavery? The thoughts raced through her mind.

"But to change another person and bend them to your will takes true power," Phlorax coughed up a laugh and blood splattered against her robe. "But, since I am interested in the blood and cannot take it from you I will restore your appearance." With a snap of his bony fingers, she returned to her old wicked self.

She released a low, inaudible sigh. Her actions had almost cost her everything trying to impress something that contained more magic in a toe than her entire body.

"Don't keep me waiting as I wish to return home this century. What do you require for that blood?"

She thought for a long time, always keeping the vial in view but just out of reach. "I want the yellow blood from the child the bearer carries," she said with a smile. "I was led to believe a lich of your abilities should be able to acquire it quite easily." Her voice grew weak. Just being in his presence started to take a toll on her body and she could feel her life draining away.

Phlorax laughed. "I wish nothing to do with mortals, as I have forsaken man centuries ago."

"But yet you take them as slaves," she fired back.

"Trophies," he corrected her.

Lucinda squinted from the fire which flared up around him. "What better trophy is there than Arlin Brack?" she asked.

In her studies she learned that unlike demons, liches were incapable of soul possession but could claim ownership of the physical form if they intervened just as death was about to occur thus trapping the soul inside the corpse, and, if they had the required component, a drop of blood willingly given to a witch for services rendered, they could claim ownership of not only the physical form but the soul as well.

"Why don't you go yourself?" he shot back. "Would it not give you pleasure to watch her hang as the lifeblood dripped away."

"I would love to, the euphoria I would receive would be most pleasurable. Unlike you though, I am made of flesh, blood, and bone, and can be killed. A risk I cannot take."

"Surely, with your magical abilities you could easily dispatch a simple band of travelers escorting a frail girl, and then devise a way to get what you desire from the mother?"

"I don't possess the knowledge to separate yellow blood from the mother, and her child," she admitted, "but you do." She bit her lip till it bled then continued. "There is one other concern I have. I do not know yet of his extent, but Elwrick had been heavily involved as well."

The lich grew sick and vomited a pile of maggots. "If you know what's good for you, you will never speak his name again within my presence, or I shall have no other choice but to strike you down right where you stand."

Lucinda studied the lich intensely, the words she spoke made him grow quite uneasy. "What do you fear?" she asked. She knew it was all but impossible to destroy a lich. Even if their physical form dies, their soul remains and in a few days, they are granted a new body.

"I fear very few," Phlorax said. "Elwrick though, strikes fear in all liches as he has the power to travel to Agathys and destroy my phylactery which in turn, destroys me. It's not as simple as you believe."

Lucinda listened diligently as he spoke and understood his concern. Elwrick was a dangerous creature and not one to underestimate. "It is my understanding that on Agathys your powers are tenfold compared to Icearaus, and you would have companions. If he did go there, would that not be the ultimate trophy?"

"You forgot one other minor detail. There is a rhythmic link between her and him and when she nears death, he will feel her pain and come to deliver aid. How will you prevent his arrival?"

"Simple," she giggled, "I've already concocted a spell of deceit that will be placed upon her and Elwrick will feel nothing as her lifeblood drains away."

"Possible," Phlorax said. "But how do you plan to cast such a spell upon her when her location evades you?" he asked, intrigued by her innate knowledge. "In order for a web of deceit to be cast successfully, it must be cast upon the individual."

"True," Lucinda said. "But I don't need them in their entirety, all I need is a piece of them. The rhythmic link is associated with the unique genetic code which makes up the body." She pulled out a rag covered in dried blood. "I recovered this before her residence was burned to the ground. I need only to cast it upon her blood, and the effects are the same as if it was upon her."

The lich clapped his bony hands together, "And what of her companions?"

"Do with them as you wish, they mean little to me."

"Do you believe they are going to let me take her, without a fight?"

"I'm sure you can find a way to dispatch them without significant loss. And even if you do take serious loses, in the end, will it not be worth it?" She held up the small glass tube containing Arlin's blood. "Do I need to remind you what you can do with man blood when it is given voluntarily to a witch for services rendered?"

"No," he answered, his voice blazed like wildfire. "I have studied the dark arts of body possession and the rights of ownership longer than you have been alive. But what I wish to know?" The lich paused for a moment as if talking to something back on the Agathys. "What I wish to know is what you understand about the acquisition of yellow blood from an unwilling subject?"

"My business is my own and what I wish to do with the yellow blood is to be kept secret."

"I think you toil in a dangerous game that you don't fully understand," the lich said. "It's one thing to alter the physical state through metamorphosis, but to tangle with the building blocks of life I feel are way beyond your comprehension."

Lucinda laughed out loud and clapped her hands. "You ignorant fool, I alter nothing, I simply harvest and replace. I just needed the right bearer and child to be chosen. Instead of forcing my plan, I waited and practiced my art perfecting it, but now, the time for action is at hand."

The lich almost seemed to sigh, he hated the fact there might even be the slightest chance a mortal was smarter than him. "I will see to it… personally, to make sure nothing goes wrong, but first, I wish to know what you plan to acquire by obtaining the child's yellow blood."

Lucinda looked at him with a dreadful stare, "salvation."

"Salvation," the lich laughed, "salvation from what?"

"Ever since I was born I've had the gift of clairvoyance. Before it ever occurred, I witnessed my own rape and birth of my only son. I witnessed me abandoning my child before he could be sacrificed. Since then, my powers have been dormant until now. Now, I have grand visions of what is to become and it doesn't bode well for the inhabitants of Icearaus. The sky burning with fire and ash, water turned to blood, everything green will be dead and rotted. Icearaus will only know pain and suffering."

"How does the yellow blood of the bearer provide salvation from what is to come? Enlighten me."

She smiled as there was no harm in telling him. He had already given away his soul for eternal life and could not use it for personal gain. "Elwrick is not the only one who can open a portal to another world, the child can as well. When the Creator places the child within the mother, he is given a specific genetic code to allow a second portal to be opened which will allow him to return. By extracting the yellow blood of the child and infusing it into my body, I will then have the ability to open a portal out of this world. It will be a one-way trip, true, but it can be no worse than the future of Icearaus."

"Except there is one minor detail I fear you have overlooked in all your excitement at the thought of escaping damnation. Yellow blood, just like red, cannot be used unless it's giving willingly."

"There is a flaw in the design. While the child is still inside the bearer, it can neither accept nor reject what happens to it. So the milking of its yellow blood is neither willing... nor unwillingly."

The lich released a wicked laugh then clasped its bony hands together. "My dear, I love the way you think but you are forgetting one element. Man yellow blood and woman yellow blood is different, you cannot use the opposite."

Shaking her head in disagreement she spoke like a scientist, "this bearer is different. I sensed it on the bloody rag."

"Are you implying?"

"Yes," she giggled. "This is the first time a bearer has ever carried a female."

The lich shook his head in amazement. She had to be the smartest mortal he ever encountered and would make a fine lich given the opportunity. "I want Arlin's blood as payment in advance?" Phlorax said. "And I will make sure you get the yellow blood you desire."

"I'm no fool," she hissed, and carefully placed the vial back into the leather pouch. "I will give it to you when I receive the yellow blood and not before."

"Or, I could simply kill you and take it."

"And I have no doubt you have the power to strike me down with a single thought, but then the blood will be useless. Remember, it must be given voluntarily," she answered his threat.

The lich snarled something in a voice she had never heard before.

"I will afford you this bit of information to sweeten the deal. I believe you won't have to wait long to cash in your reward though. Karayan sent Arlin in search of the bearer and I believe one of her escorts is the long deceased Demetrius. I personally think it's a suicide mission as I have seen both fight."

"Demetrius," the lich laughed. "It took you mortals this long to realize the lies and deceit. But then again, it was masterfully played and expertly executed so it doesn't surprise me your mortal's minds failed to comprehend."

Lucinda smiled a fake smirk, "Use this to contact me when you have the yellow blood." From her pocket, she produced a small broach and tossed it at the lich who snatched it with greedy enthusiasm. "And now I must take my leave."

Snapping her fingers, a laser thin blue line formed in midair then expanded outward to the width of a full-size door and she stepped through. Upon her exit, the thin line collapsed in upon itself leaving silver sparks fluttering into the air.

"Damn her," the lich snarled. In a puff of putrid yellow smoke, he was gone as well.

Chapter 29

egan woke screaming in a fit of rage. Frantically, he yanked away his tunic and fought with the buckle that held the thin, leather armor in place. His pale face glistened in the early morning light and large beads of sweat dripped from his quivering chin. As it snapped free, he grabbed at the small wound which appeared no more than a small slit surrounded by a reddish bruise. Pinkish streaks that resembled the gnarly roots of a tree spread out as if searching the environment for nourishment. On his back where the bolt exited, a small hole about the size of a child's finger was surrounded by dried bloody crust. Somehow, luck had gone his way, and the bolt hit no vital organs or major arteries. The wound would heal in time, it was the infection which was killing him.

"His shoulder looks bad, and the infection grows worse," Lorandrial said to Saress.

"Horrible would describe it more accurately," Saress said.

Thathra limped back from the stream having washed the crust from his eyes left behind by the poison-induced sleep. "There may yet be a way. Years ago…"

Lorandrial ignored Thathra as if he were a child. "We need to make a difficult decision." He stirred the dying fire with a stick spreading out the hot coals to form a base then dropped on a few more branches. "You three have experienced much in your time together, but what we need to consider is if Pegan has become more of a liability than an asset. A man in his condition will only cripple us."

The fire crackled and popped as the sticks ignited.

Saress looked at him with squinted eyes, "I know what you're thinking and I think it wrong. I understand the importance of getting Averie to the island, but I refuse to abandon him. If we do, he'll die from infection or the ravenous beasts that roam these mountains. There's even the possibility the Brotherhood will discover him before he passes and then he'll… I can't even think about it and I refuse to accept your reasoning."

Thathra placed his heavy fur cloak around Pegans shivering frame then headed straight for Lorandrial.

"Well, then what do you propose?" Lorandrial argued his point. "And from how it looks, I would say his left-hand remains useless. If he can't fight, then he's no good to us."

Thathra was a formidable man even with his wounded leg and never slowed as he reached the elf. With viper quickness, he snatched the elf by the tunic then began to shake him with such force his bow launched in one direction, each sword in another, and his head flopped back and forth as if the neck bone had suddenly dissolved. "Listen," he snarled in a tone that was barely human. "There's a plant. I don't know the name but my father used them when my sister was very young and became ill with infection. He would grind them up into a paste and coat the wound. He told me to always remember it as it may save a life someday but in my youth, I never thought of dying and quickly forgot it. Now, I wish I had listened."

"Can you describe it?" Saress said. "And quit shaking the man before you kill him."

Lorandrial crumbled to the ground as Thathra let go but quickly recovered and retrieved his weapons.

"They are tall, about three feet with a thin green stalk with bladed leaves that grow apart from each other. The key feature though is the bright blue flower on top. It is shaped like an up-turned bell with two yellow stalks protruding with black bulbs on the end of each stalk. I can remember my father saying if you find ones with faint white spots on the blue flowers to gather them as they are the most potent."

Saress thought for a moment, "I've seen those very plants, although none had white spots."

"Veronica Officinalis," Lorandrial said. His voice lacked enthusiasm.

"Who is that?" Saress asked.

"Not who, but what," Lorandrial said. "The flower you described, there is no other like it in all of Icearaus. The common name for it is Speedwell. Its primary use is to aid with infections and increase the healing speed of a wound."

Thathra grew livid. "You knew all along you worthless maggot," and pulled his axe free. "You want Pegan to die, don't you, admit it you stinking worm?"

Lorandrial pulled his blade free emitting an angry metallic hiss, he would not be shaken this time without a fight.

"Do you know where this cavern is and how to successfully navigate your way through it if we did happen upon it? What about the docks, you know its location? What else do you know you haven't told us?"

He drew back with the weapon to attack but was shocked to find it ripped from his grasp by Saress. "He's mine first, you can have him next." She ripped her sword free and let her flash into the thermal spectrum. With her enhanced vision, she could see the fright on his face.

Pegan stood and watched them squabble. He needed to do something as they looked to him for direction but his head swooned and he felt nauseous. Without his intervention, one member of the fellowship was going to die right here.

Saress neared and Lorandrial backed away but was too slow to prevent being slung to the ground by a wicked fast tail whip which took his feet out from under him. Leaning forward, she opened her massive maw baring her teeth and hissed something which threatened to burst all their eardrums.

Thathra smiled as he watched Saress hover over Lorandrial. "Kill the maggot," he screamed excitedly.

"SARESS," Pegan screamed, then vomited.

She turned to face him, a lust of rage filled her eyes and her body convulsed with anger.

"What are you doing?" he cried out.

Saress abandoned the fight and ran to the man's aid.

Thathra faced Lorandrial, "you ever talk like that again and I swear on my mother's grave I will cut your head off and feed your corpse to a pack of wolves, you hear me?"

Pegan's eyes were glazed over and he swayed side to side as if lost in a drunken stupor, and then collapsed almost landing in the fire. Saress bent down and placed her snout against his nose, her voice sounded more human than ever, like that of a child. "When I was poisoned you saved my life, tell me, what must I do to save yours?"

"Great," Lorandrial barked. "We'll overlook the woman whom we should focus our attention on and save a man who means nothing. He was a common criminal before this, and that's what he'll be after, regardless of our success."

"Speaking of that, where is Averie," Thathra said.

Saress looked to where she slept but the woman was nowhere to be seen. Next she scanned the glade and a fading heat came into view. "You stay here with Pegan, I'm going after her."

The trail grew brighter the closer she came and eventually Averie was discovered hiding in a large pile of fallen trees.

"Get away from me," she screamed. "Can't you see it, Karayan was right this whole time. I've caused nothing but grief, destroyed lives, and continually spread hate and discontent. I am nothing but a filthy creature that deserves nothing less than destruction. I'm surrendering to the Brotherhood."

"Over my dead body," Saress said.

"If that's how you want it." Averie snarled. She waited till Saress was within striking distance then balled up her fist, closed her eyes, and swung with all the determination of a caged animal.

Saress saw the attack coming and could have easily blocked it, but chose not to. She let her arms hang limp and waited for the blow to come. She wanted the woman to release her anger and frustration, to let it all out so she could be reasoned with. The fist slammed hard against her scales resulting in a deep thud. She pounded again and again till her hand bloodied.

Saress had no choice now but to intervene before Averie caused serious injury to herself. On the next strike she grabbed her by the wrist and twisted it till the deranged woman had no choice but to either sit or watch her arm break, she made the wise decision to sit.

"Don't ever say that again," Saress demanded. "You're not a filthy creature, you're just frustrated. You understood this quest would not be easy and there would be many dangers. There's more who would like to see us fail than—

"What about you?" Averie squeezed the words from her lungs in-between long winded sobs of anger, frustration, and fear. "I woke to see you killing Lorandrial."

"I told you, upon my life, I will protect you. That hasn't changed, not now, not ever. We fight because we disagree on matters which I view more important than he does," Saress explained. "Now we're heading back and if you run, I will carry you."

Against Lorandrial's better judgment, they agreed to stay another night and allow Pegan to rest a bit longer.

Averie's eyes were focused on the scales that lined the lizard's belly. She sat opposite her and the light from the fire made them glow like hot embers. She was ashamed and refused to make eye contact. To do so would admit guilt. Guilt in questioning her most trusted companion's loyalty, guilt from her attack, and most dishonorably, guilt of betrayal. She didn't have to look into those big yellow eyes with crescent-shaped pupils to know Saress was angry. She could feel it like a large stone bearing down upon her, crushing the life from her.

"Look at me," Saress said. There was a hint of anger, but also sympathy in her voice.

Averie complied, she anticipated the smack across the face she knew would come and tensed her muscles.

"Why did you run?" Saress asked.

Averie shrugged her shoulders.

"Well it was very foolish of you," she said. Her voice was only a whisper to keep from waking the others. "What were you trying to do? Or hope to accomplish by that selfish act?" The scales above her eyes rose and her eyes widened as she waited for an answer that never came. "Every one of us has sworn upon our lives to protect you, to see you to your destination. Nothing has changed."

Averie sighed. "Every word I said was true. Just earlier you were going to kill him for what?"

"I was—"

"Because of me. I don't understand why you won't admit it? I'm the cause of all this fighting amongst us."

"If you let me finish, I was going to kill him because of Pegan, not you."

The color drained from Averie's expressionless face.

"I knew you were going to be fine."

"How... What?" Averie asked.

"Let me explain." Over the next few hours, Saress took the time to explain in excruciating detail all the events that played out since she became victim to the tetrodotoxin. When she finished, Averie's face flushed red with embarrassment. "I feel stupid right now..." Her head drooped, "I didn't know."

"I know you didn't, that's why I am not angry like I should be. In fact, I'm elated to see life back in your eyes. Now get over here and give me a hug and this time try not to beat the scales off of me."

Saress sat perched on the pile of stones and stood guard while the rest slept, her eyes focused on a mouse across the glade searching for food. The night was dark as the heavily clouded sky had every star veiled.

"She ran because that's what she felt she had to do, to protect you," a voice said from behind her.

She recognized it instantly and never turned. "What am I to do," she whispered.

"You're her protector, her guardian," Elwrick said. "She looks to you for guidance like a mother. I suggest you start acting like it." He sat beside her on the stone.

"I'm just so mad, so angry—"

"Let it go," Elwrick interrupted her. "Pegan may not survive this ordeal, he may not survive the night. He knows this, he accepts this. You're a natural born leader. I see the same traits in you I saw in your father during the Great War. If Pegan falls, it will be up to you to lead Averie, and Icearaus to salvation."

"I don't know—"

"Look inside yourself, inside your soul, the answers will come," Elwrick said.

Saress turned to him, to plead her case, but he was gone.

The morning arrived with rain, fog, and an unsettling coolness they had not experienced in a very long time. Saress threw many logs on the fire till the flames leaped high in the sky to keep Pegan's shivering body warm, then ordered all three to come close. "As you can see, Pegan is in no condition to lead, so at this time I am claiming command of the fellowship."

Lorandrial began to complain but Saress quickly silenced him.

"If you wish to argue you can leave, no longer will we fight amongst ourselves. We've all taken an oath to see Averie through and that's what I intend to do. If you plan otherwise you're free to go."

"I'll follow you to the end, or until Pegan recovers," Thathra said.

Lorandrial grumbled but reluctantly agreed.

Averie smiled when she heard the words.

"So what shall you have us do," Lorandrial asked.

"You know the plant Thathra described, make haste and find some. I need to get that shaft out of Thathra's leg. Averie, you tend to Pegan."

Hours later, Averie applied a liberal amount of salve to Pegan's shoulder and Thathra's leg.

"We need you as a guide," Saress said to Pegan who was able to point in the correct direction but nothing more. Pegan led them west down a narrow trail of stone and clay while the rain fell in sheets and lightning lit the darkened sky. Along their travels, they encountered nothing and spoke only in hushed whispers. Occasionally, they happened upon the healing flower which was harvested to be used later. As evening approached, the trail led them through a section of dense forest of ancient trees then descended into a deep ravine where they found shelter from the rain.

The next morning the streaks had almost faded and the infection lessened while Thathra barely had any discomfort at all. Both men now stood on their own and began to argue and pointing to specific body parts.

Saress hissed a sickening groan listening to the two compare battle wound, and who had it worse.

Applying the slave quite liberally before they set out again, Pegan informed them they should arrive at the Glarahn Highway before noon and his estimate was accurate to within an hour.

The Glarahn Highway ran north to south and all the way from the Dugab Caverns to the Lost Sanctuary. It was the only trade route for the dwarves that lived under the mountain.

"We'll follow it the rest of the way," Pegan said.

"Looks like a trap," Lorandrial said. "If this is a major road, I would suspect the assassins will watch it closely. It will leave us out in the open, exposed, vulnerable."

"I have to agree," Thathra said, "is there not another way?"

"How far up the road are the caverns?" Saress asked.

"A good half day," Pegan said. His color was returning and his voice was more understandable. "There is another way, slower, and much more treacherous, especially with this blasted weather." Pegan let his vision drift to each of his companions. "There have been complaints about the paths I have chosen so I will let you all decide."

"Lead us down the other path," Lorandrial suggested. "My instincts tell me danger awaits us down that road."

Saress shook her head and looked at Pegan. "Unfortunately in your delirium I had to relieve you of command, and I have taken charge. I will gladly return it to you when I feel you are ready, but not yet."

"I understand," Pegan said.

Saress turned to Averie, "you decide, and we'll follow."

She thought for a long moment and looked in both directions, "we'll take the road. If the stories you told me are true, then the Brotherhood has lost much and are probably more concerned with trying to recoup their losses than search for us. They are leaderless and without direction. I believe we have enough time to pass and besides, the rugged terrain is hard on Pegan."

Thathra released a deep winded sigh. "The bearer has spoken, let's not toil and give them the opportunity to track us."

Lorandrial shook his head in disgust. "Not sure how you plan to make it in the new world making decisions like that," he mumbled to himself. He waited for Thathra to pass then fell in behind.

Many years ago it was obvious the road was an engineering marvel. Bricks were chiseled from stone then placed from edge to edge in an elaborate pattern. Along the edge a curb had been created by bricks stacked three high and mortared together. The top stone was chiseled round to give the whole structure a distinguished appearance. Through the decades though, time and weather had ravaged the road leaving the once perfectly placed stones upheaved and broken, and in a few places the road was completely washed out, while the remains of shattered boulders which fell from higher up the mountain pimpled the ground.

In one particularly nasty section, it appeared every stone had been carefully removed and packed away making room for wicked, ugly, deathly brown bushes with razor-sharp thorns longer than a man's finger to grow.

It was easy for Averie to see at one time this road would have been easily traveled. The grade was low even though all around them the mountain shot up to dizzying heights.

In the distance, they could see Saress returning from one of her scouting missions, a smile on her face and a gleam in her eye. "Farther up there is a fork in the road. I followed both. One led to the stairs cut into the face of the mountain, while the other went to a large cave at the bottom of the mountain. The cave isn't deep, maybe forty feet, and I could feel cool air filtering down from an somewhere above."

"The elevator shaft," Pegan said. "There was no way to make the stairs wide enough for mule-driven carts to pass, so the shaft was built to raise and lower their wares. Tradesman would arrive with their carts and for a fee, they would be raised up into Dunbar. From my understanding, the system was extremely efficient and operated day and night."

"We're going to ride an elevator?" Averie asked rather excitedly at the thought.

"No," Pegan answered. "The elevator no longer functions. The wooden platform has long since rotted away along with the ropes, cables, and pulleys. All that remains now is a massive hole that offers only death for any who ventures to close. We have no choice but to take the stairs."

A short while later in the distance, they observed an opening cut into the side of the mountain.

"Are those the stairs?" Averie asked.

"Yes," Pegan said. "The stairs of Numribelyn, named after the dwarf who spent years with the design and eventually oversaw the construction." Jogging ahead of his companions, Pegan waited on the first step. As his friends arrived, he dipped into a bow and swung his arm under his breast, "welcome, my fair traders," he announced loudly as if he were a merchant.

The beginning of the stairs appeared like an entrance to a cave and was cut deep into the side of the mountain. The left side was firm against the rocky face which was worked smooth while the right was comprised of a series of thick round stone pillar's which were chiseled round and supported the massive arched ceiling. A stone railing filled the void between the pillars which kept the traveler from falling to their death but allowed a gorgeous view of the surrounding mountainside. Slats were carved into the railing which allowed the natural light to illuminate each perfectly carved step.

At the entrance, the steps were quickly navigated but soon became treacherous and the pace slowed considerably. No longer were they level but instead cracked, broken, and covered in a thick slimy green moss that forced them to hold tight to the railing. Occasionally, they came upon areas where the ceiling had crumbled forcing them to cautiously navigate the natural obstacle.

They traveled for some distance when Pegan brought them to a halt at the edge of a rather large gap. It appeared as if a massive boulder had fallen from somewhere up above and destroyed the ceiling, taking with it a large section of the stairs.

Pegan stood at the edge and glanced down. From this high up the ground looked like a swirling haze of mist and a howling wind buffeted his body.

Pegan surveyed their surroundings then released a dreaded sigh

"Is there no other way?" Saress screamed over the howling wind.

"No," Pegan said, "we have no choice but to jump it."

Thathra examined the gap and shook his head no, "none of us here but Saress can make that," Thathra said. "We need to build a bridge."

"How?" Lorandrial asked, "There's nothing here but stone."

Saress's eyes lit up, "Thathra, follow me. You three wait here and don't let Averie close to the edge."

Nearly an hour passed before they returned carrying a large plank of wood and some other smaller pieces. Under Thathras guidance, his companions quickly constructed a bridge and reinforced it with stone's to stabilize the beam. To his companions' amazement, even a handrail was quickly fabricated for added security.

"I'll go first," Saress said. "If it supports me, the rest of you will be fine."

The board bowed and creaked under her weight but the engineering marvel held and soon she stood on the other side urging her companions on.

"You're next," Pegan said to Averie.

Each step felt like she was walking straight to the execution chamber.

"Don't look down," Pegan urged her on, "Go straight to Saress."

Averie froze part way across. Her breath was stolen by an unmerciful wind which also tossed her hair around temporarily blinding her.

"Don't stop," Saress screamed. She could see the woman almost being lifted off the plank.

"Go," Pegan screamed.

Averie looked back, then to Saress, then back at Pegan and started to back up when Saress screamed at her to stop and go the other way.

Averie looked down, the beam was no wider than her feet and the ground suddenly rushed up to meet her.

To their fear, they could see the board being buffeted by a sudden gust of wind and Averie all but lost her balance.

"Please hold... please hold," Thathra whispered. He prayed the skills his father taught him as a child remained.

Saress fell to her knees and pleaded. "Come to me... please."

Having heard the call, she turned and bolted like a ballerina across the beam and fell into the waiting arms of Saress."

Pegan all but fainted watching her cross; she had to make everything so dramatic.

Lorandrial crossed next followed by Pegan and finally Thathra.

"Will we be coming back this way?" Thathra asked.

"No," Pegan answered.

Hearing the words he undid his work and watched the beam fall into the void. "No one can follow us now."

The remaining stairs were all but destroyed which made travel slow, but the railing remained intact and eventually they arrived at a large landing with an opening carved into the side of the mountain.

The sun dipped behind the white-tipped, jagged peaked mountains casting long shadows. When Saress looked back at the distance they had come, the Lost Sanctuary appeared as small gray pebbles.

"We'll stay here tonight. We could all use the rest," Pegan advised.

Averie quickly went to work applying more salve to Pegans wound while Thathra built a small fire from the scraps of wood which lay scattered.

Chapter 30

Thathra rose well before the first crack of light. Beside him, Saress lay stretched out flat on her belly, arms and legs sprawled, looking more like a skin than a companion. The fire had died down to embers, but he could still make out the silhouette of Averie who lay beside it. Lorandrial slept just to her right wrapped in his cloak, but Pegan was nowhere to be seen.

Quiet as a landslide, he made his way towards the opening.

"Going somewhere?" Pegan whispered.

Thathra froze, then looked in all directions but was unable to locate the elusive man.

"Up here."

Thathra looked up but still didn't see him. "Stop hiding and show yourself, I hate talking to an apparition."

On a ledge about ten feet up, Pegan materialized from the shadows then shimmied down the wall to stand beside his friend.

"I was worried you'd ventured off to scout and got yourself in trouble. I don't think your shoulder has completely healed yet."

Pegan worked it in a circular motion as if testing his capabilities, "feels good as new?"

"Good luck convincing Saress," Thathra chuckled. He ran his hand along the edge of the opening. It was cold and smooth but felt good against his rough hand. His mind drifted back to what seemed like years ago when he roamed the Frozen Tundra, the snow whipped open plains and bone-chilling winds. Back to his family and the shack he called home. Never in his wildest dreams did he believe he would see the things he saw, or do the things he'd done. And now, he stood only a sunrise away from traveling under a mountain.

The entrance was wide enough for ten grown men to pass abreast and twice his height. Across the top, a thick placard spanned the distance of the opening and was populated with intricately carved symbols.

Pegan followed Thathra's stare. "Welcome one and all to the Twin Cities," Pegan said.

"You can read that?" Thathra asked.

Pegan leaned against the stone face and blended in till he vanished. It was only when he spoke did his location get revealed. "No, I can't," he said. "There are few who can. I only know what it says from the tomes I've read. I was fascinated with these caverns and took many years away from my trade to explore every inch possible." Pegan released a deep breath which shone brightly in the moonlight. "All was not a waste though. My time spent in here alone made me a much better killer, and I learned ways to conceal myself others never dreamed possible. It was the only way to survive the things that came up from below." Pegan paused to watch the elf approach.

"You've passed completely through?" Lorandrial asked.

"Numerous times."

Thathra looked at Averie who stirred then motioned for them both to lower their tone.

Lorandrial adjusted his bow, "how long can we expect to remain in this tomb?"

Pegan could see the elf had second thoughts about entering. There was a strange nervousness about him he had never seen before. The way his fingers twitched against his bow, how he hesitated when he approached the entrance then stepped back when he felt the warm air brush against him. As if it was the breath from a giant beast about to devour him. "I have covered the distance in three days, but I traveled light and never stopped to rest. I avoided all creatures and quickly disposed of those who stood in my way. For this journey though, I expect to remain underground for five and that's only if our passing goes unnoticed by those who dwell below."

"Below?" Thathra asked. "Below what?"

"*SHH,*" Pegan whispered. "You'll wake the lizard."

"I'm already awake, and have been for your entire conversation," she whispered back.

"Could have fooled me," Pegan chuckled. "The way you were snoring I thought you morphed into a dragon during the night."

She narrowed her eyes in discontent towards the human, wondering how he would taste for breakfast. "Well, you gonna answer him?"

Pegan laughed, "There is a second layer much deeper than the first known as the Middle Dark where kobolds, carrion crawlers, bugbears, and several other forms of filth reside. Luckily we won't have to go there and most things don't venture up, except for the kobolds."

The morning arrived with the most beautiful salmon colored sky Averie had ever seen.

"Hope you enjoy it," Lorandrial said. "We won't see it again for five days."

"Is it your goal in life to spread misery?" Saress questioned the elf.

"I'm not spreading misery, simply informing the woman what to expect," Lorandrial answered.

As they entered, Averie expected a world with dripping water, oozing worms, and roots that poked through dirt walls that grabbed at her dress and pulled her hair. Instead, she discovered the tunnel was rather bright and unusually clean except for small pebbles that littered the floor and a thick layer of dust that swirled around their feet with each step. Partway in, Averie stopped at the source of illumination. A steel sconce fastened to the rock wall held a plant which grew up and out of the container. The bulbous body filled the sconce and many long vines cascaded over the side nearly scraping the floor. The entire plant resonated in a strange aura that lit the tunnel in shades of reds, blues, and greens. "What a strange plant," she said.

"It's not a plant, but a bioluminescence fungus called Idrium. It comes from the lower dark and was harvested as a light source for surface dwellers. Before Idrium, torches were used but they left a thick hazy smoke, and many people avoided the caverns. When trade suffered, search parties were sent out to discover a new light source, and this was the outcome. Uses no fuel, creates light, and makes oxygen. Rather ingenious if you ask me. Since its discovery and implementation, the only fires allowed were those at the forge and for cooking, which required a complete redesign of the ventilation system."

"Lower Dark?" Lorandrial asked. "You said Middle earlier."

"There is another layer where the vilest most loathsome creatures exist. In my mind, it's the closest thing to Hell on Icearaus, but the way is sealed."

"More importantly?" Saress asked. "Does this fungus grow throughout the cavern?"

"For the most part, yes. But as we near Nendorühl, it becomes sporadic at best and nothing grows in the city."

"There are two cities?" Averie asked.

"Yes, the first remains complete while the second lies in rubble. It was there the Great War ended."

Averie released a sigh, "more death and destruction."

"What else did you expect? Name a place he's taken us that wasn't?" Lorandrial said.

Pegan shot him a wicked glance. "We should be going," Pegan said. "We'll go many days with trillions of tons of stone upon our backs and even the hardiest of men who are accustomed to living in this terrain have gone mad."

The tunnel continued straight for a good distance then snaked left, snaked right, then took a hard left opening into a perfectly square chamber. It was hand carved and contained two buildings attached to either wall with many rooms. Between the buildings were the remains of an ornate gate which now hung twisted and mangled by only a few of its many hinges.

"The entry vestibule," Pegan said as he scouted the windows of each building searching for signs of recent travelers. Observing none, he released a silent sigh. "Shall we rest here a time or continue?" Pegan asked as they wandered through the buildings but found nothing of use.

"I say we continue as I wish to remain here no longer than necessary. The underground is for the dead, not the living," Lorandrial said.

The others eagerly agreed.

"Shall we then," Pegan said. The tunnel continued for some distance then twisted a few times before opening to a large foyer. To either side, the remains of destroyed statues lay shattered. Farther ahead, the ground abruptly ended.

Pegan led them to the edge and stopped. "We need to be careful here as a simple fall will prove fatal. The sides drop away thousands of feet and with no rails, an unexpected stumble can prove fatal."

Averie glanced down at the steps and froze. They were steep, foreboding, and in many places, broken and littered with rubble that fell from a stalactite encrusted ceiling. The Idrium that grew here provided little light and the heavy angles kept most steps cloaked in shadows.

Pegan began the decent first followed by Thathra, Averie, Saress, and then Lorandrial. Part way down, the stairs twisted to the left and were slightly tilted in that same direction. To keep the horrible thoughts from entering her mind at what might happen if she fell, Averie counted every step until they arrived at a large landing. Along the edge, there were a hand-full of stone benches. Most were broken or busted and unusable, but a few remained complete. The air was warm but fresh and to their surprise, none had yet to start sweating.

"Five hundred and twenty-three," Averie proudly announced.

"What?" Thathra asked.

Pegan knew exactly what she did, for he had done that very thing on his first trip.

"Number of steps down," she said with a smile.

Lorandrial looked back the way they had come and from below the stairs looked like a sheer wall. "I feel sorry for men who had to chisel that death trap."

"This is only half-way," Pegan said. He could see a veil of despair drape over their faces like a shroud of death.

"We should rest here, and every chance we get," Thathra suggested. "Who knows what waits in the darkness to greet a weary traveler?"

"No," Averie said. "I want off these stairs now." The words came not as a statement but as a demand. She looked both left and right to make sure she remained as close as possible to the exact center.

"Well that's settled," Pegan said.

The next series was similar except they twisted to the right and angled in the same direction.

At the bottom surrounded by a ring of stone benches is a large fountain depicting an enormous dwarf constructed from beryllonite. Long water stains of many colors marred the stone, and the basin was either cracked or crumbling in numerous locations. Where there should have been eyes only dark recesses remained as both eyes had been plundered decades ago.

Thathra paused to look at the statue. "Such a shame, fine craftsmanship destroyed at the hands of thieves."

"Not thieves, kobolds," Pegan answered. "Those eyes would have been made of pyrite and any thief would have viewed them as worthless, but kobolds are drawn to anything shiny and would have given an arm to gain possession. They infest the middle dark and often venture up to pillage and plunder. And if luck prevails encounter the unsuspecting traveler."

"Think we'll encounter any?" Saress asked.

"If we do it won't be alone. Because of their small stature their quite weak. But in large numbers extremely deadly. You can bet if we see one, fifty more will be close behind waiting for the right moment to strike."

After a brief rest, they continued.

The passage continually changed in width and angle twisting and turning like an angry snake, but the ceiling always remained just out of view. Hours passed and along the way the tunnel branched in numerous locations and high above the barely traceable outline of arched bridges spanned great distances.

"You've explored every one of these branches?" Lorandrial asked.

"Yes," Pegan answered.

As if he carried a map, Pegan led them with expert skill and they eventually arrived at a natural cavern whose far end remained hidden in darkness. Large columns stood like soldiers supporting a shadow infested ceiling while a gracefully carved ramp led down to the floor of the cavern which was coated with thousands of stalagmites of every shape and size. As they neared, a worn path came visible that wound its way through the stalagmites and faded off into the distance. Poles stuck in the stone floor held baskets of Idrium which lit the path nicely, but beyond that, it grew in sporadic batches leaving large areas in complete darkness. From somewhere out in the darkness the *drip... drip... drip...* of water into a pool reverberated like a bass drum.

"Let us pass quickly," Lorandrial said. "The hair on my neck rises simply standing here."

It was hard to tell for sure how far they'd traveled in the dim light but for Averie it felt like days. Her body ached and her legs grew weary.

It was only when they came to a large opening cut directly into the stone did they finally halt.

The opening was not tall, maybe ten feet if you stood in a hole, but wide enough that fifty men could pass shoulder to shoulder and still not touch the edges. A wall sconce packed full of Idrium had been fastened to either side of the opening and a long stone placard was affixed above the doorway.

"Do you know what this one reads?" Thathra asked.

"Of course, it reads Welcome to Dünbar, a Shining Jewel Encrusted in Stone."

Farther up another passage could be seen cut into the wall of the cavern. Barely visible in the dim light and cast in foreboding shadows, the edges were barbed and looked more like the maw of a subterranean beast waiting to slam shut on any adventurer who lost their way. From the top, Saress could see wide stairs which spiraled down into the darkness and the air that filtered up was much warmer and carried the scent of filth.

"Where does this lead?" Saress asked as she started down.

"Stop," Pegan yelled. "Those stairs lead to the middle dark. I've ventured down there and what I've witnessed has left me with no desire to ever return. We need to go this direction."

When they entered, Averie covered her open mouth with both hands, her eyebrows shot to the ceiling, both eyes jerked open, her legs turned to jello, and she simply sat, or fainted—her companions were not sure. The sight was too much for her surface dwelling brain to comprehend all at once and shut down.

Forming in the dim light was a metropolis the likes of which she never imagined possible. Buildings four, five, and six stories tall or more made of stone, wood, and steel filled her vision while hundreds of meticulously carved staircases were chiseled into the mountainous walls. Some ended at doorways, while others led to rope bridges which snaked across the sky and connected with stalactites reshaped into observation towers turned upside down. Thousands upon thousands of windows looked down upon them like black hollow eyes while roads snake through the city for as far as the eye could see. They were not dark and foreboding like blackened veins but bright and inviting. On every corner, there was a post which held a long arm and from it dangled an intricately fashioned glass lamp that contained Idrium. From here she could see five massive stone bridges that stretched out like giant fingers over wide chasms and fissures. Most impressive though was the vast waterfall which was lit by an enormous ball of Idrium that hung from a steel chain thicker than a man's waist.

Thathra tried to speak but no words came. His head seemed to be on a swivel as he looked from left to right and back again. There was just too much to take in all at once.

Averie shook her head then ran her hands down her face as if wiping away an illusion, but when her hands cleared the city remained. "Th... th... th... this is not possible," she stuttered. "You could fit fifty Lynn Brooks in here."

"Or more," Pegan chuckled. "There is a building not far from here we'll rest in for the night."

"How do you know when it's night?" Saress asked.

"I can't explain it, but I will show you," Pegan said. They remained on the stairs for some time then Pegan pointed to the large ball of Idrium, "watch."

To their surprise, a perfectly shaped slab of steel that mimicked the circle of the ball suspended by four steel arms slowly circled the ball. As it blocked the light, the city began to fall into darkness and the street lamps grew brighter. "I don't know how they did it, but they got it clocked so that plate spins at the same speed as the planet rotates so the time here is the same as on the surface."

Absolutely remarkable," Thathra said.

Pegan led them partway through the city to a large four-story building with massive double doors. The rusty hinges groaned as the solid doors swung inward. Just outside Pegan snatched a lantern then led them past multiple ground level rooms to a set of winding stairs which climbed clear to the top where he followed another hall to a large room also sealed off by double doors. Once inside he lowered a large metal rod and twisted a lever. A loud clank echoed as a strange fastening system secured each door in multiple locations.

"Where are we?" Averie asked as she wandered around the large room. Near the back, she discovered another door which led out to a balcony that overlooked a deep chasm. Far below the churning water rushed past.

"The Molten Kitten Inn," Pegan said. "It's one of the few buildings designed to house larger than normal occupants. This room from my understanding was the banquet room."

"Odd name," Thathra said.

"The story goes as they were about to pour the molten stone into the forms, a kitten stuck his head out and the owner snatched the cat saving its life, and since he hadn't named the building yet, he simply called it the Molten Kitten, and the name stuck."

Saress grew worried with Averie alone on the balcony and joined her.

"It's beautiful up here, almost surreal," Averie said.

Saress nodded but kept her eyes trained in the distance for any sign of danger.

"It's amazing how we'll kill each other, and then risk our own lives to save something like a cat," Thathra said.

"It just shows where our priorities lie," Pegan said.

Averie reentered with Saress not far behind, "whatever happened to the Dwarves?"

Pegan cracked a smile, "There's not much to say, really. It all happened long before our time and no records were ever recorded of their disappearance."

"There must be something," Thathra said. "A whole race just doesn't disappear without someone saying something."

"Nope," Pegan said as he moved around a few broken pieces of furniture creating a makeshift chair. "One day they just vanished without word or warning."

"You would think they would have told someone their plans?"

"If they did, that person is long since dead and took the secret to their grave."

"One day here, gone the next? Not a trace of them has ever been discovered? Something doesn't add up here." Lorandrial said.

"I wish I had an answer, but I don't," Pegan shrugged his shoulders.

"Probably something to do with the Great War," Saress said.

"Doubtful," Pegan said. "They vanished decades after the Great War ended."

Averie began to apply more salve to the wound which looked almost healed. "You said there were two cities here, is the other just as beautiful?" she asked.

Pegan shook his head, "Nendorühl lies in ruins. Nobody truly knows where the war started, but everybody knows where it ended."

Saress located a comfortable place to lie down and sprawled out.

"Here's what I do know," Pegan said. He removed a dagger and jabbed it in the table then slowly begun to spin the weapon with two fingers. "The dwarves where actually two completely different races, not related in the least bit. The Dünbar Dwarves were beardless, couldn't grow a hair on their face if their lives depended on it. But they were master craftsmen and chose to build great structures instead of worrying about riches. Hence why the city is so big and beautiful.

The Nendorühl Dwarves were explorers, mining for gold, silver, jewels, diamonds, anything worth riches. They cared little how they lived as long as they slept on treasure.

Well, from my understanding an agreement was made that the Dünbar Dwarves would build them a city worthy of songs while the Nendorühl Dwarves would provide them with enough finances to finish building theirs, as they were low on funds and most of the city was left unfinished."

"And?" Saress asked as she raised her head.

"That's all I know, but something happened and if you ask me, it has to do with the Nendorühl Dwarves."

"What makes you believe that?"

"I can't honestly say," Pegan answered. "Just a feeling I get every time I came here and even now. It's like a thousand dwarves scream out for help and not one of them are Nendorühl Dwarves."

Saress looked at him strangely. "There's more to you than what I think you've led us to believe. I've seen you do things no mortal has ever done."

"I don't know what," Pegan said. "I don't remember doing anything strange or out of the ordinary."

"The assassin, you made his eyes melt by screaming something."

"I don't remember it," Pegan said.

They could all see he told no lie and dropped the subject.

"I suggest we get some sleep," Thathra advised.

Pegan woke to a pair of yellow eyes staring down hard at him.

"What have you done?" Saress hissed and ripped her blade free.

"You violated Averie why she slept." She jabbed in quick aimed straight at his heart."

On his feet he leaped to the side, performed a role, and came up beside the reptile, both blades sparkled in the artificial light. "Where did all this come from," Pegan said. "I would never…"

Thathra's axe came free as well.

She lunged again and he easily parried the attack then leaped back into a defensive crouch. "I have done nothing."

Saress lowered her blade and then slid it back in the sheath. "I'm sorry I had to do that. I needed to test your body, test your mind. I feel know you are capable once again to lead us and I relinquish the fellowship back to your command."

Thathra drew a heavy breath, "Next time you do that, please tell me first."

They set out in what would have been considered early morning.

For ten long hours, they walked and only took breaks when absolutely necessary. On their way, they traveled down deserted streets searching buildings, houses, and other shops but finding nothing of use. In time they crossed multiple bridges that spanned great distances where far below and out of view the sound of churning water was heard. Next, they entered the industrial complex where great forges sat cold and iron casts lay scattered waiting to be filled with molten steel to create tools, weapons, or anything else they may have needed. Next, they happened upon the residential area where row upon row of identical houses lined every street. It was here they also discovered the unmistakable scent of death.

"We should investigate," Pegan said. "Discover who or what died. They may have left valuable supplies or provide a warning to what lurks somewhere within these city walls."

"I think we should leave now before whatever killed… kills again," Averie suggested.

"Pegan's right." Lorandrial agreed with Pegan for a change. "If we must face an enemy, let us know what we face." Lorandrial nocked his bow. His eyes scanned the rooftops of nearby buildings."

Using her snout as a guide, Saress took the lead. She led them down a few more streets, round a corner, then partway down the next road before she stopped at the doorway to a large three-story complex with many windows. "It radiates from within here."

Luckily, this building was one of the larger structures and Saress managed to squeeze and wiggle her way through the doorway, Pegan, Averie, Thathra, and Lorandrial followed. Two floors down in the basement in a secluded room she discovered the source of the putrid scent.

The room was rectangular shaped with an abnormally high ceiling with a door easily large enough for them to enter through, but Saress chose to remain where she stood and block all others from entering. "There's nothing here to aid us," she said. "It would be best if we left... now!"

Pegan tried to enter but Saress stopped his every movement. "If you go in there Averie will want to follow, and I won't subject her to this kind of disgruntled, brutality."

"I need to see what died in there, to know what we may face deeper in the caverns."

Saress nodded and walked away but stopped at the base of the stairs when she heard Pegan groan.

This was not the basement of some residence; it was the tomb of an uncountable number of creatures. It was hard to get an exact count as they were completely dismembered. Arms piled in one corner, legs in another, heads in a third, and their tails in the fourth. Their torsos had been torn open and piled directly in the center while their entrails hung from the ceiling like holiday decorations and blood dripped like rain from the eaves of a building in a rainstorm.

Pegan picked up a head and examined the grotesque wound. It had not been cleanly cut off by a blade but ripped free by brute force. He knew what they were, but had never seen such savagery among man, or beast in all his life.

As he emerged, the others waited to hear what he discovered. "Their kobolds," he said. "Nasty little filthy rats of the middle dark."

"Who would do this?" Saress asked. "Killing them is one thing. But the pure mutilation performed in there is just sickening."

Hearing the description, both Lorandrial and Thathra entered the room to gather a better understanding of what kind of monster they may have to fight.

Pegan waited for them to return before he answered, "I don't know.

I have never seen such hatred taken out on any subject, even them."

Thathra shook his head at what he witnessed. "Do you think what-ever did this still lurks within this city, maybe it ventured back down into the middle or some other forsaken place not meant for man." Pegan started up the stairs when he stopped and looked back towards the room, then the stairs, then the room once more. "Whatever killed them never left that room."

"Impossible," Lorandrial argued.

"Look here," Pegan pointed to the ground. "There are faint tracks I failed to notice before. Those are the kobolds entering the room. Look at how they're pointed. But you see no tracks of any of them coming back out, or the tracks of whatever it was that killed them."

Saress nocked an arrow and peered back into the tomb. "Nothing in here is giving off any heat. Whatever did this is long gone."

"We need to be on our guard," Lorandrial said. "Whatever did this we cannot allow to sneak up on us as well?"

For the remainder of the day, they wound their way through the city and saw no sign of life. It was only when a large opening cutout in the wall came visible did Pegan stop to rest. They entered a small, two-story building and picked a room with a window which faced the opening.

"The Gate of Orethane," Pegan said. "I am not sure exactly what the reasoning was for its construction, but there's a massive gate that can be lowered to separate the two cities."

"At least it's not lowered?" Thathra said.

"Yes," Pegan agreed, "it appears luck has finally shined in our direction. Tomorrow at first light, well set out again."

That night they ate smaller rations to conserve what little food remained.

Two beady little red eyes cut through the gloom only blocks away. He had been following them ever since they started down the ramp, staying just out of sight as he was well aware of the reptile's excellent night vision. Once he was sure they would not be coming out and risk being seen, he signaled for the others to come. Upon their arrival, they slipped into a taller building that gave them a bird's-eye view of the small structure.

"I wantz to killz dem… dead," one of the odd-looking little creatures hissed.

"Noze," another replied. Judging from the strange crown he wore he must have been a chieftain or some other high ranking member. "Unlezz you wizh to be made an example like our companionz when they dizobeyed."

The kobold released a shriek at the thought.

"We are to make sure they pass through the gate then send the signal to have it closed so there can be no retreat."

When morning arrived, they set out once more headed for the large opening. Just as they crossed the threshold a loud grinding sound could be heard as if stone was being ground against stone and the whole complex shuttered. Small pebbles danced on the floor and the dust was stirred up into a choking elixir.

From the buildings and every other direction, kobolds could be seen running at them, chanting, and screaming in some strange language.

"RUN," Pegan yelled as he took Averie by the hand and they ventured down the wide corridor. Partway down they paused to look back only to find the gate was closed and hundreds of creatures climbed over one another hacking and slashing at the bars in an attempt to get through.

Saress had never seen odd little creatures like these before. They were short but stout and walked on thick muscular legs accentuated with a spiny elongated tail. Most of their skin was the color of rust except for their bellies which glowed bright yellow. Around their waist, they wore ragged loincloths with a small dagger attached on one hip while a sling swung on the other. Long elated snouts with exposed fangs curled over snarling lips and muscular jaws bit down hard. Behind it all, two beady little red eyes shone brightly in the hazy blue atmosphere.

"Thank the Creator we made it," Thathra said. "Those bars actually saved us."

Pegan shook his head no. "This was a trap," Pegan groaned. "Someone or something knows we're here, and wanted to make sure we can't retreat." Using his sleeve, he wiped the dust from his eyes then adjusted his blades to make sure they would slide easily from their sheaths. "Filthy kobolds, they must have been following us."

"If what you believe is true, we need to be alert and sleep in shifts from now till the exit," Lorandrial advised.

Chapter 31

rlin wished he'd died. For an untold number of days, he lay in a bed at a tavern in Mill Stone fighting off a delirium induced stupor, high fever, blurred vision, muscle aches, while a good portion of his body was covered in large blisters.

The witch had told him there may be some residual medical condition afterward having been so close to the demon, but she never mentioned anything like this. Had he understood, he may have reconsidered his options.

After the vomiting and dysentery ceased, he felt now was the time to head home. Weak and lethargic, he left the tavern behind and vanished into the cool night air. He moved without purpose, his mind fixed on a hot meal, warm bath, and most importantly… his own bed.

Lauden watched the bewildered man stumble his direction from across the glade. "You're late," he said.

Arlin paused, his eyes barely open, oblivious to the fact he was being watched. "I was delayed," he whispered.

"By what, a whore, a tavern and a bottle?" Lauden snapped.

"I was on a quest to discover the true identity of the man who aided the bearer," Arlin snarled back. He was in no mood to be questioned by a lesser ranking man of the Brotherhood.

"We'll, your delay has cost the Brotherhood dearly. I only hope the information you gained was worth the price."

"What price?" Arlin asked.

Lauden studied the man for a moment, then his face lost expression. "I hate to inform you of this but your father passed a few days back. He warned us Demetrius was a dangerous man, but we grew cocky and failed to heed his warning. The results were devastating to the Brotherhood.

"What... Demetrius was here?" Arlin asked with wide eyes and raised brows.

"Walk with me and I'll explain the unfortunate events which led to his demise, and the collapse of the Brotherhood," Lauden said.

It was only when they neared the sanctuary did Arlin understand the true extent of the carnage. Bodies lie strewn like garbage, their pale faces a brief glimpse into the past of an unforgettable horror. Large blue flies feasted upon the corpses and vultures circled high, waiting for them to leave before they continued to consume the dead. Eventually, only the bones would remain and those would be dragged away by scavengers and with that, their existence would vanish. Arlin turned away from the scene and somehow blocked the smell from his nostrils, but the taste lingered upon his tongue like a spoiled piece of poultry while the steady buzz in the air nearly drove him mad.

Arlin walked through the door and down the stairs then released a sigh, it felt good to be home. As he started down the corridor to his quarters, he paused. He just realized his position of authority had increased, so he headed for his father's chamber, which now belonged to him.

With directions given to the slave on how he wanted the room reorganized, he headed to the ward to say his last respects, to verify he was now Lord Brack. On his way he met Lauden once more who followed.

Arlin stood next to the slab where his father lay. The steel collar still fixed around his pale colored neck. Arlin need not ask how he died, the gaping hole in his chest that exposed busted ribs, half-eaten lungs, and a black, rotted heart explained everything.

"How did this happen?" Arlin asked. "It's as if something grew inside then ate its way out."

"That's exactly what happened," the embalmer said. He never looked up from the cart where he was preparing items. "The giant wasps of the Northern Silvers plant an egg in a living host and it grows there until ready then eats its way out. I was there when it all happened and every one of us was left in a state of shock at the sheer brutality of it all, none had the sense to kill the newborn creature."

Arlin turned away before he threw up on the corpse.

"Your father never left a statement of deceased, where shall I have the corpse sent upon the completion of my work?

"Do nothing with the body," Arlin answered. "Tonight we'll have a king's burial with fire."

The coroner dropped his tools back onto the table, "as you wish, Lord Brack."

Hearing his name said that way sent shivers up his spine and tiny bumps formed on his skin as if he had a chill.

"Since my services here are no longer needed, I will take my leave," the embalmer said and walked out.

"So how long do you plan to stay? Until we hunt down the creature that caused this?"

Arlin thought for a moment, "I'm not going after the Northern Wasps."

"It's not the wasps I'm talking about. The bearer brought this damnation upon us." Lauden waited for an answer but he could see Arlin was hesitant to speak. "You do not wish to seek revenge for your father's murder?"

"My father's death was not caused by the bearer; it was caused by his greed. I will not make the same mistake as him."

"And what of your obligation to King Karayan? I heard of your quest to track down the bearer and bring her to justice."

"He's not my King nor have I sworn an oath to him. What we had was a contract, that's all. Upon her capture and return, I would receive my reward. Since I am now Lord, the item I wanted now seems petty. I will be rewarded tenfold due to my current position and not have to lift a finger." A crooked sadistic smile found his lips.

"When King Karayan discoverers you've broken your contract, he won't be the least bit happy. In fact, I would guess he would arrive here within days to question your motives."

"My motives are my own," Arlin snapped. "The bearer means nothing to me, whether she lives or dies, I care not the least bit. His problems are no longer mine."

"To him though, your motives will look like defeat, weakness, and complete disobedience. Something he is not fond of."

Arlin came to him and placed a gloved hand on his shoulder. Even ill, his quickness was dazzling fast.

Lauden's eyes shot open when he felt the thin scalloped blade slide through the rib cage, angle upwards, then pushed all the way in puncturing a lung.

"He won't find out I abandoned the quest. In a few weeks, I will return and inform him I lost the trail and wish to cease the contract as the reward no longer matches the risk."

Lauden collapsed to his knees when the blade was pulled free. "Why?" Lauden said through gurgled words. Both eyes already glossed over.

Arlin circled the man, his feet silent on the cold stone. "Because you would have informed him to further your status and line your pockets with a few gold coins."

"I would not of…" he gasped like a drowning man coming up for the last few gulps of air before death.

"I know you would have… because I would have done the exact same thing, and you're no different from I."

Arlin watched the last bit of color drain from Lauden's face.

Movement from behind drew his attention and when he turned the shock of what he observed caused the dagger to fall from his grasp and he backed away till the cold wall pressed hard against his back. Before him, his father stood.

"I've been waiting for you," the corpse said in a much deeper voice than his fathers. When it approached, the bones popped and snapped as they broke free from the rigor mortis that had set in, yet the thing still stood.

"What do you want?" Arlin quickly branded his other weapon and held it straight out.

"Payment for services rendered," The creature hissed. The jawbone broke in the process and hung only by the ligaments.

Arlin almost fainted, he could see life in the clear glossy eyes but it was not his fathers. Something else, something wicked had moved into his father's corpse.

"What services?" Arlin screamed.

"Are you that ignorant?" The creature screamed in a high pitched, hair-raising tone. Then shot at him with lightning speed and grabbed him by the shirt. With one hand he lifted him clear off the floor and slammed him hard against the ceiling. In his other hand, a heavy piece of black material formed. There was strange gold colored writing around the edges. "For payment, I want the Demetrius's still beating heart placed in this bag."

"Impossible," Arlin said looking down at the living corpse.

"Improbable, but not impossible. If you fail, then you take the place of him, per our agreement."

"What, that's not wha—"

"Silence," the demon interrupted. "You now know what I wish for payment for the services I rendered. You agreed and are therefore liable for your actions, or inactions. Failure to act upon your part is no excuse as I have already fulfilled my obligation, and the contract shall not be broken nor release of it permitted. Upon failure to gain said item, you will take his place at the offering table."

Arlin did not know what to say, instead, he hung there limp until the corpse collapsed to the floor and he fell upon it. He laid there for a moment then grabbed the bag unsure of his next move. Regardless, he had no desire to become a demons pet.

Chapter 32

High above the ruins of Nendorühl, the tiny bat-like creature hung from the jagged ceiling with razor sharp claws which penetrated the granite with a vice-like grip. Large round yellow eyes with fiery red dagger-shaped pupils sunk back in the skull, surveyed the carnage while its pink upturned nose sniffed the air. With senses so keen it could see a flea or smell flesh from any-where within the city, nothing would pass undetected. So when the subtle vibrations of metal grating against stone reached his feet, an investigation was in order.

Without thought, the claws retracted and the thing plummeted towards the rubble below like a meteor. Seconds before impact, broad, translucent wings spread, and the creature took to flight. The invigorating effects from its near-death descent sent shivers clear to its black heart. Flapping once, then twice, it easily glided across the destroyed landscape and disappeared into the darkness of a narrow corridor which led to the Pinghä. Circling the room multiple times, it located a suitable spot atop a broken statue sunk back in the shadows of an alcove built high up on the wall.

"We need to hurry," Pegan urged them on as he looked back at the bars. The clan of kobolds grew substantially climbing over one another until it looked like one giant mass with a thousand legs and arms trying to chew its way past.

Averie never looked back, she didn't need to. The sound alone was disgusting enough to send her skittering in fear.

They traveled a great distance down the dim corridor which bent and twisted a few more times and only stopped to rest when they came to a weirdly shaped chamber with three exits.

"Which way?" Lorandrial asked.

Pegan pointed straight ahead. "But not till after we've had a break." He dug through his pack and handed Averie a flask of water who eagerly accepted it.

Saress faded off into the gloom doing what she does best.

"Are we anywhere near Nendorühl?" Thathra asked.

"We still got a good distance to travel, and many more obstacles to overcome," Pegan answered, then took a drink.

Saress returned with a horrified look on her face. "The passage ahead is completely blocked. Are you sure that's the right direction? Maybe I should scout the others."

"Are you sure?" Pegan asked.

"Positive," she answered. "It's choked full of massive stones, rubble, timbers, dirt, hardened mud, and grown over with roots the size of my tail."

"Good," Pegan smiled. "Then we are still headed in the right direction."

"Did you not hear a word she said?" Lorandrial asked.

"I did," Pegan answered then grabbed the satchel. "Shall we continue?"

The corridor continued straight for a short distance then made a sharp right but quickly switched back left then widened. It was partway down this passage they came to that which Saress described.

"Fantastic," Lorandrial mockingly cheered. "The path before us is blocked, the way back is bared, and soon we'll be forced to drink our own sweat and eat whatever filthy rats we can catch. That is if those kobolds don't break through first."

Thathra began to examine the blockage, "This was not a natural disaster. You can tell by the way it's stacked it was designed to collapse."

Lorandrial nodded in acceptance, "So you led us to our deaths... congratulations." He kicked a smaller stone and watched it bounce away into the haze.

"I don't believe so," Thathra argued. "I have learned much about this man and he would not have come this way if he knew the passage was blocked. I would guess he has something else planned we're not aware of yet."

"Correct you are," Pegan responded. "I was going to say there's a secret passage to the Pinghä. But you were all so enthralled with the collapse, I decided to let you all worry. Maybe now you will learn to trust me."

"What's the Pinghä?" Averie asked.

"The Pinghä translates into the room of many meeting. It's where the two races would converge to discuss trade deals and strike agreements."

Saress turned away in shame and slammed her fist against a wall, the resounding thud brought a heartbeat to the cold stone. "I'm sorry. Even I grew doubtful when I saw this… I should have known—"

"It's not you, it's this," Averie interrupted. She swung her arms out wide and turned in a circle. "Surface dwellers are not meant to live underground. We need the sun on our faces, the fresh air in our lungs. This dirt and stone works against us and lowers our morale. It has become our enemy and works to break us of our will to survive."

"No… not me." Saress disagreed. "I love being underground. It's just so natural, so beautiful. I just lost control and gave in to fears this may finally be the end."

Averie rubbed her belly and let out a God-awful groan.

"Are you hungry?" Saress asked.

She nodded.

"Let's rest here."

"We really should keep moving till we reach the spiral stairs," Pegan said. "It'll be much safer at the top."

Thathra opened his pack and handed Averie a chunk of salted meat and a flask, "have my portion, you're eating for two."

Pegan sat on a stone, clearly irritated by the delay.

"Can you continue just a bit further?" Saress asked Averie.

"The stairs are less than an hour from here, but the climb is treacherous and very time-consuming."

Averie rubbed her eyes then agreed to trudge onward.

Not far from where they stood cut into the wall at a strange angle was the secret passage. It was both narrow and short which forced them to bend at the waist to enter. Saress though was not as fortunate and had to crawl and still, both shoulders scraped at the walls. Luckily, the passage was not long, and they found themselves in a circular chamber looking up at a spiral staircase which vanished into the ceiling.

The stairs, shrouded in complete darkness, are uneven, fractured, and slimy from water that dripped from somewhere above. No Idrium grew here.

Partway up, Averie paused to catch her breath. "Are these things ever going to end?" she asked Pegan who waited a few steps ahead.

"Eventually," he answered.

Exhausted, red-faced, and on legs which wobbled as if made of jello, they emerged from the stairs like a rat sticking its head through a hole.

The foyer was large and only lit by one small sconce which left the majority of it cast in obscuring shadows. Beginning in the foyer and vanishing into the blackened void, a narrow arched bridge stretched like a crooked finger. Where it ended, none could see.

"We'll rest here for the time," Pegan said.

After a few hours, Pegan roused the others who fell asleep almost instantly. "We've remained here long enough, actually too long in truth. We need to get moving again."

After a quick meal, he had them gather around in a circle. "We must take great caution here. The Ancient Bridge is littered with enormous gaps, cracks, uneven edges, and a wicked wind which howls across."

"Who would build a bridge so terrible and unsafe?" Averie asked.

"It was not designed that way and time has a way of destroying everything left unchecked, and the bridge is no exception. Eventually, it to will fail, and the caves will become unpassable," Pegan said.

Pegan rummaged through his satchel and removed a small rope and tied it around Averies waist, then wrapped the unused portion around Saress multiple times. "Someone the size of Averie will surely be blown free, and I don't believe her dress will be much help when she discovers the bottom." Pegan cracked a crooked smile at Saress.

With everyone prepared they set out. At first the wind was only a howl, but as they cleared the safety of the wall, it turned into a frightful scream. Pegan led the way with Averie close behind. Saress followed, then Lorandrial, and finally Thathra. They each held tightly to the other, and they moved like a human centipede.

Averie let out a wicked deadly scream as she felt herself become weightless. Her hair thrashed at her face, dress puffed out like an umbrella, and both feet lifted clear of the stone.

Saress felt it as well and latched onto the woman and held the rope tight.

Frantically she clawed at Pegans back, which almost caused them all to take a tumble. Thathra saw the incident unfold in slow motion and sidestepped Lorandrial—who was watching in horror as the trio neared the edge and did nothing—grabbing Saress by an arm saving all three.

From here Pegan motioned for them to crawl on hands and knees.

Carefully, they worked their way around each obstacle and emerged at the far end unscathed, but drenched in sweat, dust, and fear.

After another quick break to recoup, Pegan led them down a passage which was wide but made many turns but eventually straightened, the far end of which was brightly lit.

"Are we at the surface?" Averie asked due to the brightness ahead.

With a heavy sigh, the passage broke through the wall near the ceiling onto a small balcony overlooking an octagon shaped room. Idrium grew here unchecked and the brightness of the room made them all shield their eyes. Stone steps fixed to the wall led from the balcony to the floor which was a good fifty feet below them.

The room was in complete disarray. A gigantic table hacked and slashed rested directly in the center but leaned heavy as both legs on one side were broken. Not one chair remained intact and the fabric that once covered the cushions lay ripped and torn. A great cabinet lay toppled and all about the floor the parchments it once contained laid strewn like confetti. Multiple alcoves lined the walls high above, and each contained a shattered statue. There were also a few wooden chests bound with steel straps that were broken and plundered of their valuables. The most notable feature however are the four large pillars that extend from floor to ceiling. Each one was carved with images and writing and in many places, there were visible cracks from repeated blows as if an attempt was made to topple the entire chamber.

Under the stairs were two doorways. One still held fast but had an enormous hole blasted through the center, while the second hung by a single rusty hinge.

Saress let her vision drift freely over the carnage, "Who would do such a thing?"

"Demons, and other filthy creatures," Pegan said.

Averie glanced up just in time to see a pair of yellow eyes blink shut. "Something's up there?" she whispered and then pointed.

"Probably just a bat or something similar, strange creatures inhabit this place," Pegan answered.

Having been spotted meant nothing to the creature. More importantly, the subjects had finally been located. Grinning, it took to flight.

They all watched as the small thing drifted past and out through the open door then faded into the shadows.

"Well, it's gone now," Thathra said.

"Hmmmm," Saress mumbled, keeping her thoughts to herself. She had seen something in its eyes when it drifted past, something not natural.

"Where does this lead?" Lorandrial asked as he stood in the doorway the creature flew through.

"Well, they both eventually lead to Nendorühl, but that particular way goes to a rope bridge that crosses a massive chasm then continues on to Nümrouth Overlook."

"What's it overlook—"

"We go that way." Averie pointed to the other door as she interrupted Saress.

"That way is quicker though" Pegan pointed to the opening where Lorandrial stood.

"I grow weary of bridges and wish to not cross another as long as I live," Averie demanded.

Pegan sighed, "Okay, but that way leads to the cemetery."

"The what?" Averie all but fainted.

"The cemetery. Even living underground, you still have to bury the dead. Dwarves don't live forever," Pegan explained.

"That's obvious," Lorandrial said, and then backed away from the wicked glance Pegan gave him.

"That passage will add about five hours to our travels," Pegan said.

Averie thought for a moment but the fear of being blown free again outweighed the time difference. "I don't care, I won't cross that bridge. If you decide to go that way then I will meet you all at the exit."

"You're talking foolishly now," Saress scolded her. "First of all, I wouldn't allow you to wander off alone."

"I guess that's settled," Thathra said. "I've learned to never argue with a woman who's that determined."

"We can try, but the door has been fixed tight ever since my first time here," Pegan said.

After a quick break, Thathra examined the door, then stuck his head through the hole and studied the other side. "Hmmm, I see the problem." The muffled voice came back through the hole. Reaching through with his left arm, he felt around for a few moments then found what he was looking for and yanked hard.

A loud clank echoed followed.

Thathra stepped back and pulled on the door with one finger and it silently swung open. "There was a broken weapon wedged in the door, I'm surprised you never noticed it."

Pegan shook his head, "through all my times here, never once did I ever."

This passage was tall and wide but cast in darkness as no fungus grew here. After a few bends and elevation changes, they arrived at the cemetery.

Along each side, thousands of alcoves lined the walls. Row upon row and stacked twenty high, they went on for as far as the eye could see. A few were void but most contained the vandalized remains of a race long forgotten. Caskets lay ripped open, their lids shattered, and the contents scattered upon the ground. The floor appeared to have been constructed of gray marble as thousands of bones had been trampled into a fine powder. As they walked, the grayish powder floated knee high and shrouded the floor in a swirling haze. Before many alcoves, stone benches were destroyed or vandalized. Idrium grew everywhere and lit the place with a grizzly ambiance.

"Who would desecrate something as sacred as this?" Averie asked.

"Kobolds, bugbears, hobgoblins, and other creatures from the middle dark that venture up here looking for anything of value," Pegan answered. "Unlike them though, we'll pass by in silence to pay our respects to those who have fallen."

After a few hours, they came upon a highly polished, ornately carved mausoleum that shone brighter than anything else in the room. Untouched by the dust and dirt, it seemed out of place, exotic, as if it fell from Heaven.

Positioned directly in the center, it sat in such a way that no other tombs looked down upon it. Directly before the highly polished stone door sat an unmolested stone bench.

Looking around, Averie could see no other structures like it.

Lorandrial stopped to watch Averie as she approached the structure. His bow slid from his shoulder and he waited to see what would leap out.

Averie felt herself being drawn towards it. Something called to her, begged for aid. As if in a trance, she walked around the mausoleum then ran her hand down the smooth stone. As she did, the runes that lined the door she had not noticed before gave of a faint bluish hue.

"Averie," Saress yelled in a heated panic. Having seen the structure come to life, she expected the worst and slipped her sword free.

Pegan screamed for her to back away and both daggers sparked to life.

Either not hearing them, or choosing to ignore, she kept her gaze focused on the strange rune writing. "It calls to me, screaming my name for help," she finally said after she circled the mausoleum twice more.

"What calls to you?" Lorandrial asked.

"I don't know…" She ran her hand along the rune words once more. "This is the resting place of Nümribelyn," she finally said after a few more minutes. "The great architect of his time, the true designer of the Dügab Caverns." She ran her hands over more of the rune words. "This mausoleum has a very powerful ward spell cast upon it, but by whom the words do not speak."

Saress studied Averie who seemed to be lost in a trance. "How do you know?"

"Because I can read what it says," she rubbed her pale-looking hand over the stone one more time.

"As I first stated," Pegan said. He stood beside her and placed an arm around her shoulders, a smile a mile wide upon his face. "I think you're going to be the answer to many questions that now plague

Icearaus."

"I may be the answer to the problems," she said, "but it sounds as if I won't be here to see them corrected."

"We should keep moving," Lorandrial suggested. "We've been here too long already."

"Agreed," Thathra motioned. "This place has left an icy chill deep within my bones I feel I may never recover from."

Two more hours passed before they reached the far end and exited the cemetery.

The passage continued for a good distance then emerged into a much larger cavern that was connected by three adjacent tunnels.

"That one leads to the lookout," Pegan said as he pointed towards the left. "That one there goes to the lower dark," he pointed to the right. "The middle is the one we want as it leads straight to Nendorühl."

"What are we waiting for," Thathra said as he begun to walk ahead but was quickly stopped.

"The exit to the surface is easily accessible and many creatures live there. We need to pass as quietly and quickly as possible, for things live in Nendorühl that should not be disturbed." Pegan looked at them all until they each understood the severity of his words.

The bat-like creature shot from the cave entrance like a bullet and soared over the great divide. Oblivious to the passing ground below, its attention was focused directly on the task it had been given—locate the bearer, report back.

Both wings flapped in a flurry of motion as it climbed higher and higher until it caught the air currents then stretched them out and began a graceful glide. Far below, the desolate town of Ti'ath came to view. Locating the darkened hole which led to the lair, it tucked both wings tightly against its body and dove hard into a corkscrew spiral pattern.

Tavok watched the familiar circle through marbled eyes. His naked body stood rigid upon a pedestal of searing coals. In his right hand he gripped a tome which dripped blood, and in his left, he held the skull of a small child. Upon his chest and arms symbols had been freshly carved, and long snake-like welts rose upon his back.

Across the room, an obsidian altar rose up from a pile of ash and upon the smooth top, a large skull was perfectly positioned as if it was there to observe him. It was elongated with huge eye sockets and still held a pair of overly large fangs. A thick black candle held in place by melted wax was fixed to the top of the skull and the flame fluttered in the gloom.

Deep within the skull was a large silver box adorned with gemstones and teased with just a dash of gold dust. The lid was partly ajar revealing the edge of a bone colored parchment.

With the completion of this task, his phylactery would be complete, and he would be given his reward… immortality and a new life on the world of Agatha.

Unflinching, he never moved or made a sound as the beast landed on his shoulder. Blood streaked down his back as the needle-like talons dug into the flesh.

A loud, hideous laugh escaped his lungs as if he enjoyed the pain, in truth, he cherished it. Within moments of landing, the creature reduced in size till it resembled a flea then crawled upon Tavok's neck and licked the blood which ran from the ear. The tiny snout sniffed the environment until it became satisfied then continued on its way until it reached the ear and entered.

Nendorühl was accessed by a long wide ramp. Part way down the left wall gave way and afforded them a grand view of the town. As far as the eye could see, thousands of gray stone buildings lay in ruined heaps amongst enormous mountains of ash. Not one building remained intact as it appeared each had been uprooted, ripped apart, and then discarded like refuse. What few buildings did stand where broken, split down the middle as if hit by a giant axe, or half collapsed and left in a state of perpetual turmoil. Even now, ash still fell from the ceiling like snow and the entire city smelled like molten stone, sulfur, and death. From the destruction, it was impossible to decide where one road ended and another began.

"How will we find our way?" Thathra asked.

"I know the way through, but nothing here is safe as those few remaining buildings can collapse at any moment and stalactites have been known to give way and fall. Nothing awaits us here but suffering and anguish."

To their surprise, Averie wept. If this town was anything like Lynn Brook, she could only imagine the pain and suffering that must have occurred. Gone were the men hard at work and street vendors selling food and fine garments… gone were the women who watched their children play and laugh… gone were the children. Only destruction and death remained.

Lorandrial went to speak but stopped when Pegan raised his hand as if he was going to slap him. "Give her a moment, she has never witnessed the ugly side of war."

Near the bottom, Averie motioned towards a clear section. "Let's take that road there," Averie whispered.

Pegan stuttered when he spoke. "That's not a road, but the base of a great building obliterated into dust, along with all those who dwelled within."

As Pegan led them cautiously around broken buildings and destroyed structures, none spoke as they each seemed to be affected differently. Charred remains of stone were left as piles of ash and cracked and broken walls fought to stay standing. What was once roads were now infested with enormous holes and rubble littered the ground along with splintered timbers, mangled steel, melted stone left in a state of permanent torture, glass, and burnt ash.

Somewhere in the darkness among the skeletal remains of stone and steel, something screamed. A loud piercing scream, the kind that makes your blood sizzle.

"What was that?" Saress asked. Her head jerked around to locate the noise so fast she became dizzy and almost fell.

"Who knows, Nendorühl is full of both strange and deadly creatures and many of them scream in the dark. To either signify victory… or defeat," Pegan answered.

As they moved deeper into the city they discovered bits and pieces of clothing, destroyed furniture, unidentifiable bones, numerous broken axe heads and twisted swords, mangled armor, and crushed helmets, some still held the broken bones of the man who wore it.

Seven hours had passed before they stood at a large cutaway which led to a much smaller chamber. It reminded her of the first one they had come to as it also had two buildings, but there was no gate and she could feel the cool breeze on her face.

"This was the entry chamber," Pegan said.

From here, Averie could see the natural light filtering in through the large opening.

Ignoring Saress's warning, Averie charged ahead and ran for the sunlight. The air was fresh and the sun was bright, but it was the warmth on their skin that confirmed they finally breached the surface.

Chapter 33

areful not to kill the host, the familiar moved with exacting detail around and through bundles of nerves until it reached the frontal lobe then ejected a microscopic probe which fused to the soft, sponge-like material.

Tavok never flinched even though the pain was excruciating.

Secreting a greenish serum into the brain, the familiar initiated a link between the host and his master.

Phlorax sat idle on a throne of bones and looked out over his domain. Rivers of lava flowed in every direction and fiery red lightning scorched the blackened sky. Ash floated in the dense atmosphere and the pungent smell of rotted flesh tainted everything. There was nothing green here, no trees, no shrubs, nothing of beauty only volcanic rock, charred stone, and misery for those who slithered on their bellies like worms. To a mortal it was Hell, but to him, it was home, and he loved every bit of it.

"Master…" The squeaky, mouse-like voice traveled through space and time back to Tartarus. "The bearer has passed through Nendorühl."

"Excellent," Phlorax replied, his bony hands clanked as he rubbed them together. "A perfect opportunity for my apprentice to prove his worth, to justify a position at my side as an acolyte." Fondling a large red soul stone he held it up to bask in its beauty. Contained within were the tortured souls of all those who have previously tried and failed to fulfill their master's final task.

"Can I kill her?" the familiar asked. "I have proven my worth many times over and the euphoria produced when I hear her final screams—*AHHHHH*—just the thought of it sends a shiver of excitement racing through my veins."

Phlorax stood and kicked a body which crawled too close to his throne. "No!" The words could not have been any clearer. "You are to be my eyes and ears only. If any unnecessary harm befalls her, and she loses the child thus costing me my reward, I will hold you personally responsible. Need I remind you what happens to familiars that disobey my orders?"

The familiar shrieked and almost broke the connection. "No, my Lord. I am well aware. What of the others—"

"How many?" Phlorax interrupted.

"Four total, three men and a reptilian."

"This will make the test all that much sweeter," Phlorax laughed. "Severe the connection. I wish to converse directly with my apprentice about that which must be accomplished."

The familiar did as instructed but remained inside the head. Communication was no longer possible but their conversation would not go unheard.

"Tavok…" The voice resonated inside his brain.

"Yes, my Lord," he answered back, quite surprised to hear from the lich lord himself as most of their communication was done through the familiar.

"Have you prepared yourself for this final test? To prove your worth and take a position at my side here on Tartarus and continue your training to greatness under my guidance."

Tavok smiled a greedy grin, "yes my Lord."

"And your phylactery has been constructed as instructed?"

"Every detail was followed with surgical precision. It only awaits your gift of the soul stone to be complete."

"Excellent," Phlorax said. He detected no hesitation in the young apprentice. "For your final test, you are to capture a subject of great importance. No harm is to befall her or the child she carries. With them a reptilian travels, it is to be subdued but not killed. All others concern me not."

"I eagerly welcome the challenge," Tavok cockily said.

"Heed my words," Phlorax said with a stern tone. "This group has proven extremely resourceful in their abilities to survive insurmountable odds, therefore, I will accompany you and watch your skills at work. If you falter, not only will I be forced to intervene, but you will join the others in my soul stone. But to exceed my expectations and prove yourself worthy, I will personally discuss your coronation with Queen Vhathialox and seek a speedy ceremony.

"I understand my Lord. But your time is valuable and it will be wasted watching me complete such a menial task when you could be working on something of much greater importance."

"What's more important than observing my faithful apprentice in action?"

"My sincere apologies my Lord. I simply figured I was menial in your eyes." Tavok retracted his words.

"Apology accepted, this time, but do not question my motives again. All I ask is you do not embarrass me this day on the field of battle."

"When I am finished and you have the subjects you want, you will understand I am years ahead in my training... I refuse to fail."

"We shall see... begin the summons."

Making its way back out the way it had come, the familiar returned to his bat-like appearance and took to flight back out the hole it came through.

Tavok arched his back and clutched his fingers then his whole body convulsed as if he went into a seizure. *"Come, my minions,"* he screamed out in his mind. *"Heed my call."*

Arms crossed he tapped his foot and soon the Din-Jin, which were short even compared to children, arrived in numbers far greater than he expected. They were un-ordinarily odd looking. Not dead, yet, you'd be hard-pressed to consider them living. Attenuated to the point of being anorexic, their bones stretched and manipulated their ashen gray leathery skin. Pure black eyes void of life sat recessed in their sockets and jagged teeth protruded far beyond what should have been lips. Behind them trailed the unmistakable stench of rot. To see this many, proved he had grown strong.

Chapter 34

egan remained in the shadows of the opening and watched Averie frolic in the setting sun. Her arms stretched wide like a bird in flight as she spun like a ballerina. Head tilted back, her long hair swung out wild and her dress flared out in a magnificent blur.

Saress walked passed and perched herself on a large stone.

Averie swayed right, then left, then into the arms of Thathra as he passed. The constant twirling left her dizzy, but also with a wide smile. "You can't make me go back in there," Averie proclaimed.

"I think at this point we're pretty much done with the caves," Thathra responded.

Saress shielded her eyes, and a smile came to her face as she gazed upon The Great Divide. It was a vast sea of rolling green plains only broken by sporadic patches of dense trees. A cool breeze drifted down from the north and she could just barely make out the sparkling waters of a distant river. A hard-packed road of dirt and clay overgrown with grasses led away from the entrance for some distance then abruptly turned north and faded while directly behind them the sheer mountain face rose straight up till it stabbed into the bright blue sky.

Thathra leaned against the boulder. "It's views like this that make life worth living."

Saress nodded in agreement.

Averie continued to dance and sing.

Lorandrial joined Pegan and when he spoke his voice was soft and empathetic, "which direction from here?"

The sight of watching Averie dance brought a tear to Pegan's eye which he quickly wiped away before Lorandrial spotted it. "West…." He let his eyes gaze to the distant mountains. "We'll cross The Great Divide and turn north when we hit the Broken Spine Mountains. From there, we'll follow the base north for a few days where we'll hit the small town of Talons Peak. Camp there then head west for another day and if all goes well, we should arrive at the dock before sunset."

"Excellent," Lorandrial said. "After that, all that's left is the journey home."

Pegan waited for a minute to collect his thoughts. He wanted to make sure he didn't sound like a fool. "Even when she's gone and we remain, our task will not be complete."

Lorandrial shot him a daunting glance, "I don't understand. After she's gone, Karayan will have no choice but to relinquish his rule."

"No," Pegan corrected him. "You must remember it is the child who will defeat Karayan. Not me, not you, not anybody."

"It was my understanding when the child returns it will take Karayan's place," Lorandrial argued.

Pegan sighed, "You still don't understand." He raised his hand to slap the elf but quickly lowered it. "Karayan is not a King, not now, not ever… he was only a steward who took control through fear and bribery."

"If this child is not going to replace him, then who?"

"I know what you're thinking and I've often wondered the same thing. How is Karayan going to be removed from power when this child is not destined to become king and to be truthful I don't have the answers, and neither does Elwrick."

Lorandrial went to speak but suddenly stopped as Pegan continued.

"Make no mistake, when she's gone, Karayan will not forget about us. We'll be hunted like wild animals, a bounty placed upon our heads and nowhere will we be safe, not even among friends or family. Greed has a way of changing people, even those who are closest to us. I fear none of us may see the child return."

After a spell, Pegan recommended they make camp as evening was fast approaching.

Unlike the Din'Jin that could become invisible at will, Tavok had to invoke a spell of invisibility, but nothing could mask the pungent stink of the Din'Jin and the winds sudden change to favor his opponents had him worried. To back down now would only be a sign of weakness and he had no desire to explain to his master, the test was delayed due to an insignificant breeze. "No," he told himself, the attack had to come this very night.

Averie lay cuddled next to Pegan while Saress lay sprawled out. Thathra slept propped up against a log while Lorandrial kept watch. The night was cool but the small fire produced just enough heat to keep them warm.

"What is that foul stink?" Saress asked, lifting her sensitive snout.

"I don't smell anything," Lorandrial said. He sat across the way atop a flat stone.

Less than a hundred feet away, Tavok brought his minions to a screeching halt. A foreboding warning came to him in the form of an icy chill that crept up his spine like a flesh-eating fungus, and from his mouth escaped a wicked hiss. One of the bearer's companions reeked of a dormant magic, dark magic, just waiting to be unleashed.

Saress climbed to her feet and raised her snout high. "How can you not smell that, it's awful?"

Her complaining woke the others.

Pegan rose rubbing the sleep from his eyes when he got just a faint whiff of the stink. "Did you kill something and leave it to rot?" he asked Saress.

She shot him a nasty look.

Soon, they all walked around the camp trying to find the source of the sudden stink.

The sky was still dark and they'd only slept a few hours.

"Maybe we should abandon camp and move on," Thathra suggested.

Averie was licking her lips as if she could taste the foulness.

"Maybe something died farther up the mountain and the wind changed direction," Lorandrial said. His nose twitched, it was the most disgusting scent he'd ever sniffed.

Tavok could not allow them the opportunity to leave and the time to strike was now, but first, he had to deal with the one who had him concerned. Taking a white feather from his components pouch, he laid it on his palm, whispered a few words, then blew it into the air.

"Run and hide… Fear and flight…
"You have lost the will to fight…

Pegan spotted the pure white feather first as it floated down. It moved unnatural, almost flapping like a butterfly and moving against the breeze. Snatching it from the wind, a vision suddenly filled his mind of the purest blue eyes he had ever seen. The same pure blue he had seen in the elf he destroyed so long ago.

Murderer… Killer… The words came.

"We need to go, now," Pegan screamed.

Saress froze, she had never heard him make such a shrieking cry.

Thathra's axe came free.

Then, nobody knew exactly what happened but the whole world seemed to suddenly unravel.

"AHHHHHH," Pegan screamed as he grabbed his head. His mind filled with visions of terror the likes of which he had never known. His companions transformed into grotesque creatures covered in deathly gray skin sporting festering wounds that seeped yellow pus, while maggots squirmed from their eyes. Their hands became ugly barbed claws that tore at their stomach spilling out the innards which looked like a mixture of worms, maggots, leaches, and other unidentifiable long squiggly things with fanged incrusted suckers on each end.

Run… Run, a voice inside his head screamed.

As if he had gone mad, his words were unintelligible as he looked back towards the others and screamed then ran towards the caverns.

Thathra watched Pegan retreat and was about to follow when he felt the immense slate stone beside him begin to vibrate as if the inside was brought to a rapid boil.

Throwing himself to the ground, he narrowly missed instant death as a million razor sharp chunks sizzled past only inches above his head.

Saress leaped to the side and rolled away just in time to avoid being crushed by a gargantuan boulder that zinged past as if it were weightless.

Averie thought for sure she was dead as she stood in the direct path of the boulder Saress dodged. Just before impact, its course changed as if guided by an invisible hand and crashed into the side of the mountain exploding into powder.

Thathra leaped to his feet and swung like a mad-man, but there was nothing there to attack.

"Run to the cavern," Saress screamed.

Lorandrial heeded the call and abandoned Averie where she stood and bolted for safety.

Hearing the call for retreat, Tavok laughed and ordered his minions into battle. Even though they are small and appeared feeble, they are actually quite deadly and had the uncanny ability to solidify air and propel it towards their targets at great speed.

With one arm Saress snatched Averie by the waist while Thathra followed directly behind.

Near the entryway, Saress was hit hard in the chest by an invisible force and knocked back into Thathra taking all three to the ground.

The cackle of laughter ensued.

Just above their heads they could feel an energized force of mass quickly pass and slam into the edge of the opening, then another followed by a third and the entire structure began to rumble.

Back on her feet, Saress grabbed Averie and ran in a different direction as it sounded if the entire mountain was on the verge of collapse. Thathra ran a different direction while Lorandrial moved farther back into the mountain leaving Pegan to cower in one corner of the room.

Spitting out dirt as he ran, Thathra noticed strange claw marks form on the sand as he felt something zip past. "Look at the ground," he yelled towards Saress as he set to chase after the invisible creature. Swinging high the first two swipes missed, but the third connected once he lowered the blade. Purple blood sprayed far and wide as a headless creature formed before him as it fell to the ground. A good distance away the head landed.

Saress saw what occurred and discarded Averie for her bow and fired a series of quick bursts.

One creature dropped dead instantly while another crawled around trying to remove the projectile from its chest, and a third spun in circles trying to stem the steady flow of blood from a severed artery in its neck.

Coming from the cave opening, the rumbling sound turned into a roar and all at once millions of tons of stones slid down from above and crashed around them. The cavern was obliterated and all around her the bodies of those caught in its wake formed. Twisted legs, a hand here, crushed head there, something which looked like an arm, while others were reduced to a purple stain. Somehow, she and Averie managed to avoid injury. Thathra was nowhere to be seen in the clogged dusty air, but she assumed he too perished under the rubble along with her other companions.

The fear that crushed his mind and subdued him waned, replaced only with one single involuntary thought, survival... All around him the noise was deafening as the mountain came down. Dust bellowed as stones of every shape and size, boulders, timbers, dirt and roots, pounded where he had just been moments earlier. Then without warning, the entire ceiling collapsed in one horrendous boom. The concussion was fierce and lifted him from the ground and threw him back like a paper doll.

As the dust settled, a few thin rays of light worked through the blockage.

"We're trapped," Lorandrial screamed as he reentered the partially collapsed room to observe the carnage. "And it's your fault... coward." He pointed at Pegan who stood there covered in dust.

Pegan shook his head and cleared his mind then waited for the dust to settle. For the most part, only the actual entrance was blocked, the rest of the chamber was intact. "Where are the others?" he asked.

With air still in his lungs and blood coursing through his veins, he swore never to surrender. Through the smoke and dust he could barely make out Saress fighting for her life, behind her, Averie cowered but held her sword straight out in defense. Releasing a battle cry, he charged back into the fight and sliced down two more before being hit in the chest and knocked back down to the ground.

Saress fired twice killing one but missing the other.

In a half-hearted attempt to rise, Thathra would have been hit directly in the face from another blast that more than likely would have killed him, except, his axe took the damage shattering the shaft and sending the blade sailing off into the distance. On his knees, he pulled a blade free from his boot and jabbed outward catching another creature in the throat as it ran past.

Averie screamed and shook her entire body violently as she felt something land on her back.

Saress felt the presence as well. Spinning with her blade out just above Averie's head, she felt only a slight hesitation as it passed through something invisible.

Averie screamed as she felt the warm purple substance run down her back and chest as a head formed at her feet. Behind her, a body landed on the ground with a thump.

Outside the stone blockage, the sound of war waged on.

"They're dying out there," Lorandrial screamed in muffled coughs.

Pegan stood motionless for a moment, his vision locked on the blockade—Lorandrial was right, this was his fault and the thought of what he did hurt him more than anything he could ever remember, even more so than that thing the Elf Queen called a pet. "There's another way, we have to get to Nümribelyn's private chamber."

Pegan led him back into Nendorühl to a narrow set of stairs that followed a jagged wall. They were uneven, chipped, cracked, and spiraled at a severe and unusual angle. Pegan never looked back to see how his companion faired as he scaled them three at a time till he reached a narrow landing which overlooked all of Nendorühl. From there, the narrow passage led to a room that was small but savagely vandalized. The remnants of a bed lay thrashed while a large table had been busted to splinters. All around the room lay rubble, debris, animal waste, bones, and a few unidentifiable corpses. Most important though was a steel door fixed to the wall that was secured by a sturdy looking padlock.

Pegan wasted no time on his search for a suitable rock then grasped it in both hands and slammed it firmly upon the lock. The clang of the impact echoed clear across Nendorühl and the vibration jarred the stone free from his grasp.

"You might as well bang a gong and let all of Nendorühl know where here," Lorandrial said in a rushed voice.

"We don't have a choice. This is the only other exit without having to go back deeper into the cavern," Pegan argued. Picking up the stone he slammed it down upon the clasp. When nothing happened he tried again, and again, and again, until the stone crumbled in his hand.

"This is crazy," Lorandrial complained. "Can't you just pick the lock?"

"No," Pegan answered. "This is a very complicated mechanism, I neither have the time, nor the tools to understand how it works."

"There's a reason it's still intact," he tried to explain.

Pegan ignored the words and continued to pound on it till his fingers bled.

Lorandrial grabbed Pegan's arm and their eyes met.

"What?" Pegan screamed in an irritated voice. All around him there was a pile of broken stones and powder.

"That lock, it's protected by magic, I can feel it. If we can't find the key in all this mess we'll, never get it opened."

Pegan slammed the padlock down, "it can't end like this," he screamed, there was a savageness in his eyes. Repositioning the lock he examined the keyhole looking for clues to how it functioned.

Tavok raised his clenched fists in the air and screamed, "Πονηρά χέρια εμπλέκονται."

Saress leaped to the side as the surrounding ground in a large circle began to bubble. Puffs of dust floated from tiny holes as if it were steam escaping and a gulp… gulp… gulp… sound could be heard. As she moved, the circle followed and then the tiny holes burst into fist-sized fissures and from them ghoulish looking green hands with long bony arms reached out and latched onto her legs.

Swinging her sword she sliced through them like vines, but as they fell away, more grew.

Thathra managed to find his footing and leaped to his feet but was obliterated by a series of attacks which pushed him along the ground and shoved him up underneath a large rock to where only a foot was visible. Unconscious, he lay inches from death.

Trapped, Saress looked at Averie through pitiful eyes, "run and don't ever look back."

Thwack, a pebble shattered against the wall pelting Lorandrial with shrapnel.

"Kobolds," Lorandrial yelled as he ran to the side of the door narrowly dodging another pebble that traveled just above his head. In the darkness he could see their red eyes glowing like torches, "and they're everywhere." He leaned his back against the wall away from the incoming projectiles. "Are you listening to me? We need to fight our way out of here before we get trapped." Lorandrial ducked just in time to avoid another pebble that whizzed past.

The words Lorandrial spoke fell on deaf ears as Pegan remained focused on the lock.

"Pegan!" he yelled. "We need to get out of here… now," Lorandrial demanded.

"Hold them off, I almost have it," he responded with a lie.

Lorandrial shot him an angry glance. He knew the man was lying. He also knew their chance of surviving was slim to none.

Lorandrial shot twice. The first kobold dropped dead where he stood while the second screamed out a loud squeal then retreated down the stairs. Their deaths bought enough time for Lorandrial to grab the fallen door and slam it upward into place then used whatever he could find to wedge it there. "I hope you got a miracle up your sleeve," he said, and then piled more wood in front of the door effectively securing it.

Hearing the words, Averie darted from Saress only to find herself trapped in a mass of vines that had not been there moments ago. Whipping and thrashing, they grabbed at her feet and took her to the ground. More grew and latched on until she was completely mummified in the withering mass. Doing the only thing possible, she screamed as if her life was ending, yet there was no pain, the vines simply held her immobile.

Trapped but not immobile, the sight of seeing Averie get taken down brought on a whole new anger and she hacked and slashed with the fury of a scorned woman. The attack was relentless and she overcame the ghoulish hands and leaped free but what happened next she never saw coming. Hit from behind, her bow splintered and she was slammed face down into the dirt. As she tried to rise, another spell hit her head and spun her to the left. Seconds later, and from a different direction, a spell spun her to the right. All but dead, she lay there kicking with one leg and mumbling incoherently.

Phlorax floated on a disk of onyx decorated with runes high above the battlefield. All around him the air crackled with energy and small bolts of lightning shot out from the disk. From here he watched with a smile as Tavok successfully dismantled the fellowship. When the big reptilian fell for the last time, he directed the disk lower to the ground. At head height, he steeped clear and floated to the ground.

Upon his arrival, Tavok released the invisibility spell and knelt before the lich lord. His eyes focused on the master's feet which were mostly bone, but also held a few scraps of dried skin around one big toe. "It's completed, my lord. The enemy has been dispatched, and the bearer has been captured unharmed."

Phlorax surveyed the battlefield with smoldering eyes, "and your performance was spectacular," he said." Phlorax motioned for him to stand. "It is time for your final lesson, observe closely, listen to my words and watch my movements."

Phlorax stuck a bony arm straight out with the palm facing Saress, each boney finger pointed towards the sky and was spread wide. "Εκπλυση της ζωής."

The words penetrated both flesh and bone and Tavok backed away.

When the last word ended, the hand shimmered red and a thin silver thread crept from the palm. It grew in length until it reached far enough to probe the body of Saress. As it searched, it eventually found the head then slithered between two scales, punctured through the underlying skin, then drilled through the thick skull and attached to the brain like an umbilical cord. Once complete, the silver thread pulsated with every heartbeat of the lizard. A sigh of relief could almost be detected on the face of Phlorax.

"Master," Tavok said. "What was I to learn by this lesson?"

"Remember my words and my actions. Retrieve the bearer and have her brought to the chamber. It is there I will teach you the life leech spell."

Tavok watched as the lich floated away then ordered his minions to recover the bearer.

Pegan kicked the lock and walked away. He needed to gather his thoughts, there has to be a way. Using his blade, he fumbled with the keyhole already knowing the lock would remain clasped. His companions were probably already dead, and they were soon to be as well.

Grabbing the lock with both hands he flexed his muscles and screamed, *NOOOO!*" His eyes begun to change and soon they were black as onyx and the veins in his neck bulged till they neared explosion. His whole body began to shake and twitch. At first nothing happened, and then small cracks began to appear in the metal.

Lorandrial walked backwards till he bumped into the wall, eyes, and mouth wide open, visible fear on his face.

Loud pops and snaps echoed throughout the room as large cracks formed in the steel, and chunks began to drop away and all the rubble on the floor began to dance from an unseen energy. Then, in one final outburst, what remained of the lock shattered into fragments too small to be identified.

Pegan stumbled back and fell to his knees as the door swung inward.

Lorandrial stepped out onto a large balcony that overlooked the opening of the cave far below. "How do we get down?" he yelled.

Pegan never answered as he brushed past and hung from the railing and let go, he didn't care how far the fall was, only that he got to his companions.

The ground was uneven where he landed which resulted in a twisted ankle. Behind him, the agile elf landed without injury and followed right on the wounded man's heels.

In the darkness of the night, it was hard to tell exactly what happened, but it appeared to be complete chaos. Saress appeared dead and all around her lay the mangled bodies of creatures he had never seen before. A dense fog of powdered stone still hung thick in the air along with the scent of decayed flesh. "Spread out, search the area," Pegan demanded.

Thathra was located near the entrance of the cave and carefully extracted from his would be grave if aid wasn't administered quickly. Afterwards, they searched well beyond the battle area yet Averie was still unable to be located.

Pegan could see life still remained in the eyes of the barbarian. "Where's Averie?" he asked.

Thathra tried to answer but his words came as a jumbled mess. He was alive but his mind was confused and dazed.

"Saress lives as well," Lorandrial said, he had his ear next to her snout. "Her breathing comes in gasps and her heart beats fast."

"I think they took her." The words barely escaped Thathra's lips before he began to fade.

"Who did?" Pegan asked, shaking the man to rouse him once more.

"Here, try this," Lorandrial located a flask that still held a small amount of water which Pegan poured over Thathra's head.

"Who did? Who took her?" Pegan asked again.

"I don't know," Thathra said. "Just before I faded I heard someone or something say to recover the bearer. I don't know what happened."

Placing Thathra next to Saress they set out searching for any signs that someone took her and it didn't take long to discover the drag marks.

"Well, we have a trail to follow," Lorandrial said.

"First, we need to tend to our companions. I won't abandon them to die out here in the Divide. Besides, I believe we have time. If they wanted her dead, she would be. She was taken for a reason and I don't believe she is to be delivered to Karayan. There is something else here at work, something sinister and evil, and something none of us know what we are dealing with."

A few more hours passed before Thathra could stand but a few more would have to pass before he had the strength to help his companions.

Saress had no such luck and seemed to be getting worse, her breathing became labored, and any response they could get from her had long since vanished.

"Thathra," Pegan called to him. "You need to get her to Talon's Peak. They may have a healer willing to work on her."

"And what of you two?"

"We're going after Averie," Lorandrial said.

"I would rather go with you."

"I know my friend, but we have an obligation to Saress, and left here alone she will surely die, and then be picked apart by the carrion of the Divide. Do you want that on your conscious?"

Thathra shook his head. The disappointment was deep within his glossy eyes. "How do I get to Talons Peak?"

Hastily drawing a map in the dirt, Pegan gave him the directions then swiped his foot across to hide the diagram "Five days and you should be there," Pegan answered. He clasped Thathra on the arm and their eyes met. "We need to go." The heartfelt sorrow and the pain of agony of losing a friend lingered in his voice.

"Goodbye Pegan… Lorandrial," Thathra said.

"It's not goodbye. It's until we meet again my good friend and trusted companion," Pegan answered.

With that they exchanged hugs and walked away into the morning light never once looking back.

Chapter 35

Thathra's heart sank as the shape of his companions faded. He felt alone, vulnerable… weak. Only once had he felt this way before and that was when his mother was placed in the ground. He begged her not to die… no, demanded her not to, but she seemed to ignore his request.

Fighting back the urge to weep, a thick, heavy tear trickled down his cheek at the sight of Saress lying there in a heap of blood, bone, and scales.

Falling to his knees, he cradled her big head against his chest. "Don't you die on me, don't you dare," he whispered into her big cloudy eyes. Kissing her snout, he gently lowered the head and wiped away the tears which fell like rain.

Slapping himself back to reality he knew now was not the time to grieve, each minute he did nothing was a minute she slipped closer to death.

Searching the field of battle, he gathered what supplies remained and stuffed them into a satchel, then went about collecting weapons. Recovering his axe, he was amazed to see it still held about a foot of the shaft and he fastened it to his pack, but then paused at the sight of her bow, or what he assumed was her bow. Splintered into a hundred pieces, the string fluttered in the breeze like a flag.

Loaded down with supplies and Saress leaning against him for support, they set out into the afternoon sun.

Pegan and Lorandrial traveled for the rest of that day, through the night, and well into the next day only stopping to rest or eat when the trail led them to the bank of a wide fast-flowing river.

Pegan looked up and down the bank but there were no signs of a boat having been beached or a dock to moor a vessel. "It appears the water parted and allowed them to pass," Pegan said. He sat on a log that had been washed down from farther up and removed his right boot exposing a large ugly blister.

"Or they realized we were rapidly catching them and tossed her in the river to save their own skin and fled," Lorandrial said. He knelt and splashed the cool water on his face.

Pegan studied the ground looking for signs they may have fled but every trace ended at the water's edge. "No, it's obvious nothing walked away from here, everything abruptly ends right here," Pegan said. He joined Lorandrial at the water's edge and faced west shielding his eyes to the sun, then his face suddenly went pale as if all the blood drained from his body, and he trembled.

"Do you see her body?" Lorandrial screamed. He stood next to Pegan knee deep in the water and turned to the west.

"No," he answered through a trembling lip, "but I now know where she's being taken."

"And…" Lorandrial waited.

Pegan's face had yet to regain its color. "There is only one town this direction—if you can call it that—and I will not speak its ancient name as the taste of filth will linger on my tongue long after the words are gone. It is a vile, filthy place where the living is not welcome and the dead rule. Many believe it's the gateway to Hell and there has never been a tale told yet of what lurks inside because those who have ignored the warnings to stay clear and went exploring have yet to return."

"So what is it called then, it must have a name?"

"In a more civil tongue, it's called Ti'ath." Pegan returned to the log and sank as if all the air was just released from his body and he buried his face in his palms.

"Are you frightened?" Lorandrial asked. He wanted… needed to hear the words come out of the coward's mouth, possibly to justify his own existence.

"Petrified," Pegan finally answered after a long delay. "And you would be wise to feel the same."

"You don't even know what is there?"

"No," Pegan answered. "But—"

"Then you simply fear words," Lorandrial interrupted.

"I don't know when, but someday you will learn to respect those things which do not deserve respect. You only do so because they are so vile, so savage, and so dangerous, they demand it, regardless whether they are living or dead. I only—"

"I fear nothing," Lorandrial snapped.

Pegan's face went deathly cold and lost all expression, "you will fear Ti'ath."

"Well, if you're that scared then you are no good to me, or Averie. Point me in the right direction then head north to Talons Peak. Meet up with the others and wait for my arrival."

Pegan laughed at Lorandrial. "You'll long be dead before I'm halfway there, which wouldn't bother me none," Pegan chuckled. "I only go because I see no reason to continue living knowing I didn't do all I could to save the woman I lov—" he abruptly paused, "I mean the bearer."

"Well then," Lorandrial said "If you're still willing to save this woman, then I suggest we end this delay and go directly to Ti'ath. Perhaps, there might even be a slight chance we'll arrive before whoever took her and destroy them before their arrival thus avoiding Ti'ath."

Pegan nodded in agreement but knew there was no hope. Eventually, they would have no choice but to enter the one place on Icearaus he feared the most… Ti'ath.

High above, the familiar drifted past then quickly circled to take a second look at what he believed may have been a few members of the party associated with the bearer. Upon further observation, it was indeed members of the group and he let out a chuckle and dropped into a dive to attack, but quickly stopped and circled back. It would be an easy kill and oh how he wanted to feast upon their blood and bones, but to attack without approval could lead to his own destruction, something he did not desire. Flapping his wings frantically, he regained both height and speed and made his way home to inform Tavok.

There was no trail, but Pegan led them with a keen sense of direction always following the river west. After a time, the water became stagnant and pooled in colors of deep reds, dingy browns, and slimy greens. The last living creatures they saw were fish that swam to far upstream, but they wouldn't be alive for long. Soon they would be floating on the surface, belly up and bloated to the point of eruption and contributing to the stench of decay and the nasty haze which hung in the air. The ground was hard packed, cracked, and covered with ugly brown weeds with infested with black thorns that grabbed at their ankles with each movement.

Still, Pegan led them west.

The sky grew pink and the last rays of the sun dipped below the Broken Spine Mountains when Pegan brought them to a halt at the base of a gangly looking tree. The long thin contorted branches hung like claws and the thick heavy air produced panic infested beads of sweat upon their backs and on their faces. Not two hundred yards before them the ground jolted upwards to the edge of a large rim. "On the other side of that lip, deep within an enormous crater, we'll find Ti'ath."

It only took moments for Tavok's blackened lips to curl a crooked smile after he was informed about the intruders.

"Can I kill them?" the familiar pleaded. The urge to kill flowed through his blackened veins.

"No," Tavok said. "I have a better plan. Take a few Din'Jin and go to their location. I want them captured. It will make me appear stronger on the night of my coronation. One will serve as my life support after the ceremony, while the other will become an offering to Vhathialox upon the slab. It will be a glorious time and all of Tartarus will rejoice upon my arrival."

The night sky was bright with a million stars when they made haste towards the raised ring of loose stone, boulders, dirt, weeds, and bones which hid the city from view. Tracing the edge, Pegan studied the ring searching for the best place to attack the unstable obstacle.

Having found a suitable location, he began the harrowing climb towards the lip but soon discovered the error in his thinking. The dirt under the stones was softly packed and very fine and when he pushed off, the stones were dislodged and tumbled back down the face—often times narrowly missing Lorandrial—creating quite the ruckus.

"You gonna alert the entire town of our presence," Lorandrial whispered.

Pegan looked back, "they already know we're here."

Altering his course, he led them more sideways than straight up which worked much better and soon they looked down upon the ruins of a city which appeared to have been forgotten by time.

Ti'ath is separated into two sections. The first section was mostly smaller huts which were made from mud bricks, loose stones, and thatched roofs were but were placed to surround a large obsidian sacrificial stone lit by burning torch on each corner. The remnants of blood shone brightly in the wandering light as the faint breeze made the flame dance.

From there a wide path leads to the second section which was only one large building constructed from stones which looked like they were brought up from Hell that very day. Along the path, steel braziers filled with bones—probably human—burned.

"Were too late," Lorandrial whispered, noting the condition of the sacrificial stone.

"I won't believe that till I see the corpse," Pegan said.

Behind them, the crack of stone sounded as it cascaded downward. Lorandrial nocked an arrow while Pegan eased both hands down to his weapons. When they turned, nothing was there.

For a moment time stood still, only the rustling of the wind through the dead trees far below could be heard.

Lorandrial jumped and slid partway down the hill. His whole body twitched and jerked as if his skin crawled with bugs. "Something just touched me!" he yelled.

Pegan watched the ground looking for movement but observed nothing.

Many minutes passed while they waited and no other incidents occurred. "Must be our nerves," Lorandrial suggested.

Pegan raised his nose to the air, "you smell that? It's the same stinking filth left by the caverns. I believe whatever attacked them, is watching us."

Lorandrial sniffed the air, then without a warning he was ripped from his feet and thrown over the edge vanishing from sight.

The attack was so quick the elf never made a sound.

Pegan bolted for the rim and leaped over as the attack slammed into the stony edge pelting his back with stone fragments. When he landed, Lorandrial came into view at the bottom. The elf was either dead or unconscious as he lay in a contorted heap amongst the rubble. To stop and aid now would only be suicidal.

In a frantic rush, he bolted for the town. Behind him, the unintelligible chattering of voices increased in intensity till they reached a wicked scream. The first two huts are no more than a blur as he made his way to a side door of the third hut and flung it open to enter. To his surprise, he was not greeted by darkness but instead by a pair of pulsating blue orbs set back under a dusty black cowl and a wide grinning mouth full of glistening, dagger-shaped teeth. Pegan leaped back and landed into a roll and was instantly back on his feet to run when he felt a mountain suddenly fall upon his chest and he was slammed to the ground taking the air from his lungs. Unable to move, he felt the leathery flesh of grubby little paws all over him and his eyes widened when he saw it, a large thick black club rise, then come crashing down.

The Great Divide was easily traveled with its subtle hills and low valleys. Water and food were abundant, and the weather remained cool and the sky clear, expecting to meet others on their travels they saw none.

On the fourth day, Saress took a turn for the worse and could not support her own weight and by the fifth, Thathra was forced to abandon most of their supplies and carry her. A thick glossy film coated her eyes and her once vibrant green scales faded to the color of rotten fruit. Her forked tongue had turned the color of blueberries and long strings of saliva hung from her chin like spider webs.

Near the end of the day, exhausted, and ready to give up, he saw what he believed to be the faint wisps of smoke and on the breeze came a slight hint of meat cooking. "Not much further now," he whispered into her ear but he doubted she understood. "Just need you to hang on a bit longer ol' girl." From his best guess, they were less than an hour away.

Soon they discovered the first signs of civilization in the form of tilled ground, and over the next small hill, they encountered a man guiding a large ox as it pulled a plow through the dirt.

"Help me," Thathra called out, but his hope sank as he watched the man look their direction, abandon his work, and run away screaming.

Half-way through the field, Thathra had no choice but to lay Saress on the ground. Large beads of sweat ran down his face and every muscle burned from over-exertion. Opening a flask, he downed half the contents then poured the rest down Saress's throat. Drawing a deep breath, he sat next to Saress who gasped like a fish out of water.

The pounding of many feet caught his attention as it appeared half the town approached. Unsure exactly of what to expect, many wielded pitchforks and sharpened sticks, while one older woman held tight to a rolling pin.

One man stood out from the rest, not in height or weight, but in appearance. He wore the thick fur of an animal and wielded a long pointed spear. A thick mustache and a dense beard hid most of his facial features except for two small hazel eyes which were squinted almost shut. "Welcome," the stranger said in a high-pitched, almost panicked voice… "I'm Rufus, Mayor of Talons Peak."

When Thathra stood, Rufus backed away and pointed his spear at him. It's obvious the man had no formal training and he could have disarmed him, but that would only hinder his goal. "I'm Thathra," he responded extending his large hand. Rufus hesitated, but then gripped it tightly. After all, it was his duty as mayor to welcome the guest, and they had yet to cause trouble. "My friend has fallen ill and I come in search of aid."

Rufus could see the big lizard was gripped in the coils of death. "We're a small town," the mayor acknowledged. "We really have no means by which to heal your friend. She looks as if death has already found her."

"You have no healers?" Thathra sighed.

"We have one, but she is young and inexperienced."

"Would she at least try?" Thathra asked.

"Wait here," Rufus politely said. "Let me speak with the others as I know they are concerned. I do not wish to make hasty judgments without the consultation of the townsfolk."

"I hate this," he whispered to Saress. "It's like we're common criminals."

It seemed as if an hour passed when Rufus returned. There was a bewildered look in his eyes. "We're just a farming community. We till the land and raise sheep and goats. Life here is simple. We're not fighters or warriors and have no way to defend ourselves against the monsters you've probably encountered. We value our home life more than gold or riches. Many believe that you two are warriors from a distant land and believe whatever troubles you there, is bound to follow you here… and most do not wish to bring this judgment upon ourselves."

Thathra went to speak, but the mayor raised a hand as if he was not finished yet.

"But," he paused and looked around, then back at the others who were giving him the stink eye. "Against my better judgment, I have convinced them we should help. Someday, when we need help, perhaps you will remember us?" Rufus said.

Thathra's face broke into a thankful smile.

After he finished, he barked orders to the others, "Bring a cart and ox, water, and blankets."

"Thank you," Thathra said. "We are forever in your debt.

Pegan woke in the most unpleasant of situations. Stripped naked, shackled at the wrists, and hung by a rusty chain over a pit of bubbling green slime that reeked of sulfur, he clearly understood nothing good would come from situation. The room would have been shrouded in darkness had it not been for the luminescence glow from the goo. After his eyes adjusted, they were drawn towards a small shiny steel table that sat across from the pit. Upon the top were a few rags, one long writing instrument, a glass flask containing a clear liquid that bubbled, a long-handled clamp with a large knob on the handle end, and a thin fixed blade razor. From somewhere behind him, a strange rasping sound echoed. It reminded him of metal being sharpened on a leather strap. The sound one would make just before butchering an animal.

Pegan wiggled and tried to turn so he could see who or what was behind him, but found twisting to be impossible.

Finishing his task, the Din'Jin circled studying Pegan's physique. "You'll make a fine canvas," it hissed in a voice barely human.

This was the first time he had really seen one up close and shivered from the fear it induced. "What are you gonna do?" Pegan screamed at it.

The thing never answered as it went to work looking through each instrument on the cart. Having found what it wanted it slowly turned towards Pegan.

Pegan's eyes went wide as he watched the little creature put the fixed blade razor to his skin. He expected any moment to feel the sting of the blade as the meat was sliced from his legs, but was shocked to see the Din'Jin take great care as he shaved every hair from his body. Each time a hair fell into the ooze, the bubbling mixture snarled and hissed and the pungent smell of sulfur made him gag. Next, Pegan watched as the Din'Jin soaked a rag in the clear liquid from the vial then scrubbed every inch of his naked body.

Pegan all but fainted when he observed a grubby three-fingered hand open the small wooden box, and remove a thin hooked needle. Attached to one end was a long black thread. Tying a rather large knot at the end, the Din'Jin held it up to examine the work. Satisfied, he placed it back on the table and grabbed the long-handled clamp and smacked Pegan between the eyes with the blunt end.

He woke to an intense burning pain across his face. His lips were clamped together which left him incapable of making even the slightest noise. What troubled him deeply was the fact the thing waited for him to wake before moving on to the next step in the preparation. Shaking violently, he tried everything to free himself but it was a useless, feeble attempt. To his surprise, the short skinny thing stepped back and watched him struggle for a few moments. It was only after he stopped from sheer exhaustion did the creature continue with whatever sick idea was buried deep within its scrambled mind.

Using surgical precision, the Din'Jin fed the needle through the lower lip, then pulled on it until the thread had come almost all the way through. Then, he repeated the process on the upper lip. Once forced through both lips he guided it back through the lower loop and pulled the thread tight, giving it a solid tug for good measure. The process repeated until his mouth had been completely sewn shut. Naked, cold, and hairless, Pegan hung unable to scream or speak and smelled of something in between formaldehyde and alcohol.

Pegan wanted to groan but couldn't as the Din'Jin drew strange symbols all over him, often outlining the symbols with some form of rune writing. The red ink from the pen glowed brightly in the darkened atmosphere. Completed with his work, the Din'Jin examined it one more time. Satisfied, he replaced the pen and rolled the cart away, annoying squeaky wheel and all.

Somewhere behind Pegan, a door shut with a barely audible click.

Unable to swing, he found little mobility while his arms neared the point of dislocation. Both shoulders screamed out in pain and his naked body shivered. The only sound breaking the painful silence was the occasional horrid screams of an elf crying.

Thathra was shocked at the town's simplicity. Each building was round and constructed from mud bricks and topped with tall pointed grass layered roofs, complete with a small opening at the center for the smoke to escape. There were no designated roads as enough space was placed between each building to allow people access to wherever they needed to go.

The wheels groaned under the weight of Saress as they traveled through town and Thathra could hear hushed conversations and felt the heavy weight of many stares as they passed. None seemed angered by their arrival, but he could tell there was a purpose to their caution.

At what appeared to be the center of town they arrived at a large structure with many stables.

Rufus never had to ask for volunteers as many men offered to help move the giant beast.

"Go find Ellusia," Rufus ordered a young boy with blond hair who watched from a safe distance.

The boy nodded and ran away. His tattered clothes flapped in the breeze and his bare feet slapped against the hard ground as he went.

"Normally…" Rufus stopped to look at Saress who gasped and coughed while her chest heaved with spasms. "Normally we're a very kind folk and welcome all with open arms and can't wait to hear the news from the outside world. Lately though, there have been some strange and just plain frightening occurrences around these parts that have kept us all on edge."

"Like what?" Thathra asked curiously

"Well, since you asked," he said. "There have been the most god-awful sounds at night coming up from the south. Deep within the Broken Spine Mountains, like something, or someone is being skinned alive. No other way I can describe it. Each time it happens we're forced to plug the children's ears or they're left in tears and most families cower in the dark hoping it passes quickly."

Thathra leaned against a post, "you would think a sound like that would reach deep into the Great Divide, yet I heard nothing the likes of which you described. In fact, the five days it took to arrive here the journey seemed quite peaceful."

"You would think that but you'd be wrong. These mountains have a way of holding onto sounds, especially in the still of a cold night."

"And you're sure the sounds you heard where human? Maybe they were coyotes, or wolves fighting and killing each other. In the north, they'll cannibalize their own if food grows short."

"What I… we heard were no wolves. They may not be human, but they weren't wolves either."

Thathra moved out from under the grassy cover where his eyes could study the mountains. From here, they appeared narrow jagged, and steep, while the heavy trees gave them a fur-like appearance.

"Where's this healer?" Thathra growled as he turned back towards Rufus who sat on a flipped over wooden pail.

"Patience," Rufus said, his eyes followed the large barbarian as he paced back and forth across the stable. "She'll be here shortly. I can see something else is eating at you, out with it?"

Thathra looked at him through squinted eyes, "I have three other companions that are still out there, and now what you tell me brings an uneasy feeling to my blood."

It seemed like hours had passed when Rufus finally broke the awkward silence, "here she comes now." The boy guided a petite looking woman by the hand.

"Jensen tells me we have an injured man?" She says eager to test her skills.

"If that's how you want to put it," Rufus chuckled.

Entering the stable, her eyes instantly found the feet of Thathra, then climbed till they arrived at the impossible height of his head. He was by all stature, the biggest man she had ever seen. "I am Ellusia," she stuck her hand out in a polite gesture, "Ellusia Daquell, at your service."

Struck by her beauty he almost forgot why he even came. The radiance of her skin shown in the shadows of the stable and her gold curly hair spilled down over a face that could be no more perfectly round. The penetration of her dark green eyes caused both pleasure and pain and the touch of her skin reminded him of whipped cream.

"What ails you?" She asked, having already made a visual examination and finding nothing of major concern.

"Oh, it's not me," Thathra said, shaking away the trance that encapsulated him. "It's my friend over here, she needs help."

Ellusia looked in the stall and screamed, "what the!" as she backed away stumbling over the bucket, she tumbled to the ground spilling the contents of her small medical bag. "Is it dead? And if not, kill it quickly before it wakes!"

"You'll do no such thing," Thathra snarled.

"Easy girl," Rufus said. He helped her up.

Thathra kept a close eye on her as she took another glance. It was quite obvious the way she leaned against the fence her legs had grown weak.

"They came here in need of aid and have caused us no problems."

"Do you even know what that is?" she asked. There was no use in hiding the disgust she felt towards the creature.

"Well… uh, not really—"

"Of course you don't," she cut in before he had a chance to finish.

"You've never traveled outside the Broken Spine Mountains. That thing in there," she pointed with a finger, "that's one of them reptilian folk from De'Jan Mul' Anor."

"De'Jan?" Rufus looked confused.

"De'Jan Mul' Anor," she said. "It's a swamp in the south-east. These reptilian are quite vicious, kill you simply because you don't have a forked tongue."

"You lie," Thathra said. His face flushed red with anger. He had heard enough rubbish to last a lifetime. "This woman has saved my life on multiple occasions."

Her eyebrows rose slightly and small wrinkles creased her forehead. "I just don't understand why it's clear over here, normally they don't leave the swamp."

Shaking his head in disbelief, he entered the stall and sat beside Saress. "So I take it you have no intention of helping her?"

"Oh, I know." A smile crossed her face and she let out a high pitched laugh and slapped her knee. "This is all a joke to scare the wits out of me and it worked, you brought it here to sell the skin."

Thathra crossed the stable quicker than any expected, broke through the wooden fence and snatched Ellusia by the shirt lifting her off the ground. Hatred burned in his eyes. On the outside she was beautiful but on the inside, her ugliness shined through.

Rufus latched onto Thathra's arm but the added weight did little to lower the muscular arm. "Put her down please, she means no disrespect."

"Nobody is skinning her, even if she passes," Thathra snarled then placed Ellusia down then walked away raising his hands. "I'm sorry," he said. "She and I have fought and nearly died side by side numerous times. She has been more faithful than any of my barbarian companions have ever been. The thought of her being skinned... I don't know what came over me."

Rufus looked hard at Ellusia, "this is no joke." then moved in close and whispered into her ear. Thathra never heard the words but knew it had to be about them judging from the way she refocused her gaze from Saress to him.

"What did you whisper?" Thathra asked Rufus. "I could tell just from her response it was something about us." His face flushed red and his knuckles turned white as he flexed. "We have not caused you any trouble. I only came to seek aid for a wounded faithful companion who sacrificed herself to save me. These words I hear disgust me. If you choose not to aid us, tell me and I will take my friend and be on our way."

"I'm sorry, I mean no disrespect." Rufus grew angry. "I told her you two may be associated with the strange rider who'd shown up here asking if we have seen any strange travelers."

"What rider?" Thathra demanded as if his life depended on it because it very well could. "Tell me everything you know?"

"Well," Rufus paused, wiping his palm across his face to erase the beads of sweat that formed. "About three," he paused for a moment. "No. Four days ago a strange man came here riding a pitch black steed, biggest horse you ever saw. He asked many if we'd seen any strange travelers coming around, seeking shelter, possibly provisions. Never seen the likes of him before, seemed to shimmer in the sunlight as if not solid. To be honest, he scared me, and I don't scare easy." Rufus threw the last part out to make himself seem tough but Ellusia knew the difference, giving Thathra a quick wink.

"Did he say what these people looked like?" Thathra asked.

"Nope, just that we would have known if they came this way."

"Then a few nights ago, another strange man showed up, never saw his face, always kept the cowl pulled down low, creepy fella."

"Looking for the same people I assume?"

"Yes, except he was on foot, but moved like the wind."

"Did either say when they'd be back?" Thathra asked, his attention drawn to Saress who made a wheezing sound.

"Well, the rider said he would be back, while the man on foot just slipped off into the night. To be honest, I hope neither would return."

Thathra lowered his head into the palm of his hands. Everything was in disarray. Saress was on the verge of death, Pegan and Lorandrial may be getting skinned alive, and who knows what those demonic creatures were doing to Averie at this moment. Thathra walked out to the street and fell to his knees. Raising both hands towards the sky as if to pray he screamed, "what more do you want from me?"

Chapter 36

arayan leaned against the balcony railing just off the library which over-looked Lynn Brook. He wasn't looking for anyone or anything in particular, he just had no desire to stay cooped up in the palace and lost the desire to read hours ago. Evening arrived earlier than expected and all across town torch lights and corn oil lanterns flickered to life. The sky was a sad strange color no words could describe and the steady wind from the north carried the first traces of a brewing storm.

Releasing a sigh, he was about to go in when movement on the street caught his attention and snapped him right back to the railing where he waited for the rider to reappear from the back side of a large building. The streets should have been vacant as the dusk curfew is still being enforced, yet here this man was, hunched forward on his horse and wrapped in a bloodstained mud-splattered pitch black cloak. The horse lumbered onward without a guide as if it knew the way.

It wasn't until the rider reached the stable and dismounted did Karayan finally recognize him and immediately summoned Lilith.

"Yes, my King." Her head bowed low when she spoke.

"Master Kalliphae has arrived. Make sure he has fresh clothes and something hot to eat, afterward, direct him to my private chamber. I am sure there's much we need to discuss."

"Yes… my King," she said then hastily left the room.

Somehow, it slipped his mind that he sent Kalliphae weeks earlier along with a group of his best trackers, swordsman, and archers on a highly secretive mission to hunt down the bearer. He kept it silent to reduce the risk of betrayal as a few of his men proved coins were more valuable than their lives, and he could not risk word being sent through a secret carrier they were being tracked.

Lilith waited with the door open to greet Kalliphae. "Welcome home," she said with a smile as Kalliphae rounded the corner. "I am to offer you fresh clothing and a warm meal, and then King Karayan wishes for you to meet him in his private chamber."

"Fresh clothes and a warm meal… sounds pleasant," Kalliphae said. "Unfortunately though, I have more pressing matters which must be discussed at once."

"King Karayan will not be pleased when you pollute his floor." She followed at his side and some distance away to avoid the trail of muck which leaked from his cloak.

"He would even be less pleased when he discovered I delayed this vital information to change my clothes and fill my belly. What I have discovered cannot be delayed." He shot her a perverted glance.

"As you wish."

Upon their arrival at the massive double mahogany doors, she almost fainted at what she observed. Kalliphae never knocked, he just flung them both open wide and entered as if he was Lord and Master. It was a bold move as if challenging the King's authority. She had only seen it done once prior by a man whose name was now a crime to mention and he, along with his family, was thrown into a pit of starving dogs.

"My King," Kalliphae said dropping to one knee. "I bring dire news which could not be delayed."

Karayan shot him an angry glance at the sudden intrusion. "Since you come alone and without a smile on your face, it's safe to assume you did not capture the bearer?"

"You are correct, my King."

Karayan motioned for him to stand.

"But I do not return empty-handed. I bring news which should put your troubled heart to rest. It seems the bearer and her companions encountered something along their travels they had not expected, and now her death is all but certain."

Lilith leaned against the door frame. Her heart raced and her palms became sweaty. She longed to hear the words she somehow knew he was going to say. Fearing they would both notice her excitement, she turned away to close the door which also provided the perfect opportunity for her to regain her composure.

"Well don't keep me waiting, what did they encounter?"

Kalliphae's face lost all expression and he spoke softly as if not to alert the monster, "a lich lord."

"What?" Karayan raised one eyebrow and his mouth curled into a frown, "How… when… where?" He fired off the questions.

"We tracked them to the Lost Sanctuary where they got captured but mounted a successful escape and entered the Dügab Caverns."

"Are you telling me Lord Rayne held them and never informed me?"

"It appears so." Kalliphae took a deep breath, "but then he let the one you know as Demetrius go for whatever reason, he returned and rescued the bearer."

Karayan's face fumed red with anger, "Don't let me forget to kill him."

"Good luck with that, he was slaughtered in their escape and Arlin had the body burned at the stake."

"Arlin was there as well?"

"He arrived long after the escape from my understanding, but had already departed in pursuit."

"Good, saves me from having to bloody my hands. Not that it really bothers me." He let out a sinister laugh.

"Wait… it gets stranger. After we entered the caverns, we discovered the city of Dügab was infested with kobolds. We lost many good men trying to pass and eventually had to turn back. In the process we captured a few who refused to talk but after a thorough beating, they squealed like stuck pigs. It seems a lich lord was there days earlier along with his apprentice searching for the bearer. The kobolds were given strict orders to let them pass or death would come to the entire race. And just to set an example I guess the lich lord slaughtered quite a few of them."

"Why would a lich lord want the bearer? She's no use to it."

"I don't know," he answered. "Don't make any sense to me either."

"So now we must find her before the lich lord does."

"Yeah... about that," Kalliphae hesitated. "From what else we deciphered from the kobolds, the lich lord's apprentice captured them as soon as they exited Nendorühl."

"You lie," Lilith hissed through an angered face. "Is that the best excuse you can come up with for your inability to capture one little girl?"

"You calling me a liar?" Kalliphae barked.

"Kalliphae," Karayan intervened. "She's obviously in a state of shock, as I am as well. A lich lord is a very, very powerful creature who has spent hundreds of years training in dark vile magic to perfect its art. It's rumored a few exist who have seen more than a thousand sunrises." Karayan drew a heavy breath. "The real question now lies in discovering what this lich lord plans to do with the bearer."

"I don't know," he answered. "But I chose not to stick around and ask it."

Karayan thought for a moment, "The lich lord will take her to Ti'ath."

Kalliphae shuddered from the name, "she will not escape him as she did the Brotherhood. In my mind, we can consider her as good as dead and put this whole matter behind us."

"I can tell you this without a doubt," Karayan said looking out the window west towards Ti'ath. "She still lives. I can feel her presence gnawing at me like ants on a stinking corpse."

"But for how much longer?" Kalliphae said, "That's the question."

"Gather four of your best men and ride to Ti'ath," Karayan said in a stern voice.

"Are you crazy?" Kalliphae screamed. He risked his life by the sudden outburst, but it was no less safe confronting the lich lord. "You're the gifted one, why don't you go? Or better yet, send that master assassin you hired."

A large lightning bolt flashed across the sky lighting the room an electric blue. The windows shook from the thundering boom that followed. The rain splattered against the glass making a *tat... tat... tat...* sound then ran down in long streaks blurring everything outside.

Karayan slapped the man knocking him to the ground, "I'm gifted against mortals and protected from demons, a lich is neither," Karayan snarled. "As for Arlin, I have begun to question his abilities as he should have completed his task weeks ago, yet I have heard nothing... nothing," he screamed into Kalliphaes face."

Kalliphae crawled to his feet.

"Now listen and listen well. I'm not sending you to Ti'ath to confront the lich lord. I simply wish for you to set up camp somewhere on the outskirts and watch everything which goes in or comes out. You are to stay there until either I send word I felt the bearer pass, or you see her come out and then she is to be killed on sight. No longer is this a capture mission."

"It's a long travel from here to Ti'ath. Even with the best of horses, it will take many days to arrive," Kalliphae said.

"So I suggest you pick your men tonight and leave first thing in the morning. Lilith will fix you a satchel loaded with supplies and take your pick of the horses." Karayan started to leave then stopped and turned back. "Don't be the one to tell me she slipped through your grasp," Karayan said, then walked out.

The next morning Lilith did as instructed and fixed him a large pack loaded with a few weeks' worth of supplies for him and his men and walked out to the stables to see him off. Just before he mounted she kissed his cheek. "You really are the bravest man I know," she said. "I apologize for my behavior the other night. Please be careful around that lich lord and I wanna see you first thing when you come back." I'll wait for your return," she said with a flirting smile.

He kissed her hard on the lips.

Last night was spent perfecting her spell, along with her acting. Now, she could put it to use. The very moment his tongue met hers, she passed the little maggot looking worm onto his.

Pushing her away, he mounted then looked down upon her like a slave, "get out of my way, whore!" And then kicked his mount into action and almost ran her over as he bolted from the stables.

Later that night, Lilith sat alone in her bedchamber and wondered if the magical maggot spell had taken effect yet. Whispering a few words, she watched the mirror in her room become cloudy with a steamy haze. Soon the fog cleared and everything he saw came to life right there on the glass. "Call me a whore," she whispered, and a broken smile found her face.

Chapter 37

Rufus gripped Ellusia by the shoulders, "are you going to aid the reptile?"

Ellusia let her gaze drift between the barbarian who knelt in the road, and the reptile who wheezed, gagged, and choked. All around them a large group formed, each pushing towards the front to see the great beast. "I'll do what I can," she said. "But hear my words. Any harm this creature causes will not be the blood on my hands, it'll be on yours."

"I understand," Rufus answered uncomfortably. "Somehow though, I feel these two won't cause trouble."

Ellusia called to Thathra, "I need to know exactly what happened and be honest, it might save your friends life."

"I don't know exactly what happened but I'll tell you what I remember." Over the next hour, he spoke of kobolds, assassins, underground cities, and concluded in great detail the fight with the invisible beings.

Ellusia and Rufus stood there thinking the man had gone mad.

It didn't take long for word to spread amongst those who were unaware and soon the town's populace arrived to see the giant monster whose glowing yellow eyes could see in the dark, dagger length fangs could challenge the sharpest swords, and a maw big enough to snap a tree trunk. Those that came with the thought of seeing a blood-thirsty beast were highly disappointed when she simply laid there in a trance.

As the sky darkened, Thathra forgot how famished he was, until the rumbling in his belly could be heard by those around him.

"Feed the boy, will you," Ellusia said. "I got work to do here and I can't get it done with you two looking over my shoulder at everything I do."

"She's right," Rufus let out a hearty laugh. "Come to my place and get a bite to eat and afterward, I'll set you up for the night."

"I appreciate the offer... but I'll pass. I would much rather stay here with Saress."

"There's nothing you can do," Ellusia said. "The last thing I need is for you to drop dead from starvation."

Thathra nodded. He knew she was right and he would need all his strength if things went awry. Perhaps a well-cooked meal was deserved. "And you'll get me the minute you discover something."

"As soon as I'm able," she said, "now go."

With them gone, she went to work doing all the tests a normal healer would. Counted her pulse, listened to the heart, took her temperature but found nothing wrong, but also nothing right. All her vitals are different from a human, but she didn't know if they should be the same, therefore, she had no idea exactly what to look for. She examined every inch of her scales and found damage from the attack, but nothing that would cause her to lay here so close to death. The one thing she knew was the reptile was dying and had no explanation why. Unless she found the answer, Saress would be dead by first light.

It was late and most of the town had expired when the clop of a horse reached her ears. She turned to see the flash of a man dismount; his feet never touched the ground as he landed next to her. "Get back!" he yelled, then grabbed her by the shoulder and jerked her with such force she flew out of the stable and bounced a good distance away. When the intruder faced her, his eyes glowed like lanterns and she froze in fear. "Did you touch her?" he yelled. Instantly, he was upon her and the sound of cloth ripping cut through the air as he heaved her from the ground. She remembered him from days prior.

"Yes," she said through trembling lips.

Not so much as letting her go, he pushed her away where she fell once more, "you fool," he hissed.

With cat-like reflexes, she was up and running straight towards Rufus screaming the entire way. Thathra heard the call and leaped to his feet knocking the chair he occupied to the floor. "The stranger is here with the reptile," she cried out then fell into the open arms of Rufus.

Thathra never hesitated as he bolted towards the stable. He was unsure what, or who he would face, but would meet them none the less. At a full sprint and the stable in sight, he slammed into something hard and invisible. The impact was fierce and left him flat on his back. Anger filled his mind, and he screamed something unrecognizable, a fiery rage burned in his eyes and his lips curled back exposing his teeth in a rabid snarl. His second try proved no better, but this time he remained standing.

Through the invisible barrier, he could see a man draped in a white robe hunched over Saress. Near the stable, a pure black steed stood.

Slowly, Thathra reached out with his palm until he could feel it, a wall as solid as stone yet invisible. With his hand as a guide, he traced the barrier and discovered it circled the stable and went higher than he could reach. In fact, he believed it may have been a complete dome. Another plan crossed his mind and he tossed a handful of dirt upon the surface and watched as it slid down the perfectly smooth surface. It would be impossible for him, or anyone else to pass. They had no choice now but to watch.

Elwrick reached out to touch Saress but quickly pulled his hand back, he could feel the evil coursing through her veins and he backed slightly away. He needed to find out exactly what kind of lich had placed the Life Leech spell upon her? Focusing his mind on her, he reached out and mumbled a few words which drew an ooh from the crowd as he inspected her mind for what she had witnessed.

With the inspection complete he now knew, and it would not be easy. The spectators were about to get a show worthy of songs.

Whispering the words, he doubled in size and brightness while an orange glow grew around his wrist like bracelets. As he continued to chant, inside the dome the wind increased and his long white hair whipped and thrashed at his face. Hay intermingled with dirt flung from the ground circled the enclosure. On more than one occasion, the smash of a stone echoed as it pounded into the barrier. With his palms placed at his sides and his fingers stretched outward, the glowed emitted caused the crowd gasped in shock, expecting any moment for them to burst into flames.

Throwing his head back and screaming up into the sky, the words which came could not be understand. He bent both arms at the elbow till his hands were level with his waist the twisted his wrists till his palms faced skyward. A green hue, almost flame-like, danced on his palms as he spoke. Most of the words were indecipherable, but occasionally, a few were in the common tongue.

"By the power invested in me, I command you to
Leave this shell,
To abandon this woman and go back to the foul plain
whence you came!"

After he finished, Saress rose a few feet from the ground, then spun counter-clockwise. Kicking and thrashing, she appeared to fight back. She would not surrender easily to his words.

Elwrick's face deformed with intensity as he grabbed the lizard by the head with such force, it appeared he would crush her skull. Then the hue that radiated from his hands dissipated into her skull and he spoke again.

"You don't belong here, leave this
Innocent soul and be gone!"

Inside the stable, pastel-colored beams shot out from the lizard and ricocheted off the walls, while hay burst into flames as it whipped around the dome.

They all swore a demonic ritual was happening right here in their own town.

Without warning, her blue tongue came alive in retaliation and snapped like a whip towards Elwrick, which he caught and continued the chant.

"You are not welcome here.
Release this woman to my care!"

Elwrick hissed towards the lizard. His whole body shimmered and convulsed as the wind swirled around him and his robe thrashed. It looked as if he used all the force in the universe when the light from his entire body slammed into Saress and entered her body, then exploded outward. The flash was so bright it lit up the town like an afternoon on a hot summer day, and then there was darkness. Elwrick lay motionless, draped over the body of Saress, the invisible barrier now gone.

In the darkness, they heard the lizard take a breath. Not an easy breath, but the kind you take long after being chocked.

Thathra entered the smoldering remains of the stable first with Ellusia and Rufus close behind.

Rufus pointed to two large men who stood near what used to be the stable. "Take him to my place and place him in the spare room, he'll be safe there."

Covered in the remains of burnt hay and smoldering ash, Saress lay where the ritual took place. Her breathing slowed, and she now seemed to be asleep in a peaceful slumber. After a quick check of her vitals, Ellusia flashed Thathra a smile. "Her vitals seem more on par now for a healthy woman," Ellusia confirmed. "But I recommend we don't disturb her until the morning. She is peacefully resting now."

Thathra remained at her side until the sky lightened. It was only then he saw the true extent of the damage the stable sustained. Thick wooden beams now stood only as thin charred sticks and all around him the glowing embers of what he believed must have been the roof smoldered. Most of the hay was gone, either burnt to ash or completely vaporized and the ground smoldered. He now realized why the dome was created, to prevent all those around him from being obliterated.

Thathra oversaw the movement of Saress to the Mayor's house and placed on a bed of hay in the far corner of the main living room. Here, Ellusia could closely watch the reptile's recovery.

Elwrick had no idea of the time, but he could guess by the bright sun that lit the window it was well past noon. His head swooned and his arms felt weightless as if at any moment they would float away. As he sat up, he viewed his environment and was baffled. He had no recollection of this place. Where was he? How did he get here? Last thing he remembers is fighting a war with an evil parasite hell-bent on destruction. In an all-out effort, he remembered using all the power he could muster to drive the evil entity from her body before it killed in retaliation. Outside the door, he could hear voices. Not just one, but many. His legs wobbled as he stood and he struggled to cross the room.

Rufus came to his feet and went to aid the haggard looking man.

"Stay back," Elwrick mumbled in a terrifying voice.

Rufus backed away, not sure exactly how to handle the situation, he simply slid a chair out and waved him over.

Ellusia brought a large plate of food from the kitchen while Thathra sat across from Elwrick at the table.

Elwrick studied them all and when his eyes fell upon Thathra he spoke, "where's Averie?"

"Gone," Thathra responded. "I have never been so happy to see you. Everything is in disarray and the quest is all but busted."

Elwrick seemed to ignore Thathra, "I need a large basin of ice water," Elwrick said. His head flopped to one side as if he no longer had the strength to hold it up.

"I have a large wooden bowl—"

"It must be glass," Elwrick screeched, his voice almost made their ears bleed.

"Something's wrong," Thathra said. In the short time I've known Elwrick he's always been strong, confident, but now he appeared tired and broken."

Ellusia left to retrieve a glass basin from the room and quickly returned then filled it as requested.

"He doesn't look good. I better have a look at him." Opening her bag she pulled out a few instruments.

"Don't touch me," Elwrick screamed, he looked like a rabid dog about to bite.

Startled by the sudden outburst, she backed away till her back found the wall, "is he okay?"

"I don't know," Thathra answered. "I've never seen him this disoriented."

To their surprise, Elwrick slammed his face down into the icy water. He remained there motionless for many painful minutes and they all knew he was dead. His arms hung limp at his sides and his chest ceased to rise and fall.

Rufus looked at the others, "What do we do now?"

Thathra stood knocking the chair over, "I don't know," his lower lip trembled and a tear ran down his cheek.

Ellusia passed them all and approached the corpse, "we can't leave him here." When she was an arm's length away, Elwrick reached out and snatched her by the tunic, then slung her away almost ripping the material from her body. The process happened so quickly, she never screamed.

With a violent outburst, he jerked his head back flinging his long silver hair spraying the ceiling with water. From the center of his forehead, a long silver thread emerged and entered the water. Thrashing, the entity launched large cubes of ice from the bowl and then circled looking for a place to escape. Moments later, the water turned black as ash and a foul smell filled the room.

Nonchalantly, Elwrick slid the bowl to the center of the table.

They each studied the bowl like they had just discovered an unknown species.

"Shall we eat," Elwrick said. To his surprise, everyone had lost their appetite.

Rufus nearly passed out and his face turned a deathly blue.

Ellusia slapped him on his back to get his lungs to work.

"I'm Elwrick," he said. "The food smells wonderful, compliments to the chef."

None spoke, their vision alternated between Elwrick and the bowl and the thing which swam through the water.

"Never mind that, it'll be dealt with later."

Rufus shook his head in disbelief.

Elwrick was halfway through the food when he stopped and turned to Ellusia who stood near the bowl, a long wooden fork gripped tightly in her hand. Her intentions were obvious to all. "I wouldn't do that if I were you, unless you want to end up like Saress."

She quickly dropped the fork, embarrassed she got caught.

His gaze remained focused on her and she felt naked, ashamed. "You're a very lucky woman," he said. He could see she was nervous, so he intentionally changed his gaze back to his plate of food and took another bite before he continued. "I understand you work with medicine, but in this situation you were out matched and underskilled. I must apologize for the way I treated you but I had no choice. It's not in my nature to hurt others but you did not realize the dire circumstances you faced."

Elwrick could see their interest was still on the bowl and not his words. "I didn't want you all to see this but I have no choice as you are more interested in that thing than what really matters. Do you have any holy water?" he asked Ellusia.

"A tiny vial, but it's almost empty."

"Hand it here, I only need one drop."

A quick search of her bag produced a small vial with a cork stopper which she handed to Elwrick.

"Plug your ears," he said, then popped the cork and held it over the bowl. The thing inside backed away as far as the bowl allowed. When the single drop hit the water the thing let out a demonic hiss, then screamed and thrashed as the water began to bubble as if it boiled while a putrid steam rose from the bowl. The whole ordeal lasted only seconds then the water calmed, and the thing was gone.

"Did it die?" Ellusia asked.

"Yes, a very painful death to the parasite," Elwrick said, and then the bowl suddenly shimmered and then faded from existence. "I sent the bowl to my home where it can be properly disposed of thus permanently destroying any chance of the parasites return. If you like, I will replace the bowl for you?"

They spent the rest of the day on the porch relaxing and it was only after dinner was consumed did Elwrick strike up another conversation. "Now tell me?" Elwrick asked Thathra, "What do you mean by she's gone."

Over the next hour, Thathra explained everything.

Elwrick rubbed his chin deep in thought as Thathra finished. "They're named Din'Jin. Vermin from the thirty-third plane of Tartarus. They live in subterranean caverns deep underground but are often captured by liches and turned to slaves. Any that do not come when beckoned and fail to do whatever they are asked are tortured in ways you all cannot fathom in this realm."

"What's a lich?" Ellusia asked.

Elwrick drew a deep breath and gave her an awkward glance. "A lich is an undead creature who has gained eternal life through suicide."

"Wait… what, that can't be right," she said. "Now I'm more confused than ever. You said they commit suicide yet they gain eternal life… you can't have both… can you?"

Thathra leaned forward in his chair, he wanted to hear the answer as well. Rufus wanted nothing to do with the supernatural and continued to blow the most amazing smoke rings which left the entire porch covered with a sweet cherry tobacco scent.

Elwrick leaned back in his chair, "I guess there's no harm in teaching you something," Elwrick said. "A lich begins his life as a person, just like Rufus, you, or Thathra, but spends years of training to become a necromancer."

Ellusia shuttered, "necromancers disgust me."

"When they reach this stage…" Elwrick stopped and looked in through the doorway at Saress who made a groaning sound. "They summon a lich from the Realm of Tartarus and request to become its apprentice. Once accepted, the apprentice begins an intense training ritual. When the lich feels the apprentice is ready, he provides both a soul gem and the details on how to build his phylactery.

Saress released a loud, painful screech.

"Anyway, a coronation is held and if the Lich Queen Vhathialox approves, then a Spell of Life Stealing is performed and the soul tries to enter the phylactery. If he has done everything right, it accepts the soul, but if not, the soul is contained within the gem and the lich claims ownership.

"From there the phylactery is taken back to Tartarus and in about six days the soul is granted its first corpse to claim. What we see is just a physical form that you can destroy. The soul continues to live through a newly granted corpse."

"So what would this lich want with Averie? She has no desire to be a lich, at least none that I know of." Thathra said.

"That is a question I intend to find out." Elwrick stopped to look at Saress through the open door. Her lips curled up exposing glistening teeth, and she mumbled something incoherently. Her tongue is bright and pink again and the cloudiness that once encased her eyes had faded. It would still be some time before she could travel. "There's something far more sinister here at work and I intend to find out what," Elwrick said.

"What do you mean?" Thathra asked.

"A lich will not come here on its own, let alone a lich lord. They hate mankind and everything we believe in. Because of their evil nature and perverted minds, they prefer to stay in the Realm of Agathys where evil rules.

"Karayan brought this damn thing here?" Thathra commented.

"I would have to say no," Elwrick answered. Again he turned towards Saress who made a strange hissing and a clicking sound.

"Is she going to be okay?" Thathra asked.

"The natural healing process is terrible. She will recover but it will be painful."

Rufus came out from the kitchen holding a large mug of ale for each.

Elwrick gladly accepted the drink, "As I was saying a lich, let alone a lich lord, will not just show up on their own accord. It takes someone with great powers to bring one here."

"So why is it here then?" Ellusia asked.

"I don't know," Elwrick confessed. "I only know of one man who possessed that ability, but he has not been heard from in decades. I presumed he perished performing a sick ritual."

Ellusia gulped as if she fought for air, "will it come here next?"

"I don't believe so," Elwrick said. "The lich lord has what it's after but what's troubles me more is the rhythmic link between me and the bearer. I feel as if she's fine and I know she is clearly in trouble, but somehow, her location remains cloaked from me. Right now I should feel fear from a terrified young woman."

Ellusia rose to check on Saress. "How come I could not heal her?" Ellusia asked.

"Because what ailed her was not a physical wound you could see, smell, or touch. It's a nasty vicious spell called a Life Leech," he said. "I can see the confusion deep within your eyes so let me explain. When a lich comes here, they cannot stay for that long as their physical form begins to die almost immediately. So, they need a living being to steal life from to stay. After locating a suitable prospect, the lich casts a spell and a magical parasite enters them. It then goes to work draining the host's life and sends it back to the lich through an invisible cord, almost how a mother sends nutrients to its baby through an umbilical cord. Only a true understanding of dark magic and how it functions can defeat it."

"Is that why you were acting so different afterwards?" Ellusia asked.

"No, the parasite can jump from host to host and the cycle repeats. I was acting differently because it leeched onto me and even though you saw me here physically, in the astral form, I was fighting the cursed thing. To remove it, I had to find something to contain the parasite. I am not sure why, but ice water is the best thing as it will latch onto it as if it's a new host. But it must be glass as the parasite can pass through wood. Now you understand why I had to know if you touched her."

"Yes," Ellusia said. "I am just glad the thing decided not to attack me,"

"So am I," Thathra said.

"What a nasty, hateful world we live in," Ellusia said.

"You're wrong," Elwrick intervened. "It's a beautiful world, the most beautiful I have ever seen. It's the evil acts of the man that make it appear so ugly."

"And you're positive the lich lord is here for Averie?" Thathra asked.

"Very much so," Elwrick responded. "But his intentions are dark. A lich can do nothing to Averie, not even touch her as she is carrying a gift from the Creator. She is so pure to even touch her would lead to their deaths, both physically and spiritually."

"That's why the Din'Jin was here?"

"Correct, because they can touch her and have no ill effect." Elwrick leaned back in his chair and stretched. "If they wanted her dead, they would have just killed her, but since they went to all the trouble to capture her, that tells me the lich lord has sinister intentions." Elwrick took a drink from the mug he held then placed it on the railing of the porch. "I fear great harm though will befall Pegan and Lorandrial as I do not believe they know the horrors that await them in Ti'ath. In the morning before sunrise, I will be on my way to Ti'ath"

"I'm going with you, Saress can stay here on the mend."

"No, you will not go with me," Elwrick said. "When Saress awakens and finds herself alone, I fear this town will end in shambles. Waking up from a Life Leech spell is nasty," Elwrick shook his head. "I think it would be wise, very wise for you to stay."

Hearing this Rufus demanded Thathra should stay.

"With that, I take my leave." He bid them all a good night and left for his room.

Two days after Elwrick left, Saress woke in a fit of rage. Luckily, the day before Ellusia wrapped the reptile's massive hands and feet in large mitts many layers deep to protect Thathra from being shredded alive.

She kicked with both legs as if in a full sprint and swung as if she had gone mad with disease as the two wrestled around the house. Chairs crumbled beneath them and the table shattered. Outside a large crowd gathered. No one could see exactly what was happening inside, but they could guess by the cries, screams, and moans.

What seemed like days was under an hour when she broke down crying, curled up on the floor. Ellusia arrived to give her the pre-scribed treatment Elwrick said would ease her pain. That night the mitts were removed and she walked for the first time on her own, weak and unstable, but on her own. With both arms wrapped around Thathra, she embraced the human in a long hug. "I am so glad to be back, my old friend."

Chapter 38

Alone… hung up like an animal ready to be butchered and covered in ink which slowly burned through the outer layer of his skin, Pegan accepted death. Engulfed in the pungent stench of decay, it coated him like a wet sticky fog and his stomach churned as his nostrils filled with the foul funk. With a single violent contraction, his stomach expelled anything undigested along with a creamy yellow bile mixed with caustic stomach acids. His throat burned and the smell of vomit only added to the stench which forced him to dry heave many more times.

He never devoted much thought to how his life would end, but he had plenty of time to think about it now. A painful end to a man who has caused much more pain and suffering than he could ever receive. As the faint wisps of smoke lifted from his skin and his entire body felt as if it were on fire, he accepted death with a smile. What he could not accept though was what would become of Averie. She didn't deserve to die this way. She never asked to be a bearer, it was thrust upon her.

Glancing up at the ratcheting mechanism he studied its function, then closed his eyes. *All I ask is to let it fail, give me a fighting chance*, he prayed. He never was very religious, often times mocking those that were, so it came as no surprise when the mechanism held strong. *You put the child in her, you fix this*, he demanded. *I willingly give up my life to you, I accept that, do with me what you will. She is innocent though, damn you.*

I know it doesn't mean much coming from me, but she has done no harm.

Letting his head fall forward, he closed his eyes, trying to fight back the emotional waterfall that hissed as each drop landed in the bubbling slime. *I've never prayed before, and I know it looks bad that I pray now when I'm in this situation, but I don't know what else to do. Help me to help her, that's all I ask.*

As if his prayers were answered, across the room a needle-thin green light pierced the darkness, then rapidly expanded. All around it the air crackled with energy. Small flashes exploded and long thin streaks of energy which looked like lightning grabbed the walls and held strong. The light was circular and expanded until it reached both floor and ceiling and was so bright he slammed his eyes shut, but the energy penetrated through his eyelids and he could see. Not clearly though, but as if he looked through a satin curtain. He could make out the form of someone, or something as it emerged. He tried to trace the direction the thing went, but it was gone. As quickly as the portal opened, it collapsed in upon itself exploding outward in a dazzling array of silver sparks.

Pegan went rigid with fear. He was positive whatever this thing was, its intentions were to satisfy its own lust for pleasure with his pain. The anticipation was almost worse than the pain and he nearly fainted when he heard something move behind him. Prepared to feel the slice of a blade or hear the crack of a whip he closed his eyes.

"Just a few more seconds and I'll have you down," Elwrick whispered.

Pegan's eyes fired open when he heard more movement as if stuff was being shuffled. It was Elwrick, but how, nobody knew where they were. His prayers were answered, he thought. He looked up towards the ceiling, thank you.

Below him, the hue from the pit dimmed to a faint glow as a large wooden plank was slid over the pit and the *clank... clank... clank...* of metal gears were painfully welcomed.

Pegan had never been so elated in all his life to feel the ground. On trembling legs, he stood naked. It was only now he realized how weak he'd become.

"Easy now," Elwrick said as he covered the man with a cloak then aided him towards a rickety bench that looked as if it would collapse at any moment.

From somewhere within the folds of his robe, Elwrick produced a small candle and tossed it into the air where it floated. Then with a snap of his fingers, brought a flame to the wick.

"Oh my," Elwrick said. Upon his entry, he didn't notice the thick twine threaded through Pegan's lips. "Let's see if we can't fix this." With the tip of his finger he touched the very edge of the thread and it slowly dissolved starting at one end, and as it worked its way across his mouth, the holes closed and the wounds healed. With that complete, he next focused on the thick black shackles and with a word they crumbled to dust and floated away.

Pulling the cloak tight around his naked frame he let his head sag. "I've failed you, and I've failed Averie. I deserve death."

"You've failed no one," Elwrick replied. "But what you did do was get yourself in quite the bind. Somehow you stumbled upon a lich lord and it's taken an interest in Averie, but I don't know why."

"A lich lord?" Pegan didn't know a lot about them, but the tomes he read described them as vile, wicked nasty creature's hell-bent on destruction.

"Yes," Elwrick said. "I found Thathra and Saress at Talons Peak—"

"You found them, is she going to live?"

"Yes, she is on the mend as we speak now and I was informed of everything that occurred."

"So she told you how I fled like a coward?"

"No, you fled because of a very potent fear spell that would have left many permanently insane, yet somehow you endured. In hindsight, it was a dire mistake on its part as it allowed you to survive and send Thathra and Saress to the one place I knew you would eventually arrive."

Pegan rested his back against the wall and he let his mind go over every detail that he could remember before he spoke. "I didn't stumble upon it, we were set up. That lich knew we were coming and I don't understand how?"

"What makes you think that?" Elwrick asked.

Pegan told him about the gate and how it was lowered after they passed to prevent retreat, and the kobold corpses and how they were mutilated, then drew a heavy breath, "But it can't be, a lich won't come here on its own."

"You're right, which makes this puzzle even more bazaar."

"Karayan... he had to summon it," Pegan said.

Elwrick shook his head no. "It takes a very powerful necromancer to summon a lich, especially a lich lord... which Karayan is not. Something else brought it here."

"Who?" Pegan sounded like an owl as he asked.

"I don't know," Elwrick answered, "But I intend to find out." Across the room he rummaged through a large dusty metal bound chest and located Pagan's items. "Hurry and get dressed, we need to find the others," Elwrick said as he handed him the cloths.

Pegan dropped the robe and tried to wipe away the red ink but instead he cringed in pain.

Elwrick hissed and stepped back.

Pegan froze and looked at Elwrick with terrified eyes. He knew by Elwrick's reaction something evil lurked upon his skin. "What is it?" He asked.

Elwrick went to touch the writing then jerked back as if to prevent being burned. "It's blood ink taken from a sacrificial virgin.... It appears you were to be sacrificed to the Lich Goddess Vhathialox at the coronation of an apprentice."

Pegan remembered the sacrificial stone and how the blood was still fresh. "Averie?" he asked.

"Possibly," Elwrick answered. "But we won't know until we either find the corpse or her alive. Hurry and get dressed as time now is of the essence."

"What about this ink, can it be washed away?"

"No," Elwrick answered. "It can be removed with the right knowledge and time, but right now we have neither. It may hurt for a while but luckily, it won't kill you."

After Pegan got dressed, Elwrick performed a quick healing spell.

"I thought you couldn't heal mortals?" Pegan asked.

Elwrick smiled, "I can when the wounds are caused by something not from this realm."

Outside, Ti'ath was still covered in a veil of shadows even though the first traces of dawn streaked across the sky. The air was unseasonably warm and a thick haze covered the crusty ground. All around them lurked a foul stench like an old bog. They traveled quickly and soon arrived at the large sacrificial stone in the center of town. Upon it sat a strange looking creature.

Elwrick smiled as if he just solved an ancient riddle. Right about the time he began a spell, it noticed them and took to flight, but Elwrick proved the faster and captured it inside a sphere of light which left it bobbing on the breeze. Then, as if attached to an invisible string, Elwrick reeled the bubble back to him until it was close enough to grab and tucked it neatly away in the folds of his robe. "Let's find a place to have a discussion with our new friend," Elwrick said.

"I could be wrong, but that looks just like the strange bat that flew past as we traveled through Dügab," Pegan said. "I thought it was strange looking, but those caves are known to produce some strange off-breeds so I just let it go."

"That explains much," Elwrick responded. "This is no bat, it's a familiar."

"The lich's pet. Damn," he said kicking at the ground. "I should have known better," he cursed himself.

"Even if you did, what would you have done? The way back was sealed."

"I... I would have been more prepared"

"Your fate was sealed the moment the lich sought Averie. There is no way you could have won so stop making excuses." He took a deep breath, "Nothing we can do now except rescue Averie and the elf."

At a nearby hut, Elwrick walked in catching the Din'Jin which stood across the room rummaging through a pile of clothes by complete surprise. Its attempt to blink out of sight was short lived as Elwrick traversed the room in a flash and swung his staff with blinding speed. The horrible crack of bones being crushed echoed through the room followed by a thud as something solid hit the floor.

In amazement, Pegan watched as a pool of purple blood formed first, then a gray body materialized in the puddle.

"Bar the door," Elwrick said then went about his business of removing the orb from his pocket.

With the door secure, Elwrick held up the globe and examined the familiar. The wings were still outstretched as if getting ready to glide, the mouth stuck in an awkward open position and lined with many small teeth. One eye was shut as if instantly froze in mid-blink.

"Hopefully all of our questions will soon be answered," Elwrick said, and then he reached into the globe and snapped both wings which gave off a loud crack, then pulled the thing free from the light and threw it down upon the dusty table.

"Release me," the creature hissed in a low demonic voice. "Release me now." Trying to right itself the withering mass flopped.

"Why are you here?" Elwrick asked with a voice sharper than a sword.

"Release me, now," The creature demanded. He managed to position himself upon his two small legs, his head cocked sideways, he examined Elwrick then hissed at him.

"Let's try this again, shall we," Elwrick said. "I do not have time to toy with you, you will tell me what I wish to know, or you'll spend eternity suffering."

Waving a hand above the familiar, a small white circle appeared underneath it. Magically, it expanded till the mass of the familiar was contained. Once satisfied, Elwrick snapped his fingers closed making a fist. "Shall we have another round, why are you here?"

As he finished with the question, the light upon the table increased with intensity until the hair-thin bones within the body of the creature became visible. Flopping around within the light, the creature hissed and screamed before answering "To capture the bearer... to capture the bearer." Small whiffs of gray smoke rose from the creature and the pungent smell of burnt hair attacked their nostrils.

"And what use does a lich lord have with a bearer?" Elwrick asked his next question.

The creature never responded, choosing instead to wither and twist into the shape of a pretzel.

Elwrick smiled, and the intensity increased. "Answer the question and I shall ease your suffering.

Pegan cringed at the distorted shape the familiar twisted into from the intense pain.

"To milk the yellow blood from the bearer before destruction," The creature screamed its voice pure venom.

"Why?" Elwrick snapped.

"To fulfill a contract with a witch," it snarled. "Now fill your obligation and release me."

Elwrick cocked his head sideways, "a witch… *hmmm.*"

"One more question. Where are the others?" Elwrick asked.

The intensity of the light increased until every blood vessel within the thing became visible.

The familiar screamed a blood-boiling cry. "The elf is a few buildings over and the bearer is in Tavok's chamber deep underground. But you're too late, she's dead."

"You lie," Pegan yelled as he ripped Fel Strike free.

Elwrick intervened before Pegan could act and threw the familiar back into the sphere. "I'll keep this for now in case questions arise and dispose of it later."

With the information provided, they quickly located Lorandrial in an adjacent building. Elwrick cracked the door to peer inside and what he saw startled him. The elf hung by his ankles unconscious over an open pit of green slime. Stripped naked, his entire body was covered in long snake like welts from where he had been thrashed mercilessly.

"About time you arrived. The probe has been prepared, and the subject is ready." The Din'Jin said as it stepped around the elf holding a wicked corkscrew shaped tool. His voice screamed like that of a tea kettle reaching temperature.

Pegan went mad at the sight. The anger within him boiled and this time Elwrick would not be able to prevent its eruption. With a bang, the door was ripped from its hinges as Pegan bolted through.

The Din'Jin tried to react by becoming invisible while casting a spell, but the sudden outburst left it confused and it accomplished neither. Using a nearby chair as a catapult, Pegan launched into the air and landed a kick directly to the Din'Jin's face, which left the morbid looking little creature flat on its back. Pegan let the momentum carry himself through the attack then bounced off the wall like a sprung cat and landed directly on top then punched the thing an untold number of times in the face until the blood from his knuckles mixed with that of his victim.

Elwrick was shocked at the ferocious attack. He had never seen Pegan lose his cool in this manner and he could find no words to describe what happened next.

Pegan screamed something then picked up the Din'Jin and slammed it down upon the table splitting the wood directly in the center then it all collapsed around him in a cloud of dust. Reaching into the cloudy haze, Pegan grabbed the Din'Jin by the skull burying a finger in each eye socket and dragged the pathetic whining squirming thing towards the bubbling pit.

After his arrival at the edge, he picked up the Din'Jin and slammed it down into the bubbling goo.

Screaming in pain, the Din'Jin tried to climb out as the robe disintegrated, but Pegan kicked it in the face knocking it back in.

Flailing wildly he splashed at the slime. His arms became bone as the skin slid free like an overcooked chicken leg. The stink of death coated the room like a wet blanket.

When it was all finished, Pegan turned to Elwrick who stood in the doorway eyes wide open. "I'm Sorry," he took a deep breath. "I don't know what came over me."

"I do. Your fear and anger were revealed, and it's something you shouldn't be apologizing for. It proves to me you really do care for Averie and I couldn't have picked a better man."

Pegan listened to the words of Elwrick and realized the truth was spoken.

Carefully, Lorandrial was extracted from the mechanism and placed in a chair where Elwrick could examine him more closely. The beating had taken a heavy toll on his body and it took many minutes for Elwrick to revive him, then many more before the elf could stand on his own.

Lorandrial was still in a fog as he got dressed and the words came painfully slow, "is she alive?" Lorandrial asked.

Elwrick thought for a moment, "I don't know. A well-crafted spell has been woven to hide both her condition and location from me."

"So if you can't sense her, how will we find here?"

"She's here, in a chamber deep underground according to the familiar Elwrick questioned," Pegan answered.

"If I had to guess, I would say the temple would be the best place to begin. The prayer room could easily be converted into a summoner's chamber. And if she's not there, then we'll tear this town apart till we find her."

In the distance, the temple loomed like a two story-opponent which mocked their every move. Littered with windows they looked out in every direction like evil sentries, while the large opening where doors should have been spewed a hazy mist giving the structure life.

Doing their best, they hid in the shadows till they reached the doorway to stay in the shadows until they reached the doorway which opened up to a small chamber where a large brazier burned in the middle. As they neared they could see strange words written in green blood which left long streaks which glowed brightly above an arched doorway. Beyond the doorway, a set of wide steps spiraled down into darkness. Directly before them, a large square doorway gave way to a huge chamber lined with an uncountable number of pews.

Kneeling by the brazier, Elwrick motioned for the others to join. "I'm not sure exactly what we're going to discover down there but let's make one thing clear…I will confront the lich lord."

"You can have the damn thing," Pegan snarled.

"Oh, and one more thing. I believe it's time we even the playing field. This might feel a little weird at first." Elwrick placed his palm on each of their foreheads and began a low audible chant.

Pegan lost control of his eyes and they began to spasm. Blinking rapidly out of control, he saw only darkness as if he'd been blinded, but then his vision returned and he could see many things, both wonderful and horrifying, that were not there before.

"What have you done?" Pegan asked.

"I've allowed you to see into the realm of invisibility," Elwrick answered. "No longer will the Din'Jin be able to hide and you'll see their attacks coming."

"Time for revenge," Lorandrial snarled.

The stairs were wide and easily traveled and ended at a small foyer. Across the way and directly ahead a large doorway allowed access to a circular chamber. From the foyer, they could see Averie. She was hung upside down by large hooks shoved through each calf muscle and supported by a thick, rusty chain. Inserted in each of her fingertips is a long hypodermic needle with a thin tube which fed into a larger tube and eventually ended in a giant glass beaker that was half full of a creamy yellow substance.

Directly behind her, the lich lord stood. His back to the doorway, he was preoccupied fiddling with something on a shiny steel table and unaware of their approach. Beside him stood another man, shirtless, and covered in rune words.

"Slave?" Pegan whispered.

"Apprentice?" Elwrick answered. "And seems he's on the verge of becoming a lich himself. This does not bode well, not at all."

Lorandrial nocked an arrow and took aim.

Elwrick quickly stopped him. "You'll be dead before the arrow strikes. Remember what I said, let me deal with the lich lord and his apprentice," he whispered. "You need to get in, get Averie, and get out as quick as possible. Don't concern yourself with whatever happens to me."

From where they knelt they could count on one hand the number of Din'Jin that roamed the room.

Elwrick pulled a small pebble from a pocket and cupped it in his hands. Whispering a spell, the small stone began to glow and he tossed it into the room.

Clunk... it landed near the center and bounced a few feet.

Every Din'Jin heard the noise as it hit and turned to look. Mesmerized, they all seemed to ponder exactly what it was. One even had the audacity to get on its knees and get close as if to sniff it.

Elwrick waited till the timing was perfect then snapped his fingers. The stone exploded into a flaming white-hot phosphorus ball that emitted blinding streaks of migraine causing, nausea-inducing, eyeball burning, streaks of light. Screams filled the chamber as Din'Jin scurried to and fro trying to hide from the ball which now began to pulsate giving out a loud whoop... whoop... whoop sound.

Satisfied, Elwrick charged in and screamed the words to a spell. In his hand formed a blue ball outlined in silver which he promptly threw at the apprentice. Behind it, a trail of silver sparks sizzled the stagnant air as it traveled towards its target and upon contact, it launched him backwards destroying the cart.

Lorandrial kept a blistering pace as he crossed the room and never slowed when he fired. Across the room, two Din'Jin dropped dead.

Pegan slit the throat of another before leaping across the open pit, rolled under the Din'Jin, jumping to his feet and burying a dagger in each of the burning blue orbs it called eyes.

Spinning on his heels, the lich lord cast a Shield of Protection deflecting Elwrick's next attack into the wall which caused the entire structure to tremble.

Conjuring up a series of floating red balls that crackled and hissed with energy, the lich lord propelled them directly at Elwrick.

Elwrick was not without protection of his own and weaved a barrier which deflected the missiles back towards the lich lord who in turn redirected them towards the ceiling where they exploded into fire and smoke. The entire structure shook and the sound of rock fracturing could be heard but his attempt to topple the structure and crush his adversary failed.

Running behind the lich lord in hopes of protection was a fatal mistake as Lorandrial let an arrow fly which passed through the shimmering form and buried deep into the Din'Jin's face

Pagan sat atop the last Din'Jin pulling his blade from its chest as Lorandrial ran past. The elf had discovered a new target.

Tavok recovered from the devastating attack and easily swatted away the arrow the elf slung and countered with a spell which jerked the elf from his feet and propelled him at great speed towards the far wall.

Pegan watched in horror, he knew upon impact nothing would remain but a blood splotch and maybe a few bones.

Elwrick saw the spectacle unfold as well and just before impact he raised his hand and Lorandrial fell harmlessly to the ground. "Get her out of here," he yelled. His voice boomed like thunder.

Burning with anger, the lich lord charged directly at Elwrick and they locked onto one another in a mental and physical war. Between them, you could see their faces distort as they fought.

Locked onto each other they rose from the ground and began to spin in a circle. Below them, a vortex of molten stone formed and then they both tumbled down into the swirling mass.

Shocked at what he observed, Tavok ran towards the hole to save his master when a long, tentacle looking thing reached out and coiled around his neck jerking him through as well.

Lighting erupted from the hole and fire shot straight up charring the ceiling and the entire structure shook and rumbled and then it happened. In one loud boom and a cloud of dust and debris, half the ceiling came crashing down exposing the upper-floor.

"Get her out of there." The voice boomed back through the swirling mass and then the floor solidified leaving only a smoldering recess in the stone floor.

"No" Pegan screamed as he ran to the location of the vortex and fell to his knees.

"You heard him, we need to go, there will be time later to grieve," Lorandrial screamed.

From the floor above, the sound of clawed feet could be heard as two Din'Jin looked down upon the rubble assuming all perished but were surprised to see Lorandrial standing at a distance already aiming.

The first Din'Jin fell into the room dead with an arrow in its chest, while the other tried to flee but took an arrow to the back which blew out through its chest.

Pegan removed the needles and with Lorandrial's aid they lowered Averie to the ground and bandaged the holes in her calves.

A locked chest near the cart where the lich worked held her belongings, and she was haphazardly dressed then wrapped in a blanket. Completely unconscious, she would have to be carried.

"There's no way out but up," Pegan said. The part that collapsed completely destroyed the doorway.

Repositioning a few timbers a ramp was constructed. The hole was behind them, and freedom waited.

The room was maybe half the size of the lower and in the center a partial skeleton hung. Near the back in a dusty pile lay the items which obviously belonged to the victim.

Lorandrial peeked at an angle out the window looking for any sign of movement. "I think we're safe for the moment," he whispered.

"It won't be long until they figure out where we went," Pegan said as he rummaged through the pile of items. "There has to be something useful here," he whispered to himself. "Oh wow, look at this, think it's any good?" He held up a heavy bow with intricately carved designs on each limb. Near the handle, a name had been carved into the wood, but the writing was foreign to him.

"Just an old bow, the string will probably break the first time it's pulled," Lorandrial said as he glanced back.

"Here, take these," Pegan said, handing the elf a stack of unspent arrows with razor-sharp tips.

"I'll keep it for Saress. Bows this intricate are not junk."

"If we ever get out of here," Lorandrial hissed. You're more concerned with useless items instead of our escape."

Picking up a sword, he quickly discarded it along with a few clothing items worn thin from time. About to leave, the clank of metal on stone caught his attention as a gold necklace fell to the floor, the attached diamond sparkled bright red. Snatching it up, he placed it in a pocket.

Outside they could see the Din'Jin coming in numbers far greater than they ever imagined.

"We'll never escape, especially having to carry Averie," Lorandrial complained.

"What about over there?" Pegan pointed to a small shack which looked to be in better shape than all the rest.

"I don't know, looks like a trap," Lorandrial answered.

To their surprise, something strange and unusual occurred. All the cloaks the Din'Jin wore fluttered to the ground and an eerie silence filled the air. For many tense moments they waited, but nothing occurred.

"OHH," Pegan said with a smile. "These things were slaves, I bet they saw a chance to escape as well."

"Possible," Lorandrial agreed. After many more minutes of waiting and hearing nothing, they made a break from Ti'ath taking turns carrying Averie.

By noon of the second day, they were far enough from Ti'ath, they felt comfortable finally stopping to rest. Averie began to show signs of life and even spoke a few words, jumbled and meaningless, but words nonetheless.

The crackling fire spit embers up into the night sky as Pegan gently tilted back Averie's head just far enough to pour warm broth in her mouth. He made sure she was still getting something in her gut. All finished, he pulled the necklace with the red diamond from his pocket and examined it in the firelight. Reflecting the light, it seemed to burn inside with its own intensity.

"What's that?" Lorandrial asked.

"Not sure. It was in those old clothes where I grabbed the bow. I figured I would give it to her as a gift before she left."

"Can I see it?" he asked as he held out his hand.

Chapter 39

hlorax sat on a temporary throne of bones deep in the middle dark. All around him Din'Jin feverishly worked to transform the dismal cave into something more of his liking. The hard cold stone floor was magically altered to give the appearance of broken fissures and flowing lava while the ceiling mimicked a blood red sky. Bolts of electric blue lightning sizzled through the stagnant air and the magically induced cries of a thousand suffering replicated his home perfectly. Bones, both human and animal, were precisely positioned while five braziers burned with hot coals and minuscule flakes of ash fell from above. If you drew a straight line between each brazier, a perfect pentagram was created and his throne sat directly in the center.

Phlorax held up the small vial and examined the yellowish substance. "It's amazing," he said to Tavok who stood off to his left. "How in my hand, I hold the key to life."

Tavok ignored his master, or so it seemed that way when he offered no reply. Both eyes trained on the Din'Jin as they held a young child on the ground and thrust a large barbed hook through one leg. A wicked smile broke his otherwise expressionless face as he listened to the scream. "Music to my ears," he said, right after the child was hoisted high into the air by a twig-thin rope.

"Ah yes," Phlorax responded. His chest rose as he took a deep breath and slightly tilted his head to sniff the environment. Tavok knew it was only for ambiance though as the lich needed no air to survive. In fact, the current corpse his master occupied had been dead for well over a hundred years.

Phlorax twirled the vial. The contents crept up the sides until it was moments away from being flung free. When he ceased the motion, they watched it settle back to the bottom.

"I sense you are troubled by something?" Phlorax said. He never took his eyes from the vial as he twirled it again. "Speak."

Tavok hesitated a few seconds to relish in the cries of the child before he answered. "I am troubled… troubled deeply that my coronation has been postponed."

"You must rememb—"

"What troubles me more," Tavok interrupted his master unintentionally, but quickly stopped drawing a stern look.

"Continue," Phlorax said.

"What troubles me more is they escaped without a single death. I question if I'm worthy to become a lich?"

Phlorax let out a laugh which sent the Din'Jin scattering for their lives. "Well let me ease your mind. Your coronation has been delayed because the summoners circle was destroyed. To call Queen Vhathialox here in an improperly prepared room would show ignorance upon both our parts. I will not have my name tarnished because you wish to rush the inevitable. Depending on her mood, there's a possibility we would both be destroyed as punishment for wasting her time. Your coronation will come in time. Preparations have already been put in place for the circle's reconstruction."

Tavok studied the newest victim of his master's Life Leech spell. He was enormous, stripped naked, and squirmed in pain from a severe lashing. Occasionally, a faint moan or sob escaped through his clenched jaw.

"And you feel they have escaped without injury?" He held up the vial. "It would bother me more to have them all dead and this ruined," he held up the vial then took another bogus breath. "As for killing them, did you really believe it was possible? You had the most powerful spiritual guide ever created standing right in your chamber. You took a devastating blow, yet still had the sense to realize I was in trouble. Then, without regard for your own life, you followed us through the portal. It was only there when we combined our talents that we could subdue him, and now he sits as my... our trophy."

Tavok didn't have the courage to admit he didn't follow, something latched onto him and dragged him through.

"I have waited many decades for events far less important than your coronation. The time will come and then we'll rejoice in the blood of our victims."

"I suppose you're right," Tavok answered. Deep down, the truth of what really bothered him remained unspoken.

The five men rode hard and only stopped when necessary, a look of determination plastered on each of their faces mixed with, dirt, sweat, concern, and fear. They forwent armor; speed now was of the essence, not protection.

Lynn Brook was all but a memory and Nye Lake passed as fractured images through the thick dense trees of the Majestic's. As dusk fell, the forest gave way to The Great Divide.

Kalliphae raised his fisted hand to signal their halt at the bank of a river. To continue much farther without rest, the horses would perish and they'd be left on foot.

"I can't believe you agreed to this," Kipp complained as he climbed from his mount. A long sword swung from each hip and his belt held many weapons, smaller, but just as deadly.

"What choice did I have?" Kalliphae asked as he swiped back his long hair that partially covered his dirt-stained face with a gloved hand decorated with metal nubs at each knuckle.

Kipp knelt at the water's edge and splashed water on his face then looked at Kalliphae, "none really..."

Koby took a long swig from the flask which reeked of ale, "you know you're leading us straight to our deaths. No one has ever emerged from Ti'ath alive. In fact, I don't think anyone has emerged from there dead. Foul things happen there I would rather not experience." He was not as heavily armed but bore a wicked two-handed axe that could cleave a tree down in one strike.

Kalliphae grabbed the axman by his leather armor, slapped him, and then pulled him close enough that their bad breath mingled into a deadly aroma. "What are you doing?" He grabbed the flask and threw it into the river. "Now is not the time to get drunk. We need to keep our wits. If we think that we're all gonna die, all were creating is a self-fulfilling prophecy. We need to stay strong, vigilant, and prepared to fight the enemy."

"But who's the enemy?" Kipp asked. "We don't truly know who really holds the bearer."

Kalliphae gave him a stern look. "The enemy is whoever holds the bearer, living or dead." Kalliphae answered.

"Great," Koby snarled, the sarcasm was not well disguised, "just what I wanted to hear."

"Besides," Kalliphae said. "We're not going into Ti'ath, we're to set up camp on the outskirts and watch for anything going in or coming out. If we do discover the bearer, she is to be killed on sight."

Koby released a comforting sigh.

"We got a good four more days of hard riding. As soon as the horses are ready and we get a few hours of sleep, we'll be back on the trail."

The trio traveled through the night and morning came with clear skies and warm sun, yet Averies teeth chattered.

"We need a fire," Pegan said. "She shivers as if she's embedded in ice." He held Averie tight to his chest.

"The enemy is still out there. A fire now would only reveal our location."

"We have no other choice. Either she dies at the hands of our enemies or by us for lack of care. I would rather face them... all of them, than have to tell Saress I let her die and did nothing. Besides, we've traveled far off the beaten path and none know our location."

Lorandrial understood his reasoning and had no wish to cross the reptile either, "how close is Talons Peak?"

"Not far. Less than a day, but I fear we would arrive with a corpse if we continue."

Lorandrial agreed with Pegan's reasoning then went to collect anything that might burn.

Lilith lay on her bed and looked straight up towards the ceiling and wondered how the men were doing. They had been gone for days and now felt like a good time to check on their progress.

Standing before the mirror, she whispered the words to activate the spell, and the image formed in the mirror. They were well within The Great Divide and the land was streaked with long shadows from the rising sun. She relaxed and just rode along. Her eyes scanned everything as they traveled looking for any clues he may have missed. After all, his vision was weak compared to hers.

An hour passed when the faint glimpse of smoke far to the west caught her attention. "Investigate that smoke," she whispered to the mirror, but her words reached his ears as if she rode with him.

Altering his course, they headed towards the Broken Spine Mountains.

Lorandrial jumped to his feet, his vision focused on The Great Divide. He waited to make sure his vision didn't deceive him before he spoke, "five riders approach from the west."

Pegan looked also and quickly developed a plan. "Climb that thick tree till you get a clear view of the camp and wait for my signal. They will not be expecting an attack from above so with their attention on me, they'll be easy pickings for you. If I pull my weapons, don't hesitate to fire as we don't know their intentions."

Pegan sat next to Averie and only stood when the riders approached. When they came into full view, he clearly recognized three of the five. Kalliphae led them while the brothers, Kipp and Koby, stood to either side. Behind him were two he didn't recognize.

"Welcome gentlemen," Pegan said. "What brings you all the way out here on such a glorious day?"

Kalliphae glanced around Pegan to the woman wrapped in a heavy cloak, "who's that?"

"My wife," he answered. "She's pregnant and quite sick. We're on our way to Fairdenn, heard they got a great healer."

Kalliphae scratched his chin, "remove the blanket and if it's not the woman we seek, then you can go about your business."

"She's resting," Pegan declared.

Lilith studied the man, she had seen him before. Well not as much as the man, but his eyes, she had seen those very eyes. "You fool, that's Demetrius and the bearer, kill them now!" she screamed at the glass. Somehow they had managed to escape the lich and the chance of her gaining the yellow blood was all but impossible, so she might as well die.

Kalliphae shook his head as if confused. "Surrender the bearer… now," Kalliphae hissed. His lips curled up exposing yellowed teeth while a hand crept towards the hilt of his rapier. "And I might persuade the King to grant you a merciful death."

Pegan listened intently. "I have a better plan, one that won't result in bloodshed."

"And what might that be?"

"Return and tell Karayan you never found us, or any traces of our passing, and your wives will not become widows this very day."

"I'm good with that," one of the unknown men said.

Kalliphae looked at his partner with disgust then back towards Pegan. "That's a bold claim, especially coming from a man who's outnumbered five to one by heavily armed men," Kalliphae said.

"Four to one," Pegan argued.

"How do you figure that?"

"One of you will flee to inform Karayan of the failed capture, and judging from your stance, I'd say it's you." Pegan shot the burly man a half-witted smile.

"We didn't come all this way to barter," Koby snarled. His axe slid free while he circled to better his position. "We've been gone from home a long time and our ticket home sits only feet away, yet we try to bargain."

Kipp ripped one of his swords free and circled in the other direction,

"Remember… you said to kill on sight, well I'm done bargaining."

The other two men each pulled free a weapon.

"I suggest you surrender, it would save us all the trouble of having to clean our weapons later," Kalliphae said, giving Pegan a slight wink, and a broken smile.

Pegan drew a heavy breath, he was tired of the killing but today, once more, men would die and flung his cloak back and both daggers flashed to life.

The signal was sent and Lorandrial let the arrow sail. It hissed through the leaves and branches till it found its mark in the neck of a soldier. He tried to scream but the words only came as jumbled gurgles. His severed artery spewed bright red blood everywhere, including the side of Kalliphaes face.

Startled by the attack, Kalliphae leaped back stumbling over the other guard and they both crashed to the ground. Pegan could not tell who was which as they seemed to meld together into one enormous monster that kicked with four legs and swung the same number of arms to right itself.

Koby came in hard and fast with a series of swings meant to catch Pegan off-guard, but the nimble assassin ducked, dodged, and weaved, avoiding every attack.

Kipp circled in from another angle and headed straight for the prize then swung his sword directed at Averies head, but to his surprise the blade was deflected. The loud clash of steel echoed out into The Great Divide.

Pegan spun kicking Koby directly in the chest forcing the man to stumble back barely keeping his balance.

Kipp saw an opportunity as Pegan was involved with his brother and came in for another attack, his vision focused only on the cloaked woman as he raised his weapon to strike.

Pegan though was lightning quick and returned before his plan could come to fruition and planted his blade directly into the exposed armpit of Kipp.

Restoring his balance Koby was then unexpectedly launched forward and fell to his knees. He tried to scream but only blood ran from his mouth. The weapon he carried slid free from his grasp and the shiny tip of an arrow protruded from his chest. Falling forward, his face landed directly in the fire igniting his hair.

Kipp swung with his other hand which resulted in the loss of it at the wrist. Eyes wide and grabbing at the wound, he never saw the attacker which left him dead.

Recovering from the tumble, Kalliphae ripped his rapier from its scabbard ready to attack, but an arrow altered the furious man's plans as he was forced to leap out of the way just as an arrow whizzed past.

The soldier behind him never saw what hit him. All he knew was his head was thrown back, and both eyes popped free of their sockets. The shaft blew through his mouth shattering teeth before severing the spinal cord, then erupting out the back like a rock thrown from an erupting volcano.

Kalliphae was in shock from what he witnessed. How did this small band dismantle his group of highly experienced fighters so quickly? He would figure it out later and dodged another arrow that zinged past and mounted his horse and bolted away. To his surprise, all the other horses followed.

Drawing back, he let an arrow fly missing his mark by inches. The next arrow hit its mark burying into the shoulder knocking him forward on the horse. It was not the instant kill he wanted, but it was enough that if medical attention was not acquired, he would probably bleed out within a day or two.

"I hit him, but I don't believe it was fatal," Lorandrial said after he climbed down from his perch.

"I saw that," Pegan said as he looked in the direction the man fled. "If he lives, he'll report our location to Karayan and more will come. We must hurry."

Chapter 40

The next day Lilith aimlessly roamed the halls of the palace. No words could describe the sick feeling she felt at this very moment. She simply couldn't fathom how they could escape Kalliphae and his men, let alone a lich lord.

Standing at the door to her bedchamber, she grabbed the handle with her left hand, but it passed right through as if she were an apparition.

She cocked her head in confusion and tried with her right hand, but the results were the same.

"What kind of magic..." and then she screamed as she felt herself falling. No, not falling, but being dragged through dirt, and stone. She passed thick stumps and deep roots as she traveled deeper and deeper underground until she arrived at a large chamber. All around her she could feel the weight of millions upon millions of stone.

Across the way, Phlorax sat, "Ah... good, you've arrived just in time to join me," Phlorax said.

"I ordered you to use the broach to open a portal," she snarled.

"My dear," he laughed. "I take orders from no one. And besides, a portal you could not have entered. This way you didn't have a choice."

Fear struck at her heart and she backed away clutching her chest. In their first meeting, the lich was contained within the circle and could not get to her. Here, she was offered no protection and could be bent to his will, become a slave to his every whim. From the evil grin he gave her, she knew he understood. She had not expected it to turn out this way. She figured there would just be a simple exchange of fluids and she would go on her merry way. Something inside told her she was wrong… dead wrong.

"Have you got my reward?" Phlorax asked.

She never replied. Her mouth ceased to work.

"Of course you do, I can smell it on you like fresh blood when you begin your menstrual cycle." He tilted his head back to raise what would have been his nose into the air. His eyes burned orange with Hellfire. "Come, sit awhile." He patted the grayish femur exposed through his tattered robe.

She found herself unable to resist and her legs moved against her will. Rigid as a tree trunk, she fought. Her mind raced with every possible spell she knew to get away, but he had taken control of her mind and body. Like a puppet pulled by many strings, she moved in erratic jerking motions towards him until she climbed upon his knees then her head turned towards him and she smiled.

"Ah… much better," he said. With an outstretched finger, he ran his hand down the front of her tunic and as it passed, the material tore exposing her chest. The red blood in the vial looked bright against her pale skin. His head neared hers and a long black tongue crept out through a hole created by missing teeth and licked her cheek.

She quivered at the coarse texture of it. Unable to move she felt like vomiting, but her muscles refused to work.

Next, he ran a bony finger down her cheek and as he did so, her form changed back to the witch she had been upon their first meeting. "I told you I preferred you better this way, and this is how you shall stay." With his finger around the chain, the clasp on the back unlatched and it fell from her neck. He held it up to the light, could feel the heartbeat still present within the tube. "You would suit me well at my side," he whispered into her ear, his voice almost sounded human.

She wanted to cry, but found she couldn't. Her body lacked all function except that ability to breathe. She was a mere puppet in his hands. Putty to mold as he wished.

"But I always honor my words and commitments and our time together has now come to an end. You are of no further use to me. Do not contact me again, or it will prove quite harmful to your health." He held up the vial of yellow blood and hung it in place of the blood he took. "Our agreement has been fulfilled."

Across the room a portal opened. And with unseen hands, she was lifted from his lap and thrown backwards through the portal.

She woke hours later lying on the floor of her bedchamber with her hand still clutching the vial of yellow blood. Thinking it was a lie, she glanced in the mirror and began to cry at what she saw. She was once again the witch and the spell to transform her back was erased from her memory.

Along the way, Averie took a turn for the worse, and by evening, they had no choice but to stop and build a fire. She had become so cold, her body continually shivered, her face turned a deathly shade of white, and her lips faded to an icy blue. Each breath was labored and she gasped for air like a fish out of water. She seemed to no longer even have the strength to open her eyes or even make an attempt to lift her head.

"She's dying," Pegan said.

"What do you need me to do?" Lorandrial asked.

Pegan took off his cloak and wrapped it around her as well. "You need to run to Talons Peak and get help."

"Keep the fire burning bright as a signal," Lorandrial said, and then bolted off into the waning light.

Rufus sprinted through town until he arrived back at his house to find Saress and Thathra resting on the front porch. "Our spotter informed me someone approaches from the south," he said in-between long winded gasps. "A lone man, it might be an elf."

"An elf," Saress said as she rose from the floor where she was laid out. "I best go look."

"I'm going as well," Thathra said. He had just finished making a new handle for the axe and it felt good in his hand, "I may need to test it out."

From the edge of town, she watched the small dark speck grow to a blob and then a man. It was an elf, an elf she recognized. "Lorandrial," she murmured and bolted away almost knocking four farmers over in the process.

At a full sprint, she met him halfway across the field, and it was obvious he ran himself to exhaustion. As she neared he fell to his knees. Thathra arrived shortly after.

"She's dying," he gasped fighting for air between each word. "To the south, about an hour from here, along the edge of the mountains in a huge ravine burdened with rocks. He has a fire burning."

Saress left him to lay where he fell and broke into a sprint. Using all four legs, she propelled herself easily outdistancing the barbarian who kept yelling for her to wait, but it was no use. She was already either too far ahead or simply chose to ignore him, he guessed the later. She covered the terrain quickly in large bounds as the smoke of a distant fire worked as a beacon. She didn't know if that was him, but that's where she was heading.

Pegan never drew his blades when he heard someone approach. His only concern lay with the woman at his feet. Her eyes glossed over in a deathly stare.

Saress never said a word as she passed, her tail knocking the assassin to the ground. "What happened to her?" Saress demanded. There was a visible anger in her voice.

"I don't know, the lich did something—"

"I'm taking her back," Saress said as she scooped Averie into her arms.

Pegan chose not to follow, instead, he sat at the base of a large stone and watched the fire burn. He had no desire to return only to watch her pass away.

With Averie on the bed, Ellusia went to work examining the unconscious woman. "I need you all to leave… now!"

Saress growled.

"Except you, you can stay." She knew better than to anger the lizard.

It was dark this very night as if every star was veiled and the moon refused to shine. Pegan walked slowly as he had no desire to arrive at Talons Peak only to discover she had died. Regardless, his delay would not delay the inevitable.

It was noon the next day before Ellusia walked from the room. She looked pale as if all the blood had drained from her body.

"Did she…" Pegan paused, he couldn't say the words. Behind him, Thathra and Lorandrial stood.

"She's going to live, she's a tough woman."

"The toughest," Pegan said.

"It seems they were draining her yellow blood for who knows whatever sick reason. And they had drained enough her body was starving to death and began the process of shutting down. A few more hours and we would have lost her."

"What is yellow blood?" he asked. "Every person I've ever killed has always bled red."

"It's not blood, actually, but a component of blood that's used to transport nutrients, hormones, and proteins throughout the body. It's often referred to as the gift of life. Without it, we can't survive."

"But why would they need it?"

"I have no idea what their sick intentions were. But I do know it can be useful in many situations."

"Can I see her?" Pegan asked.

"For just a moment, she really needs to sleep now."

Pegan entered the room and to his surprise she was awake. There was a life in her eyes, but she still looked frail. "Pegan," her words were barely audible.

Chapter 41

egan had no idea of his current location. The ground was made of charred stone and small streams of lava flowed past. The sky was blood red and black clouds drifted past and silver lightning split the sky. The air was dense, and it hurt his lungs to breath while the distant cries of a man pained his ears.

As he turned to take in the view, an obsidian shelf rose up out of the ground which left his eyes wide. He looked left, then right, and finally up, but there was no sign of where it began or ended. The structure is comprised of nothing but cubicles. Millions and millions of cubicles as far as they eye can see. The smooth surface is deceiving and looks cool but actually emits a heat so hot his skin roasts as he nears. He tried and failed to fight the strange force beckoning him. As he drew closer, the smell of his flesh cooking made him sick to the point of vomiting. Standing before the massive shelf, he could see each cubicle contained a contorted block of ice no bigger than his closed fist.

From the shelf, one block called out to him and he snatched it. Unlike the others, it was perfectly round and placed on a pedestal carved from one solid chunk of basalt. Encompassing the pedestal were rune-words that glowed bright purple and pulsated with energy. Inside, a man knelt, arched backwards with his arms placed in a defensive posture as if he was about to be struck by something above.

The globe reminded him of the one Lord Rayne kept in his chambers when he was a child. How he would sneak in and make it snow with a simple shake.

The globe was weightless in his hand and quite warm. As he held it up to his face, he got a better view of the man trapped inside. His face was locked in a state of both anger and fear. At first, he didn't recognize the man. He was battered and beaten, covered in ash, and both eyes were gouged free leaving bloody black tormented sockets. And then the true fear punched him straight in the gut as he recognized the captive.

"I knew you would come to save your pitiful master."

Pegan heard the words and spun only to find him standing face to face with the man from the chamber who was covered in rune words.

"Give me back the item you stole and the rest of your pitiful worthless companions may yet survive tonight. Your fate is yet to be determined."

Pegan stood there baffled at first, he didn't know what to say, what to do.

"Give me the item…" he screamed and then reached out and snatched Pegan by the throat.

Pegan woke thrashing at his blankets while outside the wind and rain lashed at the house guided by an unnatural anger. He closed his eyes and rubbed his face. There had to be more to the dream… there must be more to this dream.

Instantly the room lit electric blue as a bolt of lightning flashed just outside the window, and the entire structure shook from the thunder that followed. On his feet, he made his way to the water bowl and splashed his face.

Across the room, a faint light was visible beneath the door and voices could be heard. With both hands, he washed his face once more and looked in the mirror and saw the prettiest blue eyes he had ever seen staring back at him, he jumped when the left one blinked. Spinning on his heels, he turned to confront the woman behind him, but no one was there. Back at the mirror, they too were gone.

At the table, Rufus and Ellusia sat across from one another, the soft glow of the lantern kept them partially hidden in shadows. Between them, there was a large unrolled parchment displaying a drawing of the coastline. Ellusia was pointing to a spot on the map while Saress leaned over her shoulder and pointed towards another area.

Pegan leaned on the door frame and he wiped the sweat from his face. "Rouse the others," he said in a shaken voice. "There's an evil that tracks us."

"It's just the storm, it'll pass by morning," Saress said as she looked at him. "You feel okay?"

"No," he answered, his eyes were distant, glossy, and he held a strange gaze. "We need to go… now," he demanded.

"In this weather, are you crazy?" Thathra said from the divan where he lay half asleep. "Have you not looked outside?" Thathra rose then paused when he saw Pegan for the first time in the light. "You look pale like death found you in your sleep—"

"Have you not listened to a word I said?"

Thathra glanced towards Saress, "I've never seen him this way. Maybe we should go."

Boom… the thunder shook the small building causing the flame to do a strange mesmerizing dance, then without explanation, the color turned from a soft orange to a faint blue, almost the color of the eyes in the mirror, then it turned to black.

"GET OUT… NOW," he screamed, then grabbed Averie by the wrist and broke for the door. Reaching out with his hand as he neared, the door was blown from the hinges with an eardrum busting crack, then vanished like a playing card tossed to the wind.

Saress let her gaze follow him as he faded into the distance, still not sure exactly what she had just observed.

"This is strange," Rufus said as he looked at the lantern.

Ellusia didn't need to be told twice, she too could sense the evil which had just entered the abode and ran for her life.

Hypnotized by the strange flame which began to grow slightly while dancing around the inside of the lantern, Rufus stepped back to watch the show.

From a stable across the way, Pegan watched a lightning bolt strike the roof of the house which caused it to shake violently.

Saress heeded the warnings and quickly left along with Thathra. Lorandrial and Rufus remained behind.

The flame shattered the glass of the lantern as it sprung forth then grew in size till it reached that of a small child. Everything it touched burst into flames and within seconds the entire structure was ablaze.

Lorandrial and Rufus crawled out on their hands and knees, their clothing still smoldering.

Another bolt of fiery hot lightning shot downward blowing the roof off the structure and the boom of thunder brought the entire house crumbling down.

"We need to leave this town before whatever hunts us razes it to the ground," Pegan yelled against the wind.

"Who is here, what chases you?" Ellusia asked, raising her voice over the thunderous boom. All around them townsfolk began to gather to observe the spectacle that was taking place.

"I don't know," Pegan answered. "I can just feel it in my bones. An evil the likes of which we have never known and I can sense its fury. Perhaps next time we will depart under better circumstances," Pegan said and gave Ellusia a long hug and thanked her for all the aid she provided.

"Can't you wait until morning?" She asked.

"I would love to, but I feel if we stay here much longer there will be nothing left of this town," Pegan said.

Another thick bolt of lightning shot across the sky then branched out lighting the entire town.

"Once we're gone, life should return to normal, or as close as what can be considered normal."

"I understand," she said to Pegan.

After they each said their goodbyes one last time, they headed west.

Ellusia stood motionless until their bodies became small dots then disappeared.

The storm finally passed and by morning the sky cleared. Ellusia stood in her kitchen over a pot of boiling water and looked out the window. From here she could see the smoldering heap which just yesterday was the Mayor's house. From her bedroom came the light snoring of Rufus. She had allowed him to stay there until his place could be rebuilt, which would begin first thing this morning. Outside, far away above the mountains, she could still see the flashes of lightning. It was almost as if the storm followed them. She frowned as the last few sliced up potatoes fell into the water with a splash, then thought about her new friends wishing them well on their journey while wondering if she would ever see them again.

Near the edge of town Arlin located a suitable family and went to work doing what he does best, making people talk and causing pain. "I know they've been here," Arlin hissed as he pressed the blade against the woman's face. "Where are they?"

The man had no choice but to answer or watch as his wife's face get peeled away. "They were here," he pleaded on his knees. "But I believe they left last night. When the rains started I came back home."

Arlin slowly pressed the blade in allowing the man to hear his wife scream. "Which direction did they go?"

"I beg you," he cried again. "I don't know?"

"Who would?" he snarled.

The man never hesitated when he answered, "Ellusia, the healer. She helped them and healed the bearer. She would know."

"How do I find this Ellusia?"

The man gave very specific directions to the home of Ellusia.

Arlin smiled as he threw the pregnant woman to the ground and kicked her in the stomach. "If you lied to me, I'll return to finish what I started."

Rufus sat at the table enjoying breakfast and talking about the weather and how it was going to be nice to not have to start rebuilding his home in the rain when he suddenly slouched forward as if he fell asleep. Seconds later his face slammed into the plate and a thin dagger protruded from the back of his skull which appeared to kill him instantly.

Ellusia jumped to her feet right about the time Arlin emerged from the shadowed hallway. When their eyes met she bolted for the door.

Arlin followed and cut her off and landed a punch to the side of her head.

Dizzy from the blow, she stumbled backwards then clawed at his face as he grabbed her which left a long bloody scratch from eye to ear.

Infuriated, he pounded her until she looked as if her face had been trampled by a horse and her arms hung limp and she faded.

Ellusia woke with a horrific headache that throbbed like a bass drum only to discover she was bound to a wooden chair. Arlin sat at the table eating the food she had prepared.

"Oh good, you're awake," he said. "I was worried I may have killed you." He dragged a chair over and sat directly in front of her. "Now, I'm only asking you once, and then the pain begins, which direction did they go?"

She turned away.

He slapped her and then slapped her again. "I know it stings, where did you send them?"

Somehow, a tear managed to squeeze its way out of an eye that was swollen shut.

"Loyalty, I love that in a woman," Arlin laughed. From a small pouch he produced a series of small needles which began hair thin but quickly grew in thickness. Holding them up for her to see, he began to feed them underneath each of her long decoratively painted fingernails.

She screamed till her throat burned.

"You want it to stop, tell me where you sent them." When she failed to answer, he pushed the needle in farther which began to tear the nail away from the skin.

Her entire body convulsed and she vomited her breakfast.

Laughing in her face he moved to the next finger and started the process again until every fingernail had been torn away, then he moved on to her feet where he jabbed the needle in between two toes and began to twist it.

"Please forgive me for what I do," she whispered to her far away friends knowing they couldn't hear her plea, but the pain had become unbearable and she confessed where they were headed before begging him to kill her.

"Not today sweetheart, you'll make a fine mother for my children, that is, after you're properly trained.

She knew things were going to get worse as he ripped open her shirt.

"Please don't," she trembled.

"Shut up," he yelled and spit in her face. "Your first lesson begins with never to question me… ever." And he slapped her many times until she almost blacked out. "Your second lesson will be on how to please me." And he cut away the straps of her bra.

"No… please don't," she begged him and began to scream for help but he hit her on the side of the head with such force the chair tipped over.

He untied her and drug he by the hair down the hallway to the last room before slamming the door as loud as possible. Moments later the sound of clothes being torn away and the muffled cries of a woman filled the room.

It was well past noon, but the land was still eerily dark as thick black clouds invaded the sky blocking all but the most persistent rays of light. The trail is slick with mud, steep and toothpick narrow. In a few places, abruptly turned at the edge of a sheer drop off where death was all but certain. Hours passed while they made their way through the onslaught of water driven by an unnatural fury when they began their descent and the trail widened and turned to sand.

"It's as if nature itself attacks us," Thathra yelled, competing with the wind and rain. The thick smell of salt rode on the wind and salt water blown from the sea stung their eyes.

They walked the beach well into the evening when a dock stretched out over the water like a broken bridge. The massive structure was rickety at best, and large steps climbed partway up then swiftly turned and continued till they reached the top. Constructed of old wooden planks unevenly spaced and bound in place by a thick piece of rope that interlaced between each board in a crisscross pattern, the dock was stronger than it made them all to believe by appearance. The whole structure was supported by large wooden posts that disappeared into the water and the entire structure swayed from the angry tide.

"What do we do now?" Averie asked when they reached the top.

Pegan led them to the far end well out over the water, "we wait," he answered.

Chapter 42

Arlin cursed at the heavens at what he saw. Pegan had led them to the far end of the dock which extended well past the shoreline. From what he could see, the element of surprise was all but forgotten... or had it and a smile came to his face.

Behind him, Ellusia remained silent. Her hands and knees were both bloody and raw from having been forced to crawl the entire distance, and her partially dressed body showed the bruises from having been severely beaten. Around her neck was a thick black collar and from it came a rope which Arlin held tight in one hand.

"Sit," Arlin snapped.

She promptly obeyed.

"Not like a human." He lashed her across the back with the rope which brought forth a whimper. "Like the dog you are." He raised the leash to strike her again, but she quickly repositioned her body to imitate that of a dog.

"Good girl," he patted her on the head. "Wait here for my return. If you leave I will hunt you down and your training will begin anew, is that clear?"

"Yes master," she whispered. Her head lowered in submission. Somehow, a tear managed to leak from her swollen eye.

Arlin used the passing dense clouds and high sand dunes to his advantage and darted from one to the other as the shadows fell between them. It took more time than anticipated but he eventually arrived at his destination… the dock. Once there, he scaled a post and then hung from the ropes used to tie the planks together and worked his way down the entire length of the dock until he arrived at the end where Averie sat with her back towards the sea. Hanging there, he could see them and waited until the time was right and when they were all looking towards the shore, he made his move and swung himself up onto the dock and landed silently.

Averie let out a scream as she was grabbed from behind and felt the cold steel of a blade press against her throat.

Pegan leaped to his feet and both daggers flashed to life while Saress nocked an arrow and spun to face Averie. Thathra nearly dropped his axe… startled, while Lorandrial backed away.

Directly behind her, a man draped in a long black, hooded cloak held Averie hostage, his face masked in shadows. "Shall I kill her now? Or deliver her to Karayan and claim my reward?"

Averie struggled to free herself but ceased when she felt the blade bite into her neck and the warm trickle of blood as it ran down her neck.

"I'm waiting for an answer, my patience wears thin," Arlin hissed. "It would be so easy, a quick flick of my wrist—"

"Then you die next," Saress said followed by a low growl.

Pegan studied the man trying to figure out exactly who he was when he caught sight of the scalloped Kris as a lightning bolt tore through the sky. There was only one man who carried that style of blade and could have snuck up on them that easily. "Release her," Pegan demanded. "I don't believe she is who you seek."

"Why would I seek any other than the bearer, after all, the price on her head right now is astounding?"

Pegan slid his daggers back into their sheaths. "Because a man with your skill could have easily killed her and been on your way, having never been seen…"

"You're right—"

"Enough with the idle threats you'll never complete," Pegan interrupted him. He knew exactly who he dealt with and was in no mood to play his games. "If you plan to kill her, then do so and let's be done with it. Otherwise, tell me what you want and be on your way."

Thathra gasped at what he heard.

Arlin pointed the Kris directly at Pegan, "I want your life, I want your heart, and I want your soul. And I want all three right now."

"And just how do you intend to do that holding her captive. You think I will just lie down and allow you to cut it from my chest?"

Arlin's laugh was almost hysterical. "I have no intentions of staining my blade, I'll leave that job for your companions. Do you think they will defend you and stand beside you when I tell them who you are and what you've done. They'll want you more dead than I do. But in their eyes, I will be the savior when I release the bearer."

"You're wasting my time and yours. They already know my past," Pegan said, "and they also know I have forsaken the Brotherhood."

"All of it," Arlin chuckled, "every grisly detail?"

Saress cocked her head sideways.

"From the way the lizard looks, I'd say no."

Pegan never responded, instead, his focus remained on the assassin.

"Well… do you wish to tell them or shall I," Arlin said.

"I have nothing to hide," Pegan said. He repositioned himself to where he could see both Arlin and his companions. "The coward standing before us who uses an innocent woman as a shield is my brother Arlin—"

"Half-brother," he screamed.

"As you are well aware," Pegan continued, "I was an active member of the Brotherhood for many decades. But what I didn't tell you, and what he is referring to, is that I once worked for Karayan, and it was my job to track down and destroy the bearer."

"How could you?" Averie cried out.

"A bit hard to swallow," Arlin whispered into her ear. "The same man that aids you is also responsible for the death of so many before you."

Saress drew back her bow.

"Ah… ah… ah… don't try it," Arlin said pressing the blade hard against Averies skin. "She will be dead before the arrow takes to flight."

"I wasn't going to kill you," Saress rotated towards Pegan. A lust filled hate burned in her eyes.

"Tell me it ain't true," Thathra said.

Lorandrial ripped his sword free, "Please tell me Meriel was not one of your victims?"

"I can't," Pegan spoke softly. "I cannot go back in time and relive the past and undo my wrongs." He didn't try to move when he saw Saress draw down upon him or when Lorandrial approached. "And if you choose to strike me down, then I believe the punishment is just." Pegan looked alone, his head slightly slumped while both arms hung as if the bones had been removed. "But what I can do is everything within my power, even offer my life to get the bearer to the portal."

Thathra motioned for Saress to lower her bow and Lorandrial to sheath his weapon then spoke loud enough Arlin could hear. "Elwrick recruited this man and he must know his past. Therefore, I cannot justify killing him. I will let Elwrick deal out the punishment he feels is needed for the crimes this man has committed."

Behind them, lightning lit the darkened sky, and the rain fell in sheets blown sideways.

Arlin hissed an angry scream. He still needed the heart to fulfill the contract and to leave without it would only lead to his own demise. His reasoning became clouded and he pointed a finger straight at Pegan. "Then I challenge you to a duel, and assassins duel if you wish to save her life?

"I agree," Pegan said. "And I want your word, an assassin's word if you win you will not stop them from reaching the island. You will leave with my heart and never bother them again?"

Arlin nodded. "As for this wretched thing, I care less if she lives or dies, to me it matters not. Right here, right now, in front of all your companions," Arlin hissed. "You will die." He pushed Averie away.

Instantly, she ran to Saress.

Behind them, lightning flashed illuminating the dock.

"Just like old times," Arlin said, "you and I together again."

"No," Pegan responded. "Unlike you, I've learned the truth and realized there are more important things than the senseless murder of the innocent people."

"Good thing you're not innocent," Arlin said, then lunged his blade straight at Pegans throat.

Pegan parried the blade but never struck.

The hair on Averie's neck stood as the clash of steel reached her ears. "What if he wins? What if he kills Pegan?"

"Then he gave his life to save yours," Saress answered.

Arlin struck again, lashing out quickly at a sweeping wide angle with one blade designed to leave the opponent vulnerable while the other blade shot in expecting to find an opening.

Pegan deflected the thrust and simply stepped back to allow the other blade to zing harmlessly past then struck at Arlin. One blade fired in low aimed at the torso and he worked his way up in a series of jabs and thrusts.

Arlin danced backwards avoiding each blade then crouched in a low awkward position.

Pegan almost had to laugh, he was the one who designed and perfected the maneuver and taught it the Arlin.

Arlin could see the error of his thinking in the crooked smile on Pegan's face and rose, he would need another tactic to down this formidable foe.

Circling, Arlin stuck his arms out wide exposing his open chest. "Your movements are slow and easily predicted. You couldn't land a strike even if I left myself exposed."

Pegan kept his eyes trained on the assassin and never responded to the taunt.

Arlin grew furious and charged in striking like a man gone insane. Four daggers, legs and arms became one as the two men seemed to blend into one.

The ring of steel informed the observers most attacks from either man never landed.

When they separated, they each dripped blood from multiple wounds, but none were deadly.

Arlin didn't allow his opponent a moments rest more than what himself needed then launched a new series of attacks aimed at the side of Pegan's neck, while his other weapon came low and fast.

Pegan blocked the high blade, leaped over the low blade, and the pair locked together once more and tumbled to the deck. Grunts, groans, and snarls, could be heard as the pair clawed, bit, punched, and tore at each other as they rolled around and when they separated, Arlin spit out a chunk of Pegan's ear.

Pegan stepped back. His chest heaved as he tried to catch his breath, yet Arlin's barely moved.

"You grow tired old man," Arlin cackled, "I can see it in your eyes, in the way you move, your lack of training over the years has taken a toll on your body… on your mind."

Pegan stood silently looking into the eyes of a merciless killer. Maybe the world would be better off with his death. It would mean one less murderer, but then again, he couldn't trust Arlin to keep his word. No, he would have to go on fighting to the death.

Arlin feigned his movements, then lunged straight at Pegan's heart.

It was only his quick reflexes which saved his life as he leaped to the side and rolled under the attack then landed a thrust to Arlin's calf muscle which left the man limping.

Arlin screamed, then his eyes filled with a burning desire to not only kill this man, but make him suffer and set out a series of attacks designed to work his opponent's blade low and away leaving him vulnerable.

Pegan had no option but to counter. He designed this maneuver and knew it well, but what happened next could not be predicted and caught him completely unprepared leaving him unprotected and defenseless. Expecting Arlin to go for his throat, he devised a scheme to counter when Arlin changed the game and performed a perfectly timed flip landing behind him and coming across with a deadly strike leaving a large gash from shoulder blade to hip.

A large section of Pegan's cloak fluttered on the wind briefly before it flew away like a butterfly in a hurricane.

Pegan howled something that sounded almost animalistic.

Arlin screamed in victory but it was short lived.

Pegan ignored the pain and faced his opponent once more then launched a vicious attack that could not be countered and when he finished, Arlin was backed up to the edge of the dock and only held one weapon. His other lay on the deck along with all his fingers.

"You're beaten," Pegan snarled as he leaned to one side and stood in a pool of blood that formed at his feet. His appearance was almost ghostlike and his breathing was labored. "You can't win without both weapons."

Arlin listened intensely as he slowly moved to the side and away from the edge of the dock. "I don't need to kill you now, only survive long enough until you bleed out." He wrapped his bloody nub of a hand in his cloak.

Pegan knew Arlin was right, he could already feel himself going weak, and the two engaged again in a clash of steel. Their movements were a blur and when they parted, Pegan had his dagger through the pommel of Arlin's, and then he twirled his arm like a windmill which effectively pried the weapon from his adversaries hand and with a subtle flick, the Kris vanished over the side.

Arlin looked in horror over the side having heard the splash. Pegan never ceased his attack and buried his blade in Arlin's side clear to the hilt and begun to thrust it upward while his other came down quick at the neck to sever the spinal cord.

Instantly, time froze. The waves ceased to crash upon the shore and seabirds hung in the air as if dangling by strings. The wind stopped blowing, and the raindrops floated on the dense stagnant air.

Suddenly a flash of red light erupted upwards from the surface of the dock and exploded outwards towards the sky, and a billowing black sulfate smelling smoke filled the air, while ash fell like snow-flakes. When it cleared, a large skeleton draped in a shredded robe, that smelt of rotten flesh formed. Beside him, another man stood covered in writing.

Averie instantly recognized them and fainted yet she remained standing, held by an invisible force.

In a fraction of a second time caught up with them and Pegan was forced backwards landing at the feet of his companions while Averie collapsed to the ground.

"You belong to me," Phlorax said to Arlin who squirmed on the dock.

"No," you lie." Arlin fired back.

"Don't question me mortal." Phlorax pointed a bony finger at the withering man who screamed and squirmed as if he'd been set on fire. As he twisted in a contorted position, the grotesque popping sounds of joints being dislocated could be heard.

"It can't be true?" Arlin hissed. "You cannot possess my soul."

The lich eased his suffering enough Arlin could comprehend the words he was about to hear. "You're right, I can't you silly mortal. With your blood given to me under free will, I can take possession of your body if I can intervene just before death occurs. And If I would not have stopped Pegan, you would be dead at this very moment."

"I gave my blood to a witch, not you."

"Correct you are, but the witch bartered your blood to me in exchange for yellow blood from the bearer which I provided. So now, you belong to me. And you will stay in my possession until your death. At that time the demons from Hell will claim ownership of your soul for your failed obligation to collect Pegan's beating heart. But, I fear they will have to wait many decades to receive you as I have many things planned."

"No… God no," he begged.

Phlorax laughed, and a doorway opened in mid-air rimed in fire.

Tavok picked up Arlin by the skull and they started to leave.

"Wait! I command you," Pegan screamed. Unable to stand on his own, he leaned on Thathra for support. "I offer you a trade, one life for another."

Phlorax looked at Pegan with flaming eyes.

Pegan cringed in pain, it was almost as if the lich was looking straight into his soul. "I want Elwrick returned… I know you have him trapped in a globe of ice. I have seen it with my own eyes—"

Phlorax interrupted with a devilish laugh. "And why would I surrender my most valuable trophy?" The lich questioned. "What would a mortal have that I myself might want?"

"This," Pegan said as he reached into his tunic and pulled out a small box that dripped with blood. Using Fel Strike he slid the top free and they all watched it tumble to the deck like a flipped coin. With trembling hands, he held Fel Strike which glowed bright blue at the unseen contents. "I will let your apprentice live, in exchange for Elwrick. All the years you spent training him, gone quicker than a blink of the eye."

Phlorax studied Pegan intently. Somehow, this mortal had acquired Tavok's phylactery and even though he was not truly a lich yet, he had invested enough time that if the parchment was pierced, it would indeed kill him.

"I want him returned, alive, to the Island of Aramoor before the next new moon which will occur in five days," Pegan said. "And alert enough he will be able to open the portal for the bearer to leave this world," he added.

Phlorax looked at his apprentice in disgust.

"Keep your trophy, I give up my life," Tavok said.

"Forget him, trade for me," Arlin yelled towards Pegan, his voice broken and meek. "I will help you get the bearer to the portal. We don't need Elwrick."

"Silence," the lich yelled, the voice drove Arlin to his knees and blood leaked from his eyes. "I agree to your offer. You will have your savior returned."

Phlorax waved a hand and magically the phylactery lifted from Pegan's hand and the lid from the dock and they both floated through the air to his waiting palm where the lid fell precisely back in place.

"Never try to contact me again or you will join Arlin," Phlorax said just before he entered the portal followed by his apprentice. Before it slammed shut, they could hear the blood-curdling screams of a man who sounded like he was being torn apart

The very moment the portal closed the menacing black clouds lightened, the monsoon ceased to exist, and the angry waves that lashed at the dock calmed to a gentle slap. The sensation of burning sulfur and the stagnant stink of decayed flesh were quickly replaced by that of a fresh spring day. Mother Nature began the process of cleansing itself from the filth that stood on the dock and the rays of sun which fell upon them was warm and felt good on their wet skin.

Pegan collapsed to his knees then fell face down in a pool of blood. His body trembled and his face went pale. He had survived long enough to fulfill his task. The bearer would now be able to reach the portal safely. All obstacles in her way had been removed.

Averie ran to his aid but was oblivious on what to do. Her only knowledge of wounds was to try to stem the bleeding, but the gash was long and deep. Using her dress she applied pressure to the wound, but she knew it wasn't enough, he would soon die.

Saress knelt by the fallen man but her head turned to a dune not too far from them. "Thathra," she snarled, "there's something or someone behind that dune. Now is not the time to encounter another enemy."

Thathra grabbed his axe and set out to meet this new foe. His large arms flexed as he gripped his weapon, the new handle felt good in his hands and it was about time he tested it.

Jumping over the dune he let out a horrendous barbarian scream and drew back the weapon to strike when what he saw hurt him more than any weapon created.

Ellusia, or at least what he thought was Ellusia, sat like a dog. Around her neck, a leash hung.

"I tried to stop him," she cried out upon seeing him. "He hurt me, I tried," she choked on the tears. "I had no choice but to bring him, I'm sorry." Her jaw quivered to the point her teeth chattered.

Thathra was so angry at what he observed he screamed to the sky cursing Arlin. Her busted face, bruised body, and ripped dress, were more than he could take and a tear came from his eye. Feverishly, he worked to unclasp the collar then took her in his arms. "Shhhh," he said. "It will be okay. He can never hurt you again, or anyone else, trust me." He then picked her up and carried her towards the others.

Having heard the commotion and fearing the worst, Saress ran towards him to see if he needed help, but abruptly stopped when she saw Thathra emerge from the hole. She knew instantly who it was, and gasped when she saw her condition.

"Arlin tortured her until she brought him here."

"Judging from her dress and vacant expression, I would say he did more than torture her," Averie argued.

"Ellusia," Averie said. Getting no response, she lifted the battered woman's head away from her knees and looked into her eyes. "You need to help Pegan. I know you're hurt and I'm sorry, but we don't know what to do. I'm afraid he might die. Look at him."

Saress directed Ellusia's gaze towards Pegan who laid face down. "We need your help? He needs your help?" Saress begged her.

"No!" She said with a trembling lower lip. "He hurt me."

Saress shook her head in disbelief.

"He didn't hurt you, Arlin did. Please… help him." Averie pleaded. She alone understood what the woman felt. She had sat in that very spot, beside the pond, the day after she had been rescued. She hated every man that ever lived.

"He fulfilled his task," Lorandrial said. "He got you here, let him die in peace."

"Shut up!" Averie screamed

"I was just trying to say—"

"Just shut up!" Averie screamed till her throat hurt. "You don't know nothing about him, or what she's going through, what she's been through." She placed the bloody cloth back onto the open wound, then laid her head on his back and cried.

Chapter 43

egan lay there in a state of delusion. His chest heaved in spasms as a series of ghastly moans escaped his lungs. All over his body, small black splotches which resembled spilled ink formed while large beads of sweat percolated up through his pores. The skin surrounding each wound turned bright red and sent out deathly black feelers which looked like angry roots while a creamy yellow puss dripped from his eyes.

"What's happening to him?" Averie screamed to the world.

"Arlin must have had his blades coated with a disease, or ailment," Saress suggested.

"I don't know either," Lorandrial said shaking his head, "but it looks as if he's dying." His vision looked past them to the end of the dock. "While I wish we had more time to discover the answers, possibly even find a healer, a decision needs to be made about his fate. The boat just docked and we don't know how long it will wait."

Thathra released a half-hearted sigh, "I have seen this man do amazing things that would leave you bewildered and scratching your head, but even I don't think he can recover from this. Regardless, he would not allow Saress to be abandoned like trash to die out on The Great Divide so I will not abandon him here."

"Look at him?" Lorandrial snapped. "You don't recover from that without Godly intervention. What if we bring him and he infects the rest of us? Or worse, what if he infects the bearer? It's better to lose one man than the entire party."

"What's wrong with you?" Averie screamed at the elf. "I will not leave him. He could have left me that day in the room when I looked just as sick. If you don't want to help… fine! I'll carry him myself to the boat if need be." She tried to lift him but failed. Next, she tried to drag him but only made it a few feet before she was left winded.

Saress was furious as she walked past she lashed out with her tail catching Lorandrial behind the legs knocking him to the deck. "You disgust me," she said, then scooped Pegan up and carried the unconscious man towards the boat.

Averie sucked in her breath then released it giving off a loud oh. She had seen small boats used in rivers and lakes, but this behemoth that just docked was indescribable. She had no choice but to swivel her head to see it in its entirety as it was too big to view all at once.

When the captain was satisfied the boat was properly positioned, a large plank was lowered to the dock which landed with a heavy thump threatening to collapse the rickety structure. Next, a large section of the gunwale swung inward, and the captain danced down the plank, a prominent limp in his step.

"Greetings," he said when his feet touched the dock.

Averie was not sure how to respond. She had never seen anyone dressed so strangely yet he was quite reserved and well spoken.

"I'm Captain Bristol Royston and my vessel, *The Albatross*, is at your service." He slipped the wide-brimmed hat from his head then folded his arm under his breast and performed an elegant bow.

He was a handsome man with long curly hair the color of beach sand. A dark red satin coat hung unbuttoned exposing a light gray shirt stitched with gold thread and a slightly ruffled around the collar. Dark leather boots reached clear to his knees then gently doubled over at the top while an ornate scabbard swung on his right hip. She could guarantee the blade had yet to see combat. For a younger man, his features seemed chiseled and his deep emerald eyes could have melted ice from a hundred yards away.

Averie smiled. He had a certain charm which melted her heart.

"It's been a Gods age since I've ported here," he said. "In fact, I forgot this dock even existed. Good thing my boat remembered."

"I'm glad it remembered as well," Thathra said as he passed. "I would have been highly upset if we had to swim there."

Royston ignored the barbarian and kept his attention drawn on Averie. "I could be wrong," his eyes traveled down to her belly, "but my gut tells me you're the mother?"

"Yes... yes, I am," she answered.

Royston cringed and stepped back when he viewed the man Saress carried. "He looks terrible, you sure he's alive? I don't like corpses on my boat, they leave an eerie feeling long after they're gone."

"He's alive, just severely injured." She looked down at Pegan's face. Green foam spewed from his mouth. "If he passes, we'll have a proper burial at sea you'll be proud to say you attended."

Lorandrial passed them all and boarded but kept an eye on Saress the entire time, a look of revenge still fuming in his eyes. Averie boarded next, followed by Saress who still held tight to Pegan, and Thathra boarded last.

"What about her," Captain Royston pointed to the woman who stood expressionless at the end of the dock. "Is she going?"

Saress looked back to see Ellusia standing motionless where the red light had erupted. Around her, swirling wisps of smoke from the smoldering wood obscured her legs.

"I'll get her," Thathra said and he started back down the plank.

"No," Saress hollered towards him. "She is terrified of men right now and she may run and we'll never catch her. She'll be stranded here alone to die and I won't allow it."

"Then I'll get her," Averie said, and carefully passed Thathra on the plank.

"It can't be," Ellusia whispered as Averie neared. "It's not fair."

"We need to go and you're coming with us," Averie told her.

"How come he gets to leave, while I'm left here to suffer?"

"You're mistaken," Averie softly said. "He just didn't get to leave. A very vile creature called a lich lord took him. If you ask me, I would be led to believe the torment he put you through has been handed back tenfold by now."

"But how do I know, I can't go until I know? He needs to be punished for what he's done."

Her thoughts were irrational and her words made no sense. It was obvious the woman had become unstable.

"Trust me, I heard the screams coming through the portal. In time your wounds will heal and you will return to your beautiful self once more, but stronger because of what you had to endure. Arlin though will never be the same, ever."

"But he took something from me I can never get back."

"I know that. We all know that and none of us are angry with you. There was nothing you could do to stop him. None of us look down upon you, in fact, we're all here waiting for you and if you don't go, then I ain't either. We'll have to make a new life for ourselves here."

Ellusia looked towards the boat and with Averie at her side, hand in hand, they made their way up the plank and with that, they left the mainland.

"All aboard," the captain yelled.

The sound of chain clanking and gears turning could be heard from somewhere below the deck as the plank rose then retracted.

The boat was constructed from a dense hardwood coated in something to give it a glossy sheen. Any water that splashed upon the deck simple bubbled and ran away in long streaks. Towards the bow and stern, massive doors lined with stairs to either side broke the ship into three sections. At the bow, a long round pole stuck out over the water while towards the stern there was a third set of stairs that arced its way up to another level which looked out over all the rest.

A young man dressed in a white jumpsuit with his dark hair pulled back in a ponytail ran to the edge of the stairs and faced the captain, "everything is in order below, Sir."

"Fantastic," he answered. "Now attend to the passengers. They look famished and remember, nothing's too good for our guests."

"Certainly," the deckhand responded. "Dining and quarters are this way," he motioned for them to follow with a wave of his hand.

Thathra needed no formal invitation and disappeared through the doors.

"Think I will stay up here with Pegan and enjoy the fresh air," Saress said, then carried him up the stairs.

The top deck was small and mostly occupied by a large mast that shot straight up through the wooden floor and reached for the heavens. It was thicker than most trees, worked perfectly smooth, and ringed by a wooden bench.

"Can you please take off my boots?" Pegan whispered to Saress, his words barely audible. "If you would please." His feet had swollen to almost twice their normal size and every inch of skin below the ankle was the color of ash.

Lorandrial roamed to the front of the ship while the two women found a suitable location on the stairs between the second and third levels.

Averie could see Lorandrial at the front of the ship, one foot propped up on the railing and using his hand to shield his eyes from the sun as he looked out over the mainland. "I don't like him, or trust him," she whispered to Ellusia. "It seems like every chance he gets, he tries to have Pegan killed or removed from the leadership position. I know you don't want to help because you're hurt and angry, but Lorandrial has no reason, yet he refuses."

As if by magic, three large white square sails appeared and puffed outward as if caught in a hurricane, yet the surrounding air was stagnant and thick with humidity. Sewn into the fabric of each sail was the image of a great bird. Its wings spread wide as if drifting upon a current. With a lurch and a groan, the boat gained speed slowly at first then set into a steady cruise. The open sea air was both refreshing and chilling leaving a tingling sensation down Averies spine, and she buried her fingers in the folds of her bloody dress.

Captain Royston took notice and draped his coat over both women who looked appreciative of the added warmth. "You two should go below deck where it's warm," Captain Royston said. He could see the goose bumps visible on their skin.

"Perhaps we shall," Averie said.

"And have a warm meal first, you both look famished… Captain's orders," he concluded.

Captain Royston gained the attention of a deckhand, "Take these two ladies below deck and make sure they are fed well then given the utmost luxurious quarters. Nothing is too good."

"Yes sir," he replied, then turned his attention towards the pair. "My ladies," he welcomed them with a bow.

"If you don't mind, my good man," Saress said as she crossed the upper deck and bound down the stairs. "Where she goes, I go."

"Perfectly acceptable. Wouldn't have it any other way," Captain

Royston acknowledged. "Make that three." Royston revised his original statement.

"Ah… Sir," he looked at Saress, "the reptile will never fit."

"Then put them up in my quarters, after they have had a hot meal."

Below deck, the captain's room was large and lavishly furnished. A bed against the far wall was big enough for two, and on either side sat a plush, pillow-top chair you could melt away in. Multiple lanterns burned giving the room a nice homey feel and from an unseen location, warm air filled the room. A thick ornate rug depicting Aramoor covered the floor while a handsomely carved desk and a wooden chair added just a slight touch of feminism.

Ellusia sat in the plush chair, knees pulled to her chest, head lowered.

Averie sat beside her on the bed, "I know what you've been through… and how you feel."

"Do you?" A hint of sarcasm lurked on her words. Her left eye had yet to open.

"Yes… I do. It was not long ago I myself tried to hide in a corner. Starved, beaten, and tortured. But I was saved by a man I didn't know. He had no obligation to save me, but he did," then she told Ellusia her history.

Saress opened the medical bag and dug through the contents. Everything was labeled, but the words were foreign. Eventually, she gave up and placed everything back in the bag.

"That same man who helped me now needs my help, and I can't give it. I don't know how. You have the skills to do something, won't you help him?"

Ellusia sat for a spell then looked at Averie with one eye still stained red from the busted blood vessels. "He hurt me—"

"Arlin did, not Pegan," she interrupted. "Pegan is a good man but has a dark past, one he is trying to forget," Averie said.

"It's still not fair, why is it he gets to cause all this harm and I get to return nothing?" She pounded her fist on the side of the boat which reopened the closed wounds. "All I wanted was for him to feel my pain." The floodgates opened and her eyes could no longer contain the waters. "I want him to pay," she screamed. "Look at me?" Ellusia cried as she looked at them. "He made me ugly and I hate myself. I have nowhere to go, nowhere to live. He killed Rufus because of me. All this death, it's my entire fault, I don't care." She turned away. "If I ever return home, they'll surely finish what he started," she sobbed.

"Ellusia… Ellusia," Saress called to her then gently, but firmly slapped her across the face to bring her back to reality. She had no desire to smack the woman, but she had to do something. There will be a time to grieve, but not now. "There are places to live and you must understand what happened is not your fault. Don't blame yourself… don't you dare for one minute? Please don't think we'll abandon you either. Somewhere, somehow, we'll find you a new home," Saress said. "The man who can help you is upstairs dying from the same man that hurt you. What better way to get back at him by saving the one he intended to kill. If that ain't reason enough, then do it for you. Prove you're stronger than what he believed, and you won't be broken. Do it for the women of the world to show our strength."

"You will survive this ordeal and it will make you a much stronger woman," Averie added.

Ellusia looked at Saress with anger in her eyes having just been slapped, but then the anger turned to tears. "Okay," she agreed. Her fingers were still too swollen and hurt too much so she asked Averie to find a plain white bottle labeled Symphytum Officinale. "I need a cup of water to make this elixir," she said. Saress hunted down a clean mug and handed it to Averie who measured out exactly one cup of water, then dumped it in. It needs to be shaken until dissolved, which Saress quickly handled. "Make sure he drinks this. All of it, every drop."

"I'll make sure of it," she said. "Even if I have to sit on his chest and pour it down his throat."

"We'll arrive in two days," Captain Royston said. He was not surprised when Pegan never answered. From what he could tell, the man was already dead

Saress left the confines of the darkened doorway and made her way towards him. The mug looks small in her massive hands, "Ellusia made this for you." She tried to hand him the cup but his arm never lifted.

"Looks like we'll make it," he said never lifting his head.

Saress wanted to cry, her companion was wasting away.

"Say goodbye to Averie for me and tell her I wish her the best in her new home. And remind her to never give up the fight when things get tough, find a way, make it happen." With that, his head slumped forward and the spark in his eyes which at one time seemed so bright, diminished.

Tilting his head back she slowly let the contents fill him. He never moved or made a sound as she watched the last drop vanish. When it was empty, she threw the cup over the side and sat next to him for a while, the silence was deafening and she finally had to speak. "Don't die on me. I can't do this on my own," she admitted. "I need you here to finish what you started."

She wanted to scream, to cry out in anguish, but deep down, she knew she would have to stay strong for the others. "I can't sit here and watch you die. I feel so useless," She said.

The swells picked up and the boat took on a rocking seesaw motion. "I don't like this, not one bit." She spread her legs wide to balance herself. Madness seemed to take over and she darted from side to side watching the water slap the boat. "Can't I just swim from here?" She asked.

"There are things in the water you would like even less," Captain Royston replied to the lizard's request as he adjusted the wheel, "than riding on this old wooden boat."

Saress ignored him and ran back to the other side again as the boat rocked.

"Maybe you should get some sleep? I will look after your friend," Captain Royston told Saress.

"I think you're right. I'm going back down; you can't feel the rocking motion inside." In all reality it was a lie, she could not take the sight of Pegan sitting there slumped slightly to one side. His limp body swayed with the boat. She needed to get away, to scream and yell, but more importantly… to grieve.

Chapter 44

ilith lay on her bed and observed the small vial of yellow blood. She had no idea if it would be enough as she had not read in detail yet the process involved to transfer it into her own body or how much time it would take.

What she did know was that the bearer had escaped and was well on her way to the island and that Kalliphae sat in the medical ward awaiting the arrival of King Karayan who had been notified of his return.

She needed to buy time, something, anything to prevent him from going after the bearer and a simple plan formed, make Karayan believe the lich lord still held the bearer. By then she would have figured out the yellow blood and hopefully be gone before her deception was discovered.

She arrived moments after Karayan and would need to act fast. The door flung open with the force of a hurricane and she barged into the room. "You!" she screamed in a high-pitched squeal and pointed a bone-thin wart infested finger at the man who lay on the bed.

King Karayan stepped out of the way. He was not exactly sure what just entered the medical ward but knew he wanted no part of it.

"Don't you recognize me, my King?" she hissed.

"No… not exactly," he answered.

"It's me, Lilith, your faithful servant," she said as she hobbled past. Her frail thin body supported by a crooked cane.

"What?" he gasped. His eyes went wide as if he'd been deceived. "You lie."

"I tell no lie," she snarled. "This is the result of trying to do your bidding."

"What are you talking about?" he demanded.

Kalliphae sat up on the bed, he wanted to hear this as well.

"I went there along with Kalliphae to Ti'ath. I wanted to make sure the job was done correctly. As you're well aware of, I have limited magical abilities and I portaled to his location and what I observed drove a dagger of fear straight through my heart."

"You lie! You were never there," Kalliphae said.

"Do I? Where are the four men who rode with you?"

"Dead," he said.

"More like tortured. They were offered to the lich as sacrifices."

"You lying whore," he screamed and started to rise from the bed but Karayan stopped him.

"Lilith, now please tell me exactly what you are talking about?" Karayan asked.

"Well, I arrived there only to discover Kalliphae was striking a deal with the lich. I could not hear the conversation per se, but it appeared he had also sold out Arlin as he was already strung up. The bearer was there as well, stripped naked and locked in a cage and being tormented by the ugliest thing I'd ever seen." She had to make the story sound realistic so there would be no questions. "There was one man dead on the sacrificial stone. It was hard to tell who it was because the body was so mutilated. For all I know, it could have been Demetrius. Well, stupid me. I tried to kill the bearer to make sure the deed was done. The others did not concern me, but before I could strike, the lich transformed me into this. I barely escaped with my life, but now I fear I may be stuck like this forever."

King Karayan stood with his mouth wide open, he had no words to say.

"Sir, this is all a complete lie."

"Where are the other men?" he asked, his arms crossed his chest.

"I already told you, they're dead, we were attacked?"

"But yet you live with a non-fatal injury?"

"I know it's hard to believe, but it's true."

"If you don't mind, I will take my leave to try to find a way to reverse this spell. I just felt it would be best for you to know the truth, so I did not delay coming here."

"Thank you Lilith, and I will talk to you later. I know someone who may be able to help."

Lilith cracked a wicked smile as she left and headed back to her room. Once there, she stood in front of the mirror and whispered the words activating the spell. She had to make sure her lie was believed and what she saw and heard, made her cringe.

Chapter 45

aress entered the room to find Ellusia had been stripped, washed, hands bandaged, and then put to bed, while Averie laid strewn out across the chair. The lanterns had been turned down to a warm glow, and the desk moved to one side of the room to allow a large mat to be placed for Saress to sleep comfortably. Flopping down, she tried to close her eyes but her thoughts kept drifting back to Pegan, his appearance, and what he said just before his head slumped.

Pegan had already accepted his death so he was shocked and confused when his battered bodied began to heal, and he felt rejuvenated. Whatever ailed him was slowly being forced out. The black splotches faded to an ash gray and the swelling in his feet diminished and their color returned. He still felt the pain from the gash across his back and his ear still hurt where Arlin bit a good chunk away, but no longer was his breathing labored or his vision impaired. Still though, he was exhausted and every muscle screamed out in pain and the very thought to lift even his arm was excruciating.

Gazing towards the sky, he watched the twinkling lights drift past while the waves lapped a pleasing tune against the sides of the boat. At the wheel, Captain Royston guided the vessel.

As the horizon lightened, Lorandrial crossed the ship all-the-while keeping his eyes on the silhouette of a man he knew should be dead by now. It would be easier to explain to the others he passed through the night than to fabricate a lie as to why he was no longer on the ship. To his surprise, Pegan opened one eye and spoke.

"Beautiful night," Pegan said softly.

"Indeed," Lorandrial agreed. "And surrounded by water makes it all the prettier."

"We'll be at sea for another day, but by tomorrow morning, we should arrive at the Isle," Captain Royston said.

Lorandrial glanced out over the water and there was no land in sight, no possible place for Pegan to swim to when he threw him overboard, no chance of survival. This morning his thirst for revenge would be satisfied.

Pegan adjusted his position against the thick beam to allow a place for Lorandrial to sit.

For a long time, they sat in silence.

"I don't know why I say this—honestly, he did— but when you and Arlin fought, a little piece of me hoped he would kill you. And then when I saw the gash across your back, I knew your death was imminent, and I smiled. Yet somehow you remain. How is that possible?"

"Why would you say that. I have done nothing to you?"

Lorandrial glanced at him, "Revenge, hate, disgust, I don't know, maybe redemption for what you did to my sister. She didn't do anything to you either yet you cut out her eyes."

"That was decades ago and every day I'm left to suffer with the thought of all the pain I've caused. It's like a Hell I can never escape from. Maybe that's why I didn't die. I'm forced to remain in this world and relive the pain I've caused. To die at the hands of Arlin would have been a blessing."

Lorandrial smiled, "Now it's time to reveal my little secret as well. Before my mother came to you and told you to leave, she came to me first and convinced me to come with the promise of revenge. First and foremost, our goal was to get the bearer to the island, second, it was to end your suffering. The first object has now been accomplished."

"What are you saying," Pegan said, there was a look of confusion in his eyes.

Lorandrial laughed. "I'm saying it would have been much easier for you to have died here tonight on your own than for me to carry out what my mother has ordered me to do. That is, unless you suddenly leaped to your feet and threw yourself overboard. It would be easier for me to explain to the others how you couldn't bear to have them see you this way and you took your own life."

Pegan didn't have to say a word, the look of horror on his face at what he heard said enough.

Lorandrial rose and slipped both swords free of their sheaths, "Rise... unlike you, I won't kill a defenseless person."

"I won't fight you," Pegan said.

"But you had no problem torturing a young girl strapped to a chair. My mother was right, your nothing but a coward." Lorandrial spit in his face.

Pegan never lifted a hand to wipe away the glob that ran down his cheek. If being humiliated would satisfy his lust for revenge, then so be it."

"I said get up," and he kicked Pegan's bare feet.

Captain Royston watched with widened eyes.

"I won't fight you," Pegan repeated. "I think you need some rest. Your mind is obviously clouded at this very moment."

Lorandrial kicked him in the ribs causing the man to fold over, and then kicked him a few more times. "If necessary, I will drag you to the side and throw you overboard if you don't get up and fight me like a man."

Pegan lay there on his side gasping for air.

Captain Royston thought about intervening but he was no fighter, in fact, the sword he carried had never been used except to maybe slice an apple.

"Have it your way," Lorandrial said. He grasped Pegan by the hair and drug him to the gunwale, "This is your last chance before you take a swim. Draw your weapons."

Pegan made no motion towards his weapons, he simply leaned against the rail, head hung, arms limp, and a look of defeat on his face.

"I said draw your weapons," Lorandrial screamed, and then slapped him a few times driving him back down to the deck.

"Hit him again and you'll have to fight me," Captain Royston said. His blade drawn he stood on trembling knees. No longer could he sit back and watch the beating happen and do nothing.

Lorandrial looked him over and sneered "Your only job is to drive this boat, nothing more unless you want to have an accident as well."

"I'm… I'm… I'm warning you," Captain Royston stuttered.

Lorandrial walked to the captain, swatted the blade to the side, then punched the man directly in the face.

Captain Royston covered his face but his white shirt was already stained bright red. A look of horror in his eyes at what just occurred.

"I told you to stay out of it," Lorandrial said, then hit him in the gut dropping him to his knees.

THWACK… an arrow stuck in a beam just inches from Lorandrial's head. "That was a warning, the next one goes in your skull," Saress hissed angrily. She had returned to check on Pegan and was horrified at what she saw and heard. The elf had gone insane and was threatening all and assaulting those who questioned him.

Lorandrial instinctively ducked expecting another arrow to arrive at any moment then faced Saress. "You wish kill me and save a murderer who should have died decades ago?"

Saress thought for a moment, "yes."

"You disgust me," he snarled. "I should have killed you that day in the glade."

"Well let's finish it," she said and threw her bow to the deck and slid her large, two-handed sword free. The anger returned and this time Pegan was in no condition to stop her.

Lorandrial sprung across the deck like a feral cat lopping the head off a deckhand who got in the way.

Saress bent in his direction and opened her massive maw and hissed something that sounded more like a roar and her pink forked tongue lashed out like a flag caught in a hurricane.

Lorandrial bound up the stairs then leaped to the gunwale to gain some much-needed height. The wooden rail was slick with sea water and his feet went out from under him and he landed flat on his back. The impact was bone jarring and one sword shot straight up in the air and the other was flung out into the sea as his arms swung wildly trying to grab hold, but there was nothing. The next wave rocked the boat in the other direction and his momentum carried him over the side and he was gone.

Chapter 46

llusia woke alone but bathed in a blanket of warm sunlight that filtered in through a partially open window. Just outside, the sounds of seabirds calling and the subtle rhythmic crash of waves upon the shore could be heard. Her hands were carefully wrapped in clean bandages and even though her hair appeared frazzled, it was obvious someone took great care to comb and wash it.

The warm plush rug felt good against her bare feet as she made her way to the window and looked out. Crystal blue water led to a beach with sand the color of salt. In the distance, rolling hills gave way to heavily forested mountains which stabbed the baby blue sky. One road was visible, and it meandered through the hills before fading into the shadows of the trees. She almost felt guilty as if she spied upon a dream.

Tap… tap… tap… came a rapping at the door.

Ellusia froze as if she'd been caught doing something wrong.

Tap… tap… tap… it came again but this time with a bit more energy.

She cracked open the door just enough to see who knocked. "Hello," she whispered.

"Good morning beautiful," Thathra said. "You look simply ravishing this fine morning." His face had a smile from ear to ear and in his hand he held a large plate of food that still steamed.

She knew he lied, all he could see was her eyes and a few straggly hairs. Still, she accepted the compliment with a smile, and then her face went somber, "Pegan, did he?"

"He's fine. Sore, miserable, and complaining a lot, but on the mend nonetheless." Between them a silence formed, "more importantly, how are you?"

She didn't answer.

"Can I come in?"

"No, please no." She could not, would not allow herself to be seen in this condition.

"I'm sorry," he said. "I should have given you more time, but we've arrived at the isle. You slept for the entire trip and I'm sure you're famished, so I brought you something to eat."

"Thank you, I am," she said as she took the food. "Let me eat and get dressed and I'll be up shortly."

"No hurry," Thathra said and left whistling a tune the Captain taught him.

Hours later, they met at a large circular seating area just off the dock that contained many benches. Wildflowers grew in abundance and the air was filled with butterflies of every color, shape, and size. In the center was a large seven-tiered fountain shaped like a giant clam with cascading waterfalls and covered in a strange vine. The stem was light green which was barely visible beyond the thick dark green leaves and deep blue flowers that faded to white near the center. Many of them had closed into a conical shell shape.

After many hugs and kisses were exchanged, and a few strange looks at the large bandage across Captain Royston's face, Saress filled everyone in what happened with Lorandrial.

"I feel bad for his mother, but not him. He's hated Pegan ever since we left Rhunsiire," Averie said.

Pegan walked away, a noticeable limp in his step. It was obvious something bothered him.

"Pegan," Saress called out, "what's wrong? Are you hearing things again?"

There was a tear in Pegans eye, "Lorandrial was a plant designed by his mother to kill me after we reached the portal. The elf told me before he attacked."

Saress let her mouth fall open. "I'll kill that—"

"No," Pegan interrupted her, "There's been enough bloodshed on my part. I will talk with her upon our return and if she feels my death is the only way to appease her anger, then so be it."

Thathra went to speak but Pegan stopped him, "Enough for now with me, we still need to get Averie to the portal, we're not done yet."

"You're right, we should go," Thathra agreed.

"I'm off to scout," Saress said, her bow in hand. "Who knows what things we'll find here?"

"My dear," Captain Royston cocked his head sideways and looked at her as if she grew another head. "Transportation has already been provided and there are no enemies on the island. We simply must wait for it to arrive. Let us enjoy the cool sea breeze, listen to the birds, and relax while we wait for Master Kingsley."

After a short while, a pure white horse decorated with glossy black tack arrived. The creature's trot was pure elegance and a large white plume attached to the head harness fluttered in the breeze. The carriage though was remarkable and the glossy white body sparkled in the sun. It appeared fragile yet thoughtfully designed and quite sturdy, which caught Thathra's eye. Curved perfectly to match the wheels, the top was open except for an arched lattice work complete with flowers that kept the passengers basked in shadows. There were two seats, each facing the other to allow the riders to talk. Behind it, a second one arrived identical to the first but without a driver.

The carriage came to a soundless stop, and the driver fixed the reins to a latch then climbed down from his perch and removed his derby. Sporting black trousers, glossy black shoes, and a ruffled white shirt, he performed a gracious bow then introduced himself.

Kingsley... Nicholas Kingsley at your service," his voice sounded like a dried axle forced to spin and his wrinkled face carved out a road map of many adventures both good, and bad. Bald except for a thin patch of gray hair just above each ear, he stood with a slight lean.

"What a pleasure to welcome you to the Isle of Aramoor. I thought the Creator forgot all about us. Many decades have passed since my carriages have seen passengers."

"Yes, much has happened on the mainland you are not aware of," Pegan said.

Kingsley's eyes opened wide, "now, you must tell me your names and about your adventure on the way. I so love hearing word of the outside world."

He greeted each with a handshake except for the ladies where he offered a kiss on the check as they climbed aboard. He only stopped when he came to Averie. "You must be the mother?" Noting the enlarged belly.

"Why yes I am," she replied.

"As the guest of honor, its tradition for you to ride in the first carriage," he said escorting her and held her hand as she climbed inside.

"Ah sir," Saress called out. "Where she goes, I go."

"Well climb aboard then," he answered. "I refuse to kiss a lizard though. No matter how extravagant you look."

"I feel the same about surface dwellers," she chuckled, and then took a seat across from Averie, a smile on her face.

Only after everyone boarded and found a seat did he take his place at the helm and a subtle click of his teeth set the horse in motion. The pace was slow and before long Pegan swore Averie would have the child long before they ever reached the town. Directly in front Averie rode with Saress. He knew she would protect her with her life, but still, he felt uncomfortable not at her side.

It was dark when they arrived at a small village of only three large huts. They were each constructed of stone and covered with a shake roof and faint wisps of gray smoke drifted from each chimney. All three were placed precisely around a large dais constructed of pure white granite infused with purple and blue veins. Directly in the center was an intricately carved lectern.

A smaller path lit with lanterns cut through the dense trees and climbed a small hill where two large pillars connected at the top by a massive arch could be seen. Nobody had to tell them, they all knew that was the path to the portal.

From that path, a short woman approached with milky white skin and raven black hair rolled tightly in a bun. "Welcome to Kings Watch," she said. "I am Seraphine, caretaker of the Island and Keeper of the Portal." Her voice was like hearing a songbird for the first time.

"You have a lovely place," Averie said.

"Why thank you, it's hard work but well worth it." She looked around the compound as if admiring her own work. "You must be Averie?" She gave her a hug then placed a petite wrinkled hand on the enlarged belly. "This is a glorious time. Elwrick has told me so much about you. I simply couldn't wait much longer to meet you. The anticipation was worse than murder. So when I heard you were picked up by Captain Royston…well, my heart has raced ever since—"

"Elwrick, he's here?" Pegan interrupted.

"No, he left days ago to find you, it seems he thought you lost your way. When he never returned, I figured he would just ride back with you on the boat. He won't admit it, but he hates to dimension travel and spends most his time riding that blasted horse of his. Why he chose black, I'll never know," she rambled on. "You know there are plenty of white horses available, even a fine chestnut, but he likes that black one."

Averie gave Pegan a wink who was about to interrupt again but he figured it would just be best to let her finish.

"Where is Elwrick?" she asked.

What color had returned to Pegan's face drained away. "He fell, at the hands of a lich lord."

"Fell?" Her eyes narrowed, "how? You must tell me everything."

Pegan sat on the steps of the dais and told her of the encounter with the lich lord.

"Oh my," she said. "I must send out scouts at once. The new moon will be in two days and without him, the portal cannot be opened."

"There's more," Saress said, "tell her everything."

Seraphine shot Pegan a nasty glance for withholding information.

Pegan adjusted his position as he'd become stiff, then he told her about the phylactery and the agreement he made.

"I see," she said. "First, you should have brought the phylactery here where it could have been handled properly and second, you should have never struck a deal with a lich. They are not stupid creatures. In fact, they're very intelligent and extremely cunning. Well beyond our own level of comprehension. I just hope you have not cost this bearer the life of her child by your ignorance."

"I… I didn't know what else to do," Pegan pleaded.

Seraphine held her hand out and whistled. Seconds later, a small white bird with yellow wings landed. They seemed to communicate through a series of chirps and whistles, then the bird flew away. The whole ordeal lasted less than a minute. "We'll know more by morning. Until then, I suggest we all get some rest."

The first rays of morning light penetrated through the drawn shades when Pegan slipped from his cabin and made his way towards Averie's. With a knuckle, he tapped lightly on the door.

"What do you need?" Ellusia whispered as she looked out.

"I need to see Averie."

"Can't it wait? She's fast asleep."

"No, we need to figure this out now," Pegan almost demanded.

She released a sigh then ushered him in.

Averie lay on one side of an overly large bed fast asleep while Saress was sprawled out on a large mat with her tail twisted covering both eyes. Even though she appeared asleep, Pegan knew Saress was well aware he had entered.

"Let me wake her." Ellusia nudged Averie till she opened one groggy eye, then the other followed with a large yawn and stretch. She pulled the blanket clear to her neck while her head sunk into a big poufy marshmallow looking pillow.

"We need to talk," Pegan said, then sat on the edge.

"What's wrong?" Saress asked as she rose.

Averie blinked in confusion.

"We need to figure out what we will do if Elwrick is... well, passed on. You heard Seraphine. If Elwrick is the only one who can begin the process, you will have to have the child here. It seems safe enough."

"She can't," Seraphine said from the doorway. "My scouts whispered to me they spotted you coming here. So I had to make my presence known, to make sure there was no... well, inappropriate activity."

"I would never do anything to hurt, or endanger this woman," Pegan snarled at the accusations.

"I understand, but my main concern is with the child."

"As is mine," Pegan agreed.

"But, I can see your question is truly a concern for the child's well-being, so I will do my best to answer your questions."

"Why can't she have the child here?" Ellusia asked. "I can deliver the child, I've delivered hundreds."

"My dear, I am sure you're more than qualified, but you must understand, she's not giving birth to an infant."

Averie looked at Seraphine as if she lost her mind. "What am I giving birth to then?"

"Oh dear, Elwrick never discussed it with you?"

"No, he never said a word."

"Well, since he's not here, I don't think he'll mind if I act as his surrogate and inform you of all the gory details." She rubbed her hands together as if planning something sinister. "It all begins with the portal and how it functions. Please tell me you at least know that much?"

Averie shook her head no.

"I'm sorry," Pegan said. "But we've been fighting for our lives the entire way, we really didn't have much time for an educational class on proper portal etiquette."

She glanced at Pegan, her eyes squinted in the dim light. "Okay, what you must understand is this, the portal is not like that of a dimension door where you simply walk in one side and exit the other. The portal is a living breathing entity, and it is opened by a Ceremony called the Creed of the Martyr. This is where Elwrick comes in as he has to begin the process with the Book of Portals. An oocyte is taken from the bearer and dissolved into the Book to create the identity. Once opened, a rhythmic link is created between the portal and the mother, none other can enter and only the portal knows where the mother is sent. Your body will be altered to fit with the new environment, but your soul remains untouched. You will think, feel, and act exactly as you do now.

"But how does this prevent her from having the child here?" Ellusia asked.

"Let me continue," Seraphine said. "I've only just begun."

"When you enter the portal, your body does not stay complete. It is broken down into the lowest form possible, called the granule cell. From there, it travels through space and time and in less than the blink of an eye, you arrive at your destination. This process does not affect the mother because her body, your body, is complete and no longer changing. The fetus though, from conception till birth, is in rapid growth and any pause in its development will cause her to lose the child. Therefore, our wonderful Creator has devised a simple way to transport the child, and that is in the safety of a calcium carbonate crystal shell which develops around the child days before."

"She's giving birth to a giant chicken egg?" Pegan almost had to laugh.

"You could say that," Seraphine said. "What's important though," she suddenly turned deathly serious, and she took Averie's hand. "Inside there is a small pocket of air to allow the fetus to breathe, but only a few breaths. You need to break the child free immediately, or it will suffocate."

Averie's mind was still deep in thought about the egg, "how is that going to fit out of…"

"Simple… bones break, muscles tear, joints dislocate, occasionally, the spine will even collapse."

Averie's face lost all color, and she nearly fainted.

"I'm joking," Seraphine said. "Can't an old lady well past her prime still have some fun?" She let out a hearty laugh that sounded like a horse snorting. "In all honesty, it's not as bad as you think. The shell is not rigid like a chicken egg, but actually rather flexible and covered in a slimy mucus to ease its passing."

"And how exactly would you know?" Saress asked.

Seraphine viewed Saress through angry eyes, "who are you to question what I know and what I don't?"

"I'm sorry," Saress said. "I didn't mean what I said. It's just this is so unusual none of us can understand, let alone comprehend. Mostly, I think we're just scared."

"I understand," Seraphine said. "But your words do little to ease my suffering."

"What do you mean?" Pegan asked.

"Follow me," she whispered.

They followed her up the trail to a small garden surrounded by a rickety metal fence. At the far end of a series of stone steps sat the portal. All around it trees grew and wildflowers were abundant, and even a dove or two flew past.

Near the portal, she led them to a lump of dirt and at one end was a small tombstone.

"I once was a bearer," she wept, "and on my way to the portal, I went into labor. I tried to crawl in before it arrived, I tried with all my heart, with everything I had, but I failed. I failed because the portal closed. It's only open for a short time." Tears ran heavy down her cheeks and dripped from her chin. "I never made it. The portal closed before I could enter, then the egg came. I was alone and with nobody to help... The baby came too soon." She repeated. "I held the egg in my arms as I broke away the shell. He was so beautiful, the way his eyes glistened in the moonlight. So full of life and joy. I know he would have been a wonderful steward, but it was not meant to be. I watched in joy as he gasped for his first real breath of air and held him tight against my bosom. I knew what was going to happen, so I held him there until he drew his last. He died in my arms."

"I'm so sorry," Averie said, as she cried.

"Elwrick asked me to stay on the island and I was granted a servitude of a long life. I became the caretaker, and he swore we would never lose another child due to lack of help.

"But why did your child die?" Thathra asked. "Why couldn't it live here?"

"The portal is opened specifically for the mother and fetus, none other can pass through. It prevents others from going through to another world. A safeguard to say. Once you enter, the building blocks which make up your body is altered, this prevents the mother from returning. The shell also keeps the child's original building blocks so they can be brought back. It's very complicated. There cannot be more than one person on Icearaus at a time capable of using the portal. Therefore, if the mother does not reach the portal before it closes, nature disposes of the child so another bearer can be selected. It's like a woman's menstrual cycle. The egg is released, but if it is not fertilized, it is discarded.

"My child was destined for that portal and as long as he remained alive, another could not pass. Therefore, my child had to be terminated. It's okay, I know he is in Heaven right now looking down at me smiling, and I know someday we will meet again."

They walked in complete silence back to their huts, each deep in their own thoughts.

The morning came and passed and there was no sign of Elwrick. Tonight would be the night the portal would need to be opened and the scout she sent had discovered nothing.

To take her mind off what was to happen, Averie and Saress went for a walk while Pegan sat alone on the stone steps looking down at the road which led to the docks. Thathra offered to stay, but he sent him off to go do something, anything, just not be around him at this very moment. Reality sunk in and he understood the death of Averie's child was going to be one his hands. It was his actions, his dealings with the lich lord, his failed agreement.

"AHHHH," Pegan released a hellish cry. "Damn you… damn you all to Hell, we had an agreement. I filled my end of the agreement and gave back the phylactery now fulfill yours."

Pegan felt the eyebrows get singed off his face as a flaming portal burst open not twenty feet away and everything in the vicinity wilted and died. The sand blackened and a heavy green fog crept out and brought with it the horrendous stink of rotten corpses.

Pegan came to his feet to only stumble backwards as he tried to gain some distance between him and the most ghastly thing he had ever seen before crawl out.

It had the torso of a man which looked aged beyond belief with two elongated emaciated arms. It walked horizontally though on eight bone-thin legs that grew out from the rib cage with two toes that doubled as pinchers. The neck had been stretched like a pelican while the head was so large it nearly lay upon the sand. Void of any hair, the skin drooped like candle wax and it saw through two black orbs recessed deep back in the skull. The nose was gone and only two upturned slits remained while the lipless mouth was wide and ringed with numerous rows of serrated teeth that continually chattered. The tail was that of a scorpion with a long black stinger which leaked acid while a sickly yellow bile drool seeped from its mouth.

Next, Phlorax stepped out holding Elwrick by one leg high in the air then thrust him on the ground. "My obligation has now been fulfilled, our contract is at an end."

"Come Arlin, other adventures await."

The creature hissed and clicked then followed his Master through the portal which exploded in a huge fireball.

The noise was so horrendous everybody came running to see what in the world just occurred.

"Elwrick," Pegan screamed as he ran to aid his semi-unconscious friend.

"Is she here, is she safe?" Elwrick asked. His robes were burnt black, his skin charred, and both eyes where pupil-less white orbs.

"Yes, she's safe," he said, then screamed for Ellusia until his eyes filled with tears.

Chapter 47

Karayan scaled the stairs at a relaxed stroll with a smile stretched from ear to ear. He could still feel the bearer's presence, but knew she was in the clutches of the lich lord. Eventually she would either be sacrificed, or turned into a slave. Regardless, the child would die and victory achieved. If Lilith was to be believed, then Demetrius was dead. He chose to believe Lilith. As for Arlin, he could easily be replaced with another. Never again would he have to worry about someone with enough skill or gall to try another rescue. Never again would his rule be threatened.

He had never been so proud of Lilith in all his life. She had all but given her life to save him so he had no qualms about going to Malvo and asking him for a cure to the spell the lich lord placed on her.

The stairs led to a magically sealed door which opened upon his approach. Inside, the room was bare except for a large mirror near the far wall. The ornate wooden frame was carved with a thousand minuscule images, but when combined, created a magnificent masterpiece. Where the glass should have been, a gray haze filled the void. His pace never slowed as he stepped into the whirling mixture and vanished.

In less than a blink of an eye, he arrived at his destination. The room was small and in complete disarray. Glass from a shattered window littered the dusty floor and the furniture long since gave way to the ravages of time and rodents. The air held firm to the pungent scent of death mixed with a tinge of sickening sweetness from a corpse which still reached for the door. Karayan smiled… his ward of concealment which guaranteed death to all who tried to enter still functioned.

Beyond the door, narrow stairs spiraled downward into darkness. As he transcended, the lifeless gray stone walls faded to hard packed dirt before eventually turning to jagged natural stone. The deeper he went, the hotter and more stagnant the air became. Still, he went deeper until it seemed as if the center of the world was near.

At the bottom, he followed a carved out tunnel which descended even deeper into the ground till he came to a pair of double doors bound in steel, each with a giant fang for a knob. Beside each door, a torch burned with a blue flame which emitted no smoke. Catching his breath he waited a moment, then entered.

The room was oval shaped and directly in the center was a creature encapsulated within a crystal block. Karayan ignored the beast, he'd seen it a thousand times and headed towards a second door, oblivious to the burning red eyes that watched his movements.

This room was smaller and perfectly square. Each wall was built into bookshelves that went from floor to ceiling and loaded to capacity with tomes of every shape and size. Some were small, only a few pages, while others were so thick it would have taken both hands to carry. In the center of the room, a pedestal constructed of bones rose waist high and held a vast tome already open, and the skull of an unfortunate soul as a candle holder.

"I know you're here… I can smell you," Karayan yelled as he thumbed through the tome which meant nothing to him as the writing looked like scribbles.

"I've been waiting for you." The voice was cold and screeched like a hawk just before it swooped down for the kill, "waiting a very long time."

Karayan spun to face the voice. "Malvo," Karayan said.

The old man appeared from nowhere. Slightly bent at the waist and twig-thin, a gray cloak hung loosely on his shoulders. In his left hand, he carried a short staff constructed of bones bound in human sinew, and in his right, a small clear orb that flashed blue at random intervals. Long wisps of white hair hung down from a mostly bald scalp covered in little brown spots, while his eyes were pure white and lacked pupils. Without the benefit of the sun, his skin had grown ashen gray which gave him the appearance of a corpse.

To the unaware, Malvo appeared as a frail blind hermit who chose a life of solitude, but Karayan was not unaware. Malvo was neither blind nor frail, but wielded immense power associated with the dark arts far greater than any man who walked the surface, including himself, were it not for the power granted to him.

A long strenuous silence separated them when Karayan finally spoke, "I came to discuss—"

"Silence," Malvo snarled, "I know why you've come, don't play me as a fool. You've come here to ask me to heal your whore, but you come for all the wrong reasons."

Malvo circled Karayan, "What good is healing her when you stand on the cusp of death. No, not death, a miserable bleak future where you will beg for death but it will cease to find you."

"My future is secure—"

"Your future ends tonight, at the stroke of midnight." Malvo waved his hand, and a vision formed of Averie and Saress sitting by the portal, a smile on each of their faces. "Tonight, she will enter the portal and you will die."

"That's not possible—"

"I reveal to you no lie. You have neither the time, nor the resources to stop her now... you have failed." He let out a wicked laugh.

"Lilith told me—"

"You have been deceived. She was the one who struck a deal with the lich lord. She is the one who gave the lich Arlin, she is the one who told you a lie the day you killed Kalliphae." Malvo circled Karayan again. "She has a plan to leave Icearaus for good, even though she has been deceived and will fail."

Karayan left for the door.

"There's only one way to stop her now, to stop your damnation and secure your salvation."

Karayan paused at the door and glanced back, there was a wicked grin on Malvo's face. He knew this man was right, and he hated every fiber of his being. "What do you want in return?"

"The day the keeper was killed I knew you would fail. Many nights

I lay awake wondering. Not wondering, dreaming. Oh, how I dreamed of the possibilities. It's amazing what the mind can imagine when there's no price." A sly grin crept across his thin lips. "And no price is too great since only one of us here can stop her. You and I both know what happens when she enters the portal." Malvo took a long glance out a small window built into the door to view his pet.

"Nothing happens when she enters the portal. Life continues as it normally has."

"Nothing happens…" Malvo's eyes widened. "Nothing happens," he repeated. He let out a laugh Karayan felt would topple the entire cavern. "You and I both know that's a lie. The moment she enters, it's the beginning of the end. Eventually, you will have to pay back for all the things you've been rewarded."

"No, I can kill the child upon its return, and the agreement stands. It's just easier to do it before, rather than later."

"You couldn't defeat her or her protectors now. How will you defeat her child, you won't!"

The words stung like the crack of a whip.

"You have not yet answered my question," Karayan squinted his eyes in disgust. "What will this cost me?"

"I want to be second in command of Icearaus. To have Rain Wood Palace rebuilt in my honor. No more shall I be held captive in a cave deep underground. I want to roam the surface again, to feel the sun upon my back and have it burn my eyes if I stare at it too long. To have the people fall upon their knees when they see me as if I'm the Creator and call my name. And servants, as many as I desire so I never have to lift a finger, and a pretty little wife that will do anything I wish."

"I told you long ago, I keep you down here for your protection, to have you on the surface will only cause fear and warmongering."

"You keep me down here to prevent your rule from being challenged," Malvo snapped back.

I should just leave now, and take the risks associated with the bearer escaping Karayan thought, but he knew the words Malvo spoke were true. Without his gift afforded to him by the underworld, he would have a much more difficult time killing the child upon its return. *And who knows, maybe with Malvo once again on the surface, it will work out in his favor to drive more people towards him for protection from this crazy necromancer,* the thoughts continued.

"I have one need of my own, I want her to suffer immensely, before she dies. To feel the pain she has caused me throughout this ordeal."

Malvo released a half-hearted laugh, "consider it done."

"And you're positive the creature of yours can destroy the bearer and her child?"

"Pitboch will not fail. He is faster, stronger, more agile, and deadlier than anything that walks this world."

"That thing has a name?" Karayan said.

"Yes, don't you," Malvo said. "Pitboch is not his real name though. After months of trying, I could not pronounce his birth name correctly, so I came up with one we both agreed on."

Karayan shook his head in disbelief, "but if he does?"

"He won't," Malvo snarled.

"If he does, you will sit down in this tomb and rot the rest of your miserable existence away," Karayan hissed.

"There is one other thing," Malvo said. "I will need a single hair from your head."

"And why would that be?"

"So my pet won't kill you upon its release."

"You told me years ago you could control the thing? That you had it trained and could communicate with it as easy as you and I talk now."

"And I can, but if something goes wrong and I die, at least you will survive."

After a moment's thought, Karayan nodded his approval.

"The hair needs to be dissolved in a cauldron of boiling cow's blood, frog skin, slug slime, and five goat eyes at the precise moment. Too soon or late, and you will not be protected."

"I don't have the time, she will enter the portal tonight," Karayan angrily snarled.

"I told you I knew you were coming, thus everything has already been prepared." Malvo cracked an evil smile.

We have another problem which has not been addressed. How do we deal with Elwrick? He alone has the power to destroy your pet."

"I've already figured him into the equation. Pitboch must arrive after the portal has been opened, but before she enters. Elwrick cannot leave the summoner's table, or the portal will close. If he does, then she will have the child here and it will die, or he must stay there, and listen to her screams. Either way, the death of the child will be accomplished."

"So we are in agreement then?" Karayan asked.

"Yes, we have an agreement," Malvo said.

Karayan clenched his fist in victory, "This will be a glorious night."

"Follow me," Malvo said as he removed the tome from the pedestal, "time is of the essence."

Malvo made a waving motion with his hand and two bookshelves parted revealing a short passage to another room. Karayan didn't have to ask, he could tell this was his personal laboratory simply by the furniture which filled the room.

To one side, there was a gigantic steel cauldron blacker than coal smoke, and beneath it, a searing hot smokeless flame burned. Near it, a rough cut wooden desk was covered with vials, tubes, and other various cutting instruments. Sweeping all that stuff aside, he laid the tome on the table and methodically flipped through the pages. The parchment crackled to his touch like dried leaves. The ink was black, thick, heavy.

Karayan looked down at the pages as well. Every time a page turned he cringed, waiting for it to fall to dust.

Turning each page with agonizing slowness, Karayan almost exploded and mentally grabbed the book so he could do it himself. "She'll be through the portal and her child will be dead from old age before you find the correct page," Karayan screamed.

"Patience," Malvo said. He could see the anxiety on Karayan's face. Proper punishment for all the years he was kept away from society. Several more pages turned before he stopped, "this is it, right here."

The writing on the page consisted of no words, only symbols and diagrams. "You can read this nonsense?" Karayan asked cocking his head sideways as if it would help him understand. "And why must we do this if you can command the demon?"

"I can command him, but we still need to bring him to the surface. That clear container has kept him in a state of transition between his world and ours. He's neither living nor dead," Malvo said. "And yes, I can read this. It's as plain as the nose on your face."

Rubbing a leathery twig thin finger over the symbols, he let his eyes droop closed. What little color he did have was leeched away by the pages and the writing brightened.

Malvo looked yellow against the hue of the bubbling goo in the cauldron. "Here shortly it will be ready for your contribution," he said with a gleam in his eye. Snapping his fingers, a midget came through a small door. Stripped naked except for a dirty loincloth, he waited further instructions.

Under Malvo's guidance, the slave grasped tightly onto the gnarled end of a steel rod and stirred the thick sludge. Grinning with satisfaction as the contents thickened, Malvo motioned for Karayan to kneel, then plucked a single thick black hair. Dangling it over the brew he let it fall, then watched as it floated on the surface before slowly dissolving.

As the slave continued to stir, the concoction thickened to a black tar-like substance. Large beads of sweat streaked down his naked frame as he worked.

"It's ready," Malvo said. "The time to act is now."

The slave dropped the rod and grabbed a large glass pot then filled it to the top with a shiny ladle.

All three now stood facing the demon.

"Lift him so he can pour the contents over the block," Malvo said to Karayan.

Doing as instructed, Karayan easily hoisted the midget over the block. At the top, the little man dumped out the contents. The goo was thick and took a long time, but eventually, it completely covered the demon.

Moments later, the sound of ice cracking could be heard and then a large sickly gray four-fingered hand broke free. Each of the four fingertips displayed a long razor-sharp claw. The thick muscular arm contracted causing the fingers to curl inward. Near the bottom, another crack formed and then a leg erupted free from its enclosure. Thick with muscles and covered in small spikes, it ended in a massive hoof rimmed with tufts of coarse black hair.

A slight resonating vibration could be heard coming from the block. Increasing in intensity, the sound continued to grow until the noise dominated everything within the room. Then, suddenly, and without warning, the resonating stopped for just a moment, and the block exploded knocking all three to the ground.

Recovering from the explosion, Karayan now had a chance to see the creature in its complete form.

Twisting its thick muscular neck to look upon its environment, the creature leaped from the pedestal and in one swoop grabbed the slave in one arm raising him off the ground. With the other arm, he ran a claw along the slave's abdomen gutting him like a deer.

Screams from the slave silenced as the hand around his neck squeezed until his windpipe crushed then the popping of his neck sounded like a chicken wing breaking. Throwing the corpse aside, the demon dropped to his hands and knees and devoured the entrails, then with a long black tongue, licked the floor clean. Finished with its meal, the creature stretched out both arms, puffed out his muscular chest, then released a series of grunts, snarls, and snorts. With blood still fresh on his face, he focused his attention solely on Malvo.

"You will obey me," Malvo commanded.

The creature seemed to ignore Malvo as he crossed the room at an unimaginable speed, stopping just shy of crushing the man. With one hand, he lifted Malvo up to his face which was a good nine feet from the ground, and pulled him close enough their faces all but touched.

"Release me," Malvo spoke the commands.

Having no lips, his enlarged mouth of crooked razor-sharp teeth opened, and it appeared he planned to bite the head off of Malvo.

"Put me down… safely," Malvo commanded.

Tilting its head slightly to one side, he peered at Karayan then placed Malvo back on his feet, but when he turned, his massive tail caught Malvo in the shoulder, knocking the man flat.

Karayan took a slight step back and positioned himself in a defensive posture as the demon approached.

Pitboch reached for Karayan then quickly jerked his massive hand back. Unwilling to lay a hand on him, he squatted down to his level and using his upturned nose which exposed the nostrils, sniffed him.

"Pitboch," Malvo snarled through a clenched jaw as he lay still on the ground. "Come to me… NOW!" he yelled.

As the creature moved around the room, it left a lingering funk that caused nausea and stomach cramps. Eventually, the demon stopped just short of smashing Malvo's head with one of his large hoofed feet.

"Kill the bearer… slowly… painfully… make her suffer…" Malvo grunted.

Obviously the creature understood by the way he tilted his head sideways allowing the sound vibrations to enter through small canals on each side of his head.

"Go… now," Malvo commanded.

Understanding the urgency in Malvo's voice, the creature seemed to melt into the ground, disappearing into the cracks in the floor and was gone. Only the smell remained.

Karayan wiped the sweat from his face, "I must take my leave now, as there's someone I dearly wish to talk with." And he left out the door the way he had come.

Malvo went back to his room and knelt in a large pentagram, throwing his head back he looked at the ceiling where a skeleton hung, "Master, it has begun."

Chapter 48

ilith looked like a mad scientist as she fiddled with the numerous instruments laid out on the table. With a keen sense of detail, she adjusted this knob, tweaked that dial, and added a few drops of a blue liquid that fumed white. Satisfied with the mixture, she hurried back to the book. The pages were frail to the point she could see the writing on the next page, so she took great care as she flipped the parchment. The next chapter was the most important. This was where she would discover how to infuse the concoction within herself. A smile came to her face as she read. Tonight would be the last night she would spend on Icearaus.

"Going somewhere?"

Lilith froze when she heard the words. She was certain, no, positive she locked the door and placed a powerful ward spell to guarantee her privacy. Yet, the man she loathed more than anything else in the world stood in her laboratory.

"No," she lied. "I've discovered a cure to reverse the lich lords spell. I only need to complete this potion and I shall be restored to my beautiful self."

She shuttered as the sound of his hard leather heels intermingled with that of the bubbling potion. Any moment now, she expected to feel the bite of a blade, or a firm grip on her neck. She had neglected to have a spell of hasty retreat ready, and now she lacked the time to prepare it.

She jerked, not from the pain of a blade being thrust into her back then forced up shattering her ribs, but from a warm hand placed upon her shoulder.

She spun and faced him, in his eyes fires of rage were burning out of control. The man looked as if he'd gone insane. A white froth coated his lips and his face appeared twisted as if he was no longer himself, but slowly transforming into a demon from Hell.

She circled the table and looked at him through the numerous beakers, tubes, and needles. In her mind, she had already begun the process of preparing the spell which might just save her life. It would take a few minutes, but she might be able to buy enough time by trying to hold a civil conversation with the maniac.

Karayan scratched his chin. "Just as you are doing now, I once tried searching for a way back, but could not find one. That is, until one night a strange man came to me in a dream. He glistened like an angel, and had the most beautiful wings I had ever seen. He listened to my request as I begged him to help me return to the world I once lived in, and he told me he would, and the answer would come in a book. That morning when I woke, I discovered this strange tome resting on my nightstand… and immediately I began to read and learn the process." Karayan picked up the vial of yellow blood and studied it intensely. "What I discovered though was not salvation, but damnation."

"You're wrong," she said. "The book clearly details how to leave this world."

Karayan laughed. "You're a fool the same as I was all those years ago. All I needed to do was follow the directions in the book so I did. I killed the bearer, I acquired the yellow blood, stood in a lab very much the same as you have erected now, and let my plan unfold. That night when I went to sleep, I expected to wake up back in my old bed on a planet named Earth."

He slid the vial back into the holder.

She hoped he would keep rambling as the spell she was preparing was almost complete.

"Where I woke though was a place called The Infernal Realm—albeit I didn't know it at the time, it is the home of the Dark Master—and is the lowest pit of Hell. Fires raged out of control and the heat seared my skin. My eyes melted from their sockets and every hair was singed from my body. Words cannot describe the pain which coursed through me.

"I was there only moments before I was snatched up by something so hideous words cannot describe it, and brought to a huge citadel with enormous towers. The whole place reeked of death and suffering. It was there I was forced to kneel before the man who invaded my dreams. It was there a deal was made. In exchange for eternal life, extraordinary powers, and riches beyond my wildest dreams, all I had to do was kill the bearer and sacrifice the child to him, or I would remain here for all eternity. But there was a caveat. If even one bearer reaches the portal and leaves this world, then his blessing would be revoked."

Lilith listened intently and now she understood who guided him. Even though Karayan was alive, demons controlled every aspect of him and he was simply their pawn to use for whatever they wanted from this world. They had found a way to tap into this world through the Fabric of Odone.

"What you fail to understand, is the moment she passes through, I become mortal once more and will begin to age and in time, I will die. It is then I will have to face the Dark Master for the second time, but I won't be doing it alone."

"What do you mean?" she asked.

In his hand, a dagger formed with a crystal clear blade and a bluish liquid dripped from the sharpened edge. Instantly, she recognized the blade as a *Soul Stealer*. She would die immediately upon being pierced, but her soul would be contained within the blade like purgatory, stuck between Heaven and Hell.

He moved closer to her, "When I die and go to Hell, I won't be going alone. You will be their right at my side and suffer the same fate as me."

She screamed...

His movements were instantaneous, but her thought was quicker, and when the blade struck, all it hit was her image which slowly faded.

"*NOOO!*" he screamed and kicked over the table scattering the contents on the floor.

Chapter 49

Dinner was finished and the sky was dark when Seraphine approached them at the Dais. "The time nears," she said as her auburn eyes studied the moon. "In a few hours, it will reach the zenith. We must be ready when Elwrick calls."

Averie looked somber, the worry of the unknown obvious in her eyes.

"Your ceremonial departure dress has been prepared, and the time has arrived for you to begin preparation." She reached out to take Averie's hand.

"Thank you," Averie said. "I appreciate all you've done, but if you don't mind, I will go in the dress I currently wear."

"That old ratty worn out thing," she said as she looked it up and down. "A dress much more beautiful is waiting for you as we speak."

"I'm positive. This dress has saved my life and I would not trade it for anything."

"Well... the choice is yours. Let's at least get it washed. We can't have you going to the new world looking like that."

Averie could never remember in all her life a night this dark. Every star was veiled, and only the ominous white pearl floated in a sea of black velvet. Over the last few days, she began to relax and could see herself right here on the island. Away from all the pain and suffering the mainland was subjected to. The thoughts though were folly, she had to take the portal, the life of her child depended upon it. Lost somewhere between a dream and reality, visions of a new world filled her mind.

Tap… tap… tap… came a rapping.

Did she really hear it, or was it in her dreams? She waited to see if it would come again. Outside her window, crickets chirped, and bullfrogs croaked.

Tap… tap… tap… she heard the sound once more. This time there was no mistake, someone waited outside.

She rose from the chair and adjusted her dress. Satisfied with her appearance she spoke, "come in."

Saress remained sprawled out on the floor, one eye propped open.

Pegan stuck his head in and searched the darkness till he found her. "Good evening," he said, "may I enter?" he asked in a hushed voice.

"Most certainly," she replied, and then led him by the hand to a pair of matching fluffy chairs separated by a small round table. A single candle burned brightly.

"I can't believe this is it," Pegan said, half his face hid in shadows.

"Yes," her voice cracked. "I don't know what to say." She looked around the room as if to find the answer. Eventually, she turned back to him. "Elwrick was here a bit ago, he looks great, healthy again."

"Fantastic," Pegan said. "He's an amazing man."

"He has you to thank. If not for your actions, he would still be trapped by that filthy lich lord."

"No… it's I who have him to thank, else I would be dead by now. It was not I who grabbed that phylactery. Well, it was I, but something told me to. I can only assume it was Elwrick speaking to me. I never told anyone that before."

"Regardless, you're both here now, and you're both safe."

"Did Elwrick say where he was going?"

"No," she answered. "He simply said he had to prepare for tonight."

"And what of you…" he gave her a stern look. "Are you ready?"

"Honestly…" she waited a few moments then looked away. "No… not really."

Pegan turned her head with his hand until their eyes locked. "There are a few things I think you should know," Pegan said. He needed to tell her now as he would never get the chance again. "When Elwrick first approached me about you, I told him I wanted no part of it. That lifestyle was behind me. In fact, I told him his problems were not mine. As time passed, I discovered I wouldn't have missed this for the world. You've taught me the true meaning of love. I always believed love was pain, it's all I knew. But love is so much more, there is caring, and tenderness, to help those unable to help themselves and ask for nothing in return… You taught me a feeling I've never known before."

She went to speak, but he placed a finger against her lips to silence her.

"I have seen you grow in such a short time. I watched you blossom from the wretched creature trapped in a room till now. You glow with a new vigor of life and radiate with a beauty that will blind all those that look upon you in the new world."

His eyes had a mist to them then a lone tear ran down his cheek. "During our journey, there were many nights I laid awake and looked at to the stars. I often wondered which one you were destined for. Selfishly though, I wished tonight would never come yet here we sit."

He did nothing to wipe away the tear.

"I want you to take this." He searched through his tunic and pulled out the necklace he found and placed it on her palm then closed her fingers around it. "I've saved this for a long time, a gift for you to remember me by."

Averie opened her hand and studied the large red diamond. It was beautiful, the way the candlelight reflected off the mirrored surface brought an ooh to her lips and a tear to her eye. To keep the diamond as close to the original shape as possible, the tiniest hole was just big enough so a hair-thin golden chain could be inserted. Even for its large size, it seemed to weigh no more than a feather. "It's more beautiful than anything I have ever seen."

"If you ever get frightened, or lonely, just look at it and think of me. Who knows, maybe someday our paths will cross again, in another life perhaps."

"I would like that, but we both know it's impossible." She looked towards the ceiling as if she wanted to say something, but didn't know what. "There's something I've been meaning to tell you also, something I've felt for a very long time." She was deep in thought. "I have only talked about it with another and she understood."

Her movements towards him were slow but adamant. He knew what was coming, they both did, and no longer would she be denied what she longed for. No longer would she wait for him to come to her.

The thought crossed his mind to look away, to stand and leave. How could he ever explain? He was nearly twice her senior. Why would he need to explain, they were both adults. After all, love knows no bounds and can't be restrained with the hands of time. When their lips finally met, it was like thunder, and Pegan swore he felt the ground below his feet shift.

Quickly, they separated, and they both released a short, shallow breath.

Pegan never resisted as Averie reached up and pulled his head towards hers again and their lips became one. She let her hands slide up his muscular torso, while his explored hers. A slight whimper escaped her lips when they parted.

"Now put this on me before we forget." She handed him the necklace. Pulling her hair up, she exposed her neck, and the diamond grew bright as it rested against her milky skin.

He kissed her neck, "This I swear, when your son returns, I will be here for him." He tried to leave but something stopped him at the door. After a tense moment, he opened it and walked out into the night air.

"He loves you very much," Saress said.

"I know," she answered after a long pause, "and I love him as well."

The Ceremony...

Elwrick emerged from the hut, his white robe flapped against the breeze and he seemed lost in a trance. In his hand he carried a large book covered in strange symbols and exotic words. Without hesitation, he placed the book upon the large intricately carved wooden lectern and methodically flipped through the pages before pausing midway through. He flipped a few more before looking at the three huts, and then towards her companions.

"Where are his aids?" Averie whispered to Seraphine as she watched

Elwrick.

"He will announce for their arrival when he's ready to begin," she answered. "When he calls for you though, I will be your escort, hand in hand we'll walk out together." She drew a deep sigh, remembering when it was her that waited. "And once the portal opens, I will escort you to the portal and make sure you arrive safely."

Elwrick looked upon the darkened sky, the moon was in place, the time has arrived.

"My friends, fellow companions, guest of honor, and of course my faithful assistants."

Elwrick paused for a slight moment and drew another long breath to continue.

"It is with great honor, privilege, and pleasure, I present to you, Averie, mother of the steward."

His voice boomed with such force all of Aramoor heard it.

With hands clasped the door swung open.

Pegan almost fainted at the sight. She was the most beautiful woman he had ever seen, even outdoing the Elf Queen.

The cool night air felt good on her warm skin. Inside, the air was stagnant, leaving a sticky residue on her exposed skin. Across the clearing, her companions waited. Somehow they had taken the impossible, and made it possible.

"Please… join your companions," Elwrick said.

Seraphine released her and watched her leave.

"And thank you, Seraphine, for your help these last few days getting everything prepared. Your work here has been invaluable and greatly appreciated. By the way, the island looks absolutely ravishing." He gave her a wink.

"Thank you," she whispered, a tear streamed down her cheek.

"Averie?"

Elwrick called to her. As she neared, his eyes focused on the red diamond she wore around her neck. His eyes followed the golden chain until he reached her radiant face.

"You are about to embark upon a journey through time and space. One that none of us will ever know, or experience. It will be your responsibility to raise your child, to care for your child, to teach him right from wrong. To teach him the skills required upon his return to faithfully lead us in a direction we have become lost to and return Icearaus back to its former glory. Do you accept this responsibility?"

Averie waited a long time without answering. She seemed almost too petrified to speak.

"Say I do," Seraphine nudged her.

"I do," she softly answered.

"There will be troubled times ahead and undue hardships. You will not be able to call upon the aid of your companions. You must forge new alliances as you will create new enemies. You will be a stranger in a strange land. Are you still willing to do what is necessary to protect your child, even give your own life, or take the life of another?"

"I do," she repeated.

"Then it is with great pleasure I call you to my side to make your contribution."

Seraphine nudged her, "go to him."

Beside him, her dress flapped like a flag, and her hair danced. She stiffened as he took her hand.

"Relax," he said. "I promise you there will be no pain."

On the book she saw an image that looked like the tip of a finger, and watched as Elwrick guided her thumb into position. It was a perfect match. There was an exhilarating feeling deep within her that only lasted a few seconds, then it was gone.

"What just happened?" she asked.

"You have officially been linked to the Book of Portals. Every bearer... past, present and those yet to come, are in this book. The portal will not open until there is a part of you, and your child in this book."

Averie smiled.

"Where did you get that necklace from?" he whispered.

"Pegan gave it to me as a gift, so I would never forget him."

"May I?" Elwrick motioned to see it.

"Certainly."

Elwrick took it in his hand and squeezed it hard, then whispered a prayer in a foreign language. As he opened his hand, two small fragments no bigger than a sliver broke away, which he quickly tucked away in the folds of his cloak. "Never take this off... ever," he whispered to her then kissed her cheek. "Please, take your place back with your companions while I begin the ritual."

Elwrick looked past her to the hut and called forth his three aids that were required to complete the ritual. Upon hearing his words, they came. Each wore identical robes that covered them from head to toe. Only the tips of their fingers were visible from beneath the elongated sleeves. They each took a predetermined position around the lectern.

Elwrick took a moment to look at each of them.

"If any of you three see a reason why this woman
should not be granted access to the portal and her
child becoming a steward of our land, speak now?"

The area had become aggressively quiet as they waited for a response from any. Tension grew to the point Pegan let his hand slip down to the hilt of his dagger and he shifted his feet.

After a few moments, Elwrick broke the painful silence.

"Then it is with a heavy heart that I call upon the great
Creator, to grant me the wisdom to open this portal.
We now say goodbye to this woman and anticipate the
day when we shall see her offspring return."

Elwrick placed his right hand upon the book and a purple aura outlined the dais. His body seemed to grow rigid and his eyes glossed over and turned a milky translucent white that dripped with compassion.

With a deep gravelly voice, the words came in a language she had never heard before like. some ancient dialect from a long forgotten era. From where she stood, she witnessed the page begin to glow a light green.

Independently, each letter of each word changed to a brilliant white and small wisps of smoke filtered from the page, then quickly dissipated in the breeze. Partway through the ritual, an aid placed their exposed fingertips upon the page and joined the chant which grew quite loud. Around each letter, a silver outline was created, and the words lifted from the page, and circled around them floating in the air.

With every word outlined the next, aid placed his fingertips upon the page and joined the chant. The white letters changed to a sea blue, and almost appeared fluid.

Averie waited, any moment now she expected them to run from the sky and spill onto the ground.

When the transformation was complete, the final aid placed her fingers upon the book. As soon as they made contact, the ground shook and trees trembled as the black hole between the two pillars lightened.

"We must go now, up the trail and into the portal," Seraphine yelled over the loud whoosh of wind.

Averie turned to face her companions, tears filled her eyes, and she choked on the words she tried to speak.

"We must hurry," Seraphine screamed and tugged on Averie's arm.

Averie barely heard the plea over the howling wind. She knew they would never meet again.

Each of her companions waved and then motioned for her to go.

"Go… now," Pegan whispered but knew she never heard his words.

"The portal will not stay open forever," she said. "It is time."

She rubbed her tear ladened eyes and followed Seraphine up the trail.

Pegan watched until they vanished into the shadows, then glanced up at the moon. It was no longer white, but the deepest blue he had ever seen, and he reached for his daggers. "She's in trouble," he screamed and bolted up the trail after them.

Saress and Thathra followed at a blistering pace, followed by Ellusia.

Averie passed through the gate and looked at the pillars which no longer appeared as simple stone, but filled with the vigor of energy. Upon the surface, writing glowed bright orange and in the center, a swirling bluish-green filled everything from top to bottom, left to right. Moments later, the haze cleared and inside formed an image of a thick lush forest with strange trees of extraordinary size, and a sky so blue it hurt to look at. A sucking sound could be heard as anything close by was devoured.

Drawing what she assumed would be her last breath; she rubbed her belly, and then let the breath slowly escape. The portal was calling to her, begging her to come, to taste it, to relish in it. Beside her, Seraphine stood. "Go, walk into it and it will take you," she whispered.

Closing her eyes, she relaxed a moment as she felt the wind buffet her body. When they opened, she stumbled back and screamed till her throat burned. Before her rising up out of the grass and dirt, a grotesque creature slowly materialized.

Seraphine bolted down the trail screaming a demon is at the portal.

Once it was completed and stood at full height, it let out a bellowing screech that dropped Averie to her knees.

Crawling backwards, Averie tried to place as much distance between her and the demon thing that approached.

Directly behind him, her salvation waited.

The sky turned the color of mauve and spun in a counter-clockwise motion, while lightning fired off in every direction.

Too many times they cheated death, too many times they denied fate what it desired most. Now on her knees, she looked up towards her damnation.

As if his attention was drawn elsewhere, the creature suddenly turned.

"Run…" Saress screamed as she broke through the gate taking it off the hinges and sending it sailing through the air. She had her bow out and fired two arrows in succession at the beast.

Each arrow burst into flames just before impact covering him with ash. Sweeping his massive head side to side, he studied this new threat and backed away positioning himself between the portal and Averie.

Pegan burst in and paused, not sure exactly what to do.

The demon reared its ugly head back and screamed something towards the sky, and in his hand a flaming sword formed and as he swung it, smoldering lava was slung in their direction.

Thathra charged directly at the beast, axe pulled back, and a burning fury on his face.

Pegan seized the opportunity and broke to the side following the fence in an attempt to get the demon from behind, and deliver the killing blow.

Thathra never slowed, but seemed to gain speed as he neared, then took to flight. The silver of his blade flashed bright blue and he screamed something unknown to his deity, then brought down the blade with the force of a thousand bulls, but hit nothing.

Pitboch saw the attack coming as if he read Thathras mind, and stepped aside to allow the barbarian to pass, then followed close behind with his own blade.

As he landed his feet slipped out from under him, and fell back slamming hard onto the ground. Just above him, the flaming blade passed within inches.

Thathra closed his eyes. His face felt as if it was about to melt from the heat, and the hairs on his chin ignited.

Pitboch raised a massive hoofed foot to stomp the life out of Thathra, who rolled out of the way barely escaping instant death.

Saress fired more arrows but the results were the same, so she discarded her bow for steel, and ripped her two-handed sword free.

Pegan emerged from behind the portal hoping to surprise the demon, but discovered the demon waited for him.

With the beast concentrating on Pegan, Saress saw an opportunity and charged in from behind, and lunged with the blade where she believed the heart may be found.

The demon however spun just in time and when the blades met, hers melted and wilted like a dying flower, while his returned to end her life.

Thathra recovered and circled around looking for an opportunity to strike.

Pegan swooped in with Fel Strike which glowed bright blue and when the blade hit, there was a violent eruption which ripped Fell Strike free of his grip and sent the flaming sword back to Hell where it came from, and the demon's hand fell to the ground.

Saress dug with her claws into the arm of the demon spilling black blood, and lashed out with her tail against his head.

Behind Pitboch, the bold and bright image inside the portal began to fade as the moon began it's descent.

Averie looked for a way to the portal, but the demon stood fast directly in her path. All around the beast, the ground ignited.

"We need to hurry," Ellusia cried out. "The portal is closing."

Thathra swung as he passed taking a large chunk out of the demon's leg, and the ground at his feet stained black.

Pegan rolled out of the way dodging the spiked tail which whizzed past.

Saress ducked under a blow from a massive hand, then tore her sword free and seized the opportunity and buried the blade into the demon's torso which broke through the other side, spraying Pegan with blood. She was sure this would be the blow to send the thing back to Hell whence it came from, but the demon never faltered or slowed.

Emitting a sick laugh as if he enjoyed the pain, he brought down his closed fist upon her skull, and the bones inside sounded like a pot shattering.

Averie cried out as she watched her protector crumble to the ground.

Thathra circled back for another attack, while Pegan came in from a different angle.

Pitboch turned to face Thathra while his tailed seemed to have a mind of its own and lashed out coiling around Pegan's head and jerked him from the ground.

The force was horrendous, and he had no choice but to latch onto the tail with both hands to keep his head from being ripped from his neck. Small barbed thorns dug into his flesh and his eyes bulged as the creature thrashed him with such force, both boots were flung free of his feet.

Behind them, the portal sputtered and static filled the darkened void.

Thathra had no choice but to abandon his current course of action and concentrate solely on the tail before Pegan was thrashed to pieces.

Wanting its tail free, the demon discarded its payload by snapping it like a whip sending Pegan sailing through the air. The sound of limbs smashing and branches breaking could be heard deep from within the woods, followed by a deathly silence.

Thathra watched the man fly like a bag caught in a windstorm, completely unaware of the wounded limb as it came crashing down into the back of his head sending him reeling to the ground.

"NO!" Ellusia screamed and ran to his aid.

The demon bellowed a hearty laugh then pulled the blade free from its torso and advanced towards the bearer.

Behind him, the edges of the portal had gone black, and only a large swirling circle in the center remained.

Thathra rose once more, recovered his axe, and charged at the demon. He swore upon his life to protect her, and as long as there was still life in his body, thats what he intended to do.

Pitboch laughed as the barbarian approached.

Ellusia saw the opportunity and had to act now if it was to be successful. At full sprint, she passed the demon on her way to Averie.

Pitboch watched the woman run but showed little concern.

Thathra raised the axe to strike, but it was quickly knocked away and he found himself lifted from the ground and his face brought to within inches of the demon. Their eyes meet and deep within those red burning orbs, he saw death.

Pitboch opened his enormous maw and clamped down upon the barbarian's head, severing the spine and crushing the skull.

Ellusia picked up speed and in one swoop she snatched the petrified woman from the ground and ran. With each step she repositioned the bearer's body, until she held it high above her own head.

Pitboch realized what Ellusia was attempting to do and threw the lifeless corpse at her which slammed into her back knocking her forward and launching Averie through the air into the portal.

Pitboch screamed something that sounded between the howl of a wounded animal, and a cry of defeat. She would pay for this. He would make sure of it and in his hand a dagger formed designed to entrap her soul and take her down to Hell with him, where he could torment her forever and ever.

Ellusia's heart skipped a beat as she observed the demon standing above her, and then she watched the blade fall, destined for her heart.

Pitboch screeched even louder when the blade he held shattered just before impact.

"You shall cause her no harm," Elwrick cursed. His hands waved in strange movements.

Pitboch channeled his anger on the new threat, Elwrick.

Elwrick tried to resist but something beyond his control forced him to his knees, and he bowed to Pitboch as a servant would his master. He had no magic left for defense. He had gone well past his capabilities to keep the portal open as long as possible, but the extended effort had drained him. And what little remained he used to protect Ellusia. He would rather offer himself to the demon than allow her to become a slave.

Time seemed to stand still, and the air grew hot, stagnant, and took on a nasty funk. Elwrick wanted to look, to stare into the eyes of Pitboch and curse him for his deeds.

Pitboch released a snarled grunt, then an angry growl.

Elwrick had no idea what the demon planned, but judging from the sounds spewed forth, it didn't bode well for his health.

Pitboch grunted again, and a blackened fluid dripped from his mouth.

Elwrick felt the hold on him wane and he looked up just in time to see the demon with its back arched and both arms flailing. Fire shot from its eyes and a blackened tongue thrashed at the air. He wondered what kind of demonic spell the beast was about to cast that would make him convulse in such a twisted manner.

Pitboch released another growling grunt.

Elwrick was not sure what to expect from the demon and then he saw it, the tip of pure white blade that dripped with frost and stained black with blood bust through, then was ripped free. He watched in amazement as the demon fell to the side, dead. Behind it, Lady Alenia wiped the blood from her blade and slid it back into its sheath. She once again wore the battle gear she donned so long ago during the Great War.

"Just like old times, here I am saving your ass once again… but I don't mind," she smiled, then fell to her knees beside him and embraced him with a long kiss.

Chapter 50

verie felt herself go weightless and all around her colors swirled, midnight blues, emerald greens, and white-hot silvers. Galaxies and star systems flew by in dazzling streaks of light at dizzying speeds then erupted into a magnificent display of glowing sparks that fell like rain. In less than a blink of an eye, she found herself staring in wonder, in awe, at the future that lay in front of her. The land was beautiful, trees unlike anything she had ever seen and, sounds her ears have never heard before. The desire to go back to the world she once knew was strong, but the temptation of not knowing what lies ahead was even stronger.

Malvo twitched as if a reset button had been pressed and he suddenly felt free. The magical barrier which kept him contained waned, and then he felt it completely collapse. He released a maniacal laugh and then with a wave of his hand, a magical door opened and he stepped through it and vanished.

Karayan screamed and fell to his knees. He already felt exhausted. He could sense the failure. The moment she entered the portal, a vision formed in his mind of the future, and it was grim.

Ellusia lie on the bed curled in the fetal position covered from neck to toe with a translucent silk blanket. The window was cracked open and the curtains pulled back to allow the morning sun to warm the room, while a fresh breeze carried a heavenly scent. Across the room, Gleia sat with her feet propped on a desk and a book splayed open on her lap. She only looked up when the door opened.

"Anything changed?" Lady Alenia asked.

"No," Gleia said then closed the book and placed it on the table careful not to make a sound, then rubbed her wrinkled forehead. "I think what ails her, I cannot cure."

"Grief," Lady Alenia said.

"That… and I believe she's fell victim to melancholy."

Lady Alenia sat on the edge of the desk, a baffled look on her face.

"Let me explain," Gleia said. "I believe she has lost the will to live. Someone she deeply cared for died, and there was nothing she could do."

Lady Alenia thought back to her own husband and how it had affected her when he died in her arms, and understood now how Ellusia felt.

"There's more though," Gleia continued. "I believe she also understands she's the most hated woman in Icearaus. A bounty has been placed upon her head promising wealth far greater than that of Pegan Rhoe's. She has nowhere to go, no home to go home to, and no people to accept her."

Lady Alenia thought for a moment and had a distant stare. "So what do you propose?"

"That she remain here with the elves in Rhunsiire where protection can be provided."

"You sound like you have thought this through," Lady Alenia smiled then let out a laugh.

"I have. Ever since she was brought back from the island, I have been considering what would be in her best interest. And honestly, I see no other choice. If we have her leave, she will only be killed or given over to Karayan. Either way, the final results will be the same.

Besides, from my understanding, she's a talented young healer with promising potential. I could take her under my wing and teach her extraordinary things."

Lady Alenia patted Gleia's shoulder, "I will see to it personally that housing is provided for our young friend, and she can stay here as long as her heart desires."

Gleia smiled, "I believe she'll like that. I will tell her when she wakes. I gave her a drink to help her sleep."

"Will she be ready for the ceremony tonight? Or should she stay here under your care?"

"I think it would be best for her to go. If she never has a chance to tell her final words, then I don't believe the healing will ever begin. It will be hard, but I will be at her side for its entirety."

"Well it looks like you have everything under control. I must take my leave as I'm expecting Hulradeeh and Raestmond any moment, and I wish to greet them personally."

Pegan sat at the end of the bed and looked at Saress sprawled on the floor. The majority of her head is covered in a plaster cast with a slit for each eye, and several small holes for her nostrils. Out of nowhere he began to laugh.

"What are you laughing at?" Saress asked.

"Nothing," he answered with a grin that erupted into laughter. "I'm sorry," he pattered her shoulder. I was just thinking what Gleia said when she called you boneheaded."

"She said the only reason I lived was that my skull was so thick," Saress snarled back.

Lady Alenia entered and greeted them with a hug. From the way Saress resisted, she could tell something bothered her.

No longer would Saress allow this woman to walk around them as if she was a friend. Saress flexed her claws as if ready to strike and a low angry growl escaped her lips.

"What is the meaning of your aggression," Hulradeeh said as he entered the room along with Elwrick.

"This woman," she pointed one of her broken claws at Lady Alenia, "sent her son with the intentions of killing Pegan after we reached the island." She felt it best to expose her treacherous behavior with everyone present.

"And you know this how?" Hulradeeh asked.

"Because just before Lorandrial attacked Pegan on the ship, he spoke of the deception."

Elwrick looked at Saress as if she'd gone mad.

"Lower your hand," Hulradeeh demanded then turned to Gleia who entered to check up on Saress and Pegan. "What did you give her to make her act this way?" He asked her.

Gleia shrugged her shoulders as if to say she didn't know.

Lady Alenia almost fainted at the thought her son could have changed the outcome. "I never did that! In fact, after you left, it was determined Lorandrial was the one responsible for the lie about the uprising. Somehow, he gained the knowledge Pegan was the one responsible for Meriel's death and acted completely upon his own accord to extract revenge."

Saress lowered her hand and let her head sink, she felt like a fool.

Lady Alenia gave her another hug and whispered into her ear. "Believe me, if I wanted Pegan dead he would be, and in a much more painful way than Lorandrial could have ever accomplished."

"I'm sorry—"

"No, don't apologize. You care for Pegan a great deal and it's obvious. I would have done the same thing but probably sooner. Your actions are warranted."

"Sit," Gleia ordered Saress, and then began to examine the cast and to make sure the bones were healing properly.

"I shall take my leave now and take this old woman with me," Elwrick said as he took Lady Alenia by the hand. "I am sure your father will want to hear all the details of your adventure. We'll meet up later tonight after the ceremony."

"Thank you for sending word to me," Hulradeeh said to Elwrick.

"The pleasure is mine. Now, we must be going as I and Lady Alenia have much to discuss."

Elwrick remained quiet all the way back to Lady Alenia's bedchamber. It was obvious he was deeply troubled by something.

"Something bothers you?" she said, "I can see it in your eyes, in the way you act. You have something to say, and yet I have a feeling you don't know how."

Elwrick reached out and caressed her cheek. It terrified him more than anything else in this world to think what would become of her if his suspicions proved to be correct. "You're right, and I have no way to explain it."

"Just tell me, the best way you can and we'll figure it out together," she said.

Elwrick's face flushed pale. "I believe we face a threat much more deadly, more cunning, and far more evil, than Karayan could have ever become."

"What are you saying?" she asked.

Elwrick shook his head in despair. "I shouldn't have to tell you this but, that demon—"

"Yes... I know it was a chasm demon, one of the vilest creatures ever created by the Dark Master."

"And they bow to none but him."

"Are you saying the Dark Master is here?" her lower lip trembled. She remembered the destruction the last time he appeared.

"I don't believe so. But I believe somewhere, an agent of his walks this land and commanded that demon."

"Karayan?" she hissed.

"I thought that too at first, but then I remembered a faint shift in space and time the very moment Averie entered the portal, and now I realize what it was. It was the Dark Master removing the blessings he bestowed upon Karayan."

"So Karayan is mortal again, he can be destroyed?"

"Yes," Elwrick acknowledged. "But I fear there's more. What you fail to realize is this entity, this agent, has been here for a while biding his time, waiting for the moment when his Master called... It seems now was time to set his plan in motion."

"And what makes you believe that?"

"Because that demon let Averie reach the portal. It could have killed her with a simple thought, yet it did not. Whoever controlled that demon, I fear he feels now is time to have Karayan removed from his position."

"That can't be. I can feel the presence of a demon here on this planet, and I've felt nothing. That is, until near the end when I slain it… you're wrong"

"No, it only means that demon has probably been around since the Great War but held in suspended animation, locked between life and death, waiting to head its master's call?"

"If that's true, then this agent must have also been around since then." Her face went pale white and she hugged Elwrick, "Malvo, but where?"

A knock on the door interrupted their conversation.

"I'll tell you more after we find out who this is."

"Come in," Lady Alenia said.

Two elves dressed in ceremonial robes stood at the door. "The hour draws near, my lady," one said.

"We'll be there shortly," she answered. After the door closed, she looked back towards Elwrick. "We'll continue this meeting afterward with Pegan, and you might as well bring Saress as well."

From the funeral parlor all the way to the gravesite, elves lined the path shoulder to shoulder. Each dawned in identical pure white robes hemmed in gold thread. Each elf bowed in respect as the carriage pulled by Midnight passed. The road wound its way through the whispering woods till it came to a grassy knoll where an uncountable number of chairs had been placed.

The casket was constructed of wood then covered with a gold leaf material. So many flowers had been thrown on the wagon that the base of the casket was hidden. Poles were then slid through loops on each side and six men carried Thathra to his final resting place. Directly behind the grave was a raised platform where Lady Alenia, Elwrick, Ellusia, Gleia, Pegan, Saress, Raestmond, and Tanara were seated.

After all had gathered, the glade became deathly quiet except for the sobs of Tanara, who left the platform and held firm to the casket.

Lady Alenia waited a long time to allow Tanara to grieve the loss of her brother. It was only when Gleia aided the woman and gave her something to calm the grieving girl did she begin.

The air was calm and the darkened sky sparkled with the aid of a billion stars. She gripped the edges of the podium and her face held a somber, distant look. Then she spoke. "Good evening my fellow elves, reptilians from the Anor, Barbarians from the north, and our distant cousins... man. And let us not forget those who join us from far away." She smiled at Elwrick who promptly returned one. "Tonight, we celebrate the passing of the bearer from our world to the next, yet we also grieve the loss of those who made it possible."

More than a million tears were shed tonight as each member took the podium to give their eulogy for the fallen. It was Ellusia though who brought many to their knees when she spoke of lost loves, shattered dreams, yet through it all hope was reborn.

The hour was late when a line formed as far as the eye could see and each elf passed to pay their respects. Most placed flowers at the grave while a few placed custom made jewelry inside the coffin and whispered words of encouragement to Ellusia.

The first rays of light broke the horizon, and the sky lightened to a cloudless baby blue as the last elf past.

Later that afternoon they were all summoned to a private meeting. After everyone had arrived, Lady Alenia asked Elwrick to inform them of their earlier conversation.

When he finished the room remained quiet, until Pegan spoke. "How can we fight what we can't see?"

Elwrick drew a deep breath. "We now fight a war on two fronts, one against Karayan, and the other against a force which has yet to reveal its ugly head."

"Tell me it ain't true," Ellusia said. "I can't do this anymore."

"Easy," Pegan said, and he rubbed Ellusia's shoulder. "I will deal with Karayan... alone."

"You will do no such thing," Elwrick demanded. "He is building an army at this very moment. He does not plan to relinquish his control without a fight. The location of the dwarves must be discovered. Without a sizeable army, the elves will be greatly outnumbered and eventually defeated."

Pegan rose and stood behind Ellusia. "This young lady now has a home, a promising future, and is among people who cherish her." He next went to Saress and leaned on her shoulder "As much as I love this old lizard, her father is here to take her home." He made his way back to his chair, they all watched his movements carefully.

"These two need no more blood on their hands, I will go alone in search of a long dead race."

"They are not dead, but in hiding from something, or someone," Elwrick said. "But you are right on one thing, Ellusia will not be going. Even if she begged me, I will not subject her to anymore brutality. She has seen enough and besides, she is now under the training of Gleia. I fear her skills will be needed elsewhere in the future." Elwrick pointed at Saress. "This young lady here though, I have other plans for. Her skills with a bow and swords are remarkable. Her replacement swords are being crafted as we speak, and the deciphering of her bow, given to her by Pegan, is complete and now she understands how to invoke the magic it contains. She would follow you even if I demanded her not to, it's in her blood."

Saress agreed with Elwrick's statement.

Elwrick continued after a brief pause. "Karayan knows when the child returns, it only needs to be killed to have his powers bestowed again. So he is doing everything within his power to spread his filth, his hate, his warmongering, so the child will find no safe haven."

Pegan looked at Elwrick, "so where do we begin?"

The journey continues

with…

Birth Right

expected release winter 2020

About the Author

J.R. Harris writes action-packed, fast-paced adventure novels where often times the main characters are not of human descent. Despite going into the military right after high school then earning his Bachelor's Degree in Criminal Justice his love affair with the strange and unusual always remained strong. An avid reader, gamer, dungeon master, campaign designer and map creator has left him with a twisted and distorted imagination which propels him to bring to life strange an exotic tales in ways never before imagined possible. Born in Michigan he now resides in the Greater Pacific Northwest with his wife, dog, and two cats whittling away the days in front of his computer working on his next great adventure. **For more information visit him at JRHarris.net and possibly get a sneak peek at his next great adventure.**

www.ingramcontent.com/pod-product-compliance
Lightning Source LLC
Chambersburg PA
CBHW070927100726
47908CB00001B/128